CROSS-EXAMINATION

"Mr. Beauchamp, do you have any questions?"

I continue silently to study Kimberley, then sigh.

"Ah, well, perhaps just one. You have some examinations to write next week, Miss Martin?"

"Yes."

"May I wish you the best of luck. Hopefully you will prove yourself as fine a lawyer as you are an actor."

What I seek is there: a rosiness tints her cheeks—the product of shame? Truth does not blush, a wise ancient once said.

"Thank you," she says, smiling, and pretends to all she has heard a compliment.

As Kimberley makes her way from the stand, she hesitates, looks once again at my client, and then tears begin to stream in torrents down her cheeks.

TRIAL
OF
PASSION

WILLIAM
DEVERELL

SEAL BOOKS

MCCLELLAND-BANTAM, INC.

TORONTO

This edition contains the complete text
of the original hardcover edition.
NOT ONE WORD HAS BEEN OMITTED.

TRIAL OF PASSION

A Seal Book / published by arrangement with
McClelland & Stewart, Inc.

PUBLISHING HISTORY
McClelland & Stewart edition published 1997
Seal edition / September 1998

ISBN 0-770-42781-2

Seal Books are published by McClelland-Bantam, Inc. Its trademark, consisting of the words "Seal Books" and the portrayal of a
seal, is the property of McClelland-Bantam, Inc., 105 Bond Street,
Toronto, Ontario M5B 1Y3, Canada. This trademark has been duly
registered in the Trademark Office of Canada. The trademark consisting of the words "Bantam Books" and the portrayal of a rooster
is the property of and is used with the consent of Bantam Books,
1540 Broadway, New York, New York 10036. This trademark has
been duly registered in the Trademark Office of Canada and elsewhere.

PRINTED IN CANADA
UNI   10   9   8   7   6   5   4   3   2   1

Man is sometimes extraordinarily, passionately in love with suffering.

—FYODOR DOSTOYEVSKY,
Notes from Underground

❧ PART ONE ❧

May the countryside and the gliding valley
streams content me.
Lost to fame, let me love river and woodland.

DIRECT EXAMINATION BY MS. PATRICIA BLUEMAN

Q You are a retired minister?

A I was an Anglican bishop.

Q And how old are you?

A Seventy-nine.

Q Where do you live?

THE COURT: Please sit down if you'd be more comfortable, Dr. Hawthorne. This is only a preliminary hearing, quite informal.
(Witness sits.)

A At 137 Palmer Avenue in West Vancouver.

Q Do you live there alone?

A I am a widower. I have a housekeeper—Mrs. Mary McIntosh.

Q Okay, and your neighbour on your left, as you face the street, that would be 141 Palmer?

A Yes.

Q And do you know who lives there?

A Professor Jonathan O'Donnell.

Q He's acting dean of law at the University of British Columbia?

A Yes, I have known him for many years.

Q And do you see him in court?

A Sitting right there.

Q Identifying the accused, for the record. Now I

want to take you back to the late-night hours of last Friday, November twenty-seventh. Were you at home on that evening?

A I retired at about nine p.m. I had fallen asleep in an armchair while reading and Mrs. McIntosh aroused me and sent me off to bed.

Q And did something later awake you?

A There was a great hullabaloo at the front door. I'm not sure what time it was, in the small hours at least. Mrs. McIntosh has her room upstairs at the back, so I was first to the door.

Q And what transpired?

A It was a female voice, but the words were unintelligible. I opened the door and a young woman was standing there.

Q And did this woman subsequently identify herself?

A Ah, yes, her name is, ah . . . Miss Kimberley Martin.

Q Now tell us what you observed.

A Well . . .

THE COURT: Just what you saw, Dr. Hawthorne. In your own words.

A Well, she was, ah, somewhat in a state of nudity.

Q Somewhat. What do you mean?

A She was naked, except . . . she was wearing a tie.

Q Please describe it.

A It was very garish, brightly coloured.

Q But it was a man's tie?

A Oh, yes. I really wasn't focusing very well, but I thought it depicted a scene on a beach, with a tropical palm.

Q All right, where was she wearing this tie?

A Where? In the, ah, normal place. I mean, I know this wasn't a normal situation. Around her neck. Properly knotted.

Q Do you recognize this?

A It could be the one.

Q Exhibit One, your honour. Was she wearing anything else?

A Well, a gold necklace. Quite expensive, I thought. A large cross suspended from it.

Q Do you recognize this item?

A Yes, that looks like it.

Q Exhibit Two. How was she wearing this item?

A Right, um, between her breasts. It had somehow got wrapped around the tie.

Q What else did you notice about her appearance?

A She was covered with red, ah, streaks and daubs. Her lower body, and also her breasts.

Q Explain what you mean.

A Mrs. McIntosh later recognized it as lipstick.

MR. CLEAVER: Can we avoid the hearsay?

Q Describe these daubs.

A Well, red smears, mostly, right around her body, up her legs and thighs and pelvis to the middle of her abdomen. Where her skin wasn't smeared, there was a pattern, a jagged series of peaks and valleys—drawn as one might portray waves on a stormy ocean. And her breasts, ah, seemed to be coloured, too. With that same bright red, and her entire, ah, nipples. Excuse me.

THE COURT: Can you get the witness a glass of water? (Witness sips water.)

Q Okay, and what was this woman, Miss Martin, doing?

A Well, just standing there, shaking. It was cold. And she was yelling, "He's going to kill me. Help me." I must say, I was quite frightened.

Q And what did you do?

A Well, Mrs. McIntosh had come down by then, and of course we brought her into the house, and we found a blanket to cover her, and we made some tea.

My daughter stands sternly before me like a teacher confronting an errant child. Deborah is, in fact, a teacher—of those children we formerly called slow learners—and addresses me as such, patient and resolute.

"Father, please listen to me. You can't cook. You can't make a bed. And that old house—I don't think you've ever hammered a nail in your life. What is this, some kind of male menopause?"

"My dear, I am simply retiring from the wicked practices of the law."

Seeking safety, I burrow between the sheltering arms of my favourite club chair, a padded refuge that over the years has moulded to my sylphlike shape until the chair and I are one, whole, indivisible. To part with this chair would be to part with an old and valued friend. The chair will go with me to Garibaldi Island. My wife, suddenly in the springtime of her life, will not.

From the enfolding warm prison of my chair, I can hear young Nick, Jr., restless, prowling about the house, an eight-year-old addict of the multichannel universe. Annabelle and I have forbidden television here, the pabulum upon which he feeds at home. Nicholas Braid, Deborah's husband, who is "into" (*his* preposition) mutual funds, is playing golf on the carpet, practising his putting. He finally speaks:

"Arthur, do you have the foggiest idea what it's like to live on one of those Gulf Islands? Been to Garibaldi. Full of yokels. Potheads." Nicholas tends to burp his sentences.

"Is there even a telephone in that godforsaken place?" Deborah asks. "A doctor? What if you have a *major* stroke this time?"

"I am retiring to the country so I may *avoid* another stroke. It was just a gentle warning, my dear."

"A gentle warning you're about twenty pounds overweight."

"I intend to shape up and chill out, if that's the *au courant* expression. I am on the cusp of sixty-three. A richness of poetry has been written that I have not had the time and comfort to enjoy. I intend to hone my skills with rake and hoe." Gardening has been my one great delectation, my solace, my escape. Yes, the trials of Arthur Beauchamp are at an end. He is retiring *in corpore sano*.

"I don't suppose your wife is objecting." Deborah says this in the manner of someone who knows such person only casually. The wife, my darling Annabelle, gave her suck.

"She's in accord with my wishes."

"I *can't* imagine why."

"Deborah," warns her husband.

Out of habit, I leap to Annabelle's defence. "She has her career. I can't ask her to abandon it." Annabelle has only recently become artistic director of the Vancouver Opera Society.

"Oh, yes, mother is busy, busy, busy. That *ridiculous* facelift."

"Let's change the subject," says Nicholas, as he aims a three-foot putt at a plastic cup.

The subject, Annabelle Beauchamp, my dear wife, is in the kitchen making canapés. These two warring foes, daughter and mother, have begun to resemble each other ever more closely as one grows older, the other younger. How complimented I feel that Annabelle has shed her carapace of older skin to be a wife who looks not fifty-three but half my age. Ah, but Annabelle has ever been a seeker of that legendary fountain that washes clean the waning years, the waters of eternal wrinklessness.

"I think a time apart will be good for both of us."

As I utter this hearty banality, I realize it will only reinvigorate the debate.

"So you're . . . another separation. That's really it, isn't it? Or she's kicking you out. And you just *sit* there. You *take* it."

"Nonsense. She intends to come every few weekends after the opera season. You and the two Nicks will visit, too, I hope. Young Nick will love it. On a clear day you can stand on the bluffs and actually make out Vancouver behind the polluting haze."

A silence follows as Annabelle sweeps into view bearing a tray of hors-d'oeuvres.

"Arthur wants to try something different for a while," Annabelle says. "I can't see the harm in it, nor can I see it lasting. He'll miss his grungy old robes and his place on centre stage." She kisses my forehead with lips soft and dry. I tremble from her touch, and light a cigarette.

Deborah leans down to me. "Is this going to make you happy, Dad?"

"We shall see."

"You're okay?"

"Fine."

We nibble, we chat, we pretend, as this cheerless April day grinds to its zenith, and the hour of departure nears. My chariot is out front, filled with books and music tapes, its boot yawning open ready to receive this, my favourite chair.

But why is my throat so thick with rue, why does my chest feel raw and hollow?

§§

CROSS-EXAMINATION BY MR. GOWAN CLEAVER

Q Dr. Hawthorne, I won't take much of your time. I know this isn't a comfortable way to spend a Monday morning.

A Please don't worry.

Q You've known Professor O'Donnell here for what—seven or eight years?

A As a neighbour, yes.

Q Always pleasant, easy to get along with?

A A most courteous gentleman. We visit from time to time.

Q No wild parties?
(Witness laughs.)

A He's been over for a brandy occasionally. That's about as wild as it gets, I'm afraid.

Q And he is known to you to be a man of integrity?

A I've never heard a word against him.

Q Now, on this night of November twenty-seventh when Miss Martin arrived at your doorstep, I take it there was something else you observed aside from her unusual physical appearance.

A She was in great distress, it would seem.

Q Yes, it would seem. Notice anything on her breath?

A I would have to say her breath smelled of alcohol.

Q Strongly?

A It was quite apparent. She, ah, she seemed to have a little trouble navigating.

Q Stumbled a little? Had difficulty standing?

A I wouldn't have let her drive a vehicle.

Q She was drunk.

A Fairly intoxicated, yes. It seemed to me.

Q Babbling incoherently.

MS. BLUEMAN: I object. That's a—

THE COURT: That's a what, Miss Blueman?

MS. BLUEMAN: The innuendo is unfair. Her words should speak for themselves.

THE COURT: Objection overruled.

A I would say her speech was excited. She kept repeating the same thing over again.

Q That someone was coming after her. Did she say who?

A No, she didn't.
Q Did she say she'd been raped?
A Not in my presence.
Q She didn't have much to add to her initial complaint?
A No, she quieted down. We settled her on the couch, the blanket around her. She turned quite . . . almost composed.
Q I understand you offered to call the police.
A Yes.
Q And?
A She asked me not to. She wanted me to phone a friend of hers, a Mr. Clarence de Remy Brown.
Q Her fiancé.
A I wouldn't have known that, but I do now.
Q Mr. Brown came over?
A Very quickly—he lives not far away, in the British Properties. He seemed quite calm and in control, considering the situation, and I left it in his hands whether to involve the police. Upon their departure, Mrs. McIntosh urged me to return to my bed, and I'm afraid I was too exhausted to argue.
MR. CLEAVER: No more questions.
THE COURT: Thank you, Dr. Hawthorne, you've been of great assistance to this court.

෯෯

Standing at the aft rail of the gender-confused vessel known as the *Queen of Prince George,* I can see forested clumps of land approaching. These comprise the islands beyond the great inland waterway of the Strait of Georgia, the cold salt moat behind which I shall find refuge from the city's grasping fingers.

Below me, on the car deck, my elderly Rolls Phantom V looks quite out of place amid the clutter of rust-patched pickup trucks. In my three-piece suit, I suppose I look no less exotic to the several gentle folk of Garibaldi Island who are out here in the no-smoke-less zone. With my puffing fellow travellers, I am enjoying the silent communion of nicotine, consumption of which has become the great capital sin of this baleful age of health and purity.

Some of the smoke—that wafting from the tractor-capped young gentlemen near the lifeboats—lightly offends the nostrils with a distinctively illegal sweetness. These then must be the potheads Nicholas spoke of.

Passengers glance at me from time to time, shy, curious. Who is this stuffed shirt from the city staring foolishly at the gulls riding motionless in the slipstream? Why is he leaving the world behind? Why does he seek to abandon career, fame, life, wife, the buzzing, febrile city of his birth? Why does he seek to maroon himself among the alleged yokels of Garibaldi Island?

Dire were the warnings of my fellow inmates of Tragger, Inglis, Bullingham, that vast sweatshop of writs and wills wherein I toiled for thirty years. Take time off, rest the ticker, but stay in the city and take the odd trial: one needs stimulus to survive this world, they insisted—my mind would rot through boredom. But no member of this fickle crowd of city sophists, this *mobile vulgus*, has ever ventured closer to nature than the backyard barbecue.

I dared not tell my partners I was going to the country to seek communion with our bountiful mother, Earth. Who could bear to gaze upon their uncomprehending faces? So spiritless, so dead in look, these timid men and women prefer to be locked within the walls of their sterile, sullen city.

I might have told them this, had I the courage: that I plan to watch the flowers of spring unfurl, petal by petal. To listen to the songs of uncaged birds. To press upon a spade and feel it gently sigh into the loam. In short, I am going to ground.

And perhaps I will also recover from the pain of loving Annabelle. So beautiful, so flamboyant. So perfectly preserved. Ah, but if truth be known, the pain comes from the knife of my own impotence. I have long been unable to perform manfully for her, and as punishment for my crime have been sentenced to the lash of her infidelity.

Her last lover was a hairy-chested heldentenor, Tristan to her Isolde. But who is the latest random paramour? *What slender youth, bedewed with liquid odours, courts thee on roses in some pleasant cave?* (I lack a lyric tongue, and steal these words, of course, from Milton's translation of the *Epodes.*)

But I accept cuckoldom as my lot. Unlike Iago's victim, I am not in thrall to the green-eyed monster that mocks the meat it feeds on. I am the other kind of cuckold the Bard spoke of, who lives in bliss, certain of his fate.

(Oh, noble Beauchamp, how naked and hollow are such self-pitying denials.)

Now approach the bosky valleys and rocky hummocks of the island of Garibaldi, population 539. We purr into a long bay towards a distant ferry slip. Along the shore are clearings with scattered houses and barns, giving way to tangles of willows and cedars at the tide lines. Near the ferry dock is a marina in sad repair: crumbling outbuildings and cabins.

But my attention is diverted to an energetic woman doing the rounds with what appears to be a petition. Circling me warily like a hawk, she catches my eye and finally descends. "You're the new owner of the Ashcroft place." A brisk, matter-of-fact voice, though not wanting in music. "I'm Margaret Blake. I live up the road from you."

Though she looks older than the current version of Annabelle, she is probably much younger; she does not appear to have had a facelift. Obviously she spends much time outdoors, as her skin is biscuit brown from the sun. Although stern of aspect she is rather comely, lithe and lean with close-cropped nut-brown hair and wide-set, piercing eyes, the colour of smooth-rubbed silver. She is attired in country clothes, denim jacket, jeans, sturdy boots.

She gestures below to a half-ton truck laden with bales of hay. "I have a working farm." Do I hear a note of defiance in her voice, a challenge of some kind?

"Arthur Beauchamp." I extend my hand. Hers is dry and strong and sinewy, crescents of grime beneath the fingernails.

She extends the petition. "I don't suppose you'd care to sign this."

"A pessimist makes a poor salesman. And why would I not sign it?" I observe it calls for a moratorium on a housing development known as Evergreen Estates.

"We don't want to be like the city," Mrs. Blake says. "We're getting so many weekenders now. Look at those boxes." She points to a patchy area of A-frames and trailers on a rise above the bay, which, I take it, is Evergreen Estates. "I'm sorry, I suppose you're one of them. All for what they call progress."

I mildly resent the assumption that I am of that lowly class referred to, the city weekender. "I am now a permanent resident, madam."

"I see. Well, you don't . . . *look* permanent."

Mrs. Blake studies me intently with her fierce grey eyes: she sees an outlander, a slicker, overgroomed, overdressed. She withdraws her petition from my soft, unsullied city hands—though I might have signed it had I received a courteous explication of the issues.

"Mr. Beauchamp, I do hope you're not planning to tear down that old house. That's what a lot of them do. Put up all that ugly plastic siding."

Ah, yes, the taste police. They are everywhere.

She waves at the smoke wafting from my cigarette, wrinkling her nose in silent disapprobation. To boot, she is a clean-air fanatic. I fear she will be a forbidding neighbour.

As the ferry's horn bleats, the blunt Mrs. Blake says a brisk adieu and continues her campaign elsewhere.

Before reaching the stairs to the car deck I am again accosted—this time by a small, twitching gentleman with a miniature, well-tended moustache. For some reason he is wearing a life jacket.

"I know who you are." This is said in a tone of conspiracy, as if he has come upon my photograph on a police bulletin board. "Mr. Beauchamp. You defended that doctor killed two people."

"Allegedly." A trial of some notoriety in which the media eagerly wallowed this winter.

"Be careful of that Margaret Blake, Mr. Beauchamp."

"Careful?"

"Troublemaker." He whispers, "Drawbridge mentality." It sounds like some rare disease of the mind.

"Ah, yes, she's against progress."

"I seen you didn't sign her petition. She don't want change. We can't stand still, right? We can't stand still."

The man indeed seems to have difficulty doing so, feet, arms, and eyes shifting constantly in the manner of a witness on the stand who has been overly bold with the truth.

"I'm Kurt Zoller. I guess I'm sort of like the elected mayor here, only on these islands they call it a trustee. You got any problems, I'm the last name in the phone book. I live in that converted trailer up in Evergreen Estates—you can see it from here. We don't get many famous lawyers here, Mr. Beauchamp."

He continues to mispronounce my name: Bo-champ. "Beecham, really, that's how it's said."

"That busybody Margaret Blake . . ." Again his voice takes on a conspiratorial tone. "She's an eco-freak."

"She sounds dangerous indeed, Mr. Zoller."

I see her standing some distance away, alone, cleaning her fingernails. She glances at us, and as our eyes meet she abruptly pockets the nail file.

I escape to the car deck, where one of the tractor-capped young men who'd been puffing cannabis is standing by my faithful steed, the Phantom V, contemplating it as if it were some newly landed spaceship. The clothes he is wearing, torn and grease-stained, can best be described as third-hand.

"You goin' up Potter's Road, eh?"

"Yes, I believe I am."

"Think I can hitch a ride?"

"My pleasure. Move some of those books to the back."

"You want, I could sit back there."

He is looking at my club chair, roped to the trunk. I smile. "I'm afraid it has no seat belt."

"Nobody never uses a seat belt around here except when the cop comes every second Tuesday. This is a '60, ain't it, before they changed the grille. Love to look inside the hood one of these days, man." He clambers in beside me. "Yeah, thanks. I'm in the spare-parts business. Mechanic, do some body work. I'm like an entrepreneur. Bob Stonewell, but they call me Stoney. That's 'cause one of my other businesses is stonework, chimneys and fireplaces, stuff like that. I do everything. You're the guy bought the Ashcroft place, eh? Heard you was a lawyer, a pretty good one, defended that Dr. What's-his-face, it was all over the TV, shot his wife and her boyfriend in cold blood. Wouldn't mind talking to you—just, you know, if you get a minute—about a weed case I got comin' up. How much do you charge?"

Dr. What's-his-face, a cuckold, too, but perhaps

more impetuous than I, paid a fee of a size I am embarrassed to mention. Stoney does not await a response, and is still talking as I pull out onto the ramp, my wheels finally making contact with the good earth of Garibaldi Island.

Immediately I am rerouted into the driveway of the marina—Stoney, phoneless, must pick up his messages, which are kept for him in a weathered grey building that is the local bar, known officially as the Brig. He runs inside and emerges a few minutes later with another young man, who, after introductions, climbs into my vehicle, crawling over the boxes of books.

"We'll help you unpack your stuff," Stoney says.

This *beneficium* shall be gratefully accepted. We bear off towards Potter's Road, Stoney assuming the role of tour guide. "Now, the general store is down that road past the community hall, and it's also the post office. That's the gas station, don't *never* get any work done there. You're talking to the best mechanic on the island. Coming up, that's my place on the right. House ain't finished, but I'm working on it."

The house is a seemingly uninhabitable shell of plywood and studs, the yard a battlefield after the invading force has left—abandoned relics everywhere. I think of the taste enforcer Mrs. Blake, who must endure this stressful sight daily.

The passenger in the back, a hairy creature who apparently is known by the sobriquet of "Dog," has brought along a six-pack, and I can hear the pop and hiss of the cans, can smell the rich, addicting perfume of fermented hops.

"Like a brew?" he says, extending me a can.

My hands remain clenched upon the steering wheel. "Very kind of you, but no."

We turn onto Potter's Road, on the sunny south end of the island, where my new home—eighteen waterfront acres and an ancient house—no doubt is eagerly awaiting the arrival of its new squire.

"That's your neighbour Mrs. Blake's place," says Stoney. "It's sort of like the local zoo, chickens, pigs, ducks, sheep, and they crap all over. You need any fence work done, don't hesitate."

A rambling frame structure with upper-floor dormers and a huge balcony. Nearby, cedar sheds, pens, corral, greenhouse, a small barn. The front yard is (so difficult not to paraphrase Wordsworth) a yellow sea of daffodils. A huge garden, well fenced, with spring flowers scattered among the rows of seedlings. Spring lambs rollick in her meadow. Several goats. Pigs. Mrs. Blake, doubtless a stern Orwellian, keeps a bustling animal farm.

"She lives alone?"

"Since her old man died. Had a heart attack a few years ago. Couldn't stand the pressure."

"Of what?"

"Living on this island."

But I note his disarming grin. "It ain't so bad," he says.

Parallel ruts lead us past my gate through a grove of thick-waisted Douglas firs into a clearing where stands my own house, a two-storey frame structure, much gingerbread and leaded glass, but aging, tired, the wooden veranda like its new owner sagging at hips and stomach. The garage is in even sadder state.

"I do building, too, all phases of it," Stoney says. "Renovations. Place could also do with a paint job."

My companions help me unload my boxes and my chair. The house has not been lived in for several months, and smells musty, but the lowering April sun streams in through the west-facing windows, lending it an aureate richness. The house came as is, with some old but serviceable furnishings, a substantial fireplace, and all utilities including a freezer that makes an irregular grunting sound.

Outside, a terraced stone patio leads to a yard where a giant arbutus tree swirls her skirts, thence to a rock-strewn beach and a private dock that juts into a cosy bay where waterfowl forage amidst the kelp. At one side of the house is a garden plot protected by a sturdy deer fence. On the other side are a lily pond and a small orchard with apple and plum trees in redolent bloom, a sight not detracted from by the busy pecking beaks of chickens, escapees from the zoo, presumably, of Mrs. Blake.

Impotent I may be, but still capable of love, and this emotion rendered me quite helpless on my one previous visit to this site. I had seen a small advertisement under Country Homes and Acreages. I popped over on a weekend. The real-estate lady, a creature of utterly unbearable sweetness, had me at her mercy as I fumbled for my pen.

"Fruit trees need pruning." Stoney checks the woodshed and finds it only a third full. "You wanna cord or two, I also sell wood."

Somehow, in my bemused and innocent state, I find myself contracting with this eager benefactor for some fencing as well as structural work to shore up the veranda. Nothing to it, I am advised: "You toss in a couple of big crossbeams there, and jack that old rotting timber out." Stoney promises to start work early tomorrow.

They cannot be persuaded to be chauffeured home—Stoney knows a shortcut—and the two men wander across the sheep-cropped field, pausing to examine a broken fence railing before pushing on through the trees.

So I have met several of the island characters, the so-called yokels about whom my son-in-law sternly warned. Now begins the process of my own yokelization, the bumpkinizing of Arthur Ramsgate Beauchamp, Q.C. I take off my jacket. I gather some sticks for the fire. I situate my club chair in front of the hearth. I put water on for tea. I rummage through my tapes for the Boccherini cello concerto. I locate the collected *libellus* of Catullus. *O quid solutis est beatius curis. Ah, what is more blessed than to put cares away.*

ༀ

Gowan Cleaver, Esq.,
Barrister and Solicitor

Dear Gowan,

It is about nine o'clock on New Year's Eve as I begin this dissertation. My subject is the concept of innocence. I shall be exploring the variables of this complex conceit from a unique, personal point of view—that of one imprisoned within a nightmare from hell.

From time to time, I ask myself: Is this reality? Or do I suffer a mental disorder, a schizophrenia? Has a hereditary gene caused me suddenly to snap? (A second cousin believes he speaks regularly to God on a cellular phone.) Am I frozen forever into a state of paranoid delusion? Maybe I'm in an asylum—it's called western civilization and the inmates have taken over. That would explain why I keep hearing voices. They're all saying, "How could this be happening to me?"

Gowan, I ask that question fifty times a day. God has yet to come up with a rational explanation. Does She have something against me? Was I too ambitious, too arrogant, too cruel to Professor Mallard in a recent book review?

These are the last lucid memories I hold: It is a brisk late-November day. I have just gone for an energetic hike through the university park land. I'm happy. I'm tenured. I'm thirty-eight and I'm acting dean. I am back at work, in the library, content as a purring cat, reading the musty nineteenth-century cases I love. Enter Kimberley Martin. She says, "Promise to dance with me tonight?"

Cut. Twenty-four hours later. Close-up of Jonathan Shaun O'Donnell's fingers being pressed into an ink pad by a ham-fisted cop. Script by Franz Kafka. A Hitchcock production.

Where did this damnable woman come from? The twilight zone? Straight from Satan's stable?

I sense you may be finding me a little disconnected. I am alone, but not alone in spirit, for I am celebrating the end of the worst year of my life with a half-empty friend by the name of Jameson. My father, to whom Bushmills was mother's milk, would disown me—if he had anything left to disown me with.

I am sorry to have been so long getting this off to you. I needed the whole month of December to clear my poor twirling brain. Then I had exams to mark. Life allegedly goes on.

You wanted some personal background. I think I shared my past with you many years and beers ago back in our student days. Do you remember when we argued that moot and I developed the hiccups? You were the only one who didn't laugh. I've always liked you for that.

A quick c.v. of Jonathan Shaun O'Donnell. Born in County Fermanagh, in Ulster, and raised in the family estate until I was nine. You are aware that I am not proud to be the son of Viscount Caraway. Not just because of his extremism, though His Lordship's occasional column in the *Times* expresses a politics that makes mine seem flaming bloody red in comparison.

Which it used to be, of course. You may recall that in our student days I was heavily into left-existential politics. A confused stew of Marx, Marcuse, and Sartre. When one is young, one hungers for utopias. As you get older, the shell around you hardens; you want its protection, you care less about the hungering masses. I presume that happened to me. Or do I bear the curse of my father's DNA?

The latter, I suspect, is my therapist's pet theory. Dr. Jane Dix—the Faculty Association referred her to me. She's a hot-tempered Adlerian. Lots of encounter, although she prefers to call it reality therapy. Yes, I'm off to the couch doctor once a week. Kimberley Martin has driven your punchy client halfway to the cackle factory. I'm on a diet of Valium and whisky. I can't sleep. I found myself watching a rerun of "The Beverley Hillbillies" last night. At three a.m.

Forgive me my digressions. Back to my family. My mother is only a year departed—but of course you were at the funeral. A sweet, frail woman who rescued herself—and me—from the tyrant of Lough Neagh Close. I hear the estate has been shut down now, all but the west wing—His Lordship is nearly on the rims. Skint, as they say over there. The grounds were cruelty, the settlement handsome. Mother took custody of me, but my older brother, Bob, stayed with him. Bob doesn't inherit the title, by the way; Father is only a life peer—Maggie Thatcher decorated him for doing absolutely nothing to stop the troubles as commander of the Royal Ulster Rifles. Mother never remarried, but she moved to Canada and sent me to the correct schools. St. Andrews in Toronto, U.B.C., Oxford, though she had some help from the late good-hearted Cecil Rhodes.

You've seen my resumé. It reads a little overinflated, doesn't it? Top percentile, etc., etc., double masters in law and economics, a few years of appellate advocacy—I dreaded it, I'm utterly traumatized by courtrooms—two years with the Securities

Commission, and since then faculty at U.B.C. Acting Dean since last year. Two politico-legal books under my belt, of which one bombed, the other caused a bit of commotion. I teach property, contracts, and commercial transactions.

They say poor Jim Mendel won't recover from his prostate surgery. I could have been dean at thirty-eight, Gowan. Instead, I am about to become—in the lexicon of podspeak—outplaced. That's likely to occur even if I'm acquitted—given the tenor of the times in the politically correct institutions that our modern universities have become.

I'm actually a fairly regular bloke for a rapist. I shoot pool, better at billiards. Still play a little old boys' rugby. I drink beer with the students.

And I go out with single women. This, of course, will be painted as the crime of the century when I'm on the witness stand. There must be something abnormal about a chap who's been a bachelor all his thirty-eight years. The jury will be thinking: This character can't form lasting relationships. Let's see, he's not gay, so he must be some other kind of pervert.

Let me get under way. I'll go straight to the bone. Pardon the expression. Gowan, I was so drunk I couldn't have got it up with a tow truck. Can you call expert evidence about that? *She* was drunk. And how does *that* play out? Now, witness, you say she was passed out on your couch. Yes, she was. And do you deny you gave into your animal instincts and became a lusting beast and had your will of this innocent young creature?

Why had she painted herself red? The colour of blood—some pagan ritual while I slept?

I taught Kimberley Martin for a time this year, as you know. She's twenty-three, middle class, but rising: about to be married into excessive wealth. She's in second year, and a rather—please don't think I'd ever be *unkind* to Kimberley—less than brilliant student. She scrimped by first year. She's by no means dull-witted, but she seems to have a lot of different things on the go. The Drama Society, for one. Watch out for the stage tears.

I'm not going to pretend she was just one of that sea of shining faces sitting in the lecture hall. She is not cosmetically disadvantaged. She's a traffic-stopper, and you'd have to have a terminal case of myopia not to notice. Long ringlets of crimped russet hair, always brushing it away from those big, green, innocent eyes. Wide, pouty lips. Tall. Graceful. Self-assured. Hip. And engaged. To a handsome tycoon.

You know how students will try to avoid catching your eye for fear they will be asked to discuss, say, the rule against perpetuities. Not Kimberley. She always gave me the full frontal look. She didn't know an answer one time, so she told a joke instead. It was funny, we laughed. I liked her then.

I started getting the impression she was coming on to me. It may be she uses her looks as a tool—perhaps she thought she could charm her way to a passing grade in Property II. She started hanging about after lectures, wanting me to explain some obscure rule or other. The kind of woman who touches as she talks—delicately, always with two fingertips. Heavy eye contact and lots of come-hither erotic nuances. In the meantime, I was trying to appear hopelessly professorial.

Then, with odd regularity, I started to bump into her on the campus. Between classes. On the grounds. In the cafeteria. Oh, would you mind if I brought my coffee over? Not at all, said the fly to the spider. There was also a visit to my office in mid-November. She wanted some career advice; she was interested in family law. She carried on about how her betrothed wanted babies; she wanted a career.

And I'm about to lose mine. I love my work. I'm popular with the students. I'm a good teacher, Gowan. I was.

And here I am spending New Year's Eve by my fucking self in my fucking den. I didn't accept any invitations, to everyone's vast relief. It spoils the party when someone's pinging off the walls.

Gowan, can't anyone talk to Arthur Beauchamp again? I mean, no reflection upon you, you understand that. Can *I* talk to him? Where is he being hidden?

～

The pillared courts of the Roman magistrates become an arena where the Emperor looks down upon my nakedness, and Annabelle is the queen beside him, crying shame. Guilty, I repeat. I am guilty. A loud rapping snaps me awake from this recurring eunuch's dream, and I struggle to my feet and bump into a wall where there should be a door. And I realize I am not at home. Where am I? Are those birds I hear, and the lapping of waves? And this brilliant beam that pours through these dusty second-floor windows, could that be sunlight?

I *am* at home.

The rapping again, urgent, a shivaree of noise coming not from downstairs but from above. As I shamble to the window, I see the perpetrator, a flicker that takes flight from my shingled roof. The view outside makes me dizzy. Rosy-fingered Aurora has flung wide the gates of morn. Mists float above the pasture where three mule deer graze, like society matrons at a buffet table, daintily sampling a little of everything, grass and bush and tree leaf. To better view this Turner-esque scene, I throw apart the French windows, but in the fury of my rapture they bang against the wall, and the deer prick up their ears and look this way and that, then all three bound on springy legs into the forest.

I breathe deeply the sweet-smelling air of the country, then turn to my bathroom for my morning ablutions. The fellow who greets me in the mirror has tousled silver hair of a fullness that belies his years. Hazel, heavy-lidded eyes, glazed with sleep—one of them occasionally chooses a slightly different route from its brother. A nose too straight, too patrician (let us not bandy words: a beak). Hiding in its shadow, and not hiding well, an unwanted corpulence of form. I will immediately begin a diet.

Stoney does not show up this morning as promised, and I tire of waiting. A slave to habit, I cannot sit down for the first coffee of the day without a newspaper, so I walk the two miles to the general store, arriving there distressingly short of breath. The store is a dowdy establishment run by a laconic older gentleman with rheumy eyes: Abraham Makepeace, who informs me he is also the island postmaster.

"Mr. Beauchamp, eh? You're the one bought the old Ashcroft place. Postcard here from your real-estate lady thanking you for your business and hoping you'll enjoy living here."

He reaches into a drawer and hands the card to me so that I may read it for myself.

"Do you have this morning's *Globe*?"

"We don't get that here."

"I see. Do you have *any* newspapers?"

"Didn't come in today. This here's the *Island Echo*. Comes out twice a month."

Tribulations must be borne on Garibaldi Island, but I shall survive them with equanimity. Back home in my club chair, instant coffee instantly at hand, I fold open the *Island Echo* and read about the recent lovely tea at the home of Mr. and Mrs. Vincent Rosekeeper of East Shore Road. Aha—cream puffs were served. And many compliments were "handed around" about the tasty mulled wine punch. An anomalous concluding sentence: "George Rimbold, returning from the function, skidded off the road and is recuperating at home."

I note elsewhere the confusing news of another signal event: "Badly missed by all islanders will be the Ashcroft family. Having recently moved off the island, their farm has been bought by a prominent and well-known lawyer from Vancouver, Mr. A. Beauchamp."

Ah, yes, not merely prominent but well known, this impotent pillar of the community: the right clubs, the right people, the right wing. How exhilarating was the social and political whirl. It will be unbearably taxing to adjust to life outside a crowded elevator. . . .

I spend my first week on Garibaldi learning such skills as were failed to be taught in the abysmal private schools of my youth—the hewing of wood, the drawing of water, the turning of soil for my garden, the setting of traps for the mice that have generously allowed me to share their abode.

As I settle in to my *angulus terrarum*, my quiet, gentle corner of the world, I still feel a sense of displacement, of being a stranger in a strange land. It will take a time to adapt from the comforting sounds of night I am used to: the haunting, lonely wail of sirens, jet engines in the sky, the distant screech of brakes, the city's ceaseless, hungry hum. Instead I must endure an annoying swish of waves upon my beach, the incessant gossiping of the little green frogs that inhabit my pond, the cold-hearted inquiries of the distant hunter owl. I awake not to the alarums of a garbage truck in an alley but to the impolite nagging of song sparrows trilling their tunes of the unfolding spring. Ah, but I will overcome these frowns of fortune. *Nil desper-andum.* I will prevail.

The weather remains inconstant. Though close to Vancouver—a thirty-minute flight by float plane—I am in a drier climate zone: the clouds shun us, preferring to huddle against the mountain ranges that guard Vancouver to the north. Often I see clouds forming the rim of a great hat above the Gulf Islands, but the hat is topless, the scalp bare to the radiance of that busy old fool Donne complained of: unruly Sun. *Why dost thou thus, through windows and through curtains call on us?*

But of late he cometh not. Today I have deserted my muddy garden and I remain indoors while murky clouds from the Pacific Ocean send wet warnings about the state of disrepair of my house, tiny puddles that collect upon my floor. I may wish to recruit Stoney to do some roof repairs as well, but, alas, Stoney continues not to show up, as regular as clockwork, on each succeeding morning. I am beginning to despair not only for him but for the two hundred dollars I advanced for materials.

More businesslike are the two young women from a firm known as Mop'n'Chop, which advertises in the *Island Echo*. Janey Rosekeeper and her partner, Ginger Jones, announce on arrival that they clean houses, cut wood, do yard work, and, "like, you name it."

"Ah, yes," I tell Janey, "you must be of the Rosekeepers of East Shore Road. I heard you had a splendid tea."

"My parents did, yeah. Turned into a major drunkathon, actually."

Doubtless this is the cause of hapless Mr. Rimbold driving off the road.

The two lasses, buxom both and glowing with country health, spend two days spring-cleaning my house whilst gossiping about who is "doing it" with whom on the island. To hear them, this community would seem a snake pit of sin. Not only does everyone know each other, everyone apparently copulates with each other. Each spring, I am told, after a hard winter of increasingly cheerless fidelity, there occurs a mass migration to new beds. Most active in that regard is the manager of the marina, a woman of apparently insatiable sexual thirst. I am warned to stay away from her.

As the days pass I develop routines. I walk each morning to the general store where I pick up my mail and pretend to buy a newspaper, then return to sip my coffee over a back issue of the *Echo*. (Mop'n'Chop has found a box of these in the basement crawl space.) I develop a curious fondness for the prose of one Nelson Forbish, publisher, editor, and, it would seem from the by-lines, sole reporter for this worthy gazette. "Recuperating at home is George Rimbold, who tried to jump through a plate window at the Brig dressed as a frog." Sadly, that tantalizing item is not developed to its potential. Who is this frogman Rimbold?

Militant Margaret Blake seems to be in every issue, a news item here, a letter to the editor there, mostly about that intrusion of the corrupting city, the Evergreen Estates subdivision. Aloof, distrusting, she has yet to pay a visit, though her house is only a hundred yards away. Often I glimpse her near it, busy as a whirlwind with her many chores.

I have given up on that fellow Stoney, who has been most visibly absent of late. One would expect to bump into him at one of the various centres of commerce on this island, but no.

My daughter telephones me on alternate evenings, surprised to find me still alive, chatting with the strained merriment of someone seeking to uplift the weary and the downtrodden. Why must she assume I am so unhappy?

Annabelle phones, too, full of spirited gossip about the city, her work, her current production of that weepy potboiler *La Bohème*. She is much in demand, it appears, and has contracted to be artistic director of a summer production of *Götterdämmerung* in Seattle. She has not visited yet because, she explains, she wants me to develop my "space," a concept I find confusing. I enjoy these calls, but afterwards feel unsettled, my mind too full of her.

She says she will try to get over soon, but I worry that her visit will be awkward—she is of a certain refined taste, and I will be embarrassed for my island, lacking as it does in art galleries, concert halls, and Shakespeare festivals.

Dear Annabelle, how I miss you, love you, fear you. Be strong, Beauchamp. Be of metal.

♪♪

Boy, I feel a little *worn* today. How much wine did we have to drink? Hello there, Patricia Blueman, it's me, the victim—oops, *alleged* victim of the *alleged* sexual assault. I hope this is what you want: a full, unblemished account of the perils of Kimberley, dictated onto cassette during a few quiet moments of reflection.

So where I'm at right now is my parents' cabin on Grouse Mountain. They've owned it for years, from back when there was only one mostly brokendown old chairlift up here. Now Grouse is a fullblown destination resort, all sky rides, bright lights, and Japanese tourists. Still lots of white stuff, even though it's the middle of March, and I have my skis and my season pass. Some advice for the lovelorn: You should take up skiing, Patricia, as there are lots of single men here. Brainless jocks, but what the hell.

Am I ever glad you're on the case. Until we met, I'd been wondering, like, what's going on, is anybody out there in *charge*? I mean, God, I had a couple of interviews with some grinning jackals in plain clothes who drove away in tears. They were laughing so hard. They never even took a written statement. Couple of morons who couldn't investigate their own flat feet. And then nothing, until out of the blue you called me last week. Now I have a prosecutor. Things are looking up.

Frankly, Patricia, when I first came to your office, I thought you were sort of, um, you know, *formal*. I thought, okay, Patricia Blueman, barrister, here's a real stiff lady, no sense of humour. But you really loosened up over lunch, and then last night . . . gee, you were funny. I still laugh when I think of your imitations of all those old-fart lawyers.

Anyway, I think we sort of bonded—are women still allowed to do that, or is it reserved only to men?—and I feel I can finally *purge* myself of the whole mess.

Though it will be hard to talk about. . . .

This joint is heated by a funky old potbellied stove, which I have roaring pretty good—it's a clear, brittle night, and icicles hang from my eaves like Christmas ornaments. Vancouver looks so majestic, spread like a magic carpet below me, its lights like stars, a galaxy.

Puts me in a sort of mood . . . I hope I can study here. Six days of hell coming up: final exams. Why, oh, why did they set the preliminary hearing so close to exam time? I'm going to be frazzled when I take the stand.

Sorry, I'm all over the lot here. You wanted some background. Okay, I'm in my second year studying to be a lawyer, and otherwise I'm normal—a happy, healthy, wholesome twenty-three-year-old Canadian woman who loves her father and mother and kid sister and happens to be seeing a shrink. I told you about *that*. Dr. Kropinski—he's helping me work through the awful nightmares I've been having. Our secret, okay? That smarmy defence lawyer—what's his name, Hatchet, Cleaver—he'll use it in court. Claim I dreamed it all. Religion: Catholic, though I'm sort of lapsed. I wear that cross-on-a-pendant to keep the folks happy. My dad's a mining engineer with the Goose Bay Copper Corp.—that's a division of the Brown Group—and they live away out in Labrador now.

It's through Dad I met my fiancé, who is actually his boss, full name Clarence de Remy Brown, and I call him Remy—he's a brawny, brusque businessman, a sort of constantly on-the-go kind of guy. I like him because he's not spoiled, he's his own man. No, I am *not* marrying him for his money, though I *know* somehow that's going to come up in the trial. I'm sort of living with him, but not full time—you saw my hovel in Kitsilano. This is partly because his parents are strictly from the seventeenth century, but also because I need my own space. Remy isn't exactly on the cutting edge of contemporary thought, either. But he's, you know, *secure*. And he loves me. And I love him.

So what else? I like skiing, sailing, Chinese food, and going to the movies. Yikes, this is starting to sound like a high-school yearbook. Or maybe an ad in the personals column. Wishes to meet movie star with sense of humour. My extracurricular thing: amateur stage. Played in *Saint Joan* this year. Yes, deah, it's Sarah Bernhardt here. Otherwise, I go to classes five mornings a week. I'm not one of the wonks, I don't spend all my afternoons in the library. I get my passing grades. Most of the time.

All right, which brings us to the subject of a certain, um, fringe-oid representative of the opposite gender, Professor Jonathan O'Donnell. He was—past tense—teaching me advanced property this year. Because of what everyone calls The Incident, he had to turn the class over to a loutish woman who picks her nose when she thinks we're not looking. I'd rather have O'Donnell. Stare at him. Make him uncomfortable.

Did you know his father is some kind of British noble? Baron or duke or some big deal like that. Pal of Margaret Thatcher, so you can see where Jonathan gets his right-winginess. He's an incredible teacher, I give him that. He could get you interested in the most awfully boring things. Brilliant, I guess. You see him on the tube on the *après*-news shows, reaming the Supreme Court for being too liberal. And I'm not going to pretend he's some ugly-looking troll. He's not, you know, what you'd call *pretty*—sort of ravaged-looking. He has this dark, moody thing—sort of like Remy, actually. Something vaguely dissolute about him—those deep lines on his face? Anyway, he started giving me the eye in the lecture room. I was a little flattered, I guess. I'm human.

The downside of all this was he always seemed to be picking on me, you know, like, Ms. Martin, please give me the ratio of Engelbert versus Humperdinck. I felt like some kind of special-needs kid. Give that poor girl extra attention.

And then he got so he would ask me to stay a few minutes after class on the pretext of talking about my work. I'd be all prim and proper, giving him the message as bluntly as I could, but I don't know—was he getting it?

Then once he asked me into his office to advise me on quote career paths unquote. Which he hardly talked about at all. Personal stuff, instead, what I liked to do in my spare time and that sort of thing. Oh, gee, let's see, I like skiing, sailing, and going to the movies. Kimberley Martin is this year's Miss Conviviality and she wants to be a lawyer when she grows up. I have something awful to admit. I was a cheerleader in high school. Hope *that* doesn't come out.

I'd see him on the campus a lot and I had this . . . it was a notion—but it didn't turn out to be so wrong—that he was stalking me. You know? Not like everywhere I go he's on my heels, but sort of Hi, there, mind if I bring my coffee over?

At some point we finally got onto the subject of the diamond ring that I kept waving in front of his face. So I told him about Remy. Told him what a special person he is. Invited him to the wedding— by the way, it's this fall, Patricia, and you must come, you can do your impersonations. Anyway, he never lost a beat. Kept coming on with those bedroom eyes.

So, getting to November twenty-seventh, the Law Students' Association, the LSA—I'm chair of the social committee—planned to have a dance. Okay, strike against me: I did personally ask Jonathan if he'd like to come. But you know, it was a money-raiser; we were asking all the faculty, selling them tickets.

Remy had gone away for a few days to South America with his father—the family has some investments there—and wasn't coming back until late that night. So I went alone—I can just see his lawyer making hay with *that*. O'Donnell's defence has got to be that I was a willing party, right? Is he going to deny tying me up? The lying bastard, I want you to tear him apart on the stand, Patricia. So I danced a bit—we had a live band—and when Professor O'Donnell came in, he made his usual beeline, and he bought me a drink and I . . . well,

I asked him to dance. It wasn't like a waltz where he'd be climbing all over me.

I assume there's going to be a great hue and cry about what I had to drink that night, so let me get my two bits in right now. I had exactly two rye and 7Ups at the dance. Don't you love that drink? It's so *common*. Now, the one he got me may have been a double, but I did *not* get loaded. Didn't touch any of the pot that was going around, either. I don't do drugs. Marijuana especially, I get too scrambled.

So, back to the dance. Well, Jonathan and I chatted a little. I was sort of interested in his background, how his father became a knight, or whatever he is. A viscount. Don't think he cares much for him. As his son, he's entitled to be called Honourable Jonathan O'Donnell, did you know that? Right. *Honourable*. I mean, he wasn't putting on the dog or anything—but it's sort of impressive, isn't it? To us commoners.

Anyway, I was about to leave before the last number and I was on my way to get my coat when he magically materialized right in front of me. So we do the last set of dances, slow rock, oh-oh, I'm thinking, here's the old high-school rub dance. But, you know, he was okay, kept a gentlemanly distance. He told me that the lecture theatre—these were almost his exact words—seemed to fill with a brilliant light every time I walked into it. That's what he said. I remember thinking, maybe he's not such a bad guy. Maybe a little crush on me, that's all.

Then he asked me if I was going to the afterparty. . . .

After a period of rain, a reluctant Apollo has finally spurred his fiery horses beyond the fleeing clouds, and today I have donned my coveralls. Steeling myself for the tasks ahead—a row of beans, a plot of potatoes (the carrots are in, the radishes are up!)—I light a cigarette and lean on my spade and contemplate my coming bounty, picturing it as the sylvan fields Virgil sang of. *Fortunatus et ille deos qui novit agrestis. Happy is he who knows the rural gods.* But my green reveries are interrupted by the noisy, belated arrival of Stoney and Dog, who show up—one month late—in a grunting rusted flatbed. My visitors look no healthier than their vehicle—both are bleary of eye.

"Got a timber here to shore her up," Stoney says. "Couldn't get nobody to mill it."

The timber, roped to the flatbed, is a sticky, freshly skinned trunk of a fir tree, still bleeding its sap.

"It'll add a kind of funky look."

He is unusually muted, perhaps because I am scowling. He offers no explanation for his long absence, and I refrain from asking if he was serving a jail sentence for house-renovation fraud. But my grumping subsides. The true Garibaldian, I have learned, is not beholden to the cruel dictates of time. After a few courtesies, he and Dog gather their tools and advance with determination upon the veranda.

But before I can return to my georgic chores, the sound of a small aircraft rents the placid air, and it settles in my little bay and taxis to the dock. I sense immediately that the firm has sent bounty hunters to return me to justice—as it were—and indeed the passenger who alights is Hubbell Meyerson, old friend and senior partner at Tragger, Inglis, Bullingham. (Tragger and Inglis now haunt from their graves, though Bully, over eighty, wanders in occasionally in the flesh. He is the spiritual leader of a firm with 110 lawyers.)

Hubbell seems ill at ease, but wears a mask of bonhomie as I show him about the grounds. "Fabulous outfit you're wearing, Arthur. The hick look. Where's the straw between your teeth? I'm kidding, you have a very nice spread here. The word bucolic springs to mind. Arthur, you got out before they could destroy your soul."

"The Lord maketh me to lie down in green pastures. As you see, I can offer something spiritual but, I'm afraid, nothing spirituous."

"Good, you're sticking to it. You're to be admired, Arthur."

We take tea on the patio lawn chairs while, presumably, the meter runs in the chartered plane at the dock, its pilot squatting on the port float, staring down at the minnows. There are larger fish than those in that bay. A boat must be purchased somewhere.

Hubbell stares at my two workers, who are both scratching their heads as they contemplate their task.

"Seems to me I heard somewhere there's a lot of inbreeding on these islands."

"Nonsense, those are skilled factotums of the many varied country crafts. What brings you here, Hubbell?" I cast a wary eye upon the plump briefcase that sits by his feet. "I fear you. You come not empty-handed, as a friend."

He pretends not to have heard me. "Quitting at the peak, it took guts, Arthur. Here's the best trial lawyer in the country sitting in front of me in goddamn coveralls. All those people who say you had a nervous breakdown, I tell them, hell, you just had a minor stroke, you want to slow down for a while. And in the meantime you're giving a chance to some of the others. Cleaver, he'll be doing most of the major trial work."

Gowan Cleaver, whose surname suits his art. Why is this name dropped so casually in conversation? From a corner of my eye I can see Stoney working with a pry bar, wrenching out a rotting board. A robin carols from the pear tree. A turkey vulture patrols the sky above the bay. I wait for Hubbell's second shoe to drop.

"By the way, I'd like you to glance at something, Arthur."

"Wild horses will not drag me, Hubbell."

"The preliminary hearing's complete except for the complainant's evidence. Kimberley Martin. She had a bad time with her exams, has to rewrite a couple, so the judge adjourned her evidence to this summer so she can get her school year out of the way. Gowan will finish the prelim, then hand it over to you to do the trial. Probably this fall. Three, four days, maximum a week. You whiz over, demolish a couple of witnesses, and you're quickly back digging your farm-fresh potatoes."

A heavy banging. The house shudders a little.

Hubbell opens his briefcase: accordion files, volumes of transcript.

"He wants you, Arthur. Honourable Jonathan Shaun O'Donnell, the acting dean of law at U.B.C. He wrote that savage attack on the Supreme Court—*A Law Unto Itself*. His father is Lord Caraway, a British viscount. Juicy trial. Big headlines."

"I know Jonathan O'Donnell. I have already declined his retainer."

"Yeah, but there's some real money here. The Faculty Association has agreed to pay the whole shot. It's become a cause to them, out-and-out harassment of a prof by a young lady who for some unknown reason cried rape. It's not a consent defence, Arthur. He didn't *do* it. You've never had a more innocent client. Just, you know, glance through the file. Christ, what else do you have to do out here in the godforsaken middle of nowhere?"

He has raised his voice in frustration, as if my placid countenance has suddenly confirmed for him the utter futility of his task.

"Hell will freeze over, Hubbell."

"Look, I'm going to leave you these transcripts. Police, forensics, O'Donnell's neighbour, they've already testified at the prelim. An interesting read. Hey, you'll get a kick out of some of this stuff." He brings out a few cassette tapes. "You have a machine to play these? . . . What are those guys doing?"

Stoney is noisily at work with a chain saw, Dog with a sledge hammer. "They are repairing the veranda."

"Well, they—"

The remainder of Hubbell's reflection is drowned in the roar of the veranda roof collapsing and shingles cascading from it. The rest of the house has taken on a slight starboard list.

As dust swirls and settles, Hubbell cannot restrain an infuriatingly smug smile. "Why do I have this feeling you'll be back?"

For a long while after the float plane takes off, Stoney and Dog stand by staring dully at the wreckage.

Dog kicks at the shingles. Stoney pulls from a pocket what I take to be a marijuana cigarette and lights it.

"Toke?" he says to me.

"No, thanks."

Wild horses, I repeat to myself.

�

DIRECT EXAMINATION BY MS. BLUEMAN

COURT CLERK: State your full name and rank please, for the record.

WITNESS: Constable Fourteen Gavin Oswald Peake, West Vancouver Police.

Q And were you on duty on the early hours of November twenty-eighth last?

A I was.

Q Tell us what you did and observed.

A On that day, as I was working midnight shift, I received a call at oh-five-forty-eight hours to attend at the home of a Mr. Clarence de Remy Brown at 4214 Kildonan Drive in West Vancouver.

Q And what did you do there?

A May I refer to my notes made immediately afterwards?

MR. CLEAVER: No objection, but I'll want to take a very careful look at them.

THE COURT: No question about it. You'll have full opportunity later.

MR. CLEAVER: I'd appreciate that, your honour. My learned friend has been keeping her evidence a little too close to her chest.

THE COURT: You are entitled to full disclosure, Mr. Cleaver.

MR. CLEAVER: Of her chest?
(Laughter.)

THE COURT: Oh, dear. I'm sorry, Miss Blueman.

MS. BLUEMAN: If Mr. Cleaver wishes to continue making me the butt of his humour—

MR. CLEAVER: Not the butt, Miss Blueman.
(Laughter.)

MS. BLUEMAN: I think it hardly appropriate—

THE COURT: Order.

MR. CLEAVER: Oh, I'm sorry, just trying to relieve the tedium.

THE COURT: Order. Let's carry on with the witness.

MR. CLEAVER: Well, since the subject of disclosure has been raised, I am giving notice I will be seeking production of some tape recordings the complainant apparently dictated to my learned friend, Miss Blueman.

MS. BLUEMAN: Long after the fact.

THE COURT: You know the rules of disclosure, madam prosecutor.

MS. BLUEMAN: Yes, but—

THE COURT: Let's have no more buts.

MS. BLUEMAN: Your honour, they're very personal.

MR. CLEAVER: We haven't a single written account from the complainant.

THE COURT: Do these tapes contain a narrative about the case, Miss Blueman?

MS. BLUEMAN: I'd be prepared to edit them—

MR. CLEAVER: She has to be joking—

THE COURT: Order. Miss Blueman, are you familiar with the Stinchcombe decision? The required rules of disclosure?

MS. BLUEMAN: I—

THE COURT: Everything. You have to give the defence everything.

MS. BLUEMAN: I can't—

THE COURT: You will! That's an order!

Q My objection is on the record. Constable Peake, you told us you went to Mr. Brown's house in the early-morning hours.

A Yes, I knocked on the door—

Q Can you describe this house?

A Well, it was pretty big. Three floors, I don't know how many bedrooms. Posh area, the British Properties. I was met by Mr. Brown at the door and he led me in. I noticed his hands were smudged with what looked like lipstick, and his clothes, too. He was pretty angry. He said his girlfriend—

THE COURT: It's hearsay, Miss Blueman.

MS. BLUEMAN: You can't tell us what he said.

A Well . . . that was it for a while. We just sat there in his living room and he carried on talking in an angry voice. She was sleeping. His girlfriend. Kimberley Martin.

Q Did you do anything as a result of your conversation with Clarence Brown?

A I phoned headquarters and instructed them to send an officer to 141 Palmer Avenue.

Q Did you ultimately interview Ms. Martin?

A I told Mr. Brown we should wake her up, or otherwise I am wasting my time here. So he left and eventually he came back and he led me upstairs to one of the bedrooms. Miss Martin, the complainant, was sitting up in bed in a nightgown with the sheets over her legs.

Q Okay, you can't tell us what she said to you, but did you make any observations about her person?

A She showed me some bruises on her wrists and ankles—the skin was torn there, on her left ankle. She said she had bruises on her chest—

MR. CLEAVER: Well, here we go.

THE COURT: Miss Blueman, get your witness under control.

MS. BLUEMAN: Just what you saw, officer.

A Sorry. The thing is, normally we would have a female officer, but we're usually short of manpower on the overnight shift. And, well, after some discussion, she showed me her breasts.

MR. CLEAVER: The complainant makes better disclosure than my learned friend.
(Laughter.)

MS. BLUEMAN: Mr. Cleaver, really, this is a *very* serious matter.

THE COURT: Order. Excuse me. Order.

Q And what did you see?

A I saw a small area of discolouration on the inner, ah, surface of her left breast. Check that . . . My notes have it as the right breast.

Q Then what did you do?

A I asked both of them if they would like to accompany me to the North Shore Hospital for a more thorough physical examination and some tests. We then proceeded to that hospital and I left her there while they called in the examining pathologist.

Q And did you have anything further to do with this case?

A No, I turned it over to the detectives.

Q Please answer my learned friend's questions.

⌘

CROSS-EXAMINATION BY MR. CLEAVER

Q Constable Peake, as you examined Miss Martin, did you observe any of the usual physical indicia of rape—scratches, cuts, that sort of thing?

A No, I did not.

Q Any signs of what might have been lipstick on her lower body?

A No.

Q While Miss Martin was displaying herself to you, did you get close enough to smell her breath?

A She smelled mostly of fresh soap. But I also detected a faint odour of alcohol from her breath.

Q Soap. I don't understand.

A It appeared to me that she had bathed recently.

Q Bathed?

A Her hair was wet. There were damp towels in an en suite bathroom.

Q Constable, did you not find that unusual?

A I didn't find anything usual about this case.

Q Did you seize the towels?

A No. I took a tie. Also a gold necklace.

Q Pretty odd that a supposed rape victim would crawl into bed after her ordeal and have a nice nap.

A I thought so.

Q Did you believe a word she said?

MS. BLUEMAN: This is becoming too much—

THE COURT: I will decide who is to be believed, Mr. Cleaver.

MR. CLEAVER: You said Mr. Clarence de Remy Brown spent a fair bit of time with Miss Martin before he ushered you to her bedroom.

A It seemed quite a while.

Q Time enough to have a good long conversation with her.

A Well, I wasn't there.

Q You said Mr. Brown was angry. He was fuming, swearing, carrying on like that?

A Like that.

Q Okay, I take it you knew that Mr. Brown's father is a wealthy industrialist. The Brown Group of Corporations.

A I didn't at the time. I do now, yes.

Q Did you see an engagement ring?

A A big diamond, yes, on her finger.

Q The heir to a great fortune would be quite a catch for any young lady, wouldn't he?

A I guess so.

֍

Arms folded, Mrs. Margaret Blake stands sternly at my doorstep amid the rubble of my former veranda. Her cocker spaniel, an energetic creature named Slappy, sniffs me with contempt.

"So you *are* tearing down the house."

"Merely alterations, my dear Mrs. Blake."

"It's a historic old place. There should be a law against this sort of thing."

"I am sure you will find one if you look hard enough." I intend to say this in a jocular tone, but the words emerge with gruffness. I am not in a good mood this morning.

"Well, I'm afraid I've had my fill of laws and lawyers."

Perhaps the source of her enmity to me is some wound suffered at the hands of my ever-maligned profession. But she doesn't elaborate. Slappy keeps sniffing at my feet, as if detecting something unusual or foul.

I try to be pleasant. "Can I offer you a morning coffee?"

Her tone softens slightly. "Thank you, but I have a zillion things to do. I just dropped by to ask if you've seen one of my sheep."

"I presume that's the animal I chased away this morning upon finding it defecating on the back porch."

"Oh, dear, I don't know how they get through the fence."

"Perhaps they use the holes."

Again I have been brusque, and this comment riles her. "Mr. Beauchamp, I have built and rebuilt that fence with my own two hands and I think you should be prepared to take some responsibility for your share of it. I mean . . . you obviously have money to burn."

The resentful tone, together with her apparent fondness for rules and regulations, suggests this feisty woman is some manner of socialist. She seems determined to distrust me, and I find no reason to apologize for or explain myself.

But as she and Slappy take their leave, I reproach myself for my unkind thoughts about her. She lost her husband not many years ago, and grief shows its colours in ways often harsh. Eventually, perhaps, she will learn I am merely a harmless pouf who prefers to be alone with his dead Latin poets.

Her visit, however, causes some inner rumblings of disquiet that remain with me through the day. In former times, the antidote was usually a bracing tumbler of Beefeater gin, a cure that sad experience taught me was worse than the disease. But as the days pass, I feel a slow ebbing of strength, of will. In every cell of my body, I can still taste that dulcet syrup, can sense its seductive offering of warmth and courage.

Oh, what a worshipper of Bacchus was I. Until one night, nine years ago, locked out of my house and vigorously seeking audience with a wife temporarily estranged, I fell through the skylight and onto her exercise bicycle. Promises were made at my hospital bedside. (I kept mine; she broke hers. She tried. I believe she tried.)

After a few days of doubtless pensive rumination, Stoney and Dog return to their tasks: sweaty, resolute work, pouring concrete pads and nailing up supports for the new veranda. They patch the roof, too, though in a fashion they assure me is temporary, much plywood and plastic sheeting. The house begins to look like something a hillbilly might inhabit, Ozarkian, ungainly. I suffer a temptation to have the place torn down and a new house built by a reputable city contractor. But I cannot bear the thought of having to confront my current crew with layoff notices . . . and Mrs. Blake lurks down the lane.

On an afternoon as I watch my veranda rise Sistine-like from the rubble, I am visited by the local media, one Nelson Forbish representing the *Island Echo*. A man of impressive girth, he emerges awkwardly from his compact car, armed with notebook and camera. He is about thirty-five, his cherubic face sheltered by a felt porkpie hat, the brim turned down in front.

"Mr. Bochamp, I've been waiting till you settled in to call. Like to do an interview." He has a high, whining voice, a nasal dentist's drill.

"Beecham is how it's pronounced. The name became corrupted after my ancestors raped and pillaged Anglo-Saxon England."

Nelson Forbish seems to have some difficulty absorbing this concept. "Would a good time be now?"

"As you see, the house is in disarray, so shall we just sit outside here? It's a splendid day. Would you care for a refreshment?"

"Something to eat, if you got."

I bring out a bowl of fruit and some slightly burnt homemade biscuits and lead Forbish to my dock, where I have set a table and a plastic chair. I have been fishing, offering fat worms from my newly spaded garden.

"Caught two very tasty perch the other day. Possibly that could be your headline, Mr. Forbish."

The reporter peels a banana and lowers it down his throat as if into a food blender.

"I've been reading your newspaper, Mr. Forbish, and I was wondering—if it's not subject to journalistic privilege—about Mr. George Rimbold, who tried to jump through a window at the local bar dressed as a frog."

"That was at Halloween. He's a bit of a tank."

"Ah, I see."

As he wolfs down a biscuit, he takes a photo of me, then produces some clippings from various Vancouver journals.

"Says here you've won fourteen straight murders in a row."

I hear echoes of his idiosyncrasies of composition in the *Island Echo*. Fourteen straight in a row.

"I have had my losses."

"This here magazine article says you left your office for a couple of years to work with bums on skid row."

Two years dimly remembered, two years of bibulous fog when Annabelle had separated from me.

"It was an interesting time."

"And the article goes on to say you're really colourful in court." He is on his second banana now, and eyeing an apple.

"Much exaggerated."

"You used to keep a pitcher of vodka on your table when you were on a trial. The judges all thought it was water."

I ponder his odd interview technique—he has yet to ask a question. "An utter lie. It was a pitcher of Beefeater gin. Nor did the judges suspect it was anything else."

"So there was also this time when apparently you were drunk in the middle of a trial, and you began reciting the Ruby . . ." Nelson is studying an obscure word in the magazine article.

Was I also drunk when being interviewed for that piece of literary embarrassment? *In vino veritas.* No, it was later—newly admitted to the Trial Lawyers' Chapter of Alcoholics Anonymous, I tended in those days to indulge in frenzies of truth and openness.

"*The Rubáiyát of Omar Khayyám.* 'Fill the cup that clears today of past regrets and future fears.' I once sought escape in such a cup. I am an alcoholic, Nelson."

"So what are you doing here on this island?"

"Making peace with God and nature. I am retired."

"So, for our readers, why did you choose Garibaldi?"

"I'm not sure. I think my brain may have snapped."

Nelson finally sees this as a joke and stops writing it down. He removes his hat, wipes his sweating brow. I note that my various comestibles have by now entirely disappeared down the man's ravenous maw.

"So, that's it? For your career? No more cases?"

"In fact, I just turned one down."

"What sort of case?"

"Oh, a sexual assault—"

"It isn't that law professor's case?"

I am sorry I have stumbled into this, but Nelson seems hugely titillated, his eyes bugging slightly. "I heard he kidnapped one of his students, took all her clothes off and chained her up, and took a bullwhip to her until she was bleeding."

"I ought not to discuss it."

"Then made love to her over and over until she couldn't take it any more. Do you think he did it?" There seems something almost obsessive about his interest.

"Nelson, I judge not my fellow man. And one shouldn't really discuss a matter that is before the courts."

His only response is a burp. Oh, pompous Beauchamp. Making peace with God and nature. Judging not my fellow man. But how innocent in God's eyes is our dashing acting dean of law? Does that matter? Do I care?

I am retired. That's all the news that's fit to print.

৵৵

DIRECT EXAMINATION BY MS. BLUEMAN

Q Your name and occupation for the record?

A Sergeant Henry Chekoff, detective, West Vancouver Municipal Police.

Q You've been a police officer for how many years?

A Going on ten.

Q Tell me what you did in connection with this case.

A Well, your honour, I came on duty at nine o'clock on the morning of November twenty-eighth and there was a message on my desk to go to 141 Palmer Avenue, complaint of a sexual assault.

Q This complaint had not been investigated earlier? During the night?

A Well, I was told the allegations—

THE COURT: Just what you saw and did, sergeant.

A We're pretty badly understaffed during the graveyard shift, so I guess I was the first officer to attend the, ah, alleged scene.

Q Okay, so you went to 141 Palmer Avenue that morning?

A Well, I did. Um, I attended at nine-twenty hours and there was a gentleman out front there raking some leaves.

Q Do you see that person in court?

A Yes, sitting beside Mr. Cleaver.

Q Indicating the accused. Can you tell us about his demeanour?

A Well, he seemed normal. He was clean-shaven. Casually dressed. He was surprised when I identified myself, but he wasn't unpleasant.

MS. BLUEMAN: Entering a voir dire, your honour.

MR. CLEAVER: Not necessary. For the purposes of this preliminary hearing I agree the statements are voluntary.

THE COURT: Very well.

Q What conversation did you have with him?

A Well, I said I was here to investigate a complaint about an incident that was supposed to have happened the night before. I asked him if he knew a Kimberley Martin. And he said, "Yes, she was here last night." And he said . . . Can I look at my notes?

THE COURT: Go ahead.

A He said, um, "Has something happened to her? I was worried. She disappeared." I then related to him the substance of the complaint that he had confined her and assaulted her sexually, and he didn't say anything at first, just looked kind of puzzled. And then he said, "Is this some kind of practical joke?" and I said, "No, not that I'm aware." He went sort of white, and said, "I did no such thing." I said, "Are you saying you didn't touch her?" And he said, "Didn't touch her? Of course I touched her. I took her to bed."

THE COURT: Just a minute. "Of course I touched her. I took her to bed."

A And he then added, "She was very drunk."

Q Was there any more conversation?

A Well, basically no, because he wanted to call his lawyer, but he invited me into the house while he did so.

Q And what transpired there?

A While he was in another room making his call I looked around the living room, and I could see a rumpled sheet on a couch there, and, ah, there was an end table beside it on which I found two women's earrings, which items I seized. Oh, and I found a woman's coat. Also on the table, a small black lady's purse.

Q Did you look inside it?

A A wallet, with Miss Martin's identification, credit cards and so forth, and $115 in cash.

Q Was there a makeup kit in the purse?

A Yes. I took note that there was a tube of bright-red lipstick that was worn down to the end.

MS. BLUEMAN: That's shown as Exhibit Nine on the admission of facts, your honour. A tube of . . . a product I ascertained was called Shameless.

THE COURT: Shameless? Carry on, witness.

A Mr. O'Donnell came back, and while we were waiting for his lawyer I asked him if he minded if I looked about his house. He didn't say no, so I checked in all the rooms, and in a bedroom closet upstairs I seized a woman's dress hanging there, um, along with some undergarments, panties, panty hose, and a brassière, and a pair of high-heeled shoes on the floor.

THE COURT: May I look at Exhibit Eight?
(Exhibit handed to the judge.)

THE COURT: This is what would be called a mini?

A I guess so.

THE COURT: And these are the panties?

A Yes, bikini briefs, I guess you call them.

THE COURT: Scanties. Okay?

A And there were sheets on the bed there, which looked like it had been slept in, and I also seized them.

Q Describe this bed.

A A queen-sized brass bed with posts at either end.

Q Then what did you do?

A Well, I went out to the car to call headquarters and I had a conversation with the chief, and, ah, well, it was decided I would ask Professor O'Donnell if he'd mind if we took a few pictures in there. And that's what we did.

MS. BLUEMAN: Your witness.

CROSS-EXAMINATION BY MR. CLEAVER

Q Sergeant Chekoff, I am curious about a phrase Professor O'Donnell used in your interview. Do I have your words right? "Of course I touched her. I took her to bed. She was very drunk."

A That's right.

Q So it appears from your notes. When did you make them?

A Uh, some time later that day.

Q Not immediately afterwards?

A No, back at the station.

Q Is it possible there was an error?

A I don't think so.

MR. CLEAVER: Excuse me, your honour, may I consult with my client?

THE COURT: Of course.
   (Mr. Cleaver consults with the accused.)

Q Did he not say, "I put her to bed"?

A Um, that's not what I wrote.

Q "I never touched her. I put her to bed. She was very drunk." That makes more sense, doesn't it?

A Okay. Yes, it does, I guess.

Q Thank you.

THE COURT: Excuse me, Miss Blueman, you're pulling a face—do you have a problem with this?

MS. BLUEMAN: No, I . . . well, of course, I have a problem. He's changing his—

THE COURT: Police officers have the right to change their mind, Miss Blueman. Just like members of the fair sex.
(Laughter.)

THE COURT: Sorry, Mr. Cleaver, we've interrupted.

Q Now, sergeant, you found her dress and some underclothes hanging neatly on hangers, her purse and jewellery carefully arrayed on a table?

A Yes.

Q The dress didn't seem rumpled?

A Not that I could tell.

Q When you looked around the house, did you see anything of interest you haven't reported?

A Well, I saw a man's brown suit lying crumpled up on the bedroom floor. I didn't take it.

MS. BLUEMAN: Of course he didn't.

THE COURT: What was that?

MS. BLUEMAN: Never mind.

Q See any ropes or bindings?

A No, none.

Q You *were* searching for some means whereby she could have been tied up.

A Yes.

Q And saw nothing.

A No.

Q No whips or chains.
(Witness laughs.)

A No.

Q Out in the yard, when Professor O'Donnell asked you if this was some kind of joke, you said, "Not that I'm aware." Why?

A Well, all I knew about the complaint was from this note that had been left on my desk. Naked woman covered in lipstick, claim of assault. I thought maybe it was a practical joke.

Q You never did arrest him.

A He did come by that afternoon with his lawyer, and we had a clearer picture of the allegations then. And, ah, I met with my superior officer. And I charged him. And we did the fingerprints and the art.

THE COURT: The *art*?

WITNESS: Sorry, it's an expression. Mug shots.

MR. CLEAVER: A term of art, your honour. No more questions.

THE COURT: Anything arising from that, Miss Blueman?

RE-EXAMINATION BY MS. BLUEMAN

MS. BLUEMAN: When you were looking about his house, did you check the fireplace?

A Yes. There was ashes in it, some burnt sticks.

Q Could you tell if it was a recent fire?

A I never got that close to it.

Q And I suppose you never thought to take a sample of the ashes—

MR. CLEAVER: She's cross-examining her own witness.

THE COURT: Now, Miss Blueman—

MS. BLUEMAN: Shoddy, disgusting—

THE COURT: I can't hear you.

MS. BLUEMAN: Never mind, I'm through with this witness.

MR. CLEAVER: Perhaps we should take a Valium break, your honour.

THE COURT: Fifteen minutes.

∞

After my photograph and interview appear in the *Island Echo* ("Mr. Arthur Beauchamp, Q.C., a former colourful lawyer, pictured here on his dock"), several of my shy fellow islanders begin emerging from their dens: neighbours with gifts of homemade bread and pickles.

So it appears I am being finally accepted as a permanent. (Lower in class are the weekenders. The lowest and most contemptible class is that of the mere visitor.) Like my fellow permanents, I have developed a complacent scorn for the spiritually impoverished inmates of the city. These are men who must daily adorn themselves with that floppily hanging wedge of decorative cloth known as a tie. These are women who daily must put uncomfortable shoes on their feet. They must all enter small, rectangular spaces known as offices and remain there however pleasant the day.

But prisoners are allowed weekend passes, and on this breezy Saturday in May as I mingle with my fellow Garibaldians, we see them, our friends and kin, furiously waving at us from aboard the ferry churning towards the dock. The vessel finally jolts to a shuddering stop and a swarm of cyclists pours over the ramp and begins pumping up the hill—young men and women in multicoloured garb that clings obscenely like an outer skin. I, in drab contrast, am in my garden grubs; a John Deere cap is perched cockily on my head. Ah, yes, I am melding into the community, and proudly wear its uniform.

Now debouch the foot passengers. Advancing towards me are Nicholas Braid, mutual-funds specialist; wife, Deborah, educator; and eight-year-old Nick, Jr., looking grumpy.

Deborah hugs me furiously. Her husband grasps my hand and Nicky stares up at me with eyes already laden with the boredom he is about to endure. No television, no computer games.

"Wasn't easy to get away from the pits for a weekend," says Nicholas. "Going nuts. They made me manager of a new fund. Resources, oil and minerals. Neck's in a noose if I don't get it up twenty points in a bull year." His staccato half-sentences tend to lack pronouns.

"Oh, *please* change the subject, darling," says Deborah. "It's quite boring. Dad hasn't the faintest idea what you're talking about. He saves his money under a mattress."

"Better off leaving it there than investing so heavily in land, Arthur. It's overpriced. Heading for the downhill run."

"Ah, but I have made a clear profit already. Note that lines of worry have disappeared."

I lead them to my shining carriage, all recently washed and waxed by Mop'n'Chop. But Nicholas, doubtless missing his weekend trot around the golf course, is determined to walk the three miles to the farm, and he manages to challenge his son's virility sufficiently to force him to join him.

My daughter peers at me closely as if examining me for skin disease. "Well, your complexion is okay. And you've lost some excess baggage, that's good. Still smoking, though. You haven't had any dizzy spells?"

I explain to this keeper of my health that I am in excellent shape and will soon be subsisting on my own garden greens, and then I stumble my way onto a topic less comfortable. "And how is your mother?"

"You saw her the last time I did. So she hasn't come out to see you once?"

"She has phoned a few times. She sounds well."

A long, desperate silence.

"I think . . . I'm going to say it—you should let her go, Dad."

"Perhaps we ought to find another topic—"

"Stop doing it to yourself."

"Deborah—"

But she suddenly lets flow a torrent. "I suppose she

loves you in a way. It's a form of possession, though, isn't it, keeping you flapping on the line. It flatters the shit out of her to have you down there kissing her boots before she kicks you in the face another time."

"Deborah!"

"I'm sorry, the venom is leaking." A pause. "I care for you, Dad. Really. I love you. It's just that I wish you'd stop being such a—"

"Masochist."

It is one of her favourite terms of loving abuse towards her father.

"Oh, my God, I'm just being rotten and cranky. It's a beautiful day, I'm in a beautiful place, and I'm happy and you're happy, and I'm sorry."

"Ah, yes. Did you bring the onion sets?"

"They're in my bag."

"That's all that matters."

The weekend with my kin must draw mixed reviews. Deborah, I feel, enjoys herself, but her husband spends most of his time practising golf strokes with an imaginary club. He is disgruntled to learn I am not on-line; I have neither fax nor computer. But he makes do, spending many hours on long-distance calls to the bourses of exotic capitals of finance: Tokyo, Hong Kong, Paris. He is handsomely off, but has earned his money the hard way, the Canadian way, a life of unrelenting worry, fear, and pain.

Little Nick surprises himself by finding things to do: trees to be climbed, stones to be hurled into the bay, the neighbour's stray chickens and sheep to be chased. After he is finally led exhausted to bed, his parents and I chat near the fire over our evening tea.

"How goes the work?" I ask Deborah. "With those young . . . What is the acceptable term of the day? Clearly not mentally handicapped."

"Just call them challenged, Dad. Exhausting. I can hardly wait for summer break. Two months in Europe, right, dear?"

Nicholas lifts a golf ball, sending it down the fairway of my living room. "Busman's holiday. Tax-free."

I regale them through the evening with tales of Garibaldi and its oddball cast of characters. As we are about to depart for bed, Nicholas asks if I'll be handling Professor O'Donnell's case.

"Why would you ask such a question?"

"Just that I heard your name mentioned. Happen to know one of the characters involved in the case."

"Indeed."

"That girl, what's her name . . . Kimberley Martin?"

"The complainant."

"Met her fiancé. Clarence de Remy Brown. Brown Group of Companies? Owns some gold mines in South America I'm thinking of taking a flyer on. Hard-nosed chap, temperamental. Brought the subject up over lunch at the club. Knows your reputation, of course. Asked me if you were taking the trial. All sort of awkward."

"No, I shall not be involved in that case."

Today's visitor is our island trustee, the twitchy Kurt Zoller, who is again, for some enigmatic reason, apparelled in a life jacket. Perhaps he suffers a phobia of drowning. Mr. Zoller is enlisting support for a public meeting soon to be held for a rezoning, an expansion of Evergreen Estates.

"Fifty more lots, Mr. Bo-champ. More people, more clout. New and better roads, more tax money to pay for them. We need your voice, because a lot of people are going to be there who want to live in the past. They don't want to enjoy all the comforts. I see a day coming when we will all have a mall, our own police office. Cablevision."

"Ah, yes, that will be a boon. But, Mr. Zoller, I am a newcomer—it might be seen as brash of me to loudly add my voice."

"We have to stand up to them."

"Who?"

Though we are alone, he lowers his voice: "Margaret Blake and the eco-freaks." This has the sound of a popular music group. "There are quite a few of them here. Most of them don't advertise it. They look and act just like us."

I ask Mr. Zoller how he came to be chosen to represent his fellow islanders.

"I was their unanimous choice."

"How remarkable."

"I won by acclamation."

"Ah, no one was willing to run against you."

"Exactly."

Testing a theory that plants respond to fine music, I have set speakers out on the back deck so that my peas and carrots may enjoy Bach and Vivaldi while I hack away at the uncultured thistles with my hoe. The flowers of late May are making a vigorous show: daisies, foxgloves, lupines, purple roadside sweet peas. The song sparrows are in full-throated ease. The days are growing longer; summer waits anxiously in the wings for her grand entrance.

In response to a notice in the *Island Echo* ("14-foot runabout with engine and canopy that runs like new for sale at marina, just ask Emily"), I stop by the marina office. Emily is fetched from the Brig, where she has been tending bar, a woman of middle years who wears tight jeans that make a swishing sound between her bounteous thighs as she walks towards me with extended hand.

"Hi, I'm the manager here. Emily Lemay."

Ah, this is the seductress I have been warned against. I will strive to keep my honour intact.

She leads me to the boat, which is tied to one of the slips. It is homely, but looks serviceable and safe. During a demonstration of the thirty-horse engine, the arms of Emily Lemay entwine with mine, and I am overcome with the smell of ripe peaches with which, apparently, she has perfumed her ample bosom.

"I'll sell it to you cheap," she says. "One of the local characters gave it to me to pay off his bar bill. George Rimbold? Met him?"

"I have read of his exploits."

We negotiate a price, and she offers a drink to seal the bargain.

"Thank you, but I don't. Any more."

"Well, then, a coffee."

"Tea, if you don't mind."

We repair to the Brig, which is empty in the afternoon of all but a loud table of four who are debating politics, hotly castigating the government for reducing welfare benefits. These I am told are the local drunks. Is one of these lads the notorious George Rimbold?

I survey with trepidation the many alluring labels of bottles arrayed on the counters behind Mrs. Lemay. I wonder if there is not, on this sinful island, a chapter of Alcoholics Anonymous.

Mrs. Lemay is a woman without secrets, and she babbles merrily on about various marriages she has suffered—brutish, callused men, none of them the gentleman she perceives me to be. I am rather flattered by her attentions, for she is attractive, open and gregarious, a full-fleshed woman of the type celebrated by the Dutch masters.

She extracts from me the confession that though I am married I am currently living alone, and as I rise to leave she offers to come visiting one day. I am too polite to demur to this, though I suspect her intentions are dishonourable. But why should I, the impotent cuckold, worry? No stirring of the slumbering weakling below answers her call.

In the men's room, I unleash my fearsome weapon (spineless soldier, when last did you go forth to battle?) and piss into the urinal, a stream the colour of cowardice. Am I different from other men? I always marvel at the locker-room tales of multiple conquests that I have heard, of concupiscent appetites, of night-long rigours between the sheets. Oh, there was a time when I could rut with adequate if not extravagant vigour. Enough to perform my duty to the species. But soon after my wedding, a series of humiliations proved I was unequal to the task of responding to Annabelle's womanly wants, and I went as dead as the poets of antiquity.

And yet—as I keep proclaiming (can anyone hear me?)—I hold this unyielding affection for Annabelle. Call me ill, call me twisted. I love her.

I was thirty-three and she was twenty-four. She was newly graduated from a prestigious school of fine arts, with a budding career as a set designer, but when we met, her role was as a Crown witness in the courtroom. A fraud case, something to do with an arts grant: the dreary details are forgotten.

I cross-examined her for two hours. She stayed on in the courtroom and, as she said, "watched me" for the rest of the day. Afterwards she complimented me on my victory. I stammered out an invitation to buy her a drink.

Three months later we married. We quickly parented a child of whom neither of us saw enough. Little Deborah was entrusted to a nanny while Annabelle furthered her career—set design, art direction, the stage, then opera—and while I busied myself gaining fame and fortune and a reputation as a wonderful fellow to have a drink with.

But I presume she became progressively bored with windy Arthur Beauchamp, with all his bloated, orotund posturings. I was about as romantic as the sacking of Rome. I didn't know until later on she'd had a series of suitors. As sharply tuned as I may have been in the courtroom, I was a blind witness to the transgressions of the woman with whom I had sworn to share my life. But upon one wine-soaked evening, overcome by an unguarded desire to repent, Annabelle reeled off her list of lovers and I died as many deaths.

ॐ

I am sorry, Gowan, if I have seemed so self-pitying. As I have admitted, I am slightly under the influence. Okay, let us make haste to the dance. It was well under way when I arrived. Kimberley spotted me immediately, pounced like a cougar, grabbed my hand and yanked me onto the dance floor, where we staggered around for a while in imitation of Astair and Rogers. Afterwards—I will admit this, however incriminating it might be—I offered to buy her a drink. A rye and ginger, that is what she asked for. I should have realized right then she was not a well person.

I had a double whisky. I was packing it away, frankly, getting sloshed. It had been a tough week of marking midterm papers. Was that it? I don't know what my excuse was. Maybe it was the strange electricity in the air. Maybe I should worry about my drinking. . . .

God, what's my father going to think? Or would the old roué even give a sodding damn?

So I escaped from her, circulated, joked it up with the jocks, talked football—the Grey Cup was on Sunday—but every time I turned around she was in my face. Making merry conversation, all bright green eyes and bright red lips (a product called Shameless!) in a huggy little basic-black mid-thigh mini. I actually had a good time with her. She keeps coming at you from places you don't expect. She's a stitch. She has incredible timing.

Gowan, she is going to be brutal to cross-examine. She has an élan. Blunt. Chatty. Makes lots of eyeball contact. She'll play to the jury; she'll have all the men smitten. I don't think we ought to have too many males on this jury, Gowan. I fear we are the more stupid sex. There's a tendency among members of our endangered gender to think more erratically than erotically when dealing with matters carnal. Don't you think women are more likely to see through her?

I began thinking: O'Donnell, old sport, is she offering her body for a passing grade? Be on the alert. But all the time she has this gold chain around her neck with a cross on it, and a ring on her finger as big as a stop sign. Where was her fiancé, I asked. She said, "We're enjoying a little time apart together." Apart together. We both realized how odd that sounded. We laughed. You know how people sometimes connect? I *liked* her.

Gowan, I'm not going to lie. I had *thoughts*. Any normal human male would have thoughts. But that's all. It's not as if I've been forced to make out with Man Friday on a desert island for all my years of manhood. I date. I've had girlfriends. We commit consenting acts.

I didn't pursue her. *I* am the victim.

In current time, as I write this, it's almost 11:30 p.m. In half an hour I'll put on my funny hat and blow one of those paper whistles that curls out like a snake and bops someone on the nose.

Happy New Year, Gowan. I look forward with joy to the unfolding events of the coming year. I'll finally emerge from jail talking like a greeting card. Best wishes to my favourite parolee on his seventieth birthday. You'll have to forgive some of my typing errors. My fingers keep slipping between the keys.

We had the last dance together, a slow one, but I managed to keep her at arm's length. She carried on in this deep, melting voice of hers about how she enjoyed my classes. Thought I was a wonderful teacher. Such understated wit. So cute with my little half-moon spectacles perched on my nose. I think I said something flattering, too, which no doubt will be used against me.

"Thank you for the dance, Kimberley." "Oh, no, Jonathan, thank *you*." She doesn't like to be called Kim, by the way. Kimberley.

For a reason I cannot fathom, I accepted her invitation to an after-party. No, that's not fair. There was a reason. I was having a good old-fashioned time. It was Friday night, I had a weekend to recover.

So a throng of us went in my car. I was still sober enough to ask someone else to drive. Charles Stubb, a young Liberal with an obscene ambition—he wants to be prime minister. We were crammed four in the back seat, and I was thigh on thigh beside the Dragon Lady. I remember us both being sweaty from dancing. She began reciting lines from *Saint Joan*. Yes, Gowan, Kimberley is the shepherd maid of the battle of Orleans, the heretic saint. But it is I who shall be tied to the stake. . . .

Do you know, despite everything, despite the supposed trauma of being bound and raped, she gave four performances of that play? In the middle of January at the Frederick Wood Theatre. Shaw would have been proud, he loved his plucky heroines. Gowan, if *you'd* been tied up, and had your loins girded with Shameless lipstick, and been buggered and raped, could *you* sit around and memorize all those exhortations about going into battle with God on your side?

We went to some great shambling house in the West End where several students were jointly renting the ground floor. I think I was mostly talking to Charles, explaining how his beloved Liberal party was a collection of fuzzy ideologues in politically correct multiculturalist drag. Kimberley kept hovering. She had at least one refill. They didn't have ginger ale, so she mixed her rye with Sprite one time, and if I'm not mistaken with lemonade a second time. We're up against some dark forces here, Gowan. Satan rules.

After a while I said, okay, someone drive me to my house. There was a debate about the mechanics of this, and I agreed to pay for a taxi home to whoever volunteered. Several of them offered, and ultimately five of us left in my car, Charles Stubb driving again, and a young girl Charles was with—I forget her name, Asian Canadian, first-year arts—and a notorious sluff-off by the name of Egan Chornicky—I don't know how these people find their way into law school. He was blowing about a .30. And of course Kimberley Martin came along. The next scene plays out at my house. . . .

Have I wronged Arthur Beauchamp in some way? We used to chum socially. He's had dinner at my place, the very scene of the crime. He and his wife, Annabelle. Gowan, I beg, arrange for me to see him. Please.

§ §

Annabelle gives me no warning, and I am flustered beyond words when, having driven over on the early Monday ferry, she materializes in front of my woodshed, incredibly beautiful, radiant and cheerful, carrying on as if it were only yesterday we parted. She wears a colourful *décolleté* sundress while I, of course, am adorned in the authentic garb of a rube, tractor cap, work boots, unshaven, unshorn, sweaty. I have been splitting wood.

Undeterred by what she sees and smells, she kisses me full on the lips, and I let go the axe and it falls on my foot. (The blunt part, but it pains nonetheless. A pain that can be endured.)

"Bristly. Are you growing a beard, darling?"

"What? Oh, no, I hadn't thought so."

"I think you'd look lovely in one."

"I'm quite discombobulated."

"What an awful word."

"I'll clean up. I was . . . I'll show you the garden and . . . I have a boat now. My goodness, it's delightful to see you."

I lead her past my vegetable patch towards my leaning tower of Pisa. As the construction of my new veranda advances, the house seems to heave ever more to one side. Fortunately the girls from Mop'n'Chop were recently here and cleaned up the construction mess.

Annabelle sails inside and looks about with what seems an expression of approval—Janey and Ginger swabbed the inside as well.

I shower. I change. I make lunch. I am grateful Annabelle is in a talkative mood, for I can find nothing worthwhile to say. She is in excellent spirits, teasing me gently about my hitherto-unappreciated survival skills with axe and hoe and kitchen stove.

It is a perfect June day under an effulgent sun, the island wearing a fresh green dress with floral decorations, so after lunch I take Annabelle touring in the Rolls-Royce, visiting many of the charming bays and overlooks.

My island does not receive the cynical review I had expected.

"It seems all so calm and clean and pretty," she says. "Such a sleepy little island. I get so weary of Vancouver. Everything is so unnecessarily hectic. Arthur, you know, maybe I could come out here for a few weeks this summer. Maybe after *Götterdämmerung* gets under way."

"I'd love that. Come and enjoy the sunset of the gods here on Garibaldi. A spectacular performance every evening."

Do I mean this as devoutly as it sounds? Do I still desire the pain? There are narcotics fiercer than alcohol, more tenacious.

I suggest a cruise over the waters next, but Annabelle is either leery of my seamanship or, as she says, prefers to exercise her legs, so our next journey leads us up an old fire road and through the forest. Annabelle, fitter than I—she has played tennis through the winter—is waiting at the bluffs at the top as I struggle around the last bend. Panting, wheezing, I light a cigarette.

The rocks on which we stand are thick and soft with moss. Chickadees scamper among the fir and arbutus. From somewhere the perfect silence is broken by the elegiac, distant bleat of sheep. Garibaldi lies beneath us, seemingly lifeless, torpid. There is the general store and there the school and there my house and my demesne. Sailboats struggle on the wind-calmed ocean. But above, a more skilled sailor floats on outstretched wings, a bald eagle canvassing its vast, wide world.

Annabelle seems spellbound.

"That's Vancouver." I point to the brown haze to the north. "Behind us are the Olympic Mountains." To the south, in the State of Washington, a towering barricade, cloud-capped. " 'Many-peaked Olympus, the abode of the gods, ever unchanging.' That's from Homer."

I wonder why I have such an unwavering compunction to be so patronizing and pedantic. I know she finds it tiresome. But she smiles.

"'Abode of the gods' . . . Makes you wonder, Arthur, doesn't it, if the things that seem important really are. Oh, God, I'm getting contemplative. It must be the clean air."

"You ought to come up here with an easel. You've always wanted to get back to the palette."

"You're such a dear, Arthur. We should . . . well, I think we are getting along a bit better, aren't we?"

"Ah, I remember when we used to go for walks like this."

"Stanley Park. Prospect Point. Every Sunday. And you with your poetry. I remember thinking you were trying so hard to be romantic. In your way."

"In my own stuffy way, I suppose you mean."

"Well, you were always a little . . . not pompous. Donnish."

"Pompous."

"You don't mean to be."

"Surely you can stay the night."

"No, I have to get back tonight. Dress rehearsal tomorrow."

"Oh, I regret that."

"I'm going to take along a friend."

From a distant copse a woodpecker shrieks and laughs at me.

"Little Nicky. It'll mean a day out of school, but I think we should expose him to some of the good things, don't you?"

I fear she sees how flustered I am.

"It's the last production, then I'm off to Seattle. *Salomé*."

"Oh, he may enjoy that. Suitably bloody."

"It'll keep him away from the idiot box for a few hours."

"Have a chocolate chip cookie. I made a batch." I have brought along a bag of them.

"Arthur, you astonish me."

She munches it daintily, afraid for her figure.

"So, Arthur, are you going to take Jon O'Donnell's case?"

An odd turn in the conversation—this seems to be the major topic of our times. "Of course not. Why do you ask?"

"Oh, I talked to Hubbell. He flew over here to try to strong-arm you, didn't he?"

"Yes. Tell him he can have his files back."

"Arthur, you know Jon O'Donnell."

"As do you." I had given guest lectures to his classes. We had shared the odd martini. Annabelle knows him from a few dinner parties we attended—once at his house. I have nothing against him, although I remember being mildly put out by Annabelle's tendency to act the coquette when he was about. And he seemed to be heeding her siren's song. . . .

Nonsense. My years with Annabelle have filled me with suspicious imaginings. He is an engaging fellow, not without wit, though gallingly sardonic when in his cups. I suspect he drinks too much: I see something darkly hidden in haunted eyes that tells me he is a prospective member of my tribe.

"Arthur, you know he couldn't do a thing like that."

"Do I, indeed?"

"Well, *I* know . . ."

She hesitates, and now I am suffering a vague unease.

"I mean—you know him as well as I do: tying a girl up, raping her—those allegations will always be a terrible slander to his reputation. He . . . called the house a couple of times, asking for you. I didn't give him your number, because I promised you. Well, actually, I bumped into him. Downtown. We had coffee."

"I see." I clear a throat that is suddenly tight. "Did he ask you to speak to me on his behalf?"

"He . . . asked about you. Well, Hubbell is very insistent. He really wants you to do this one more case."

"Do you, as well?"

"I . . . think you should do it."

Oh, for a tall glass of something cold and powerful. The juniper taste of gin is strong and needy in my nostrils. I watch below as a squadron of Mrs. Blake's sheep trudge their weary way across the fields. They are on their way, of course, to seek breaches in my garden fence.

I have developed an unreasoning distaste for the O'Donnell case.

Wild horses.

§⚬

My friends in the next cabin said they saw a bear yesterday. I mean, Patricia, here we are looking straight down on one of the busiest port cities in the world, and we have friendly neighbourhood *bears*. They come out of their dens this time of year, grumpy and hungry, and head for the nearest McDonald's. I had an awful nightmare, a big bear coming into the cabin and jumping on me in bed. Awoke screaming. *That* will give my shrink something to keep his mind occupied.

Study in restful surroundings, says Dr. Kropinski, and I'm not to think about The Incident. But every time I pick up *Proctor's Real Transactions,* there he is, Professor O'Donnell, my law lecher, staring up at me from the pages.

Remy is supposed to come up for a day or two, but he's not sure when he'll make it. We had a bit of a skirmish after you left us, I'm afraid. Nothing heavy, just a polite exchange of words, but he thought I got a little too—loud, he called it—at dinner. Hints I can't quite hold my booze.

But I'll forgive him anything. Remy's been right there for me, one hundred per cent, through the whole trauma. He loves me to bits.

How's *your* love life? Did you do what I suggested? Give the hunk a call. Ask him out. It's the '90s. Be bold. And stop calling yourself plain. You're gorgeous. *Think* gorgeous. I sound like Ann Landers.

Patricia, when I get back down the hill, let's go out for dinner again. I won't invite Remy and his cell phone this time, it's like having a whole boardroom of executives join you. I'll give you these tapes, but let's just have a good time and not talk about the trial. And you can do another imitation of that sexist judge . . . funny name. Judge Pickles. He's going to preside over the preliminary? Egad. Sounds like a real modern, aware, illuminated man. The pigs still run the farm.

Back to business. All right, a bunch of us leave the dance together and I get talked into going to this after-party. I was going to jump in a taxi, but Jonathan practically pulled me into the back seat of his Jag. I don't mean like I was in danger or anything, Charles Stubb was driving, and he's suitably straight and safe and totally L7, and there was a whole mob of people packed in there with us. But you know, there's like his arm around my shoulders and all this hot professorial breath on my neck.

He called me Kim. I hate that.

We went off to where these students rent a ground floor in the West End, and we sort of joked around and had a good time there. I don't think I had much to drink, maybe one. I had rehearsals that weekend. *Saint Joan.* "Who is for God and his maid? Who is for Orleans with me?" Great stuff, huh? Anyway, I didn't want to be hung over, and all I had was a little rye and something. . . .

Why do I have to justify myself? Why do I have to explain I was all so sober and childlike in my innocence? Like, you know, I was wearing something very chi-chi and short. So I must have led him on. Top two buttons weren't done up, can you forgive a man yielding to his natural urges?

And I suppose Mr. Cleaver is going to ask why I agreed to go up to Professor O'Donnell's for a nightcap. I don't know. Maybe I was curious, wanted to see his place. Like, you know, why does a bachelor son of a British lord choose to live alone in a big house? Sort of odd. I suppose that's going to make it sound like I was interested in him. . . .

God, I'm going to be a mess up there on the witness stand. Cleaver will sense blood, my dear, and tear me to shreds before your very eyes.

Anyway, I figured what the hell, why not. And he'd promised everyone a free taxi home, and his place was on my way, and I figured Remy was really going to be late getting back from his trip. . . .

Why *am* I explaining myself? What is it, women have been conditioned since the Pleistocene Era to feel guilty about not wanting to get laid by every grunting mouth-breather who wanders into the cave? I was having a good time. That's it. Period. Wanted to party. I don't know, Patricia, it's . . . life with Remy doesn't actually swing sometimes, and we *were* enjoying a little time apart. . . . Apart together, I can remember us laughing. . . . Never mind, that's not important.

So it's the dead of night as we pull up in front of this Bauhaus fascist-looking structure. Dark. Neighbours have all turned off their old Katharine Hepburn movies.

And we go in, and . . . let me describe the

place, because I wandered around a bit in it. It's not *huge* huge. Sort of rectangular and Mondrianish, if you know what I mean. Split-level. Bedroom and some kind of guest room on top. A sprawling living room, and a sort of library-cum-parlour—that's where he took us—with literally walls of books and a big fireplace and a big chesterfield and some padded chairs and lots of little lamps. All sort of stuffy, actually—not, you know, somebody's pad. Musty—you could smell the bachelor dust. No family heirlooms, no big, florid portraits of his father, the aristocrat—that's what I was expecting.

Okay, I sit on an armchair, stage left, facing Charles and Paula on the chesterfield. Jonathan draws the drapes and puts on some music—something soft and electronic—and he starts a cosy fire and brings out some five-star cognac, and some Benedictine, which I like to mix it with. I told him just a light one. He gave me this massive brandy glass with a teeny bit of liquid in the bottom.

Egan Chornicky was wandering around—I don't know how, he could barely stand. This doesn't have to get out, I hope, but he was taking lots of trips to the bathroom, and I don't think to pee, and coming back rubbing his nose. Charles and Paula were being all very twittery in the presence of the Honourable Jonathan O'Donnell. Laughing at his jokes until they could die.

And O'Donnell was *pretty* loaded. Not to the extent he could ever deny he knew what he was doing, but he was being very loud and comical and right wing. He's really a political dinosaur, Pat. Also thinks he's quite an intellect with his humungous library. I was sort of poking around in it, being a spy. Always felt you could tell a man through his books. He had all the correct stuff, though, even some feminist writers. De Beauvoir. Friedan. Paglia, of course, right on his wavelength. Lots of plays, all of Shaw, two copies of *Saint Joan*.

So somehow that inspired me to get everyone reading lines. Except Chornicky, of course, he was too swacked. I thought they could sort of help me rehearse. We really got into it—I mean, they were *good*. Charles was the bishop. Perfectly suited to the role. Jonathan was my friend Dunois, the bastard of Orleans, and we did another scene where he also played the inquisitor. I'm afraid I flounced about a lot, waving on the troops against the English goddamns, being all rousing and saintly. And I remember saying, "Everyone has to wear a costume," and during a pee break I went upstairs and put on one of Jonathan's suits . . . how embarrassing.

So, anyway, now we get to where things get weird. I was doing a speech; it goes something like, "My voices have deceived me; only a fool will walk into a fire"—and suddenly it was as if I were hearing voices myself, strange voices, and I remember I was crying. . . .

I wonder if he put something in my drink.

I'm not sure if I can tell you about the end part without ralphing. The end part—maybe that's not the expression I want to use. The private part. As my little sister says, gag me with a spoon.

Anyway, that's all I remember, until . . . he was on top of me . . . not on top, behind . . .

I can't do this, it makes me sick.

Let's just get together over dinner, okay, I'll give you the whole blah. After you've eaten.

❧

Through the "Bulletin Board" column in the *Echo*, I am pleased to learn—and not surprised—that Garibaldi boasts its own chapter of Alcoholics Anonymous. Its bimonthly evening meeting at the local school is already under way when I arrive. The eyes of a dozen of my brothers and sisters turn to me as I squeeze into a seat behind a child's desk, and I nod and smile.

"Please carry on," I tell the speaker, a scraggly bearded man of about fifty, spare and vigorous. His head is heavily bandaged and his arm in a sling. Yellowed fingers hold a burning cigarette.

"Aha," he says, "our ranks swell. Shall I begin again? My name is George and I am an alcoholic and, if I may say so, a very fine one indeed."

Is this that infamous tank, George Rimbold? Not the image I expected. There is an air of theatre about him, his free arm dramatically gesturing as he speaks. He has a sonorous voice accented with an Irish lilt, and possesses the confidence of a man used to an audience.

"As many of you have heard, I suffered a bit of an accident driving home from the Rosekeeper tea party. But don't believe the rumours. I was completely sober."

Hoots of disbelief.

"Suddenly a deer ran in front of me, but I had the presence of mind to swerve." He acts it out, turning an imaginary steering wheel, braking.

"Tell it to the cops," someone says.

"To be sure, and I did that very thing. The next morning."

He sees that I am chuckling. "Are you the gentleman who bought my boat?"

"I am that person."

"I must drop by and show you the holes where the ling cod lie in wait."

"Then we'll be in the same boat. But we already are, aren't we?"

This merry dialogue breaks the ice. I introduce myself. (My name is Arthur. I am an alcoholic.) Hands are extended. I am accepted.

"I fall off my boat—or wagon—too easily," Rimbold says. "And you, Arthur?"

"Haven't had a drink for nine years."

"Good grief," he says. There is applause.

I am of course called upon to make confession and do so with high energy, raucous tales of my Baudelairian performances in that infamous parlour of debauchery, the El Beau Room on Hornby Street, a coin's toss from the Vancouver courts and the haunt of many of my fellow litigators. The time I stood on a table and recited from Juvenal's *Satires*. The time I dumped a pitcher of Guinness upon the head of a prosecutor who'd had the audacity to call me a poor loser. The time, in court, when I'd attempted to make a citizen's arrest of the judge.

I have done a bit of amateur performing in my time (I really must join the local theatre group), and I release the inner actor, playing a merry, fustian Falstaff, punching the air with my fist, slurring and titubating in sardonic imitation of my former self.

Well, I am a fine orator when I let loose, though I will never know where the skill comes from. (My father was chief university librarian and went about his days in whispers and silence. Books we had, however, hundreds of system discards, bruised, rancid with age.) The audience is an eager jury, anxious to acquit me. Though we come from differing backgrounds, we are all peers in the great democratic addiction to alcohol. As Homer wrote, "There is a strength in the union even of very sorry men."

By the end of the meeting I am enveloped in the warmth of comradeship, and George Rimbold and I stroll out together, lighting cigarettes.

"What brings you to our little haven?" he asks.

"I came searching."

"For what?"

"Peace. Health. For the remnants of my tattered soul. And you?"

"I came to escape the trade in souls. The Reverend George Rimbold, that was my title. I am a fallen priest, sir, and shall rot in hell." He shrugs. "But in the meantime there is the delightful purgatory of Garibaldi Island."

"Ah. And how long have you been here, George?"

"To tell the truth, I'm not sure." He pulls at his beard. "In fact, I can't even remember how I got here."

On driving home that night I observe that one of my headlights has died. No matter: Garibaldi is a lawless state, the policeman comes but once a month. But impaired with the euphoria of new friendship, I am a distracted driver. As I take a turn past Mrs. Blake's house, a plump white shape moseys into the unlit foreground of my Rolls. Unable to brake in time, I feel a sickening bump.

When I exit the car, my heart racing in panic, I observe that a small pig lies in smiling, lifeless peace at the side of the road.

Oh woe, this promises another great collision, that with the fearsome Margaret Blake. Behind the gaptoothed fence of her yard, the house sits in utter blackness, with not even a porch light glowing. Her truck is in the yard, so she is doubtless abed, dreaming her Fabian dreams of the future perfect state.

In fear of her, for a moment I contemplate fleeing the scene of the accident, but I still my terrors and advance on the silent, ghostly house. After I rap several times on the door, Slappy barks, a light comes on, and Mrs. Blake greets me on her front deck with a heavy-lidded look of suspicion.

"I hope it isn't something that was bound to happen, Mrs. Blake, but I struck and killed one of your pigs."

Wordlessly, she marches in slippered feet to the road, followed by her spaniel, who sniffs at the dead animal, then looks up at me reproachfully.

"It's Betsy."

"Yes, I'm afraid neither Betsy nor I saw the pig-crossing sign." I attempt to say this in jest, but my smile dies, impaled by her fierce look. Lamely, I add, "She wandered into my path."

"Well, Betsy just cost you a hundred dollars, Mr. Beauchamp."

I have been planning to make good, but her gruffness not only gets my back up but stiffens my spine.

"I would suggest we each take our responsibility. Fifty-fifty."

"Why? We weren't sharing the steering wheel fifty-fifty."

Her dressing gown is loose around her chest and she tightens it, then steps towards me and lifts herself up on her tiptoes, hiking her face close to mine. For a flutter of a moment I think she is going to bite me, but realize she is only taking a sample of my breath.

"Madam, I have just returned from an A.A. meeting."

"Stale smoke. Okay, you have until tomorrow to pay me."

"Or what?"

"Or I take you to court. I'm not accepting half. I put a lot of work into that animal."

She drags the beast by its hind legs across the road into the yard. "Good night, Mr. Beauchamp." Slappy casts me a sad sideways look, lifts a leg, and pisses on my left front tire.

❧❧

Q Your full name?

A Egan Matthew Chornicky.

Q And you are in first-year law at the University of British Columbia?

A Just barely.

THE COURT: Mr. Chornicky, what do you have in your mouth?

WITNESS: Juicy Fruit gum.

THE COURT: Well, take it out.
(Witness removes gum.)

Q I want you to recall November twenty-seventh last. You attended a student dance that evening?

A Mm-hmm, I did.

Q And did you see the complainant, Ms. Martin, and the accused, Mr. O'Donnell, at this dance?

A I think I saw them. I was working the bar.

Q Okay, well, after the dance, did you go somewhere with them?

A I remember we piled into a bunch of cars, I can't remember who I went with.

THE COURT: Mr. Chornicky, do you have a handkerchief?

A No, why?

THE COURT: You are playing with that gum.
(Witness drops gum in glass of water.)

THE COURT: Thank you.

Q Where did you go?

A I don't know, actually. Some house these guys were renting. Seemed like it was in the West End.

Q And what happened there?

A Basically not much . . . Well, the one thing I remember is Kimberley showed up dressed like a man.

Q She showed up . . . What?

A I remember her giving a speech from a play, *Hamlet* or one of those. To be or not to be.

Q And Professor O'Donnell was there?

A No . . . Yeah, he must've been, 'cause we dropped him off at his house in a taxi.

Q Did you go into his house?

THE COURT: Witness, are you having some problem?

A I'm trying to recollect how we ended up there—I guess he invited us in for a drink.

Q Who was with you?

A Charles Stubb, I remember. A couple of girls. Maybe someone else.

Q And did you see Kimberley Martin there?

A Uh-huh.

THE COURT: Uh-huh doesn't register, Mr. Chornicky.

A Say what?

THE COURT: Say yes or no. For what it's worth, this all has to be transcribed.

Q Do I take it correctly that you had something to drink that night?

A You take it correctly.

Q Do you remember anything that happened in his house?

A I remember he gave us fifty dollars to get rid of us.

Q Fifty dollars to get rid of you . . . and you were going to leave Ms. Martin behind?

A No, I don't think that was the deal. Didn't she come with us? I think we sort of had to carry her out. . . . Or maybe that was somebody else.

Q Maybe it was you, Mr. Chornicky.

A Maybe.

MS. BLUEMAN: No further questions.

THE COURT: Mr. Cleaver?

MR. CLEAVER: I don't dare.

THE COURT: Witness, you may be excused.
  (Witness leaves.)

MS. BLUEMAN: I call Mr. Charles Stubb.
  (Witness is duly sworn.)

DIRECT EXAMINATION BY MS. BLUEMAN

Q Mr. Stubb, you are a second-year law student at U.B.C.?

A Yes, I am. I'm also vice-president of the student council there.

Q Okay, will you turn your mind to November twenty-seventh last year, and did you attend a dance that night?

A Yes, sponsored by the Law Students' Association, of which I am the treasurer. I went with Ms. Paula Yi, another student, though not studying for our chosen profession—

Q Thank you. And did you see any of your professors at this dance?

A Oh, several—we asked the whole faculty.

Q Professor Jonathan O'Donnell in particular.

A He was there. He was—well, he still is—acting dean.

Q All right, did you observe him that evening in the presence of Kimberley Martin?

A I saw them talking and laughing together.

Q Did they dance?

A They did. I didn't see anything unusual about it. She danced with a couple of the other lecturers, too.

Q Okay, after the dance you went somewhere. Tell us about that.

A Well, everyone had been invited to a house party on Broughton Street in the West End. Professor O'Donnell thought he might have had a few too many drinks and asked me to drive his car.

Q What was his condition?

A He was wise not to drive.

Q How much had you drunk yourself that night, Mr. Stubb?

A I was sticking pretty much to soda water.

Q And what about Ms. Martin?

A She'd had quite a few.

Q Carry on.

A We went to this party—it was about one o'clock in the morning, and I think we stayed for almost an hour, and then it was arranged that we would take Professor O'Donnell home and he would pay for our taxis.

Q Yes.

A And then he invited us in—Paula, myself, Egan Chornicky, and Kimberley—for a last drink. And everything was . . . normal, comfortable, the professor and I were engaged in quite an interesting political debate. And then Kimberley gave us all parts to recite from *Saint Joan*. I thought it was quite enjoyable. Then she did something I thought was a little odd at the time. She disappeared and came back in the room wearing what looked like one of Professor O'Donnell's suits. I have since realized upon reading the play—

Q And then what happened?

A And, ah, she was being very theatrical—she'd found this terrible tie and was having fun with Professor O'Donnell over it—and we carried on with the play some more, and she suddenly just fell asleep.

Q Kimberley Martin.

A Yes, on a big chair by the fire. And we called a taxi, and it came in a few minutes and that was about it.

Q What time was that?

A About three-thirty in the morning.

Q And what about Ms. Martin?

A We left her behind.

Q Why?
A Well . . . no one wanted to wake her up. I think Professor O'Donnell was getting a blanket for her when the taxi came. I wasn't afraid for her, if that's what you're hinting. Professor O'Donnell isn't someone I would dream of acting in any improper way.
Q That's all.

CROSS-EXAMINATION BY MR. CLEAVER

Q You can't conceive of him doing this.
A Not really.
Q Did you ever see him, at any time that night, act towards Miss Martin other than as a complete gentleman?
A No, sir.
Q He did not seem to be pursuing her in any way?
A If anything, the reverse.
Q No leering, pawing, suggestive words.
A Nothing like that.
Q By the end of the night, you would have to say Kimberley Martin was heavily intoxicated?
A Yes, I think she'd had too much.
Q And people in that condition have a habit of imagining things that never happened, don't they?
MS. BLUEMAN: Oh, good God.
MR. CLEAVER: You'll need His help. Nothing further.

RE-EXAMINATION BY MS. BLUEMAN

Q Mr. Stubb, are you by any chance related to Professor O'Donnell?
A No, why?
Q Just curious. Tell me, please, were you ever interviewed by my learned friend, Mr. Cleaver?

A Yes.

Q When and where?

A A few days ago in his office.

Q So he asked you up to his office to have a little chat about how your evidence might shape out.

MR. CLEAVER: Your honour, I'm aghast, she can't—

MS. BLUEMAN: No further questions.

§§

Discovering that Betsy wreaked substantial vengeance upon me for her death—a large bruise on the right front fender of the Phantom V, a pig-shaped indentation of metal that presses against the tire—I seek consultation with Stoney and Dog as they apply stain to my new veranda.

"I can straighten that fender, eh?" Stoney says. "Just enough so you can take it into a garage in town. But, what the hey, let me bang it back in shape. Save you a ton of money. It's my number-one specialty. Body work."

I remember the last time minor repairs had to be done to my Rolls. The bill from that pertinent Cockney thief came perilously close to five figures. But I have lost some naiveté and no longer live under the fanciful apprehension that Stoney is the artisan-of-all-trades that he claims to be.

"Ah, yes, straighten the fender a little, Stoney. Don't do anything else. I shall get an estimate before I decide." And perhaps countersue Mrs. Blake for the damages. Though I admit to a grudging respect for that woman—does she think she can take on Arthur Beauchamp in his own arena?

Stoney uses a pry bar to bend the fender away from the tire and we motor off to his shop. I give him permission to drive, but sit beside him like a stern chaperone. I have a great attachment to this vehicle.

As we arrive at his charnel house of dead cars, he

gestures with pride at the various rusting hulks. "Look at all these beauties. Yeah, I'm thinking of installing a big outdoors screen and speakers in all the cars, eh, a kind of used-car drive-in theatre."

I observe he does have a shop, however greasy and unkempt. Welding equipment, an engine up on pulleys.

"We'll just move her inside here after I make some space. This is yours to use for the time being, eh?"

He slaps the hood of an elderly Dodge pickup that sits beside his workshop.

"It's gotta new engine. Well, sorta reconditioned."

The beast is painted purple where the rust doesn't show through. The passenger door is held closed by a rope. The windshield is decorated with a large spiderweb crack. It is a fine traditional vehicle of Garibaldi Island. I will not be ashamed to drive it.

The engine starts with a throaty, mufferless growl, and I take to the road, riding high and proud upon the truck's springy seat, and I wind down the country roads to the general store.

"Postcard here from a lady friend of yours working at the opera in Seattle," says Mr. Makepeace, the postmaster. A photograph of Mount Rainier. A scrawled sentence or two from Annabelle, telling me she is swamped by her work, but enjoying herself. "Warmly yours, Annabelle." Warmly yours. How passionate, how wanton. Was it too difficult to telephone?

"And Margaret Blake dropped off this double-registered for you. Summons from Small Claims Court. Over that pig you hit."

§§

George Rimbold arrives at my house at five a.m. and is surprised to see I am ready—a Thermos of coffee at hand, armed with pole and line, ready to do battle with the cunning codfish. "That's the spirit, old son," he says. "You've got to get them when they're hungry. Are you joining the club?"

"The club?"

"You look to be growing a beard." Rimbold strokes his own beard, grey and stringy beneath his thin face.

I ponder this. "I'm not sure . . . well, yes, I think I am." Do I not recall artistic Annabelle giving her blessings to this hair-raising project? I, Beauchamp, who have never spent two continuous days without shaving, now wear an itchy symbol of my new-found freedom.

"I see you are healing, George."

He is no longer encumbered with an arm sling, and his head bandages have been removed.

"To be sure, I have felt the touch of Jesus, and cast away my dressings."

At the dock, he looks at his former boat with such melancholy that I am racked with guilt. But he insists that I pilot the craft and directs me out to the middle of the bay. There are reefs below us here, he says, good fishing grounds.

The engine is stilled and we drift, and Rimbold teaches me the simple tasks of jigging for cod. The air is cool, but our bodies are warmed by cigarettes and coffee and by the first rays of a sun approaching the solstice.

I am curious about the history of my companion, but too polite to broach the subject. A former priest: a plunging leap from grace?

After a while, Rimbold pulls a plastic bag from his pocket.

"Would you be liking a little puff of this?" he says, crumbling a small dried portion of green plant material into a cigarette paper.

"George, I am shocked beyond words."

"Last summer's crop, lost some potency, I'm afraid.

It's grown all over the island, Arthur. Biggest industry here, actually."

I turn down his offer, but watch fascinated as he expands his lungs with smoke and holds it in for at least half a minute, then coughs a little.

"Garibaldi Gold, they call this. Hard on the lungs, but easy on the soul. Or what remains of my soul. Still, I've read nothing in the scriptures about pot." He becomes garrulous. "Not on the list. 'Thou shalt not covet thy neighbour's wife, nor his manservant, nor his maidservant, nor his ox, nor his ass.' I coveted my neighbour's ass—that was my sin."

He does not elaborate. One must assume he refers to an episode with one of his female parishioners. He is thoughtful for a moment, rhythmically bobbing his fishing rod.

"What matter, I was losing my faith anyway. It is far easier not to believe. And I am one for the easy road. Ah, there's nothing better to be doing than to laze about with a little pot and a fishing line. It's what I do best now."

Under the apparently benign influence of Garibaldi Gold, Rimbold seems unable to still his tongue, and rambles on about his former life, his current doubts, his many alcoholic lapses. Until he washed up on Garibaldi's shores several years ago, he had served in an inner-city parish in Montreal. Born in Dublin, studied for the priesthood there.

The discursive Rimbold continues to bounce from topic to topic, but is finally silenced by a tug on his line. He pulls in a fair-sized rock cod. I am envious, and fear I shall prove to be luckless at this sport.

But it is a pleasant time. Mists caress the water. A pair of cormorants sweep by. The surface of the Gulf of Georgia is a shimmering pane of glass.

Now as we drift, Margaret Blake's farm comes into view, and I am inspired to describe to Rimbold my run-in with the pig and subsequently with her. He emits a deep rumble of laughter.

"Well, Margaret has no love for lawyers. Always taking the island despoilers to court, or the local government, then running into a brick wall of lawyers. She was sued for slander once, I believe, and had to take out a mortgage to pay the legal bills. And with her husband's death . . . They were childless. We should be charitable to her."

"Did you know her husband?"

"A fine man. Used to be our trustee, before Zoller. Played a hell of a fiddle, entertained a lot at parties. They came out here in the 1960s, hippies hoping to live off the land. The Blakes were among the few who succeeded at it. But poor Margaret has to do the work of two to manage things—I suspect she's finding it quite a chore."

George has portrayed a brave woman. I feel badly now. I will work something out with her to avoid embarrassing her in court.

A seal pokes its head above the water, then disappears. The competition. The mists swirl and rise and melt in the rising sun. A gull swoops down and analyses us and is gone.

I am jolted from the reveries that these sweet moments induce by a tug on my line. A bite!

"Good on you," says Rimbold. "Easy does it now."

The creature surrenders after a brave struggle and soon I haul it aboard, a ling cod weighing at least five pounds. Well, perhaps I overstate. But exaggeration is a part of the fishing business, is it not?

Rimbold rolls up another marijuana cigarette and offers it, and in my elation I toss care to the wind and take a tiny puff. But the marijuana—which I must say is vastly overrated—neither clouds senses nor encourages that talkative state of euphoria I have observed in Rimbold.

As we motor back to the dock I am seized with an unaccountable panic about the state of my Phantom V.

When I arrive at Stoney's garage, I observe that parts of my beloved car are scattered to all corners of his work space. Even the seats are out. I stare at my car's remains as one might an old comrade lying in a casket. I indulge in a few quiet moments of meditation.

Finally, Stoney breaches the silence. "Found mice in it."

I am not sure if I have heard him correctly. My mind seems fuzzy.

"Quite a few, actually. Coupla families."

"Mice."

"Well, now, Mr. Beauchamp, that old garage of yours—and you wanna maybe think of replacing it soon—is probably overrun with them and they must've got in the car and started nests."

"But, Stoney, why is it in a thousand pieces?"

"Well, here's the thing, they got into the wiring. Why they didn't go for all the leather in here, I dunno, but they chewed up the wiring. You see, that's probably why one of your headlights wasn't working, and, uh, there was a nest behind the back seat, and you maybe been driving without tail lights, too."

He continues with a long, baffling speech about electrical systems. I sense he is nervous, in fear of me.

"Can you put it together, Stoney? Do you know where everything goes?"

"No problem. It's all in a map in my head. And I'll redo the wiring, eh? It don't take a genius to rewire a car, whether you're doin' a VW bug or some kinda luxomobile. I can do it, Mr. Beauchamp. You gotta believe in me. I know you think I'm full of talk, but one thing I do know is electrical systems."

My mind forms a picture of myself describing this woeful scene to my mechanic in Vancouver. His look of confusion gives way to barely concealed mirth, and the sinister gleam of avarice shines from his eyes. But I must call him today, and be prepared to pay an arm and a leg.

How to explain to Stoney that I shall be sending my trade elsewhere? I commence with a lie. "Stoney, it's not that I don't have confidence in you . . ."

But suddenly I stay my tongue. Oddly, it is as if an angel of peace descends upon my weary shoulders, and I find myself relaxing. It is a mere possession, a material thing, a chattel.

"Let's see if you can get it on the road again."

"And I'll do the body work on the fender."

Incredibly, I find myself smiling. I clap Stoney on the back, offer him some reassuring words, then return to my 1969 Dodge pickup with the passenger door that won't shut.

ॐ

DIRECT EXAMINATION BY MS. BLUEMAN

Q Your name is Dr. Rosa Sanchez.

A Yes.

Q And you are a qualified medical practitioner—

MR. CLEAVER: I'll admit her qualifications. District pathologist.

THE COURT: Okay, proceed, Miss Blueman.

Q On the early-morning hours of November twenty-eighth last, did you examine a certain Ms. Kimberley Martin?

A Yes, at the North Shore General Hospital, at six o'clock in the morning. I was called in.

Q Okay, and state the results of your examination.

A I noted some redness on the interior aspects of both wrists and both ankles, an inch-long latitudinal lesion on her left shin, and some chafing there. On the inner aspect of her right breast I also found some recent bruising, two protruded areas, slightly purple. Also some slight haematoma of her exterior vaginal area, just a faint reddening, really. And . . .

Q Yes? What else did you find?

A Some recent bruising in the area of her anus.

MR. CLEAVER: Her . . . Just a minute, I don't have any particulars of this. . . .

MS. BLUEMAN: I think if you'll look at the copy of Dr. Sanchez's report—

THE COURT: Mr. Cleaver?

MR. CLEAVER: Um, yes, well, is the complainant saying she was buggered?

THE COURT: I don't see a charge of buggery on this information, Miss Blueman.

MS. BLUEMAN: Good Lord, is it necessary?

THE COURT: Miss Blueman! This is no place for profanity. . . . The charge is sexual assault, so I suppose it subsumes a case of anal penetration. But that slight reddening could be from anything, couldn't it, doctor? A rash. One often gets . . . Oh, never mind. Excuse me, I believe she's your witness, Miss Blueman.

MS. BLUEMAN: Yes, your honour, you can cross-examine her after I finish.

THE COURT: I wasn't—

MS. BLUEMAN: I'm sorry, perhaps your honour was seeking some private medical information.

THE COURT: Miss . . . Oh, just carry on. It's getting near the end of the day and I'm tired. Get on with your witness.

Q Doctor, did you do any tests for sperm?

A Yes, I took a swab sample from within the patient's vagina and subsequently examined it under a microscope. I found no sign of sperm.

MS. BLUEMAN: Please answer my learned friend's questions.

CROSS-EXAMINATION BY MR. CLEAVER

Q No sperm. But if sexual intercourse had occurred several hours later you would expect to find thousands of the little beasties, wouldn't you? Alive and kicking.

A If there had been discharge, yes, I would expect to find motile sperm. Assuming no condom.

Q Did you see any cuts, bite marks, anything you could really call a wound?

A Nothing that I would consider serious.

Q Many things can cause bruises?

A Of course.

Q Sure. I have one on my bottom from my wife's shopping cart. Hardly a sexual assault.

A Well, I don't know your wife, Mr. Cleaver. (Laughter.)

Q And some people bruise more easily than others. Sometimes just a touch will do it. Am I right?

A Some display more obvious haematomas than others.

Q If they have soft or sensitive skin.

A That's a factor.

Q And reddening in the pelvic area is not all that uncommon, is it?

A I would find that difficult to answer.

Q I mean there are rashes, as his honour suggested, or maybe a person doesn't clean one's self, or abuses one's self . . . well, whatever.

MS. BLUEMAN: My friend seems to be heading into an area of his own expertise.
(Laughter.)

MR. CLEAVER: I don't . . . Forget it. Thank you, that's all I have.

MS. BLUEMAN: Your honour, Mr. Clarence de Remy Brown is on an extended trip to Latin America and I won't be calling him until the trial.

MR. CLEAVER: If there's a trial.

MS. BLUEMAN: Likewise, Paula Yi, the other student witness, I give notice I'll be tendering her at the trial. And finally I have Mr. Paul Stanton here from the serology lab.

MR. CLEAVER: I'm prepared to admit the serologist's evidence so we can get to the end of the day.

THE COURT: Thank goodness for that.

MS. BLUEMAN: Mr. Stanton will say he examined the sheets removed from the O'Donnell house, Exhibits Six and Sixteen respectively, from the living-room couch and the bed upstairs. He found no semen stains, but he'll say they both smelled of having been freshly washed. That brings us to the end of the Crown's evidence until Ms. Martin is available this summer.

THE COURT: How much time are we going to need, Mr. Cleaver, a day?

MR. CLEAVER: I wouldn't count on my being brief.

THE COURT: Well, what's it look like, madam clerk?

CLERK: If we're talking two days, your honour, we'll have to go to July. The seventh and eighth are open.

THE COURT: Adjourned to July seventh, ten o'clock in the morning.

๑๖

The *Queen of Prince George* is only an hour and a half behind schedule on this drizzling late-June Saturday, and while awaiting its arrival I mingle with my brother and sister yokels: Nelson Forbish is here, and Janey Rosekeeper, and the allegedly insatiable Emily Lemay, and we are giving each other moral support for the task ahead—the entertaining of urban dwellers who don't know enough to take their shoes off in a country home. Also in attendance, seated in her pickup truck, is Margaret Blake. I wish to talk to her, to seek rapprochement, but she will not meet my eye.

Now the ferry is berthing, and foreign troops are landing on these shores.

Once more unto the breach, dear friends. Stiffen the sinews, summon up the blood, for today I shall be in hand-to-hand combat again. Hubbell Meyerson and Gowan Cleaver would normally have come by chartered plane, but the firm's aging godfather, Roy Bullingham, is joining in this expedition to harangue and beguile me into taking on the O'Donnell case. Phobic Bully boasts he has managed to live eighty-three undamaged years without once boarding a flying machine.

Cyclists descend like locusts and just as quickly disappear, leaving Hub and Bully and the thinly smiling Gowan Cleaver striding forward in their wake. And if I am not mistaken, bringing up the rear is Honourable Jonathan Shaun O'Donnell. These are the potential wild horses. I had rather expected them to arrive by car—it's unusual to see lawyers walking.

We gather by the rock-strewn beach at the side of the ferry slip, and I offer my farm-hardened hand to their silky city ones.

"You look like a man hiding from the law, Arthur," says Bully. He has a high voice, tightened by the stress of his life's work: maintaining our law firm's stainless, haughty image.

"Arthur," says Hubbell, "do you realize you have some kind of growth on your face?"

I wear a fortnight's worth of whiskers; my feet are shod in gumboots; my T-shirt advertises the Brig "As The Place To Go." My partners look upon me despairingly, as if at one who is lost to civilization.

"Don't think I've ever seen you outside a suit," says Bully, and he begins grumbling, "Couldn't get the damn car on the ferry. Meyerson here didn't make reservations." The senior partner is reedlike in build, in a neat, crease-free three-piece suit. But even Hubbell and Gowan wear ties: Bully enforces a strict dress code. Jonathan is more casually attired, in slacks and a short-sleeved shirt.

"Yes, I'm afraid reservations are often required on summer weekends."

"My secretary screwed up," says Hubbell. He looks exasperated. I can see that Bully has been badgering him.

"Ah, well, it's a complex life, gentlemen, when you have to rely on others for the simple things. I have no secretary, no servants, no wife in attendance. But now I can remember where everything is. Jonathan O'Donnell, your presence is an unexpected pleasure. You are looking well."

"You're too kind, Arthur. I look like one of the walking dead. Sorry, but I just had to talk to you." Jonathan seems fit, but has a tormented look about his dark and deep-set eyes. He is restive, agitated. I detect a faint odour of stale spirits on his breath.

"Well, gentlemen, I suggest we repair to the manse. We will have tea and tour the grounds."

I spy Margaret Blake standing outside her truck in earnest conversation with Nelson Forbish. The roly-poly newshound spots me and chugs in my direction.

"Mr. Beauchamp, wonder if I can get your reaction on being sued." He is munching a large, sticky chocolate bar.

"Not now, Nelson."

"Sued?" says Bully. He senses scandal.

"A minor altercation with a neighbour."

"Margaret Blake says—"

"As I explained to you, Nelson, it is quite improper to discuss a matter that is before the courts."

"Yeah, but, Mr. Beauchamp, I have a duty as a journalist, it's a thing I can't cover up."

Bully blanches. "What in heaven's name is this, Arthur? What's to be covered up?"

Forbish is relentless. "It's about him and a pig called Betsy."

"A *pig*," says Bully. "Did you say a *pig*?"

"Calm down, Bully," I say. "Restrain impure thoughts." I am one of the few in the firm who doesn't have to measure his words with Bullingham. "A minor road accident. A pig in a poke. Two titans are about to clash in a court of law."

I try to steer my visitors up the hill towards the parking lot, but Forbish keeps apace. "So what's up? I see you got some guests here."

I wearily halt the procession. Civil behaviour demands introductions. Bully, ever polite, extends his hand to the reporter, then quickly withdraws it and stares with repulsion at the chocolate that stains his palm.

"O'Donnell," says Forbish. "You're that *professor*." He seems in awe.

Jonathan reacts oddly; the soft, resigned laugh of one who is surrounded and must surrender. "Yes, I'm that professor."

"Please, Nelson. Not now."

"Sure like to do an interview."

"Nelson, not now!" Patience has flown, and Forbish scuttles off in the wake of my wrath.

Hubbell and Gowan are stifling laughter, but their smiles are replaced by looks of consternation as we arrive at my rusting, purple half-ton truck.

"God almighty," says Hubbell. "What manner of beast is this?"

"A courtesy vehicle. Bit of a bone-shaker, sorry about that."

"Arthur," says Bully, "are you sure this machine is safe?" He looks intently inside the cab as if to satisfy himself the truck has a steering wheel and brake pedal.

"Jump in, Bully. No, this door, the other doesn't open. The others will have to ride in the back."

"Surely that's against the law," says Bully. He is worried now that the firm may be disgraced with a traffic ticket.

"There is no law on Garibaldi Island," I say, "except on the second Tuesday of every month."

Gowan, Hubbell, and Jonathan climb over the tailgate and sit upon some tires I keep there for the many island hitchhikers, and we bounce off to Potter's Road. Yes, I will give this mob of city slickers a pungent taste of Garibaldi. Perhaps they will wish they'd never come—there are some who simply cannot handle the stress of country living.

"We took you back in the firm, Arthur." Bully has to shout, a birdlike screech above the unmuffled engine roar. "When you hit the rocks, we were there. We gave you the helping hand."

Bullingham has slid low in his seat, as if seeking refuge. Perhaps he does not wish to be seen.

"It was big of you, Bully."

"I'd like to think we gambled a bit on you, Arthur." He is referring to my hiatus from the firm a decade ago: two years spent on skid road, defending my fellow derelicts. The office took me back when I agreed to join A.A.

"And it paid off handsomely, I'm sure you'll agree." I need not remind him of the considerable retainers I've since brought into the office.

Bully realizes I have a thin sense of gratitude and resets his sails for an assault on my pride.

"Staying power, that's what makes the world move forward. When I was sixty-two, I felt I was a young man. I remember thinking there was so damn much yet to accomplish. Don't believe a lawyer comes into his prime until his sixties. What a waste, Arthur, what a waste."

Small green swallows flip and dive above roadside

hedges of wild roses, and I am overcome with nature's perfumed scent. We enter the atrium of a green cathedral and proceed up the aisle beneath a steeple of giant cedars, their fronds dancing in the breeze. A deer starts, then bounds into the white-blossoming salal. Look around you, Bullingham, see the appurtenances of my wasted life.

Bully continues his whining, hortatory discourse. "We do a good deal of business with the university, Arthur. The Faculty Association refers its members to us. We could lose them. They might go down the street to Hansworth and Company." An appeal now to guilt, duty, and obligation. "I should tell you, while we have this moment together, that O'Donnell doesn't seem very happy with Cleaver."

"Nonsense. Gowan is an astute counsel." I see him in my rearview mirror, squatting uncomfortably on a tire, a thin-featured man, a pencil moustache beneath a narrow nose, hard-eyed and slim-lipped.

"Oh, he's quick of mind," Bully says. "Doesn't have the common touch, though. Too abrasive."

"May I make a suggestion then, Bully. Perhaps a woman barrister . . ."

"No one experienced enough. Can't take the chance."

But whose fault is that? The firm of Tragger, Inglis, Bullingham remains for the most part a male bastion, and has not advanced its women far up the ladder.

I wave cheerily at a passing motorist and take a turn past Stoney's yard and its many wheeled hulks. Now I watch for four-footed jaywalkers as we rumble past Mrs. Blake's gate. My skewed house comes into view, my imperfect, cosy palace.

"No, Bully, I should as soon jump into a vat of boiling oil as enter a courtroom one more time."

Ah, yes, I fear the firm's venture will end dismally. Jonathan O'Donnell has yet to look me in the eye. Nor had Annabelle when she told me she had recently "bumped" into him downtown. Was the bump pre-arranged?

I would not decline his retainer, of course, for any such base reason as jealousy. That debilitating disease no longer infects me. And thoughts of Annabelle have ceased to paralyse my mind. I hardly think of her . . . hardly ever.

৵৶

Gowan, I can't rid myself of the picture: the bishop and the screaming painted nude in a ridiculous tie. "He's going to kill me"—is that what she said? Is it possible she was just having a nightmare? A good old-fashioned delirium tremens?

The tie's mine. A birthday gift from a prankster friend on faculty. I have to assume Kimberley had been poking into all my drawers—it was underneath my underwear and socks. She's an outrageous snoop. Before I forget, earlier she ordered a special drink. I had this Martell Cordon Bleu, and she wanted to mix some Benedictine with it. Apparently some people do this sort of thing. Anyway, she had quite a splash of it in a large brandy glass. A few inches.

So she came clumping down the stairs in my size-ten Oxfords, white shirt, suit, tie. I didn't know what to think. Some kind of fetish? I remember wondering if she was also wearing my Stanfield briefs. Then she was waving her arms and shouting, "I am a soldier! I will not be thought of as a woman! I will not dress as a woman!" I got the joke: *Saint Joan* as medieval cross-dresser.

We laughed. Frankly, I just split my sides. Then she started performing this hideous imitation of me. God, do I sound that churlish in the lecture theatre? But I guess she had me down pat, my inflections, my patronizing insolence. It went something like:

"My name is O'Donnell and I'm here to ram some property law into the yawning vacuum between your ears. Who wants to tell me what the Magna Carta was all about? Anyone who says human rights, you're out of here. You there, Miss Martin, when you've finished tidying your hair, tell me about the early English land laws. . . ."

I felt—it was odd—*naked*. She'd taken on my clothes, my persona. And to be incredibly honest there was a kind of sexual tension in the air. You would have to be a decaying tree stump not to feel it.

But I was damned if I was going to give in to it. Academia is strewn with minefields these days; you tiptoe around for fear of having your legs blown off. They shut down the whole damn political science department because a few instructors used politically indiscreet *language*. Words. Bedding with a student (however sexually voracious she or he may be) is on a level these days with mass murder and ethnic cleansing.

I'm sorry, I'm wandering. The subsequent events become a little foggy in my memory. People seemed to come and go. I put on some music, the Baroque Ensemble, I think. I know we carried on with the play. I was the inquisitor, demanding she repent. "Take off that impudent attire!" And then suddenly we all noticed Kimberley wasn't responding. She'd passed out.

When the taxi came I honestly assumed the others were going to arouse Kimberley and take her with them, but they didn't. She looked such a *rara avis* lying there in my suit, but (I have to say) incredibly lovely, and she had this impish sleeping smile. Mischievous. I recall standing there, looking down upon her, wondering—what? Who she was, what fires had shaped her, what intriguing secrets did she hold.

And then the last act is shrouded in an alcoholic haze. I know I found a sheet, and I carried her into the living room and I laid her—you will notice I have scratched that word out—placed her gently on the couch. Christ, Gowan, I know I'll blurt out something asinine like that on the stand. I may as well just cop a plea.

Anyway, I must have gone to bed. I don't remember doing so.

I hear horns hooting. I hear shouts of joy. A new year is born, squalling and wriggling and gasping for air. Time to put on my paper hat. And take another cup of kindness yet for auld lang syne.

Yours despondently,
Jonathan

৳৳

A chilly southeasterly wind is coming off the water, bringing clouds across the choppy bay, so after the obligatory tour of beach, orchard, and garden we assemble in my living room, where I ask my guests to be comfortable. Jonathan, who has been lugubrious and silent, plunges into my favourite chair, doing little to improve his desperate chances to win my favour.

Exhausted from too much fresh air, Bullingham nestles into my old chesterfield as Hubbell and Gowan join me in the kitchen ostensibly to help boil water for tea.

"Look, Arthur," Gowan begins, "there's been a bit of a rupture between O'Donnell and me. I don't know what his problem is, I'm on top of it, had the provincial judge virtually licking my dick all through the prelim. Anyway, the professor and I have been having a little nose-to-nose combat, and, ah, he's thinking of taking his trade elsewhere."

"He wants you, Arthur," adds Hubbell, "that's

what he really wants. Hell, a week of your bloody valuable time is all we ask."

"It might not take more than a day," Gowan says. "Case might not even have to go to trial. I mean it, the judge is in our back pocket. Impressed by Honourable Jonathan O'Donnell. Aristocrat. Son of a life peer."

I remain mute. From my refrigerator I bring out a bowl of my special peanut butter cookies.

Hubbell takes over. "You see, Arthur, the preliminary continues next week. Set for two days. That . . . ah, what's-her-name, Kimberley Martin, she's the only witness left. There's a feeling we could avoid a trial altogether if the girl is handled right. The provincial judge just might discharge him then and there."

I say wearily, "At preliminary, the judge must give benefit of the doubt to the Crown. Since he won't hear any defence witnesses, how can he not send Jonathan to trial once she's given her evidence?"

"He *could* dismiss, Arthur, if the girl is . . . you know, damaged enough," Hub says.

"She's seeing a shrink," says Gowan. "I don't think she's very tightly wrapped, Arthur. You hear her tapes?"

"I played them, yes."

"Yeah, and don't you think she's a few bricks short of a full load? If you could get her to collapse under the weight of her own lies, she might recant and that's an end of it. I could do it—I'd *love* to do it—but O'Donnell says he doesn't want me to touch her. He's *also* seeing a shrink. Guy needs a brain surgeon. A lobotomy."

"Arthur, it's not as if it's a consent defence," says Hubbell. "I know you don't like to take those. I'm with you on that. You know, prying into a woman's sexual history, having to show she came across. But it's not like that. O'Donnell didn't *do* it."

"He never laid a finger on her, Arthur. She lied to

keep her goddamn fiancé, it's as obvious as a knock on the head."

"I see. And why does our innocent paragon seem in such an abysmal funk?"

"Wouldn't you be depressed?" says Hubbell. "His whole career is on the line—whatever happens, win or lose, his name is scarred for life. He could have been dean. A Supreme Court judge. He's smeared all over the press. He's got feminist coalitions forming up against him."

"He's become a symbol," says Gowan. "Male power figure versus cowering, helpless female student."

"Ah, the kettle is boiling. Take up the tray, Hubbell. Those pickles are from the Koroluks, they live down by West Shore Road. This is goat cheese, from the Willinghams in Oyster Bay. The cookies come from my own oven."

On our return to the living room, we find Bully upright but snoozing on the worn chesterfield and Jonathan pacing morosely beside my wall of bookcases. His trousers pocket shows a pint-sized bulge—I have a trained eye for hidden bottles.

I offer him a teacup. "It won't bother me if you touch it up. Or I can get a glass."

He doesn't blush, pulls his bottle out: Dewar's, I remember it well. "Normally I only drink on weekdays," he says. "Anyone care to celebrate with me?"

Gowan declines, but Hubbell, after a glance at the sleeping Bullingham, says, "Sure you don't mind, Arthur?"

"Not at all," I say heartily.

"Just to be sociable." Hubbell goes back to get a glass, but Jonathan merely pours a dollop into his tea.

"You are well on your way, Jon."

"Oh, God, no, it's only my third this morning."

"You're becoming a problem drinker."

"I'm only an alcoholic when I drink, Arthur."

"He was pissed as a newt, for instance, on the very night in question," says Gowan, his tone censorious. "Tippling away when he composed his statement to me."

Jonathan studies my dog-eared collection of poetry. "Show me anyone with a better reason." He turns to me. "I never understood yours, Arthur. You had everything, fame, friends, future. I don't have a future. I only have fame."

"You seem not to lack for friends. The entire populated universe has been over here to speak on your behalf." For a moment, I ponder adding, "Annabelle, among them," but restrain myself.

Hubbell returns and pours a dram from the Dewar's bottle into a glass—just as Bully opens his eyes.

"A little early for that," he says.

I intercede. "Come now, Bully, it's a weekend. Here, I poured you some tea."

"Arthur," says Jonathan, "I just want to hear it from your own voice—why won't you take my case?"

"Because it's too preposterous," I say.

"What do you mean?"

"Sit down, Jonathan. No, please, take the club chair. Be comfortable."

I stare solemnly out the bay windows of my living room, where a calliope hummingbird samples the snapdragons in my window box, hovers briefly, then disappears in a wink. In the bay, a frothy surf, a family of little sandpipers pursuing the retreating waves, seeking the ocean's leavings. My guests clink their cups and wait in silence for me to begin.

"Bizarre," I say, "the woman running off like that to the neighbour's."

"Into the bosom of the Church of England," says Jonathan. "Poor old Dr. Hawthorne. A lifetime of service to God doesn't prepare you for streakers in the night."

"Otherwise a straightforward case. Your word against hers. No reason yours ought not be believed, is there?"

"God knows."

"No proof of intercourse. No sperm, no semen stains. Yet . . . well, Jonathan, you act like a man already convicted."

He looks directly at me, then quickly away.

"The accusation has driven you not just to drink but to shrink. This strikes me as an unlikely reaction. Anger, yes. A righteous anger might be appropriate. The anger of enraged innocence."

"I tried anger. Punched a hole in the closet door. It cost three hundred dollars to replace. Depression is cheaper. Arthur, my bloody career hangs in the balance."

"Ah, yes, and I sympathize. You enjoy teaching, and you are good at it. Popular with the students, that's ninety per cent of the battle, I suspect."

"Helps."

I tear myself away from the window, and observe my associates shift noiselessly in their seats, their faces shining up at me, expectantly.

"According to your account, you were particularly popular with Miss Martin."

"She seemed to have a shine for me."

"But at the same time were you not attracted to her?"

"I'd prefer to put it more passively. I found her attractive."

"A traffic-stopper was the expression used, I believe. A traffic-stopper with a sense of humour. You enjoyed her company."

"Sure. Okay, I'm guilty of being human. Where are we going with this, Arthur? Is this some kind of cross-examination?"

"Yes, perhaps it is. Before a jury of friends. Do you mind?"

"Of course not."

Bully, our foreman, nods. They are on the witness's side, eager to acquit.

"It wouldn't be going too far to suggest you and she flirted a great deal that night?"

"No, I wouldn't say that. *She* flirted, yes."

"You did not seem to be making any strenuous efforts to avoid her that evening."

"I am often accused of having an ego. I was probably flattered."

There is no point in skating about. I go directly to the nub, to the wobbly part of his story. "At your house, she disappeared for a while, then came downstairs wearing your suit."

"That's right. She'd been in my bedroom closet."

"So she apparently undressed in your bedroom. And where did she put her clothes?"

"I don't remember seeing them until the next day. They were hanging in the closet."

"She had disrobed near your bed; she had hung her dress in your closet. Surely, you took that as a clear invitation?"

"It's pretty hard for me to remember what I was thinking."

"I'm sure you remember what you were thinking."

O'Donnell shrugs, shifts about, crosses his knees.

"There was, as you put it, an air of sexual electricity."

"She was generating it, yes. I wasn't about to take any chances, Arthur."

"You were aroused, Jonathan. Very *firmly* aroused."

I say that with an ignoble snideness that is tinged with envy. The witness, it is known, has a hard-earned reputation with the ladies. But impotent Beauchamp will win the day: the verdict will be in his favour; he will not have to don his robes and belt on his gun and ride into town.

Jonathan is a long time rising to my bait. The only sounds are the irregular grunting of the freezer and the scritching of a mouse somewhere. I fear he will prove a poor witness in a courtroom.

"I couldn't have done anything about it anyway, Arthur. I was drunk."

"Ah, the defence of drunkenness. I know it well. That night you were reading from a play."

"Yes."

"No difficulty with that, I take it."

"No."

"You were animated, expressive."

"I suppose so."

"Earlier, you were hectoring Mr. Charles Stubb about his political ambitions."

"I was doing a lot of babbling."

"I suspect you had your wits very much about you."

"What are you leading up to?"

I sigh. The day is wasting. There are thistles in the carrot patch.

"Where is the suit, Jonathan? The brown suit she was wearing?"

"Back in my closet."

"Has it since been dry-cleaned?"

He looks at me sharply. No answer.

"Jonathan, did you take it out later to be dry-cleaned?"

"Yes."

"When?"

"That day . . . . the day after."

"After you found it lying crumpled on your bedroom floor."

"That's right. She'd badly creased it."

"That's the reason? There were no seminal stains on it?"

"Of course not."

"Presumably, if the suit were lying by your bed, at some point that night she again disrobed beside it?"

A long, painful pause. "I don't know."

"The suit she had worn was on your bedroom floor. Were you not present when she took it off? Did you not say you went to bed after settling Miss Martin on the downstairs couch? Did she sneak upstairs while you slept, then undress and paint herself with lipstick, then leave in sudden hysterics?"

Jonathan looks at his feet and does not answer. How sorry a spectacle he is. Still, there is something to be said for a man who lies so hopelessly; ironically, there is a certain honesty about him, a lack of facileness.

"It has been a while since I read *Saint Joan*," I say, "but isn't there a line to the effect that he who tells much truth is sure to be hanged?"

Jonathan's head remains bowed.

"I'm afraid in this case it's bad counsel."

Slowly, he drains his cup of laced tea. "I didn't rape her, Arthur."

"Your version of the events is not to be believed, Jonathan. I repeat, it's too preposterous."

Just then, ghoulish sounds from the kitchen, a mousetrap springing shut, the little rodent's death throes, a brattle of wood on the floor. The freezer makes a groaning sound, then silence.

"Oh, shit," says Jonathan. The phrase is repeated several times, softly, in utter capitulation.

I turn to the others. "Well, gentlemen, what is your verdict?"

None but Bully can look at me. "I'm sorry, Arthur, maybe we've been wasting your time."

"I apologize if I have ruined everyone's day. By way of benefit, you have learned your client is a poor witness and a worse liar." But I am feeling pity for the forlorn fellow sitting in my favourite chair. I soften my voice.

"I assume, Jonathan, that the reason no evidence of semen stains exists is that you burned the used sheets in your fireplace and replaced them with clean ones."

"Actually, I used a safe." The voice is hollow, distant. "But, yes, I did burn them. Just in case."

"A *safe*," says Hubbell. "You used a condom in the course of this . . . this . . ." He cannot find the words to express his revulsion.

"And I suppose that item, the used condom, isn't to be found anywhere among your personal memorabilia?"

"Burned it."

"Along with your bridges. You might as well have thrown yourself into the fire, too, Jonathan. You have done the work of the prosecution. You have almost convicted yourself. What a pity."

Gowan extends an arm like a traffic officer. "Okay, whoa, everybody, let's stop and reconnoitre. *Almost*, that's the word. *Almost* convicted. Nothing's been proved, and we're not in a court of law. The defence still holds, we can salvage it, it's still his word against hers, and for the record we didn't hear what the brilliant Professor O'Donnell just admitted to. I didn't hear it. Did anyone hear it? The presence of the suit in the bedroom can be explained—"

"Shut up, Gowan," Jonathan says.

"Shut up? *You* shut up. You've already said too much. Telling bald-faced lies, screwing around with the evidence—you don't *deserve* a defence—"

Jonathan begins to rise. "When's the next ferry back?"

I restrain him with a hand to his shoulder. "Gentlemen, please—"

"I got it," Gowan says. "He had to tie her up so she

wouldn't run off while he was putting a rubber on. He's a gentleman, didn't want to knock her up—"

"Gowan," says Jonathan, "I'm about two seconds from stuffing your teeth down your throat."

"That's enough!" My bull roar subdues this contumacious group. "This is *quite* unseemly."

"Sorry," says Jonathan.

"All right then, let us be fair to Jonathan. After all, he has been proven guilty only of the capital sin of lying to his lawyer. If all were hanged who had done that we couldn't find graves enough. But guilty of rape? I think not."

I bend towards Jonathan, and he cannot escape my eyes. "She hadn't really passed out, had she? She was waiting for the others to leave. The two of you then moved on to the final, unscripted act of your play."

He nods.

"She consented," I say.

"More than that."

"Then why the hell did you cover up?" says Hubbell.

"I think he expressed his overriding concern," I say. "To admit he bedded one of his students ends his career no more finally than if he'd actually assaulted her."

"That's the current diktat from the harassment committee."

Gowan comes out of a sulk. "Well, that's a damn lot better than ten years in the joint. Okay, we're doing better—so what the hell happened?"

Jonathan purses his lips, examines his hands. They are shaking a little. He responds in a slow, monotonic voice. "When I brought the sheet, she was still asleep on the chair—and I draped it over her. As I bent over her, she . . . well, she awoke. And we kissed. She became animated. I couldn't stop her. I couldn't stop myself. I couldn't stop *it*."

Jonathan slowly rises from the chair and begins to pace, not looking at any of us.

"We found ourselves on the living-room couch. Didn't talk, just, well, we necked. Then I led her upstairs, and I got the condom. We undressed, and . . . I'll spare you the vivid details. . . . She seemed starved for it. She had an orgasm and it kind of startled her. And then we, um, we continued at it. Had another bottle of wine."

"She shared in this?" I ask.

"Yes. Later, I got rid of the empty, washed the glasses. Anyway, at some point I went to the bathroom, drew a tub. I was there for a few minutes, and when I came out she was gone. I assumed she was just prowling around the house, and I flopped on the bed, waited for her . . . and fell asleep. Or passed out. And the next morning when I awoke—she wasn't there. That's it."

"And the lipstick on her lower regions and on her breasts? Her curious behaviour upon leaving your house?"

"Sleepwalking, nightmares, maybe Egan Chornicky dropped a tab of acid in her B and B. Maybe she was having a divine experience. À la Jeanne d'Arc. Maybe she forgot to take her Prozac. Who knows?"

"I like it," Gowan says. "It works."

Jonathan gapes at him. "You like it?" He erupts, a burst of unleashed pique. "What do you mean, it works? Blow it out your tailpipe, you smarmy bastard!"

"Easy, pal," says Gowan, and he looks to me for support.

Jonathan puffs his cheeks and slowly releases air. "Sorry. Get it together, O'Donnell. Get it together." He pours himself another large scotch, sips it, winces.

A strained silence follows, broken only by Bully clearing his throat a few times.

Jonathan has now taken a book from one of the shelves and is leafing through it.

"There's a line in here somewhere. . . . Here: '*Quisque suos patimar Manes.*'"

The Aeneid. He reads the ancient verse well.

Jonathan replaces the book. "'Each of us bears his own hell.'"

I ask, "Where did you study Latin?"

"Oxford. And earlier. Six years of it."

I return to my vigil at the window, look out upon my humble garden, my orchard thick with small green bulbs of apples, my pond where a wren trills sweetly on a reed.

Jonathan's hands are trembling. I sigh again and pick up his bottle and shake it. Just about empty.

"Welcome to the fold. You are an alcoholic, Jonathan."

He doesn't respond.

"Can you abstain?"

"Why?"

"Because otherwise I will not act for you."

Jonathan raises his glass, but doesn't drink. He scrutinizes the remaining liquid in it, then stands and pours it out the window.

"Deal."

"Ah, yes. Well, gentlemen, the case is more difficult and complex than first we supposed. There is a question now whether we dare put Jonathan on the stand. The preliminary hearing recommences . . . a week Tuesday?"

"Yes, July seventh," says Gowan.

I retrieve Jonathan's written statement. "Perhaps we should destroy this. And begin with a *tabula rasa.*"

I realize I have not been a good host. "Cookies, anyone? I'll be in utter despair if you don't try them— I baked them myself."

Each in turn takes a peanut butter cookie.

♪ PART TWO ♪

A man should be upright,
not be kept upright.

—MARCUS AURELIUS ANTONINUS

Thoughts of returning to the city—even for a short while—cause me a discomfort in my lower recesses, and for several days after General Bullingham's forces storm and capture me, I remain in a dour funk. After three months on tranquil Garibaldi the hurly-burly of city and courtroom seems as distant as the moon. My melancholy stems from my weak resolve—I allowed them to break my will.

But impelled by an alcoholic's code of duty to his brother—and perhaps by some misplaced sense of solidarity with a fellow Latin scholar—I could find no escape. Perhaps I see Jonathan as an ally in weakness. I so admire the self-destructive. At all events I suspect he is innocent, and despite his sins deserves public proof of that.

Sadly, the weather refuses to cooperate in my determination to be gloom-ridden. The month of July enters hot, lazy, dreamy, and altogether unnecessarily pleasant. I spend these halcyon days sitting on the back stoop while a fan of water plays over my garden, and I reread the transcripts and listen again to the spunky, chirruping voice of Kimberley Martin. And I wish again and again I had never agreed to do this. The case reeks of disaster, of damaged lives.

But my decision has brought great comfort to Annabelle, who has returned from Seattle. She telephones to say I am doing the right thing for "poor Jonathan." Though she will be delighted to have me back in the house for a few days during the preliminary, she does not propose a more extended stay. In three months she has visited but once, and she has not again mentioned joining me for that promised few weeks this summer.

Ah, well, we are enjoying this time apart together. Perhaps she is loosening the bonds. Possibly in giving me what she calls my "space," she is also tendering freedom. Or is Deborah right? Will her mother continue to reel in the puppet strings every time I try to dance off the stage? Am I tied to her in some unhealthy—dare I say—masochistic way? In bondage for my sins of weakness. Ah, yes, the ties that bind.

George Rimbold drags me off fishing one morning, and I find myself talking to him about my marriage, giving solemn confession. He listens Buddha-like, stoned on his marijuana, then tells me my impotence is a blessing from the God he refuses to acknowledge. "Oh, to be freed from the chains of lust. Look how it has brought me down. I envy you." What luckless event caused his downfall? Coveting his neighbour's ass, he'd said.

On a miserably bright and cheerful Saturday, as I am entering the fifth straight day of my malaise—the preliminary hearing looms but a few days away—George again interrupts my busy schedule, this time to fetch me to a public meeting at the community hall, the hearing into Evergreen Estates' plans to expand its subdivision.

"Drama, intrigue, high emotion, unbridled anger. You don't want to miss it, Arthur, these meetings are the island's only form of live theatre. Could see Zoller get punched out."

Kurt Zoller, our paranoiac trustee, has been urging me to attend and offer my voice to the Cause of Progress: *Mr. Bo-champs, we can't stand still.* But I have decided I am one with the eco-freaks. I will take a stand. Margaret Blake will realize I am not a lost cause after all, and will extend her hand in contrite apology for her many rudenesses.

And I will offer to settle—let's say sixty-forty in her favour on the pig. A moral victory for her.

Because George and I tarry too long over tea and talk, the meeting is well under way when we arrive. The community hall, a barnlike edifice built with donations of local money and labour, is high on an arid ridge called Breadloaf Hill. A notice on the front door advises: "Please use the facilities outside, as the toilets don't flush as there is no water."

At least half of the adult population of Garibaldi is in attendance, most of them looking rather surly as the developer, a sleek Cassius with a manufactured smile, tries to pitch his goods. Mrs. Blake is at the back, listening intently, coiled as if about to spring into action.

Several empty chairs are at the front, and, as we sit, Chairman Zoller nods and smiles and winks at me. Mrs. Blake, thinking I am allied with him, is no doubt looking knives in my direction.

But I am suddenly elsewhere, in a court of law, facing young Kimberley Martin. Listening to her tapes I felt like an aural Peeping Tom, an invader of private space. Ah, yes, how shrewd of Gowan to have forced their production; how noble it made me feel to listen to her incautious ramblings. *As my little sister says, gag me with a spoon.*

The provincial judge presiding over this preliminary is one William Pickles, a charm-free preening martinet. Gowan proclaims he is in our pocket, but I am not sure that matters. A judge's role at preliminary is a limited one: he may commit the accused to trial by higher court or—rarely, when the prosecution falls short of a prima facie case—may discharge him.

But unless the complainant recants, that will not happen next week.

The bar manager, Emily Lemay, speaks in support of the rezoning—"I need the business," she says frankly. But she is booed. Other members of this cranky audience rise in opposition: several stands of fir and arbutus must go if the subdivision passes. Septic seepage will foul adjoining farms. A rare flower, the chocolate lily, is endangered.

Kurt Zoller moves from his table and plumps down into an empty chair beside me.

"The natives are restless," he says. "Now's a good time for you to speak."

"The majority seems in opposition," I say.

"Yeah, but *I* make the decision. Got to listen to them, that's my democratic duty. But I was elected to make the hard choices."

He seems unusually edgy. Perhaps that is because he is without a life jacket today. Rising, he pats me on the shoulder, a public gesture of the camaraderie he believes we share. I have obviously been too subtle in my dealings with him.

But again I am in my courtroom. Patricia Blueman is at the other counsel table. A tense, striving woman whom I had always considered quite humourless. I am rather pleasantly shocked to know she has a repertoire of judicial impersonations. She's adroit enough. She certainly bested Cleaver at the preliminary, though that vulgar pouf would never dare admit it.

She must be handled with some delicacy, and more dignity than Gowan displayed.

Margaret Blake is on her feet now. "Kurt Zoller, do you deny you have an interest in this development?"

"You're out of order!"

"You're in bed with them, aren't you, Kurt? You have a house up there in the Estates. If you can call that ugly trailer . . . . I just bet they paid you off."

"This is a libel! I warn you, Margaret Blake, we

have a lawyer here of high upstanding. Mr. Bo-champ will explain you are guilty of libel."

I decline his invitation for a legal opinion and lower myself a few inches in my chair.

"Oh, sure, you have *him* all snuggled up in bed with you, too."

Zoller now launches into a shrill condemnation of the enemies of progress. I am somewhat alarmed, and conjure an image of the Führer in his bunker, railing against his many conspirators. After several minutes of this he recovers a semblance of dignity and retakes his seat. The developer, whose patch-on smile has become a strained *risus sardonicus,* clears his throat and says, "Does anyone have any more questions?"

Benumbed, no one rises, so Zoller hammers his gavel and adjourns the meeting.

I follow George outside, fumbling for my cigarettes. "Good God," I say. "Poor Zoller."

"A superb performance tonight," says George. "Must be off his medication."

"Mr. Beauchamp, I wonder if I can get a reaction from you." It is, of course, the man in the porkpie hat, Forbish of the *Echo.*

"Not now, Norman."

I am looking about for Mrs. Blake, hoping to satisfy her that I am not Kurt Zoller's bed companion, but the pesky, rotund reporter doesn't let up, and wants to know "my attitude" about the subdivision.

"Let's say I'm antipathetic."

Spotting my quarry, I bolt from him. Margaret Blake is already in her truck, but sees me approaching and studies me with an expression of either pity or disgust.

"Very interesting meeting, Mrs. Blake."

"I'm glad you liked it."

"In case you had the wrong impression, I am one with the chocolate lilies."

"You seemed awfully chummy with Kurt Zoller."

"Kurt is like a brother to me."

She doesn't join with me in smiling. Perhaps she believes I am serious. I wonder: Why have I become so concerned that she think well of me? Truly, she is a pain in the behind, and lacks the redeeming grace of a sense of humour. Yet . . . I am growing to admire her spunk.

"Though we are neighbours, Mrs. Blake, I never seem to bump into you—"

"That's probably because I work from six in the morning until sunset."

The implication: I am a layabout with my amateur's garden and my many hirelings. "I wanted to talk to you about eliminating one of the small frictions that seems to hound our relationship. As you know, Blake versus Beauchamp is set for Small Claims Court this month."

"Mr. Beauchamp, I am only asking a hundred dollars for that animal. If I put in for all the hours I spent feeding, giving shots, building pens, and generally mucking about, I could be asking for about five times that."

"Now, look, I've done some research. Betsy is worth sixty dollars on the hoof at fair market value. I'm prepared to dicker."

"There's emotional pain and suffering. Betsy was like a pet."

"Emotional . . ." I am lost for words. This woman will not be reasoned with. Again I feel my heart harden and my spine stiffen. It is becoming a matter of principle—I will not let this fierce farmer walk all over me in her mud-caked gumboots.

"Well, let's sort it out in court then, Mrs. Blake."

"Okay, well, bye-bye then. Have a pleasant evening."

I give her a resigned salute and she drives off. Very well, I will have some sport with this stubborn plaintiff. The judge will apportion blame fifty-fifty, but with a magnanimous gesture intended to shame her, I shall pick up the entire tab, including court costs.

🙙🙟

Dear Mr. Brown,

It was a pleasure to meet you, and I will try to carry out your wishes the best I can. The fee we discussed is agreeable.

May I confirm my instructions, so there will be no misunderstandings. 1. Never are you and I to meet while the investigation is in progress. 2. Our only contact will be through a post-office box for which both of us have keys. 3. I will gather information on Professor Jonathan O'Donnell to aid in his conviction of the rape of your fiancé, Miss Kimberley Martin. 4. Miss Martin must not be made aware that I am making these inquiries on your behalf.

However, I must advise you that without access to the central figure in this case I will be working at some disadvantage. I will try to be discreet, but I am well known to the police and to many lawyers.

I would much prefer that you consulted with Miss Martin about my role. However, you are the client, and mine is not to reason why.

My activities to date may be summarized as follows:

Having read the complete newspaper files about the case, I drove Wednesday morning to Professor O'Donnell's home in West Vancouver.

Watching from my car, I observed Professor O'Donnell leave the house in shorts and sweatshirt and begin running down the street. He returned half an hour later and went into the house.

It was not long before he reappeared, dressed in a shirt and slacks, and he backed his Jaguar car from the garage and drove past me while I hid below the dashboard. I then pulled out and followed him over the Lions Gate Bridge, into downtown, and ultimately to the False Creek area, where he parked beside a three-storey medical office building. I saw him standing at the building's door, checking his watch. I observed his hands were shaking. (The time was 1:50 p.m.) I deduced he had an appointment or meeting of some kind, but he seemed to lack courage, for he did not go directly into the building but into a cocktail bar down the street. However, he only consumed a tomato juice.

He then proceeded outside and returned to the medical building, taking the elevator to the top floor, which houses a dentist, a physiotherapist, an ophthalmologist, and a psychiatrist, Dr. J. M. Dix. It was in the waiting room of this office that I saw him talking to the receptionist. I do not know what the problem was, but he did not wait to see Dr. Dix, and almost immediately left. I sense the subject is trying to come to grips with a drinking problem and perhaps has enlisted a psychiatrist to help him.

I then followed his car to the University of British Columbia, where he went to his office, remaining until evening, when he returned to his home.

My next task will be to seek out among Mr. O'Donnell's acquaintances someone not fond of him. I find that enemies are often productive sources.

I remain yours truly,
Francisco (Frank) Sierra,
Licensed Private Investigator

§§

I rise this Tuesday morning after another dream of impotence, myself on bended knee before the Roman magistrates, *in puris naturalibus*—stripped bare, humiliated, begging them to censure me. Somewhere in the shadows of this dream a woman lurks, probably Annabelle—but I am not sure.

After I bathe, I study in my bathroom mirror the naked hero who plays the starring role of my dreams. The news is not so bad. Clearly I am trimmer—the exercise and the fresh salads are working well. Here we see evidence of outdoorsmanship: the stark outlines of a farmer's tan. Truly, I have become a redneck—though the nape of that neck is hidden by an untended garden of unruly hair. Roberto, my barber, who is waiting in Vancouver with his clippers, will have a fit that will rival the tantrums of Kurt Zoller. But Judge Pickles must not think he is dealing with some old hippie lawyer.

It's eight o'clock. Outside, I hear an aircraft throttling down, gliding into Beauchamp Bay. *Jacta est alea.* The die is cast. Today I shall cross the Rubicon—or at least the Strait of Georgia, beyond whose swirling waters lie the brutish city, its predators, its victims, its ruthless courts of law.

But my visit will be short, time enough to be reminded of the useless things I left behind.

I attend at my bedroom closet, seek out underclothes and matching socks. I have but one suit here, the one I wore when I arrived, though fifteen others grace my massive closet in Vancouver.

As I don my suit, I am overcome for a moment by a mental picture of Kimberley Martin: Joan of Arc in male armour. Maybe I should buy a garish tie for today's hearing. That would certainly set a nervous tone.

I take up my briefcase. I grit my teeth.

Gowan Cleaver, weighted with his burden of anxious city energy, is at the ramp beside the chartered float plane.

"We're set for ten-thirty, Arthur. Not much time. We should go over some things."

We climb aboard, and the pilot taxis into deeper water, then throttles, and we are airborne. I watch my little farm shrink into the distance, and the island recedes, and a sadness overwhelms me. I shall return *sine mora*.

As the aircraft churns across Georgia Strait, the muddy outpourings of the Fraser River pass below, then its diked embouchure and alluvial plains, the flat, squared suburbs, Lulu Island, Sea Island, the international airport, and now the great clay banks of Point Grey, the buildings of the university perched high atop them. I can see the law school, where Jonathan O'Donnell and Kimberley Martin took their first faltering steps towards their ultimate strange encounter.

We sweep over the steel filaments of the Lions Gate suspension bridge, then coast into Vancouver's busy inner harbour to the float plane dock. Surrounded as I am by monoliths of glass and concrete, immersed within the city's roar and clatter, I feel an ill foreboding, a loss of bearing and balance, a queasiness. The passage was too quick; I have been thrust within minutes from field and forest into the unforgiving bowels of the city. I step from this flying Wellsian time machine onto the dock, where Gowan, haranguing me like a high-school coach, leads me to one of the firm's limousines.

"Don't use kid gloves, Arthur. I think we have to work on the reasonable assumption she's lying through her teeth."

"I think we ought to try to avoid bloodshed, Gowan."

"*Au contraire*. You should do the slice and dice. Look, let's say O'Donnell *does* get committed—you do a job on her today she'll be shitting in her drawers, she won't want to push this thing to trial."

He carries on in this scabrous vein all the way to the Commonwealth Tower, the forty-three-storey phallic extrusion on Georgia Street wherein the minions of Tragger, Inglis, Bullingham perform their daily drudgery. Five entire floors we occupy; I have met but half the lawyers we employ. *We.* I am back in the firm. But I am not stopping at the offices this morning. Roberto's Salon is just off the lobby, facing the street. He has been barber to the firm for thirty years.

Gowan tells our driver, "Pick us up in twenty minutes, no later," then continues to offer advice as we walk to the building. "Don't be fooled by her. I think she'll probably come on all batty-eyed and winsome."

"I have done this before, Gowan." I am becoming brittle of temper. It's the city. I can hear its tin music, its sirens, its loud, backslapping laughter. I can smell its dense air.

Roberto, whom I remember when he was Bob and his salon a shop, has cancelled a morning appointment to squeeze me in for twenty minutes. Upon recognizing me—after some early doubt—he indulges in an effulgent display of nose-crinkling, hand-wringing, and stricken moans.

"Mr. Beauchamp, we simply don't want you looking like they found you wandering about in the Sahara Desert. I'll never do this in twenty minutes, it's impossible. That beard is utterly immoral, it ought to be against the law."

"I'm keeping the beard, Roberto. Just trim it and tidy me up on top."

He settles me into his chair with a great show of disdain, enshrouds me with a rubber cloak, takes one last despairing look at the tragedy of my hair, and goes to work with scissors and clippers.

"We *could* make a nice ponytail."

"That will not be necessary."

Gowan hovers near. "You want to go over your cross-examination notes while you're sitting there?"

"No, thank you."

"You *made* notes."

"Ah, yes, well, they're mostly in my head."

"Pat Blueman, I should warn, is very pissed off that I got hold of those tapes of the complainant. Wait till Judge Pickles hears them. When his honour finds out Blueman's been doing sendups of him, he'll want to send *her* up. Roberto, you're not listening to this, okay? We're short of time, I have to go over some tactics."

I say, "A man ought to trust his barber."

"Oh, my, cut out my tongue," Roberto says.

"Okay, the scenario plays out like this," says Gowan. "Kimberley Martin is engaged to a wealthy bore. She's in love with Remy's money, so she doesn't want to blow the marriage, but at the same time she's developed this infatuation with a prof—from whom, by the way, she needs a passing mark to get her into third year. She gets drunk, she gets loose, her hormones start to rage out of control, and before she can think about the consequences, she's busily humping the acting dean of a prestigious law school."

I hear all this. But what could have caused that supposedly healthy, happy, normal twenty-three-year-old woman to claim he tied her up?

"Now it's the wee hours, and suddenly she remembers her fiancé has just returned home from a business trip—where was he, South America right? She panics—she probably told him she'd be home no later than midnight. And she's plastered, her brain isn't exactly functioning with cool precision. Her only hope of saving the marriage is to yell rape. Following this?"

"Yes, Gowan."

"So she runs next door, makes a big show of having been attacked."

"Why all the lipstick on her body?"

"Oh, God, who knows, some sort of fetish. Shameless—it's the colour of blood. Primitive self-decoration. Remember: She's drunk, she's abnormal, she's seeing a shrink. And it's only on the tits and the lower parts of her body, places she can reach. Does she call the police? No. She's tied up and raped, and she doesn't want the police involved? She probably hopes her boyfriend will listen to her tearful explanation and, because he doesn't want embarrassing controversy, he'll advise her not to pursue it. But he does. *He*, Clarence St. Remy Brown, calls the cops. There's no backing out. She has to play out the farce to the bitter end."

"Why does she embellish this story with an account of being tied up?"

"To divert any suspicions Remy may have that she willingly put out. She chafes her ankles a bit, bruises herself up just a little to make the whole thing credible. Okay? See any holes in it?"

"It's not totally implausible, I suppose."

"So, okay, Arthur, don't forget to ask her about her tapes: where she says pigs like Judge Pickles still run the farm. He'll be smouldering, and he might just buy a pitch that the case is an abuse of process."

I am having difficulty staying tuned in. The mention of pigs has me wandering into a different courtroom. Should I subpoena a swine broker to testify as to Betsy's value on the hoof? Should I counterclaim for the total value of my recently disassembled Rolls-Royce? My small claims case seems much more fun than this atrocious business, with its inherent peril of blighted lives.

"Long in the back, Mr. Beauchamp? Something suave? Yes, I think the beard is beginning to work. Bit of salt and pepper. It says we are robust, manly, lusty." Roberto is in a much better mood as his sculpting has progressed.

"Long in the back," I say.

"Blueman hasn't been warned you're taking over as the senior. Wanted it to be a surprise. Bringing in the home-run king to pinch hit in the ninth. It'll keep them off-balance."

From the street outside, a sudden squeal of brakes,

the sound of crunching metal. Loud curses. Roberto doesn't miss a clip. He is humming to himself. He is an old warhorse of the city, inured to urban sound and fury.

Joining Gowan and me in the limousine are two students-at-law from the firm, excited, fidgeting hod-carriers bearing valises filled with law reports that I will never use. But they are young and innocent and believe the law has to do not with human foibles but with musty precedent.

We whisk along the causeway through the preserved wilderness of vast Stanley Park, then slow to a crawl on the clogged First Narrows Bridge. The preliminary is being heard in the courthouse of West Vancouver, a wealthy suburb on the North Shore, its pompous eyries terraced upon the rocky slopes above English Bay. High up live the *haute bourgeoisie*; those who have not quite made it to the top; *arrivistes* and mere professionals, like Jon O'Donnell, live lower down.

Several media vans are parked in front of the court building, and cameras follow us to the doors. A quarter after ten: there is time for a last cigarette in the free fresh air. Gowan goes inside to track down our client while I joust good-naturedly with some of the reporters about matters irrelevant and frivolous. They are here solely upon a watching brief—evidence at preliminary may not be reported.

All heads turn as a taxi pulls up. Patricia Blueman steps out, followed by a striking woman in brown braids, obviously the traffic-stopper Kimberley Martin, then followed by a man in his mid-thirties, of medium height, handsome in the manner of a model for a Jockey shorts billboard: a dimpled chin, a square, almost prognathous jaw. Dark glasses. A cellular phone in his suit jacket pocket. Mr. Clarence de Remy Brown, I presume.

Kimberley is smartly dressed in a white blouse and a long skirt that catches the tawny colour of her hair. She is smiling, but I detect she is doing so with effort—the rims of her eyes seem slightly raw, her posture strained and rigid. Her hair is done up in those strange Jamaican braids—what do you call them? Dreadlocks. There is a kind of Hollywood panache about her. The actress Kimberley Martin.

For some reason, she halts her progress and looks at me with an intensely quizzical expression. I smile. She rears a little, like a startled colt, then quickly follows her fiancé into the building.

Patricia Blueman shoos away the press so we can talk.

"And what brings *you* here, Arthur? I thought you'd retired."

"How better than to spend my twilight years sitting around courtrooms, Patricia."

"So O'Donnell finally had the good sense to fire that obscenity Cleaver. I have to give him some credit for brains after all."

Patricia Blueman is in her late thirties, spare and spindly legged. Myopic behind monstrous black-rimmed spectacles, she has a presence that can be best described as bookish—though why that adjective should have a pejorative meaning, I don't know. I have always found her brittleness and self-consciousness appealing.

"I have been dragged by wild horses, Patricia, into this *opéra bouffe*. Kicking and screaming."

"I am complimented. The defendant must be feeling the heat."

"No more than Saint Joan, I suspect. You have her all fired up and ready?"

"She's telling the truth, Arthur."

"And why are you so sure of that?"

"For one thing, last week she volunteered for a lie detector test and she passed with flying colours."

"Oh, have they figured out how to make those things work?"

"For another, I *believe* her. I've spent some time . . . oh, you know all our secrets, don't you, Arthur? You heard her tapes. Candid, isn't she? No, I don't mind at all that I was ordered to copy them for you. That's Kimberley Martin, unrehearsed and real. Same as you'll get in court, chum. Ready when you are."

She is about to go inside, then pauses. "Oh, do me a favour. When you're cross-examining Kimberley on her tapes, bring out that business where Judge Pickles is called a sexist pig."

She goes inside. I butt my cigarette and follow her.

The waiting area is thronged with gawkers, mostly older women who have abandoned their morning soaps to take in a live performance. I have been warned that a cadre from the Women's Movement would be here, Ms. Martin's support group. I see her standing there, sheltered among them, Venus amidst her mischievous train of Loves and Graces. Clarence de Remy Brown is talking on his cell phone but glowering fiercely at Jon O'Donnell.

I join Gowan and my client, who are sequestered in a hallway, our students standing a respectful distance away. There is little time to waste on idle chatter—a sheriff's officer is summoning us into court.

"Ready, gentlemen?"

"Show time," says Gowan.

"Barnum and Bailey," says Jonathan. "Bring on the clowns. I'm the high-wire act."

His manner is relaxed, but his demeanour grave. No glazed-over eyes, no essence of intoxicants. He seems in better mental health now that he is purged of his former deceit. I will do what I can for him. I may wear the horns for him, but he is my client, and knows some Latin poetry.

Jonathan's attention is suddenly elsewhere, and I turn to see Kimberley Martin, on the arm of her swain, hesitating at the courtroom door. She looks at Jonathan, then at me, then at Jonathan again. Suddenly, with a cocky toss of her head, she smiles, then turns away, and walks in. I cannot read this smile: confident, vain, a mask to hide her fear?

In the courtroom, William Pickles is at roost upon his dais, bawling out a sullen young revolutionary who apparently defaced a bank building with a spray-on slogan encouraging the eating of the rich.

"Thirty days," says Pickles. This stoop-shouldered, rheumy-eyed gentleman long ago rose to the level of his incompetence—he has been gracing the low-court bench for at least fifteen years, watching younger and brighter men and women pass him by.

"Regina versus O'Donnell," calls the clerk.

I stroll to the counsel table, my client in tow. Pickles looks surprised to see me.

"Mr. Beauchamp, you're appearing in this case?"

"Quite so, your honour. I shall be counsel for the accused today, assisted by Mr. Cleaver."

"Fresh blood. That should promise some entertainment. Always delighted to see you. Miss Blueman, are we ready?"

"Yes, and I call Kimberley Martin to the stand."

I sit, and Jonathan joins me to my left, Gowan to my right. Kimberley walks to the witness box with seeming self-assurance, yet something tells me she is not as relaxed within as she appears *in exterior*.

She responds to the standard opening questions about age and background with a voice that is measured but musical, reminding me of a precisely tuned cello. Well rehearsed? It is difficult to say. William Pickles, the judge-in-our-pocket, stares sternly at her over spectacles riding low on his nose, then busies himself with pen and bench book.

A transcript will be available, so I am making only mental notes—it is more important now to observe the language of the body and the eyes.

"You are about to move into your final year of law?" the prosecutor asks.

"If I pass two exams next week. I'm being allowed to rewrite them."

"Last fall you were taking lectures in property law?"

"Yes, I was."

"And who was your teacher?"

"Professor O'Donnell."

"Do you see him in court?"

Her eyes slowly turn to my client, and she studies him solemnly.

"That is him."

"Identifying the accused."

Curiously, her look does not waver for several seconds. Nor does Jonathan's in response—and I have a sense of some silent, angry conversation.

In a subdued, unfaltering voice, the complainant relates, with little embroidery, her early dealings with O'Donnell, in the classroom, on the campus, in his office—sketching a series of scenes of avid though not discourteous male pursuit.

I catch Jonathan at one point shaking his head. "But she brought her coffee to *my* table," he whispers.

I softly admonish him not to show reaction.

As to the events of November twenty-seventh, her version varies little from that of her tapes, though she is more forthright about the amount of alcohol she consumed—doubtless Patricia Blueman has cautioned her to avoid straining her credibility on that issue. Clearly, Kimberley is a witness prepared to amend her lines. But most witnesses, even the fundamentally truthful, tend to repair and varnish their stories. One waits and watches for the big lies.

"Did you at any point that evening consider that his intentions might be dishonourable?"

Kimberley responds oddly, with a flicker of a smile, as if finding the question rather florid and Victorian.

"Well, I had the sense he was coming on a bit strong, if that's what you mean."

"But you were not in fear for your safety?"

Gowan snorts and stirs, and whispers, "Bloody well leading, don't you think?"

"Very much so," I respond. But I am comfortable in my chair; an effort to rise would be unduly taxing.

"I wasn't afraid of him. I trusted him."

"And is that why you agreed to go along with the others to his house?"

Gowan moans, "Arthur, are you going to allow this to continue?"

"No harm is done."

"I felt perfectly secure. And he asked me to come, and one doesn't say no . . . Um, what I mean is, he was my professor, the acting dean, actually, and I thought it would be polite. . . ." For the first time, she is flustered, but she quickly recovers. "And I was curious." A smile, a shrug.

"Left herself wide open," says Gowan. "You don't say no when the prof asks you to come."

I wish he would refrain from the running commentary while I try to concentrate. Jonathan, to his credit, remains still, though his limbs are stiff, and he stares at her over his glasses like an owl, wide-eyed and sombre.

Patricia leads her witness into the taxi, into O'Donnell's house, into his library. Cognac is poured. ("I had . . . I guess it was an ounce—with a little shot of Benedictine.") Jolly political conversation takes place. ("Professor O'Donnell was being very . . . you know, crusty and curmudgeony.") The zombie Chornicky wanders about. ("He pretty well had his fill.") Kimberley browses through the library. ("I thought we could have a little fun with a Shaw play I was involved in.")

There follows a minor production of the last of G.B.S's great plays, with all but Chornicky taking roles.

"Okay, and at some point during all of this you left the room."

"Yes, well . . . actually, I went upstairs to the bathroom. Then—I don't know what was in my mind, maybe I felt this ought to be a dress rehearsal—so I, well, I went into Professor O'Donnell's closet and I put on one of his suits. It sounds silly now."

William Pickles's eyes darken with confusion—and possibly with the distrust I suspect he feels for this woman.

Kimberley attempts to help him out with a nervous *eruditio* about Shaw's image of Saint Joan as a mannish dresser. She concludes, "Joan has this thing about male armour—and a suit . . . well, it's sort of male armour, isn't it?"

I note the men in the room take this too seriously, but I smile, and Kimberley sends a quick and almost appreciative look my way.

"What did you do with your dress?" Patricia asks.

"I put it on the hanger where the suit had been. I mean, I had my bra on and underpants. But I found a white shirt of his, and—I guess I have to say I poked around—I found this absurd tie in a drawer." She glances at the ceiling, as if seeking help from above, then makes a rueful face.

Pickles is looking hard at me, perhaps wondering what I make of this. If I were to respond, I would say I'm not sure.

"And I came down, and—I don't think the others knew exactly what kind of statement I was making, and maybe I wasn't sure myself—but Professor

O'Donnell said something like, 'Ah, the maid of Orleans in her male livery,' and I knew he understood. He obviously knew the play. And I did a kind of funny, I hope, imitation of him giving one of his lectures, and we went back to the play—Professor O'Donnell was the inquisitor—and we were getting very dramatic. . . . I'm sorry, I'm just rambling here. Somebody help me out."

I am having difficulty not liking her. It will be painful when her words turn false. And I must assume they will, or I am in serious doubt about my role in this courtroom.

"Okay," says Patricia, "after you carried on in this manner for some time, what happened?"

"Well, I don't know. The drinks, the lateness of the hour, whatever, I just kind of went to sleep."

"Where?"

"On a big easy chair. I remember I was making a speech from the play . . . and then, pow, I was gone. Just like that. It was really strange. I remember hearing voices, and . . . that was it."

"Had you felt dizzy?"

"Not really."

"Did you sense there might have been something put in your drink?"

Gowan slaps his hand on the table in remonstrance, and looks pleadingly at me. "Are you going to let this go on?" he says.

"You are fussing like a child, Gowan," I whisper, quite sharply. "Stop it."

"No, I can't say if I did. If he . . . well, never mind."

"And what's the next thing you remember?"

Kimberley Martin bites her lip. She closes her eyes as if to shut out memory, then reopens them and, after an intake of breath, says, "I was being physically attacked."

She is playing to an utterly silent house.

· 135 ·

"I know it may be hard," says Patricia, but her question ends with that preface as the dam bursts for Kimberley Martin, and words start flowing, then rushing.

"He was on top of me, and I was lying on my stomach, I was naked, completely naked on a bed, and my hands were tied together, and my ankles were tied to some brass bedposts, sort of spread-eagled . . . oh, God, am I going to get through this? And he—"

"Just a minute—"

"And he kind of raised my bottom up and I felt him inside—"

"Inside what?"

"Inside . . . this is awful, I feel like I'm on exhibition here, it feels absolutely obscene to be standing in front of everybody talking so stupidly about . . . about the mechanics of getting raped, it—"

"Miss Martin," Pickles admonishes, "just answer the questions."

"I'm sorry, it just feels *wrong*. I've been over this and over this, and I know I'm supposed to say he put his penis in my vagina, and make it sound all dry and clinical, like something out of a high-school sex manual, but I was screaming, and no one could hear me. I was helpless. Have you any idea of the feeling? It was utterly degrading, and you don't know and you'll never know because you weren't *there*."

"She's losing it," Gowan whispers.

"Absolutely not," I respond. But I cannot decide whether these emotions are genuine or if this is a skilled performance of the illegitimate theatre.

Pickles's voice softens. "This is very stressful, I'm sure, Miss Martin, but it has to be done."

"I know. I'm sorry, I'm very tense."

"Okay, let's calm down and regroup a little here," says Patricia. "Now let us get this clear. When you awoke you were on a bed?"

"Yes."

"In a bedroom."

"You know, I didn't even notice what kind of room at first. It was dark, there was just some kind of night light on, or maybe from another room. But obviously it was a bedroom."

"And you were not on your back but in a prone position."

"Yes."

"Were your hands tied to any object?"

"No, just my feet. My hands were tied together."

"With what?"

"I believe it was a bathrobe cord. It was knotted around my wrists."

"And the bindings on your feet?"

"I . . . I honestly can't remember. I was in a frenzy. Some kind of cord or . . . actually, it felt silky."

"And what was happening?"

"I felt him behind me, lifting me up by the hips with both hands. And I felt his penis enter my vagina, and he began thrusting. This is so absolutely . . . I'll continue. As I said, I was screaming, and I was telling him to stop, and he wouldn't stop, and then I felt him trying to penetrate my, um, my anus—"

A gasp from somewhere in the gallery, the rustling of shifting bottoms.

"And I screamed louder, and he didn't say anything, just kept pushing at me, pushing and pushing, and I began twisting this way and that, he was hurting me, and . . . and he said something, I can't remember, and suddenly he was gone, and I was frantic, and, I don't know, I managed to free my hands, and then twisted around to release my ankles—"

"Ms. Martin," says Patricia. "Please. Slow down."

"Sorry."

"Are you all right? Would you like some water?"

"Please."

As the water is fetched, I see that Jonathan has his

eyes tightly closed. The expression on the face of Judge Pickles, as he regards the witness, has undergone a metamorphosis, a sagging, a softening. I have a sense he is no longer our steadfast ally.

"Would you like a break, Miss Martin?" he asks, his tone solicitous.

"I'd like to get this over and done, your honour."

Patricia Blueman shows a wetness of eye. Emotions here are riding uncomfortably high.

"Now exactly who was it who was on top of you?"

"Who? . . . Professor Jonathan O'Donnell."

"You saw him."

"I think so."

"What do you mean?"

"I guess when I twisted around, I . . . well, I wasn't actually memorizing details for court or anything. It was *him*."

"The accused."

"Well, it wasn't the Queen of Sheba."

The remark is too flip, and Judge Pickles stiffens.

But Kimberley recovers from this *faux pas*, and says, "I'm sorry, that's a terrible way to put it. I shouldn't try to be funny. I'm just . . . very nervous."

"Was he wearing any clothes?"

"Not that I could see. I mean, I was in . . . an hysterical state. I didn't know what was happening at first, I didn't even know where I *was*, or where I'd been, who I'd been with, I hardly even remembered my name. I was just being . . . well, I was being raped."

"Okay. Did he ejaculate?"

"I haven't the faintest idea. You'll have to ask him."

"Well, Ms. Martin—"

"I wasn't . . . this is so awful. I wasn't wet. Okay? But I felt, what? . . . Greasy. It was the lipstick all over me, I guess, I don't know why he did that. I thought it was blood at first; I was terrified, I thought he'd . . . he . . . well, never mind."

"All right, did you consent in any way to the sex or to being tied up?"

"Are you being serious?"

"I'm asking you if you consented."

"Of course not."

"Very well. And so he left you alone for a while."

"He disappeared. I could hear water running, in the en suite bathroom, I guess. Sounded like a tub filling. I had this feeling—he was going to drown me. And I was struggling to untie myself for, oh, I don't know, it seemed like an eternity, but was probably only a few minutes, and I could hear the tub filling and filling, and I . . . guess I just shot off the bed and ran out the door. And I still wasn't connecting very well, still wasn't sure where I was, but I found the stairs, and the front door, and I ran outside and to the house next door."

"And can you remember what happened there?"

"All I know is I was screaming, and this older gentleman came to the door, and then a woman—I thought they were married, but he's a retired minister and she's his housekeeper—and I remember they were being very nice, and comforting me, and I was crying, and all I wanted was to have Remy with me, my fiancé. So I phoned him, and he came over. I don't remember very much after that until—well, he took me home, and later that morning a policeman came over."

Patricia idly leafs through some notes, and I assume she is stalling a little, mulling over whether to leave matters as they sit or try to plug some of the leaky holes: How had she so easily freed herself? Why is it no neighbours heard the screams? How had her abdomen and her breasts been painted with lipstick as she lay prone on a bed? Why hadn't she called the police immediately?

Then Patricia sits. "Those are all the questions I have."

Gowan leans towards me. "You have no other choice now, Arthur. Go for the throat."

I sit, musing, trying to work all of this through my mind. I tell myself: She must be lying. Surely she is the Cleopatra *splendide mendax* of whom Horace wrote—splendidly false. Yet a worm of doubt wiggles within the rational, cynical mind. But I am becoming soft. Too long on a placid island, too many weeks away from the courtroom.

"Mr. Beauchamp?" says the judge.

I scrape back my chair and rise, scanning the watchers in the gallery; eager, expectant faces. In the back a woman knits, and I think of Madame Defarge and the guillotine. I find myself agreeing with the witness: the processes we are involved in seem wrong, obscene, a defilement.

Jonathan has his chin cupped in his hands, and he is staring at Kimberley Martin as if in a trance. What had Gowan told me last week? "O'Donnell says he doesn't want me to touch her." Why? The client seems oddly protective of his tormentor. But he has witnessed Cleaver's rough handling of witnesses, and must feel a subtler touch is needed.

"Mr. Beauchamp, do you have any questions?"

I continue silently to study Kimberley, then sigh.

"No, I don't have any questions," I say.

"*No* questions?" Pickles is taken aback.

"Ah, well, perhaps just one. You have some examinations to write next week, Miss Martin?"

"Yes."

"May I wish you the best of luck. Hopefully you will prove yourself as fine a lawyer as you are an actor."

What I seek is there: a rosiness tints her cheeks—the product of shame? Truth does not blush, a wise ancient once said.

"Thank you," she says, smiling, and pretends to all she has heard a compliment.

I sit. Patricia seems flustered, but recovers. "That's the case for the Crown, your honour."

I turn to Gowan Cleaver, who looks confused. Jonathan, if anything, seems quite relieved.

As Kimberley makes her way from the stand, she hesitates, looks once again at my client, and then tears begin to stream in torrents down her cheeks.

"Perfect," says Gowan Cleaver. "A master stroke. Ask no questions and you don't give the defence away. Save it all for the trial, brilliant."

Earlier, Gowan had been broadly hinting I was derelict in not cross-examining the woman, that I was plotting a speedy escape to my island farm. But he has now become effusive as we wait in the prosecutor's office. Patricia Blueman is elsewhere giving comfort to her charge.

"Complimenting her on her acting—just the right touch. I would have spent half the day banging away at her about her stage training and got one-tenth the impact. Christ, you're smooth."

Jonathan has been formally committed for trial by judge and jury upon a charge of sexual assault causing bodily harm. The proceedings of the day took no more than an hour. And truly there is no need for me to spend any more time in the city than politeness demands. Though in honesty that wasn't my plan. Let Gowan believe I was saving my ammunition for the trial—but, in fact, I couldn't bear the thought of going for Miss Martin's unguarded throat. She seemed too vulnerable. (Or do I guilelessly misread a splendid job of acting?) Am I losing my touch, the so-called killer instinct? Or has my hiatus from the courts made me more humane? Either way, I am the poorer lawyer.

"She collapsed, Arthur, she fell apart, what more can I say?"

"Probably just a release of tension."

"I doubt it. Guilt was written all over her. *She* should be the accused. We should bloody charge her with perjury and public mischief. *Public* mischief is more like it." He is grinning. "You want to grab a bite after?"

"Well, I think I shall be meeting Annabelle for lunch."

I have called her; we will meet at Chez Forget, one of my former haunts. I expect she will be relieved to learn I am planning a flight back to Garibaldi this afternoon.

Patricia Blueman bustles in, purposeful but smiling.

"That was very good, Arthur. She's literally terrified of you. Of course, she's heard of your reputation."

"All those wasted hours preparing her for cross, eh, Pat?" says Gowan. "Arthur decided not to give her a free dress rehearsal."

"Frankly, I thought she sounded very fresh and convincing," Patricia says. "But I wanted to talk to you gentlemen about the trial date. Normally we'd be looking at midwinter, right in the middle of her school year."

"Oh, and you want to put it off until what, spring break?" says Gowan.

"No, I don't think it would be fair to either party to make them wait too long. I'm thinking about the beginning of September, two months from now. There's a hole in the fall calendar, some kind of skid-road murder has fallen through."

"No, that's pushing it," says Gowan. "We have a hell of a lot of prep, and anyway I'm booked all through September. She'll just have to muck through and do it during her classes."

"And who would the judge be this September?" I ask.

"Mr. Justice C. Walter Sprogue. He's handling the first two weeks of the fall assize."

"*Mr. Justice* Sprogue?"

"You're not keeping up, Arthur. He was appointed two weeks ago."

The elevation of Wally Sprogue to the trial court bench had not made the notices in the *Island Echo*. When he was in practice I shared many courtrooms with him. Though surpassingly vain, he is a fellow of liberal temperament, a firm believer in the concept of a reasonable doubt. I cannot let this chance slip away.

"The first of September will be fine," I say.

"Wally Sprogue," says Gowan. "You're not going to throw a ringer at us—we show up and it's suddenly Attila the Hun."

"I can live with Justice Sprogue," says Patricia. "It'll be the jury who'll decide. He's away until August. Can we do a pre-trial with him then?"

"Most happy to oblige," I say. "Gowan, a minute of your time?"

This awkward moment cannot be avoided. As we walk together to the parking lot, I struggle to think of a way to let him down gently.

"September trial," Gowan grumbles. "Means I'm going to have to adjourn a couple of things."

"I don't think you should, Gowan. In fact, I'm wondering if I might ask you to step aside for this one. For, ah, political reasons, I feel I ought to be assisted by a female barrister. Any problems with that?"

The disappointment works through his face, but he comes through bravely. "Excellent idea, Arthur. In fact, I was thinking of suggesting that very thing. Solves a lot of problems, and you won't have O'Donnell and me going at each other's throats."

"I'll consult with you, of course. I'll need the benefit of your keen mind."

He makes the effort of a smile. I feel for him. It is an important trial for an ambitious lawyer.

※ ※

As I enter Chez Forget, its owner, Pierre, a small, vigorous man, swarms around me before I have a chance to wave to Annabelle, who sits in the back, playing with one of the roses in the vase that decorates her table.

"How do you not visit me any more? You do not like the food? You do not like the service? Try the McDonald's, they have slides and ladders for the children. Madame is here. She is starving, you can see, she is so thin. You will have the lamb paté, and the baby asparagus salad followed by *saumon fumé,* and then I give you the choice, either the tenderloin Avignon or the duck. Both are perfect."

He propels me to my chair opposite Annabelle. She is dressed with her usual flair, bare-shouldered in something silky. Her smile is soft and distant, and I have the sense that she is distant, too. In another place.

"Something wet, Monsieur Beauchamp?" Pierre extends a bottle of mineral water and I nod my agreement. Then he tops up Annabelle's half-empty glass of red wine and flies off to the kitchen.

She is still toying with the rose. She casts me a look and a shy, un-Annabellic smile.

"I love the beard. You look sort of Hemingwayish in it."

"Hides the jowls."

"Oh, but you've lost some weight."

I beam. "Yes, the belt tightens at a speed of one notch per month. Well, as I told you on the phone, my work day has concluded somewhat earlier than expected. We can relax."

"Yes. I've taken the afternoon off."

"I am flattered."

"But you're going back this evening?"

"I think that best." Don't you, Annabelle? But I hear no protests. Why does she seem so far away? She keeps running a finger along the surface of those rose petals, studying them, not looking much at me.

"Are you happy with the way it went?"

"I'd rather have been weeding my garden, frankly. But it went well enough, I suppose. Jonathan seemed oddly relieved that I didn't cross-examine Kimberley."

"You're getting along with him?"

"Of course."

"You seemed a little miffed that I was pushing his cause so hard."

"Not at all." I have the sense she is about to confess to something, and I become busy, lighting a cigarette, perusing the menu. What secret is she about to share: is she about to tell me of her love for Jonathan? Impossible. The absurdity of it would render me stuporous.

She reads my mind. "There was never anything between Jon and me—I hope you didn't get that impression." She muses, "There could have been. He's quite attractive in his dark, surly way. But there wasn't."

Should I presume she offered? I drag hard on the cigarette. I can't think of anything to say. I feel relief, of course, though I have wronged Jonathan in my thoughts, and must seek his forgiveness. I shall try to do this by proving his innocence.

Pierre bustles in with his plates of appetizers, refilling glasses.

"The tenderloin," I say.

"I can't, Pierre," says Annabelle. "No entrées."

"Madame will shrivel to nothing."

"The salad is beautiful."

"You are beautiful. The salad is only pretty."

"You're awful, Pierre."

After he leaves, Annabelle pokes at her salad a bit,

then says, "Well, it's now or never. I have something to tell you."

Her fingers touch the back of my hand. They feel cool and soft, fingers that have been caressing rose petals.

"I've met someone else."

The phrase seems banal, a cliché of Gothic scope. I am having trouble breathing. I have a flash of memory of mowing the lawn in the front of my house. I was gasping. My lungs felt as if they were caught in a vice.

"We're in love."

Love. That word seems too abstract. I cannot fathom its meaning. But I decide, no, I am not having another stroke. I am probably surviving this.

"Arthur, you knew something like this would happen. I think we stopped pretending long ago. I can tell you're in shock, but there's some relief there, too, there has to be."

"I'm . . . I'm sorry, I'm caught a little aback."

"I sort of felt . . . well, that you were giving me permission, Arthur. Moving off to your island as you did. I think you needed freedom from me. I was hurting you."

"I cannot find apt words, Annabelle." I fumble for a cigarette, though smoke curls from another in the ashtray.

"Then don't say anything. It's been going on I guess for a couple of months, Arthur. He's a very good man, awfully dashing and, well, gaudy. I suppose you'd find him pretentious, but he has a gooey centre."

I grind this information through the mills of my mind. Gaudy? Gooey centre? I picture someone gilded, ornate, superficially sentimental.

"It's François Roehlig, Arthur. The new permanent conductor? You've heard of him. I think you have some of his recordings from when he was with the Düsseldorf Symphony."

I hardly hear this. I am listening to my heart. But I am doing fine. Just fine. No reason to worry.

"*Eine Kleine Nachtmusik*. Yes, I think I saw his photo in the newspaper." Gaunt and fiery-eyed, wearing not a tropical palm-tree tie but an ascot. A rising star, a wunderkind.

"He's divorced, two children. He's . . . a little younger than I am. It doesn't seem to matter. I think he worships me. I don't know why. We share a lot. Obviously. He was conducting *La Bohème* for us, of course. And, um, he'd like me to go to Bayreuth with him this September, and he insists that I straighten it all out with you. Naturally he wants to meet you—I've spoken so admiringly—and I've been pretty frank with him about our difficulties, about how it hasn't really been a marriage for many years. . . ."

Annabelle is on an expressway and cannot find the brakes. How noble and gallant is the gaudy, gooey François Rochlig—he wants to meet the vanquished foe, the impotent Arthur Beauchamp, for a friendly after-duel drink. I am feeling some jealous ire—it is a healthy sign. I have emotions. I am well.

"Deborah will be furious, I suppose. I don't know what to do about that, she's so unforgiving. Maybe she'll find it in her heart if . . . if we finally make the break, Arthur, if I stop causing you pain. I know I do that."

She looks down, picks at a baby asparagus.

"I've been a sorry excuse as a wife. But I care for you. I want you to be happy."

She can say nothing more. She is waiting for me to accept her gift of happiness. My mind is clouded by a picture of this effete conductor, Roehlig, swiving my wife.

"Happy. Yes. Well, I am happy, Annabelle. For you."

"I'm so sorry, Arthur."

Numbly, I hear myself chattering, matter-of-fact

and falsely brisk. "I would like you to have the house, of course. I have my island farm. It is home now. I think we both have enough to keep ourselves comfortable—those funds Nicholas recommended are doing very well, really."

As Pierre descends upon us with the tenderloin Avignon, Annabelle begins to weep. He beats a quick retreat.

"I do love you, Arthur. In my way."

Annabelle suddenly rises and rushes off to the ladies' room.

I fight my own tears and stare for many agonizing moments at the half-filled glass of Bordeaux that sits beside her plate. My hand itches, moves forward, withdraws. Oh, God, what I would give for that cup of wine that clears today of past regrets and future fears.

We stop at the house—the silent, rambling structure in Point Grey I inhabited for twenty years—and I fill a large suitcase with items I'd earlier failed to bring: my favourite slippers, my collection of pipes and soapstone carvings, some gardening books. I do all this in a stupefied state, as if anesthetized.

My memories of the house seem more sour than poignant. I cannot remember too many happy days. It shall be hers now, and François Roehlig's. A picture of them seated together over breakfast composes poorly in my benumbed mind.

Lugging the suitcase out, I stop at the doorstep and say a silent, final goodbye to my former house, my runt-sized city garden, my former life. I heave the bag into Annabelle's Alfa-Romeo—she has taken the top down; the day has turned sunny. Annabelle's clouds have parted, too, and she is smiling behind the huge panes of her Italian sunglasses. Smiling. I suppose she feels an immense relief that it is over.

"Starting new lives—it feels good in a way, doesn't it? Like a fresh chance. Like finally getting the mortgage paid off, and knowing that the rest of your life is interest-free. God, I'm talking like Nicholas. Listen, François wants to meet Nick and Deborah, so we'll have you all over. You'll do the mending, won't you, Arthur? Try to convince Deb I'm not the wicked witch of the west."

My smile is fixed, glued on.

We descend the ramp to the harbour road, past Canada Place and the steamship dock, past one of those massive tourist tubs that ply the inside waters to Alaska. Annabelle races over the speed bumps that lead to the float-plane docks of Coal Harbour.

"It's a charter flight?"

"Billed to the client."

"Well, hell, I'll join you for the flight." She has had a few wines on a decidedly empty stomach. Her tears have dried. She is happy, in love, overflowing with it—there's enough to spare for me, and she hugs me after she parks the car, hugs me again as we cinch our seat belts in the back of the four-seat aircraft.

As we take to the air I maintain a conversation of sorts, some meaningless drivel about turning another bend on life's highway. I wear a mask of tranquillity—it hides the emptiness I feel, the yawning gulf within, the pathetic, self-pitying inner self.

Below us, a dozen container ships sit at anchor in English Bay, low, close to Plimsoll lines, awaiting their turns to disgorge their cargoes. Vancouver bustles. Its streets are clogged with cars—it is half past four, the city's downtown is emptying. The plane sweeps low around Spanish Banks, Point Grey, Wreck Beach, and now in the distance I see the islands of the Gulf. The exile returns, world-weary, anomic.

I direct the pilot into my cove, and the plane settles

into the water and drifts to the dock while I prattle mindlessly to Annabelle about how calming it has been for me here, how joyful to return.

"Maybe I'll bring François out here some weekend. Would that be too uncomfortable, darling? Not this summer—later, when things have settled down."

After the divorce. After the remarriage. He is younger than Annabelle—by how much? Did I not read he is in his thirties? Well, Annabelle is only fifty-three, less the many busy years her surgeon so skilfully whittled away from beside the eyes and beneath the chin.

She joins me on the dock and presses her lips firmly to mine. I have a sense of completion with this kiss, of finality. Last wifely kiss. The kiss-off.

"Scratchy," she says. "But I do like the beard. It makes you . . . interesting."

A hug. A smile. A wave. A kiss blown through the cockpit window. She turns to the pilot and starts chatting with him.

I watch until the aircraft becomes a mote on the horizon.

I walk into the house. I telephone George Rimbold, a call for help.

"She's an extremely strong woman. I think that's what first attracted me to her. Not her physical beauty, nor her style or flair or talent. Her strength. I still have no idea why I put up with it for so long, the unfaithfulness, the feeling of being diminished as a man. It's almost as if I have some *need* to feel put down."

George nods, listening to my logorrheic outpourings with the grave mien of the father confessor that once he was. It is midnight, and George has been steadfast through the evening. We have smoked to dangerous excess and have sampled three kinds of tea and various fruit juices, but I have beaten back the need, the compulsion; I haven't had to summon Scotty Phillips, the island bootlegger, who lives but a telephone call away.

"My daughter, who has some training in psychology, says I'm masochistic. I'm beginning to think she's right. To satisfy my unconscious wish to be mistreated, I attach myself to a domineering woman."

"Blather," says George. "Cheap pop psychology."

"Where does this come from? I suppose some clever therapist would point to my mother. She was domineering, too. Generous, outgoing, sharp-witted, but caustic. Very hard on my father, a quiet man. I identified with him a great deal, I suppose."

"Loved your father, did you? No wonder you're so screwed up." He says this dryly, with a smile.

"The beard, she said, makes me interesting. Am I so dull otherwise? I suppose I am. A rather boring person, really. I lack passion."

"You're certainly being boring right now," George says.

"Thank you, George."

"I mean it. Stop putting yourself down, old son. How do you dare call yourself boring? You're a celebrated lawyer, a winner of famous trials, a man of refinement, not some gaudy fop like this obviously mediocre conductor she's taken up with."

George has taken to referring to the conqueror of Annabelle's heart in acidic tones. George is my friend. My enemy is his enemy.

"It's different in court. I change. It is theatre. I play a role. I become the role. So powerful a role that I sometimes feel within me the strength of Hercules. I don't know why that's so. Then I doff my cape and resume life as the tedious, humdrum Mr. Beauchamp."

"Who gardens, who reads poetry, who plays fine

music. These are the avocations of a great and noble mind, Arthur."

The therapy is unsubtle, ego-inflating, but it works. I am feeling much better. I am free of her, and with our final disunion may soon be free of my need for her. But why do I feel so empty?

"I think I must have fed on her strength, George, in some unhealthy, parasitic way. Weakness loves strength, I suppose. It's a shameful thought, but I think I'm attracted to dominant women."

"Like who else, for instance?"

Dare I admit it? But why have my thoughts so often drifted over the fence to the neighbour's yard? There is so little I hold in common with Mrs. Blake, yet her aggressiveness, her spunk, seems to . . . excite me. How absurd.

George looks at me with a knowing smile. "How are you getting along with Margaret Blake?" He is too astute, too insightful.

I blush. "I have neither impure thoughts nor the wherewithal to do anything about them."

"Blarney," he snorts. "The reason you couldn't get it up has just vanished from your life. Performance anxiety, I think it's called. Fear of failure—compounded in your case by excessive drink. As to Margaret Blake, the best thing you could do right now to start filling the void would be to call on her. Start off by negotiating terms of peace."

"Believe me, I've tried."

As the night winds down and as I continue my recovery, our conversation moves to more neutral, less personal subjects: future fishing ventures, island gossip, my day in court.

George knows something of O'Donnell's father, the viscount from Ulster. "Mad Dog O'Donnell, they used to call him in the old days. Commander of the Ulster Rifles. Vowed to end the troubles and only created more."

Viscount Caraway is a notorious right-wing cur-mudgeon, as orange as a tropical sunset. He makes the news from time to time, even in the far-flung colony of British Columbia, with his jeremiads against such dis-parate enemies as the Pope, the prime minister, and those who feed at the public trough. Perhaps it is no wonder his son seems such a troubled man.

As I walk George from the house, he says, "If it gets tough again, smoke some of this."

He presses a small plastic bag containing some marijuana cigarettes into my hand, and he climbs into his car and disappears.

I wend my way to bed, seeking the solace of Som-nus, god of sleep. Who among his nocturnal spirits will visit me tonight—the gentle Dreams or the barba-rous Nightmares that lurk in the dark corners of my soul? As I descend into the silent cave of the Goddess of Darkness, she raises her whip. I am naked, hot, keen to feel the lash. Hurt me, I plead, hurt me.

৘৖

Tape number seventeen. Subject, Kimberley Mar-tin. Wednesday, the eighth of July, eleven-fifteen in the morning . . . Ursula?

Yes, Dr. Kropinski.

Will you cancel my lunch? Dr. Duguid from the Forensic Foundation—would you ask her please to delay until next week? Is Kimberley Martin there? Send her in . . . Good morning, Kimberley.

Morning, doctor. And thanks.

And for what do you thank me?

Fitting me in like this.

Oh, there is no problem. How did everything go in court yesterday?

If given a choice I'd have done a month in hell. I'm exhausted. Can I take my favourite padded chair? Oh, God. Kimberley Martin, the neurotic couch potato. Give me my teething ring and my teddy bear.

It was stressful?

Yeah, but it was funny, because the defence lawyer—oh, O'Donnell has Arthur Beauchamp now.

I read this in the paper.

He has this mondo reputation, I was shaking in my socks. But he didn't ask me one question. Except for some breezy little comment about my acting ability. At which moment I entirely disintegrated. They had to pass out umbrellas.

Why do you think that happened?

I don't know. Pent-up anxiety. I'm sure it looked awful to everyone, as if I were guilty of something. But the worst part was just *being* there. On the witless stand. Raving hysterically in front of all those drooling ghouls in the gallery. About it. *It*— what a nice little neutral word for being stripped and physically trashed. I felt naked in court, like some slave being prodded onto the platform to be auctioned off.

But you got through it, yes?

Not exactly in one piece. Patricia Blueman had to collect me with a dustpan. She's such a . . . well, she's a mensch. Anyway, Jonathan O'Donnell just sat there looking at me through the whole thing—he has these coal-black Rasputin eyes—staring at me as if I were some kind of creature from the lost lagoon. A few times, I just looked right back at him—he doesn't scare me. . . . I'm babbling.

That's fine.

I know what you're writing. "The patient was in a somewhat manic condition, her thoughts freeflowing, though disconnected."

How is everything else for you, Kimberley? How are your exams coming?

Constitutional law is a bitch. I'll pass it, I think.

I'll somehow ooze my way into third year. And what else? Oh, I have a part in a new play at the Granville Island Workshop. It's a sort of bush-league deal, experimental theatre, but it'll be fun. *Switch,* it's called. Comedy of morals. I play the dumb blonde who goes along with anything. You can tell it was written by a guy. But it's a lead part. . . . You know, Dr. Kropinski, I almost feel guilty about winning the audition. I'm a famous rapee. I guess the theory is my name is going to sell tickets. God, do you think I'm capitalizing? Yuk. It's so *American.*

I will make a point of going.

Bring your wife, I'll put you on my freebie list.

That is very kind. How is Remy?

Oh, he's fine. You know, I adore him, but he's so . . . what word am I looking for? Detached? Sometimes it feels like being engaged to a fax machine. He sat with me in court through the whole morning—that was sweet of him—but I could tell he was suffering heavy work withdrawal. He'd rather have been somewhere buying up mining properties.

Has anything else been bothering you?

I had another nightmare about being attacked. A man came creeping into my bedroom, into my bed.

Tell me about it.

It's so ugly. A smelly old man with a beard. He . . . Oh, God. Why is this happening? It was just a dream.

Here, take a Kleenex.

&

Now we are in the very heart of summer, long, lan-guid days of fattening gardens, of wild berries and dragonflies, of sunflowers following with rapturous upturned faces Apollo's daily westward toil. Quiet days: the little frogs have croaked and croak no more, and the bedlam of songbirds has abated, though the air is rent occasionally by the loud gronks of ravens or the piercing shriek of a pileated woodpecker swooping through a clearing in the forest, a flash of punk-red hair.

In the mornings before the dew turns into mist I take my constitutional, up the hill on Potter's Road, down a woodland path I have discovered, up behind the community church and around the bend to the general store, arriving usually as Mr. Makepeace unlocks the door. Often I tarry there over the coffee urn with friends, jesting, complaining about the government, sharing worries about the lack of rain. Wells are running dry in the hills and in Evergreen Estates.

I ask for a newspaper and occasionally receive one that is two days old. I buy groceries and stuff them in my backpack. I pick up my mail. ("Postcard here from your daughter in Paris, having a good time, says she's heading off to Italy.")

I take another route home. After breakfast, I toil: in my garden, in the woodshed, in the yard. I feel the fat melt away like butter in the sun. On a sweltering day in late July, I brave the ocean. Naked, I swim in the salt sea foam above Neptune's coral caves, and emerge to dry like a seal on the rocks. I am smoking less, no cigarettes, just an occasional pipe.

I have joined a local tai chi group that meets weekly in the community hall. I have also joined a drama group, the Garibaldi Players. I continue to go to the A.A. meetings. I have visited our septuagenarian physician, crusty old Doc Dooley, who pronounces my heart and arteries fit and dares me to outlive him. I fish on weekends with George Rimbold. I make other new friends, fellow elopers from the city. Among them are the arty and the crafty: painters, potters, poets. A writer of science fiction. A mad inventor. A burned-out rock guitarist. A burned-out broker. A burned-out traveller in cyberspace.

At home, I cook, I read, I darn my socks.

But is there pretence in all of this? How am I able to block out Beauchamp versus Beauchamp, soon to wend its way into the divorce courts, and the even more hideous case of Regina versus Honourable Jonathan Shaun O'Donnell?

As to the latter, quite easy. Mr. O'Donnell and Miss Martin live in another country, another planet. I stubbornly refuse to accept their existence. I intend to have my summer. As to Annabelle: yes, I still suffer bouts of self-pity and jealousy when I think of François Roehlig, my replacement, the younger, leaner model for the current year. More horsepower, faster acceleration. Something that Deborah can drive with pride. Do I sound bitter? Arthur Beauchamp? Never. What are thirty years of a man's life worth? A trifle in the eternal warp of time. How many of those years were happy? The first two, perhaps.

Yes, pain persists, but the wound seems clean and does not fester. I try not to pick at the scab; I have rendered myself into the care of time, misery's healer. I suffer depressions, but occasionally feel light-headed, as if a great weight is lifting from me, the baggage of the past.

Deborah and the two Nicks will be all summer in Europe—her husband is seeking new investments in the Old World. When my daughter phoned on the eve of their flight, I couldn't find it in my heart to tell her that the final nail has been pounded into the coffin of her parents' marriage. Quietly, I have left the matter of its dissolution in the hands of Hubbell Meyerson. Annabelle has a lawyer, too. It is all unbearably amicable.

In the meantime, I have not got around to mending fences with Margaret Blake, though on one of my walks to the store, I encountered her in her driveway apprehending an escaping goat—and received the coldest of shoulders. Her expression read: You are a typical two-faced lawyer—I couldn't fathom why.

But then I observe that the latest edition of the *Island Echo* has me misquoted: "Prominent island resident A. R. Beauchamp, Q.C., when asked about where he stands on Evergreen Estates, said he's sympathetic." As I recall, the word was antipathetic, but Not Now Nelson Forbish has not the keenest ear for the nuances of the English language.

But good news. On a bright afternoon near the end of the month, Stoney appears in my driveway, grinning like a chipmunk at the controls of my Phantom V. Somehow he has managed to fit all the pieces together.

"Rewired, greased, washed, and waxed, Mr. Beauchamp."

"Put it in the garage, Stoney."

"You don't wanna use it?"

"I would like to buy the truck."

I feel at home in my old Dodge. I will save my Rolls for trips to town—it is part of my former life.

∮∮

Ah-hah, the absent-minded professor.

Please, Jane, that's one of those judgmental phrases that cause people to feel oppressed. I am a temporally inconvenienced professor.

You're in a sarcastic mood.

I'm sorry. You're displeased with me, I don't blame you. The reason I didn't come last Tuesday was that I lost a day somewhere. I thought Wednesday was Tuesday. When I came by, your receptionist said you were out.

You *are* suffering time confusion. I ought to bill you for it. You know, Jonathan, one of the primary causes of short-term memory loss is overconsumption of alcohol.

Haven't had a drop in two weeks. I've enlisted in the self-improvement army. I'm running every day.

You're awfully sweaty.

I just did six miles. Almost killed me. But just when it hurts the worst, it . . . well, you get a kind of high.

Hmm. Be comfortable, Jonathan.

Should I assume the usual position?

I prefer my patients to stand at attention. Yes, Jonathan, sit down, lie down, relax.

Okay, I'm comfortable.

Something tells me you're not.

How so?

You showed up on the wrong day last week. You cancelled the week before. A little avoidance problem, Jonathan? You said on the phone there's something you wanted to tell me.

Yes. I guess I'd better do that. Get it over with.

I'm listening.

I lied to you. I did go to bed with Kimberley Martin.

You . . . How do you mean?

We performed acts of sex.

I'm sorry, I'm . . . She consented?

She? I was the seducee.

This is . . . Why am I hearing this now, after months of on-again, off-again supposed therapy based on what I took to be a truthful history of this incident, why am I . . . Why was I lied to? For God's sake, Jonathan, my time is valuable!

Um, what can I say? I wrestled with it, Jane. Partly it was . . . I guess I didn't want to believe it *did* really happen. I was sort of blocking, in denial—

Bullshit. Don't give me your amateur

psychobabble, you were conning me. I feel like a failure.

No, no, not at all. You've challenged me. I've got a better sense of myself, I . . . that's one of the reasons I was drinking, I was afraid to face up to the truth, and now . . . look, I'm sorry, I thought since I was lying to my lawyer, I also had to lie to you, I just . . . I was . . . afraid of losing everything, my career, my name. That sounds so fucking self-serving it makes me sick.

Okay. Okay.

Sorry. Self-pity is such a boring indulgence.

Your pain gives me hope for you, that's all I can say.

Hope. I don't need hope, I need a miracle. She was bloody brilliant on the stand last week. Stanislavsky Method—she became her role. Maybe she's become convinced by her own lies. Refused to admit she was coming on to me.

Is the pot calling the kettle black?

Okay, okay. We both indulged in some flirting. But safe-sex flirting. She *was* engaged. . . .

And you were her professor.

Yes, but *I* wasn't acting the slut.

Slut is a word that says more about the teller than his tale.

Sorry, but . . . Look, I regard myself as a modern person, I'm not some stuffy crock who'd prefer we all live in the eighteenth century. Equality of the sexes? Let me at the ramparts. I'm a director of the Civil Liberties Association, I'm pro-choice, persons of colour are my brothers and sisters. I was raised as a child in a very conservative home—old Tory aristocracy where sexism and prejudice came with breakfast, dinner, and tea. I've conquered that as best I could. There are remnants I haven't got rid of, inappropriate words like slut. Okay?

Why are you *so* defensive?

Sorry. That was an ugly thing to say. I don't suppose she's really . . . that kind of woman. It's a word that came out in anger. Do I hate her? I don't know. I'm confused by her.

Okay, tell me about that night. I want to know how you felt about it.

We, ah, okay, after the others left, I told you Kimberley was curled up asleep on a chair, right? I didn't know what proper protocol was. I brought a sheet to cover her, and then I just stood and stared at her. She was . . . well, never mind. It's hard to express.

Please do your best.

She was so hauntingly lovely with her Mona Lisa smile . . . and looked so absurd at the same time, in that suit and tie. Her skin in my clothes. The whole thing was kind of . . . well, I felt prickles all over. It was all too damned erotic. Soft music. The fire flickering. I can't really describe how I felt—I just felt overwhelmed; it still seems like a mystical moment. I wanted so much to touch her, but I was afraid that would make her disappear, vanish like the Cheshire Cat, fade from my life like a puff of smoke. You're drunk, I told myself. Your mental functioning is impaired. You must not do this. You are her trustee, she is your guest, your student, she is in love, engaged. But I did it.

What, Jonathan?

I kissed her.

That's all?

A stolen kiss, the slightest touch of lip on lip, that was my crime. But it must have awakened her, Jane, because she smiled, even though her eyes were still closed. And then she put her arms around me, and her eyes blinked open. And I was blinded by these huge green traffic lights. They said, "Go." And we . . . The rest isn't going to be easy.

Why?

Well, ultimately we sort of did the whole gamut, so to speak.

Did you tie her up?

Christ, no. What for?

What do you mean by the whole gamut?

The whole *Kama Sutra*.

I see.

Anal coitus, no. I definitely didn't penetrate her, um . . . There was no act of pedication, as she claims. You don't want all this stuff. I mean, do you need it for my personality profile, or what? Basically, I'd rather talk about sibling rivalry or something.

Just tell me what happened and stop putting up your barricades.

I'm sorry.

And stop being sorry. Be real.

༄༅

Suddenly the word is out that I am to be disjoined in marriage. I have leaked the news to no one but George Rimbold, but the leak has become a river at flood, and my friends have begun soft-shoeing around me, offering looks of sympathy, dropping by with gifts of cakes and jellies while making jocular conversation meant to keep my spirits high. The news has become distorted in the retelling: my once-a-week housekeepers, Janey Rosekeeper and Ginger Jones, asked me if Annabelle had really run off to Germany with an aging rock star. Another acquaintance was led to believe she's marrying a train conductor.

And worse is not only yet to come—it is on its way: advancing, waving, towards my dock. On a hot late afternoon, as I squat there, baiting a few crab pots—an art learned from George Rimbold—I see Emily Lemay, the lusty manager of the Brig, waving to me from her cabin cruiser. There is no escape, and I hopelessly await her arrival.

She aims her craft in the general direction of the dock, and thuds into it with minimal damage. She tosses me a line, and then is upon me, clasping me to her ursine bosom. I am astonished, speechless. She is more than a little tipsy.

"You poor man. You must be sick at heart." She is wearing blue-jean cutoffs and a shirt a size too small through which the vastness of her bosom strains. "I heard she's run away to Beirut with some rich Arab." Again I am overcome with the scent of peaches, over-ripe, fermented. As she unclenches me, I stagger and backpedal nearly into the water.

"I brought a picnic lunch and I'm going to take you out on a romantic cruise, just you and me."

"Ah, yes, well, I was about to set these traps." Within them the glassy eyes of fish heads warn me: There is danger on the high seas with this alcohol-impaired woman of forbidding reputation.

"Hey, well, you just let me help." She starts hauling the traps to her boat. There are life vests in it: if she attacks me, I will simply have to resist manfully—as it were—and swim for home.

Somehow we manage to transfer the cargo without either of us going overboard, and we then embark. As we putt into the bay, Emily Lemay chatters away cheerily about the emotional bruises she herself has suffered at the hands of untold faithless men: she knows exactly how I feel; she's an expert mender of broken hearts.

From time to time she swigs from a bottle of the peach brandy that she keeps in the cooler, along with sandwiches, pickles, and hard-boiled eggs. I munch nervously on those as we sit together on the bench seat. I try to inch away, but she pursues, squeezing my arm, my knee, my thigh, as if checking to see whether I am ripe.

Now I become nervous as her route takes us near the shore of Margaret Blake's farm. What if she sees us out here—what will she think? It's that two-faced eco-enemy Arthur Beauchamp, a wanton roué, he's cuddled up to a vocal supporter of Evergreen Estates.

Horror of horrors, there is Mrs. Blake indeed, feeding her ducks. She looks up, places a hand over her eyes to shield them from the late-afternoon sun. I try to shrivel, to disappear. But Emily rises and waves energetically.

A curt wave back from Margaret Blake, and she returns to her tasks. I am mortified.

"There's a quiet little bay around the corner. We could just anchor out and . . . you know, enjoy ourselves."

I am incapable of resistance, woozy in the alcoholic heat that emanates from her as we slowly motor beyond the Blake farm, past a rocky outcropping and into a tiny cove.

Emily helps herself to another big swallow of her brandy, then turns a pair of large, wet eyes to me and announces, "Arthur, I am a woman."

"I should think that's obvious," I say with a strained, almost strangled, chuckle.

"A woman. A *real* woman. With feelings. With needs."

"Ah, yes . . . " In my panic, I look towards the shore as if for help—and I see another boat in the bay, two men in it fishing. One of them is looking at us and frowning.

"Emily, I—"

Too late, she is pulling her shirt over her head, and I am confronted with the massive orbs of her breasts, and as she lunges at me I fall backwards, onto the deck, she on top.

"There are some people out there!" I shout. She lifts herself from me and peeks over the gunwales.

"Oh, God," she says. "It's Sam."

She crawls over me, finds her shirt, hurriedly dons it. "Damn."

I sit up. "Who is Sam?" This hefty, slope-shouldered man is staring at me with an expression of absolute enmity. I have seen him around, as well as his friend, who is looking on with a malicious grin.

Emily is at the wheel, accelerating away from the cove. "I've been sort of seeing him. Aw, heck."

As we head back to my dock, she says, "Don't want you to worry any, Arthur. His bark is worse than his bite."

၅၆

Though innocent in deed and mind, Arthur Ramsgate Beauchamp has quickly become the latest victim of this island's major industry, the gossip mill. The version I hear from Stoney has me not only disrobing Emily Lemay but thereafter being in the throes of naked connection aboard her boat.

"Sam was carrying on at the bar last night," he says. "But don't worry. It's all bullshit talk."

If I blot out all thoughts of the man called Sam, my satyric notoriety might permit a sense of self-esteem. At a neighbourhood potluck dinner the night after my fabled sexual conquest, men wink and women flirt. Margaret Blake shows up, avoids me for an hour, gets into an argument with someone, then vanishes in a cloud of petulance without partaking of dinner.

I drive home early, too, before dark, seeing Sam lying in wait around every bend.

To amplify my apprehensive mood, roiling black clouds shoulder over Vancouver Island from the ocean, a rare summer storm with pelting rain and gusts of wind that cause my house to shiver. Then the bolts of Jupiter begin to carve the sky above the ocean, and the guttural rumble of his thunderous voice is everywhere.

The power goes out, of course, as it tends to do whenever there's any kind of weather. I find my way to the kerosene lamp and light it, and sit in my club chair and read the works of dead German poets while *Götterdämmerung* continues unabated.

My reading is abruptly suspended when a great rending sound occurs outside. I rise to investigate. Starkly lit by the flashes from the sky is the gnarled old alder tree that grows just beyond my kitchen window. It has split vertically along the trunk, and half of it hangs menacingly over my roof.

I anxiously await the passing of the storm, and when finally the wind abates, I feel more relaxed—the tree is holding. Skilled lumberjacks will be on the scene tomorrow. There is naught to do but to say a little prayer and go to bed.

⅌

Dear Mr. Brown,

Though I have been watching Professor O'Donnell daily, I have gained little information of use. To summarize, he follows regular routines. In the morning, he runs. In the afternoon, he works at the law school. He returns home in the evening and doesn't go out after that. He does not seem to be drinking—except for tomato juice.

In talking to his fellow staff and teachers, I have learned he is held in high repute—almost no one thinks he is capable of this crime. (As cover for my visits at the university I have enrolled in an adult-education course in oriental religions. Very interesting.)

My search for someone who might tell tales out of class about Professor O'Donnell has occupied most of my time. Long hours at the university library have, however, finally produced a small nugget. It is in the form of Professor O'Donnell's harsh review in a learned magazine of a book written by one Dr. Curtis Mallard, a professor in the U.B.C. philosophy department. He is the author of *A Dearth of Justice,* a book accusing our court system of being unable to change with the times. Professor O'Donnell called it "pompous," "beyond infantile," and "laden with musty Marxist dogma."

I called Dr. Curtis Mallard. He told me he would enjoy talking about Professor O'Donnell. I will report to you after I have seen him.

By the way, I hope you will excuse me, but in your last note you suggested I pose as a policeman and "shake down" some of the people you believe are protecting him. I think this is not a good idea because I could be charged with impersonating a policeman.

Yours faithfully,
Francisco (Frank) Sierra

๑๑

A brisk breeze, the dregs of last night's storm, is shredding the clouds, but is also causing the split alder to sway dangerously near my roof, so low that its branches caress the shingles. I have brought in the dangerous tree removal team.

"Piece of cake," says Stoney. Dog nods his agreement. He is holding a chain saw that is almost as long as he is tall.

"You fellows are *absolutely* sure you know what you're doing?" But Stoney, after all, did rescue the Phantom V from the ravages of mice, and returned it in speckless condition. I have tended to underestimate him.

"Dog here's an ace," Stoney says. "Half-human, half-chain saw." He drops two coils of thick rope at the base of the stricken tree. "It's all a matter of levering it away. Question of simple geometry. Or physics, or whatever."

I must assume that neither of these gentlemen carry liability insurance. What option is there but to trust my wobbly house to their overconfident hands? And if the house be damaged—why then I have ample excuse to build anew and defy the preservationists. At all events, I have turned off the power and water and removed all combustibles from the house.

"How long will this take? I intend to be present, but I want to run up to the general store before it closes." I am expecting word from an astute young lawyer by the name of Augustina Sage: I have asked her to junior me for the O'Donnell trial.

"We got at least an hour's prep," says Stoney. "I think we should tie a line to that beam on the garage, Dog." His taciturn companion nods again. "Another line about a third the way up that cedar tree. Should go down smack in the middle of the driveway."

He pauses to roll a cigarette from his packet of Player's tobacco, then looks sideways at me.

"Now for this we gotta charge skilled-labour rates. But I been thinking, Mr. Beauchamp, remember that old pot case I was telling you about? I got busted last summer for a few plants? It's coming up next week, and I figured maybe in return for this job, you could sorta defend me on legal aid."

"I'm afraid I'm not doing pot cases any more, Stoney."

"Gee, I thought we could do a little barter."

"I will pay the going rate."

I cannot watch. I leave them as they start uncoiling their ropes, and head off in my pickup to the general store for my mail. "Looks like your grandson caught a little bug over there in Venice," says Mr. Makepeace, handing me a postcard from Deborah. "Feeling better now."

Here is also a four-day-old letter from Augustina

Sage (the mail service here is less than prompt), accepting my offer to assist in the O'Donnell defence—and advising she is arriving on a ferry that should have landed an hour ago. Accompanying her will be the students Charles Stubb and Paula Yi, who Augustina informs me have new and helpful information.

The *Queen of Prince George* cannot always be depended upon to be late, but thankfully she has lost one of her engines today—so I am informed by Nelson Forbish after I park behind him at the drop-off-and-pick-up line.

"I hear you and Emily Lemay are an item." A lecherous grin. "She's hot stuff, eh?"

I am about to instruct this master of the misquote as to the laws of libel, but he quickly says, "Don't worry, Mr. Beauchamp, my paper doesn't handle sex. Otherwise, I'd have to go ten extra pages with what goes on around this island. You should see the stories that don't make the light of day." A wink. "I have my sources. Don't worry about Sam, Mr. Beauchamp. I explained you were a lawyer with Mafia connections. Anyway, he's a chickenshit. So what's up? What's the hot scoop on that professor's case?"

I sigh. "Well, Nelson, you'll just have to come to court to satisfy this prurient interest of yours."

"Wish I had the time."

He returns to his car, and I watch as the *Queen of Prince George,* tilting to port, shudders into reverse. The boat banks hard against a rubber-tired buttress and crunches against a piling, sending its resting gulls aloft, fuming and wailing.

After the vessel finally comes to a full stop, Augustina Sage marches eagerly onto the dock, waving at me. I have borrowed her from the esteemed small firm of Pomeroy, Macarthur, Brovak and Sage, practitioners of criminal law. She is in her mid-thirties, a darkly attractive Métis woman, bright, energetic, single, though with, as I recall, a sorry history of romantic misadventures.

She drops her briefcase and reaches up to kiss me. "Arthur, you look like God in that beard."

"I am often mistaken for Him. So good of you to find the time for this. Were you able to adjourn your other cases?"

"I'd have adjourned the rest of my life to do the O'Donnell trial with you."

"You've read all the files?"

"Yes, I picked them up from your office."

"Excellent."

A young couple are standing by the ferry waiting room, the male bright-cheeked, bespectacled, with elephantine ears, the woman petite and sloe-eyed, subdued and pensive. Obviously Charles Stubb, the future prime minister, and his girlfriend, Paula Yi. Augustina makes the introductions.

"Mr. Beauchamp," says Charles, "I'm tremendously honoured. I've heard so much about you. Actually, I was at one of your trials—"

"We'll have time later for the passing of compliments. You don't mind hopping in the back?"

Charles and Paula look at the truck, look at me. They are deciding that I am eccentric. Perhaps I ought to have brought the Rolls.

Augustina climbs in beside me. "Love this truck. I love it. You're looking great, Arthur. I thought you'd be a wreck. I mean, I heard . . . about you and your wife. Sorry. What can I say?"

"I feel fine, Augustina."

"Marriage is such a rotten institution anyway, I think. Never made it that far." She sighs. "I never will. This case a winner, Arthur?"

"Normally I'd say chances were excellent. But we can't put O'Donnell on the stand."

"Uh-oh."

En route home I explain the problem to her: his lies

to everyone—including the police—about his not-so-knightly behaviour with Kimberley, lies that severely compromise any defence that the woman consented.

"He went to great pains to destroy evidence: he burned the sheets between which they frolicked. He lied to the investigating officer, denied intercourse. If we call him as a witness, he will be forced to admit to these untruths, and the Crown will have a field day. The jurors will ask themselves: Do we believe the candidly open complainant or the admitted liar?"

"Arthur, if he doesn't answer her charges, the jury is going to wonder why. They'll want an explanation—you know, for the bruises and the lipstick."

"Quite true. The defence will be difficult."

"Unless you can trap her into a lie."

"That may be a Herculean task, my dear."

We ride in silence, Augustina watching the scenery roll by.

"Not much happens here, I guess. Do you ever get bored?"

"Only between crises."

The latest of which is still unfolding in my yard, where Stoney is practising his own peculiar form of bondage—he is tangled in his ropes high up the cedar tree, which was to be the anchor for the damaged alder. Somehow he has managed to loop one of his legs to a dead branch. Dog is at the base of the tree, holding one end of the rope and calling up instructions.

My passengers alight and stare wordlessly at this scene, perhaps thinking I have arranged some mild entertainment for the morning. I offer a half-hearted explanation about the prospect of my house going the way of my former veranda should the alder tree plummet onto the roof.

"Please join me in my office. I have told my secretary we're not to be disturbed."

I remove my guests from the danger zone, leading them to the beach—the forecast has promised a sunny day in the wake of last night's storm. We comfortably array ourselves on the bleached driftwood logs that are piled like benches.

"Well, this is sure different," says Charles Stubb. "It's really odd to see you like this, Mr. Beauchamp, because last time I caught your act you were in your silks. That doctor you defended last year? A bunch of us students took a field trip. Your speech to the jury— I'm telling you, it had me trembling."

"It was that bad."

"Oh, God, no, it was—"

"Cease and desist, Charles, I'm embarrassed. Now, you apparently have something to tell us." Augustina brings out pen and notepad.

"Well, Paula here does. I pretty well said my piece at the preliminary hearing."

Yes, this floppy-eared young man was a solid rock of support for his beloved acting dean. My impression is that he has been prevailing on his girlfriend to aid the cause.

"But Paula was never called at the prelim."

"I can speak for myself, Charles."

"Sure. You explain it."

Paula pauses, lights a cigarette. She is nineteen, small-boned, attractive, and soft-spoken. A badge is pinned to her khaki shirt that says simply, "Equality." Doubtless a radical of sorts.

"I don't feel good about this, Mr. Beauchamp. I sort of feel I'm on the wrong side somehow. I think I'd better tell you—I was assaulted once myself. Romance rape, I guess you call it. I'm definitely not into protecting Professor O'Donnell if he did it."

"If he didn't do it, you wouldn't want to see him wrongfully jailed."

"No, I guess you're right."

"That's why she—"

"Never mind, Charles." Paula seems the dominant figure here.

I pack a wad of tobacco into the bowl of my ancient Peterson bent. "Have you been interviewed by the prosecutor yet, Paula?"

"An officer came by for a few minutes. He didn't take any notes. I have an appointment to see Ms. Blueman. I don't know what to tell her. . . ."

"The truth. Just as I hope to hear it."

"Okay, well, I don't know Kimberley Martin. I'm in arts. I'd met a few of Charles's friends in law school, but not her. And the night of the law-school dance . . . Well, frankly I was confused. For a while I thought she and Mr. O'Donnell were going together. I didn't even know she was his student."

"What gave you that impression?"

"Oh, just the casual way they interacted, like they'd known each other a long time. The way they joked and touched each other. I was thinking: Do they live together? I'd heard he wasn't married."

"Did you have a sense that one was making advances to the other?"

"She was all over him," Charles says.

"He was giving her *attention*, Charles. It's something quite normal that men often do. I really hate getting involved in this trial, Mr. Beauchamp, but this has been grinding away at me a lot."

"Well, you tell me about it and let us see where we go from there."

"Egan Chornicky had a couple of grams of cocaine with him that night."

"I think I heard something about that."

"And I, ah, I had a couple of lines."

"I see. Where did you consume these lines?"

"I got a kind of hand signal from Egan, and I followed him down into a little rumpus-type room in Professor O'Donnell's basement and . . . we did the dust. The coke. And . . ."

"And?"

"Kimberley came down and joined us."

I puff my pipe and ponder this. "She partook?"

"A couple of fat ones. And it was high quality. I do it once in a while, a little dope. It's no big deal. I'm a rec user."

"I don't approve," says Charles. "It's her business."

"Kimberley was already loaded. She'd had quite a few drinks."

"And did you notice if this drug had any effect on her?"

"More animated, I guess, than she was before. Louder. Pushy. Got everyone up performing parts. She was overacting, I thought. She thinks pretty well of herself. I'm sorry, but that was my impression. But then . . . half an hour into this she just fell asleep . . . well, I didn't believe it at all. Coke's a truck-driver's drug. You *can't* sleep."

The song of a chain saw intrudes.

"We will continue this conversation."

I abandon my guests to return to the job site. Dog is working at the alder while Stoney stands by, testing the tautness of lines strung to cedar tree and garage post. They quiver like bowstrings.

As the chain saw cuts, the tree shudders, then leans ever so slightly towards its intended trajectory, the driveway.

"Timber!" Stoney yells.

But the tree does not fall. Now I can see that Dog is having trouble with the chain saw, and its roar suddenly abates. I hear the words, "It's pinched."

I venture closer, but Stoney warns me away. "Better stay back, Mr. Beauchamp, we got a chain caught here. Trunk is severed right through, but she's still standing. Don't know how, but that's the way it is. Okay, Dog, let's ease off on one of these ropes. We'll let her down gently, Mr. Beauchamp, neat as a pin."

Though I was never much of a student of physics, I have a sense of something amiss in the configurations of tree and fastening posts, and when Stoney and Dog release play on one of the ropes, the stricken alder tree does a slow, grotesque piroutte, falling as it turns.

It collapses onto my garage and, with a great clatter of splintered wood, caves the roof in.

I stoke my pipe and fire it up again. I blow a perfect smoke ring. I watch it wobble and lose its shape.

I join Stoney and Dog at a window of the garage. The roof of the Rolls has managed to hold up fairly well, but the windshield has popped. An entire can of green paint has spilled on the hood.

After what seems a very long while, Stoney says, "Little paint and body work and she's good as new. You defend me on that weed charge, I'll do it for free."

Though I emphatically decline the offer, I can't help but admire his gall. I leave them to clean up the rubble. I return dolefully to my guests.

After their interviews are done, Charles and Paula, perhaps to escape the continuing embarrassment of my sulking company, decide to walk to the ferry. Augustina stays—carefully avoiding topics that cause pain, such as alder trees and Phantom Vs—and instead rambles on about the O'Donnell case.

"He gives them taxi fare," she says. "They all take off. They leave Kimberley behind. I'll just bet that Mr. Goody Two-Shoes Charley Stubb knew they were going to make out. He *could* have removed the temptation, but he probably wanted to be able to hold something over the professor. Feels guilty now, that's why he's being so helpful."

"Does cocaine—with some people—cause them to go over the edge? I don't presume you're an expert."

"I don't think so. But maybe. I'll do some reading."

Good afternoon, Jonathan.

You've cut your hair, Jane. I like it.

Different look. There's a current trendy theory it alters personality. New look, new persona.

It's so *short*. Makes you seem younger.

Thank you. You look much better yourself these days. Jonathan . . . look, let me say something at the outset: I was upset last time you were here. I wasn't in very good form. I'd like to blame it on PMS or something facile like that, but I was just bloody taken aback when you admitted you had lied to me. I have to get that out of the way.

I deserved it.

Okay. So I want to ask you: Are there any other secrets?

Um, no, Jane, there aren't.

Jonathan, how many relationships *have* you had?

With women?

Do you have affairs with men?

Of course not. We're not counting women I've merely dated.

We are not counting one-night stands.

I'm not very good at keeping relationships going, Jane, can't seem to find the right woman.

Well, that puts the blame squarely where it lies, doesn't it? It's their fault.

I've never lived with anyone. I'm not very good at love affairs. My longest relationship? About seven months.

Who was that?

Part-time lecturer in the fine arts department. That was a couple of years ago. A sort of bohemian painter. Exotic woman. I think I like exotic women.

Actually, there's something of that quality about you. That's not a come-on.

Really?

Yes.

It was just a compliment?

I suppose you think I'm a bit of a womanizer.

I'm more interested in *your* self-analysis, Jonathan.

Is there something horribly dysfunctional about being attracted to women? I'm single. Married rules don't apply.

Sure. But you're not a very successful womanizer, are you? You're attractive enough. You're bright, you're engaging when you want to be, you have this world-weary sense of anomie that appeals to many women. But it only adds up to a bunch of occasional dates and seven months with a bohemian artist. Isn't that about it?

I guess a phobia about marriage runs in the family. My brother never married. And you know about my father. He's on his fifth try.

The sins of your father are not hereditary.

Maybe I'm afraid I'll be like him, promiscuous in marriage, chasing after younger and younger women, thinking I'm thirty when I'm seventy. Or taking a fling at marriage, and failing miserably and hurting a good woman—someone like Mom. The old warhorse never found a woman he ever loved. And neither, I'm afraid, will I.

You don't think you're capable of love?

What's the diagnosis? I'm emotionally castrated, aren't I? Obviously unable to relate to women on any committed basis. I consider them mere objects and playthings, don't I?

Stop making up false images of yourself. I'm not saying that. I think you're perfectly capable of love. I think you also may be afraid of it. I'd like to know why.

Fucked-up childhood.

That's often such an easy excuse, Jonathan.

We had such a strict moral code, except when it applied to my father. I suppose the seminal event in our loving relationship was when I walked into the bedroom and caught him and Mother in the act.

How old were you?

Six. He spanked me raw. I was seven when I was graduated to the whip. Sign of manhood. If it was good enough for Viscount Caraway, it was good enough for his sons. He got whipped as his forefathers got whipped. I can hear him carrying on: "Trouble with Charles and Diana and that lot, no one's ever applied a nice bit of leather to them."

Did he abuse your mother?

He never raised a finger. It was his whoring around that tore up the marriage.

Yet you sound ambivalent towards your father.

I used to be angry at him.

Because of his strictness?

No. For ignoring me. Christmas cards and the odd letter, that was all. For almost twenty years. But there was a kind of rapprochement—after Mother died. He tracked me down when I was in London, asked me up to his club. Turns out he's been following my career, had both my books. I remember, we were laughing about the most recent cabinet sex scandal. Little did we both realize . . . He said he couldn't figure out why I turned out so well while brother Bob became a lazy playboy. Bob's one of those hilarious Brit snots. You have to like him.

Have you heard from your father since this business with Kimberley?

No. I hate to imagine what he thinks. They'll be talking at the club. "I say, old boy, sounds like something out of the sodding House of Commons."

Do you think your father ever loved you?

I don't know.
Did he ever say so?
Of course not. Wasn't done, you know.
How do you feel about that?
I don't have any feelings about it.
Bullshit.

᭥᭥

On this last Monday of July, the day when justice pays
its bimonthly visit to Garibaldi Island, the weather
continues uncommonly hot. The grassy spaces outside
the community hall—our jury-rigged courthouse—
have been toasted sere by unrelenting Apollo, who
rides naked and high in the heavens. Though I arrive
late, I see no sign of plaintiff Margaret Blake.

What must she think of me now? That ugly episode
with Emily Lemay is all about the island, magnified,
twisted into many farcically obscene versions. I disgust Mrs. Blake. I am the lecher who lives down the
road. My hopes for comity with the woman—and I
expect nothing more—have been dashed.

Inside the hall, profusely sweating, fuelling himself
with sugared doughnuts, Not Now Nelson Forbish of
the *Echo* sits at a small table. About twenty folding
chairs—several of them occupied—are set haphaz-
ardly about. Near the front is that miscreant Bob
Stonewell, alias Stoney, toppler of trees and garages.
I'd forgotten: He faces trial today as an accused cannabis gardener. His case has just begun, and on the
witness stand is his arresting officer, Constable Horace Pound, the lawman who controls crime on Garibaldi every second Tuesday of the month. He is a
serious young man with a permanent frown.

The circuit judge for these islands is his honour
Timothy Wilkie, judge of the provincial court, a former small-town Lions Clubber whom I recall as lazy
and slow of thought. He recognizes me and nods, but

almost surreptitiously, as if embarrassed to see me as a common defendant in his court. He is in his shirt sleeves—the metal roof of the building radiates heat like a convection oven. But ·Constable Pound is bravely uniformed.

"Upon arriving at the premises, which I have visited on several previous occasions, I observed numerous scrap vehicles as well as a workshed and a partly built house with only one room closed in. I ascertained that no one was present in the woodshed, though I noted the presence within it of a hoe and some garden tools and fertilizer. I then proceeded to the house."

Why do so many officers tend to talk in this stilted foreign tongue? What fussy master of the particular and the correct trains them in their speech? I can picture the RCMP instructor who is charged with the teaching of strangled English: stern, incorruptible, and humourless.

"Did you have a search warrant?" the prosecutor asks. She seems too young to have had much experience.

"I was in possession of same based on information received. On proceeding to the front door, I knocked, and upon obtaining no response, I walked around to the side of the house, where I observed a garden hose attached to an outdoor faucet on the wall. I followed this hose to where water was running through it into a shallow ditch in which twenty-three items were growing which I recognized as being marijuana."

Stoney's plaintive voice: "How does he know, your honour? They coulda been tomato plants—is he an expert?"

"I tender as exhibits twenty-three certificates of analysis from the botanical laboratory," says the prosecutor.

From my chair at the side of the hall, I can see Stoney in profile. He has a hangdog look. He is confused by the courtroom, lost in a sea of forensic mystery. Now he turns to look at me, reproachfully: I have refused to help him in his time of need.

I am retired, why cannot anyone understand this? True, I have been manipulated into making one exception: but Jonathan O'Donnell didn't fall an alder tree on my Rolls-Royce. I shall remain unbending.

The gallery of half a dozen locals becomes restless during the interminable marking of exhibits. Turning, I see Margaret Blake take a seat at the back. How smartly dressed is this feisty woman: her best city clothes and—can it be? Are those slender firm legs wrapped in hose? How elegant she looks, willowy and svelte. To my surprise she smiles at me. I am too flustered to smile back, and turn away to hide my blushing face.

She is laughing at me. She is evoking visions of Emily Lemay's body entangled with mine in sweaty embrace.

"Okay, constable, continue," says the prosecutor.

"I subsequently encountered Mr. Stonewell hiding beneath one of the vehicles—"

"I was installing a rebuilt transmission," Stoney says.

"Mr. Stonewell," says Judge Wilkie, "you will give evidence later."

"I didn't observe him to have any oil or grease on his clothes. I subsequently in his presence proceeded to seize the evidence, and as I was pulling out the plants, he said, if I can quote from my notes, 'That was going to get me through the winter, man.'"

"No more questions," says the prosecutor.

"Mr. Stonewell, now you can ask the officer anything you want." Judge Wilkie seems distracted, unaware that prosecutorial blunders have been committed here.

"Naw, I don't have any questions."

"Well, do you want to give evidence?"

"Not much point. I'm dead."

"Do you have any submissions?"

"Well, except only half those plants was female; the others I woulda just turfed out."

"Okay, well, unfortunately for you . . ."

Can it be Wilkie is about to convict? On *this* paltry evidence? I find myself propelled to my feet as if by an external force.

"If I may be so bold, your honour . . ."

"Yes, Mr. Beauchamp?"

"May I speak as *amicus curiae*?"

"*Amicus*? . . ."

"As a friend of the court."

"Well, okay, go ahead."

"I'll be short. There is absolutely no evidence connecting this accused to the plants that were seized. He was simply under a car. Not a scrap of testimony that he owned that car. Or that property. Or that he even lived there. And the statement made to the officer is clearly inadmissible as not having being proved voluntary."

The judge calls upon the prosecutor for help.

"He was hiding under a car, that's evidence of a guilty mind."

"I can't see how that's enough. Not enough for me, anyway. I think I have to dismiss this one." He looks at me with an expression that says he does not forgive my disruption of the flow of justice in his court. "I would have done that anyway, but thank you."

Somewhat red of face, Constable Pound gives me close inspection as he walks from the courtroom. He may be one of those many prideful members of the force who tend to take their losses as personal humiliations.

Stoney just sits in his chair wearing a big smile as the morning carries on: an agenda of the typical detritus of a country court—setting dates, adjournments, a couple of guilty pleas to driving offences.

"I'm really thirsty," says Judge Wilkie. "Why isn't there any water in this place? I want to take a break, and I'd like someone to get me some water. We'll do the small claims cases after."

I wander out with Stoney for a smoke. He is in a merry mood. "This year my grow ain't on the property. They'll never find it. For this, a whole new paint job on the Rolls and I'm gonna build you a garage that's like a palace. I wanna stay and watch you in action. Hey, man, if there's any way I can help you in this thing with Mrs. Blake's pig, you tell me, eh?"

Like all readers of the *Island Echo*, Stoney is familiar with the pertinent details of the case. The betting on the island is that I will win hands down. Though Margaret Blake is popular—despite her occasional bite—her wandering animals are not. Friends have parted with her on this issue. So the pressure is on me to win this test case, to make a stand against the Garibaldi Island obstacle course.

I puff my pipe and ponder my dilemma. By winning, I will do terminal damage to any hopes of closing the rift with Mrs. Blake. But no, I will not play dead for her. My current win streak stands at fourteen: it shall not be broken in Garibaldi Small Claims Court.

But I see I am facing no unworthy foe. Mrs. Blake is truckling to the judge, pouring him ice water from a Thermos. She can't be faulted—it is a clever act of generosity, but now I must work from a slight disadvantage. To boot, I am in poor mental condition. I still have *l'affaire Lemay* on my mind: it is not concentrated.

But that will change. When the case is called I shall become another person. I will doff the garb of Walter Mitty and don the cape and tights of the man of steel.

Judge Wilkie wipes his lips and effusively expresses his thanks to Mrs. Blake, and we follow him back into the building.

"Blake versus Beauchamp," the clerk announces.

I hear Margaret Blake coming forward, her heels tapping on the wooden floor. I cannot meet her eyes. I feel oafish, clumsy.

Mrs. Blake is forceful in her description of that fateful night when the defendant came to her door to confess. She speaks caringly of Betsy, and attempts to justify her outrageous claim for a hundred dollars on every basis but the relevant one: current market value of a pig.

"Do you have any questions, Mr. Beauchamp?"

I rise, pulling on my braces then snapping them, a habit of mine when commencing cross-examination. "Mrs. Blake, I shall go right to the point. You have received dozens of complaints about your animals being loose and wandering onto the road."

She speaks without a tremor. "I have free-range chickens, Mr. Beauchamp. I can't pen them up. I run a farm. I have animals on this farm. People have to be careful. Most people *know* they have to be careful."

"The animal that struck my car was not a free-range chicken."

"Betsy must have tunnelled out from her pen. I don't know what speed you were going, though I suppose you will say you were under the limit—"

"Quite so. I was."

Here Judge Wilkie interrupts, in a fashion I consider unkindly. "Was there any indication the defendant had been drinking?"

"He was quite sober. He had all his senses. He should have seen my pig at the side of the road, and he didn't. Or couldn't."

"I could see perfectly well, Mrs. Blake. Had the pig been in front of me, I would have braked. I assume the animal darted from the side of the road."

"From your right-hand side."

"Yes."

"You knew my animals sometimes strayed."

"All too well."

"Did you know you were nearing my house?"

"I saw your house. Your yard lights were out, making it all the darker."

"Well, if you were looking at my house you weren't looking at the road."

Touché. I am stunned. I glance at Stoney, who seems to have lost some of his respect for his hero. I attempt to compose myself with a display of forensics. "Madam, I am supposed to be cross-examining you, not the other way around."

"Okay, ask me what you want."

Suddenly, as I stare into her dark, pulling, confident eyes, I find myself at a loss. I can think of not a single question. She has quite confounded me.

"Fine. I have no questions."

"Do you have any other witnesses, Mrs. Blake?" the judge says.

"I'd like to call Mr. Stonewell."

My mind roils in confusion. Stoney? What could he add to her story?

As he is being sworn in, he looks at me and shrugs.

"Stoney, I heard you did some repairs on Mr. Beauchamp's Rolls-Royce afterwards."

"There was a dent in the fender I straightened, yeah. And some other things."

"One of which was the right headlamp." It comes back in a rush. I had totally forgotten. My headlight was out. "It wasn't working at all, was it?"

"Yeah, well, yeah. I'd have to say that. The right headlight had been kinda burned out."

"And it was the right bumper that was dented?"

"Yes. I admit that." Stoney looks at me guiltily.

It is a rout. I, the indomitable Beauchamp, am being chewed alive in this courtroom. I sag into my folding chair like a whipped dog.

"Your honour," says Mrs. Blake, "you have heard

Mr. Beauchamp say he could see perfectly well. But he was driving blind in one eye."

"Mr. Beauchamp, do you have some evidence you want to call?"

"No, your honour. I surrender."

I am seized by a barely controlled urge to burst into laughter. I must struggle to maintain control.

"Well, Mr. Beauchamp, I think you're in some trouble here."

"I agree, your honour." A small sound escapes from my voice box: a self-disparaging chuckle.

"You could be fined a hundred dollars for that front light, and I'm going to add it as punitive damages on to the hundred dollars you owe Mrs. Blake. That may be a little steep for a pig, but that's what she says and I haven't heard anything to the contrary."

He is smiling, too. He is enjoying the humiliation of the city-slicker lawyer. "Plus costs," he adds. "I'm afraid I have to make an example of you, Mr. Beauchamp."

Stoney, looking very serious and awkward, squats beside me. "Gee, sorry about that. Should I have lied?"

I find myself trembling, enduring an agony of stifled laughter. It breaks free, at first in little rumbling chuckles, then in a rich thunder.

My laughter is astonishingly infectious, and clerk and judge give in, then Stoney, and those in the gallery, even Nelson Forbish. And even, ultimately, Margaret Blake, a musical laughter, like bells.

I cannot remember when I have enjoyed myself more than on this last Monday of July.

The court finally adjourns, and I find myself outside, packing tobacco into the bowl of my pipe while still suffering the aftershock of my mirth attack. Margaret Blake is standing by the open door of her truck—she is smiling, too.

She slings her bag into the cab and walks briskly over to me.

"Congratulations," I say. I shake her hand—I am used to the soft hands of city women; hers is firm, callused but warm. No dirt underneath the fingernails today.

"I'll probably spend most of it on fencing."

"If you ever decide to take up law, Mrs. Blake, I shall be glad I retired."

"Law? God, no. I see you've traded in your cigarettes for a pipe."

"Am I to be sued for that?"

"No, it's better. I like the smell of it. More organic. They put saltpetre in cigarettes to keep them burning, did you know that? It's an ingredient of gunpowder, so you can imagine what it does to your insides. Don't call me Mrs. Blake. It makes me feel old."

I want to say how youthful and attractive she looks, but again she has me tongue-tied.

"I liked what you did for Stoney, Arthur. That was decent."

She proffers her hand and we shake again, and she returns to her truck, then cocks her head and casts me a sideways look. Have I aroused in her at least some mild curiosity? Or is that smile a secret one, inspired by images of me and Emily Lemay in gross combination?

Nelson Forbish hones in on me as I make for my own vehicle.

"Mr. Beauchamp—"

"Not now, Nelson." I escape.

She is in front of me all the way down Breadloaf Hill, along Centre Road, up Potter's Road. I can see the nape of her slender neck. I can see her smile in her rearview mirror.

Good morning, Kimberley.

Morning, Dr. Kropinski. Well, it's over. I wrote my second paper yesterday. Con law. Gee, that sounds like a course on how to be crooked. Constitutional law.

How did you do?

I think a B-minus at least.

This accounts for your good spirits, yes?

Now I can spend the rest of the summer trying not to think about my trial. God, it's just a month away.

You will not be able to stop *thinking* about it. Do not let it consume you.

No. I'm just going to go in there and tell the truth. And I *am* telling the truth. I got straight A's on their lie detector. So I'm not going to carry the trial around with me like some kind of monster on my back. Anyway, I've got Cynthia to keep my mind busy. She's the new me. She's the character I play in *Switch*?

Oh, your play. How are the rehearsals coming?

I'm pretty good, I'm surprising everybody. We open in a week. . . . It's just a little tin can of a theatre. Just four main players and several bit parts. Oh, here's some tickets for you and your wife. Opening night.

You are most kind.

Don't be offended—there's some tart language.

I will steel myself.

I had a fight with the playwright—he thinks he's such an intellectual with his satirical, jaded outlook and all. Some of his stuff is witty, but he just can't write for women. I'm going to refuse to do the Marilyn Monroe routine, the blonde with tits for brains. Let's reinforce that stereotype, guys, the cut-out cardboard doll. So I'm helping him rewrite the lines—we've come up with a couple of zingers. I'm now sort of sexy but clever, with a kind of flower-child edge. There's a little nudity, but it's necessary to the script. The play's about two swinging couples. It's coming together, there's a nice undercurrent of jealousy: the men get possessive as the women bond.

It sounds intriguing.

Remy and I had this humungous battle over it the other night, just after my last exam. I was feeling very up, happy as heck, and I was regaling him about the play, and suddenly he screamed at me: "You mean you're going to be half naked on a public stage?" He used the word obscene, ranted about how he was going to be disgraced in front of all his friends. Sometimes Remy really gets centred on himself. *His* friends, *his* fiancée, *his* fucking career. He thinks a public revealing of a breast or two will be used to embarrass me at the trial. I'm not going to censor myself because a man attacked me. Remy doesn't want me on the stage at all. Doesn't want me to *have* a career. Wants babies. I don't intend to be locked away in some goddamn nursery for the next ten years. I have a life. Well, we didn't sleep together *that* night. Is this what you call ventilation? God, I can't stop, I'm on a roll.

I . . . I am sorry, you make me laugh.

I'll settle down. I'm kind of hyper today.

There is nothing wrong with that.

So, what else? I woke up with the sweats a few nights ago after a dream. I couldn't retrieve all of it. It starred Jonathan O'Donnell, but it wasn't one of my run-of-the-mill nightmares. He seemed sad and lonely, and he was trying to talk to me, but I couldn't understand him; I couldn't hear his voice. But I wasn't scared of him like I am in my nightmares. I'm angry. I want to hit him, but I can't reach him. It's as if we can't communicate. And my mother showed up, warning me to stay away from him. You're making notes. Am I revealing something significant?

It is of interest. Has Professor O'Donnell been in other dreams?

Yes, he comes to me . . . I mean, he shows up in the oddest dreams sometimes. But not as someone menacing . . . I don't know how to explain.

These are not like your nightmares about being attacked. Have you had any recently?

Bad one last week.

They have been more severe since this business with Professor O'Donnell, yes?

They were for a while.

But he does not appear in them?

Not in those dreams. But, you know, I've had them since I was a kid.

Have you ever been hypnotized?

Uh-huh. Once. Do you think there's something back there, hiding? Is it like some terrible little alien monster is inside me, trying to come out?

I would not put it so vividly. I do not know, Kimberley. There may be, yes, pushed deep down. The usual signs of post-traumatic stress disorder, these you do not exhibit, but there may be some amnesia—this is what we call a dissociated memory. If so, there is nothing to be afraid of to try to recover it, yes?

I'm not sure about being hypnotized. When I was fifteen, I went to this show. Some charlatan, I guess he was, made me into a chicken, and I was clucking and flapping all over the stage. Apparently I tried to lay an egg. Utterly mortifying.

I work in a different way, yes? No chicken, no egg.

❦

I have finished my tai chi (the Repulse Monkey: cross hands, roll back, transfer weight onto right foot) and am now sitting on a divan on my front porch, leafing through a pile of old *Echoes*. I am bathed by a sun still hot but falling to the horizon, its light burning upon the softly rolling inner sea and painting the clouds pink beneath a cerulean sky. Only the pained cries of nails being wrenched free from boards mar this perfect evening. Behind the house, Stoney and Dog are working late disassembling the remains of my garage. It is the day after Margaret Blake and I shook hands in agreement to war no more. Tomorrow I will visit her with the cheque.

Ah, here we are, in the *Echo,* an edition from September three years ago: "We all console the tragic departing of Christopher Blake, aged 49, a resident of our island for thirty years leaving behind his wife, Margaret, 43, and no children. Chris had a heart attack while he was chasing a dog off his farm that was going after the sheep. The doctor said he was dead on the spot and it was one of those things that happens to the healthiest of us."

I picture Not Now Nelson Forbish munching his way through a bag of Fritos as he writes this bleak obituary.

"Chris used to be one of our trustees and was a favourite at parties with his ever-present violin. He and Margaret came here in 1968 with the old Earthseed Commune and stayed on after it disbanded. Margaret says she's going to run their 101-acre farm by herself. The funeral was at the community church, which everyone agreed was beautiful."

Elsewhere in this journal: a photograph of the Blakes together, obviously taken some years earlier. He is tall and rugged, she in a flowing flowered dress, smiling up at him. It is a poignant photograph. There was love here.

Lost in thought, I am hardly aware that Stoney and

Dog are rattling off in a truck loaded with scrap wood. They wave at me as they head out the driveway. A stillness descends, and a veil of loneliness. I fold the *Echo* closed, unable to look again at the love in Margaret's eyes for her husband. I watch the sun hiss into the distant ocean, spraying the sky with colour, and now a songbird trills at evensong.

The setting sun, and music at the close, as the last taste of sweets, is sweetest last. . . . How does the line end? Remembered more . . . *than things long past.* I close my eyes and begin to recite the Bard aloud, in full-throated vanity, resonant and sonorous. Then the Romantics, remembered from childhood, Shelley, Keats: "The murmurous haunt of flies on summer eves . . ."

I reopen my eyes in mid-stanza to see, before me, holding a carton of eggs and a tray of steaming tarts: Mrs. Margaret Blake.

"Excuse me. Am I interrupting?"

I quickly stand, my face turning the colour of the western sky. "How embarrassing. I was reciting some poetry. It is a bad habit of mine."

"It sounded lovely."

"Otherwise, as you can see, I am engaged in that indolent but agreeable condition of doing nothing."

"It sounds like fun. I'll have to try it." She smiles. She is in an excellent mood, no doubt still flushed with her victory. "I brought over some peace offerings." She extends the eggs and tarts. "My black currants are ripe."

"I am overwhelmed. Will you join me for some tea? I have herbal, if you prefer. Mint."

"I'd love some."

I lead her into the house, and bring out teacups and set the water to boil. She joins me to help, selecting her tea, then opening refrigerator and cupboard doors, examining the contents somewhat as a health inspector might.

While the kettle heats, I usher her into the living room with its groaning shelves of books, its padded chairs, its smoky ambience, its total aura of bachelorhood.

"Very little sign of a woman's presence here, I'm afraid."

With the back of her hand she whisks some loose strands of tobacco from the arm of a chair. "Those girls don't do a very thorough job, do they? More chop than mop."

At my desk, I tear out a cheque and make it out to her. "An extra fifty dollars ought to cover the costs."

She holds it proudly before her eyes. "Sorry, but I feel I have earned this."

"I was the unwitting victim of my own stupidity, though of course you had the judge in your pocket." I feel exceedingly shy, and I suffer an absurd urge to assure her I did not savour the fleshly pleasures of Emily Lemay. "Well. It's a splendid evening . . . beautiful colours. Shall we sit outside?"

"That would be nice. Let me help you get the tea."

"I wouldn't think of it. You are my guest."

She returns to the front porch, and when I finally join her there with tea and black currant tarts, I see she has the three-year-old *Echo* open before her, and she is looking at herself in that long flowered dress. Now I am doubly embarrassed.

"I was curious." It's all I can find to say.

As I join her upon the divan, she stares at me solemnly, then lowers her eyes and stirs her tea.

"I've been very bitter about Chris's death. He was forty-nine. He was healthy. He ate granola until it came out of his ears. Half his life was stolen from him."

"You loved him deeply."

Her look is almost fierce. "Yes."

"Would you rather not talk about it?"

She doesn't respond, but sips her mint tea in silence. I feel I have committed a gaffe, and know not how to make amends, and so I just stare dumbly into the fading light of the western sky where Hesperus, god of the evening star, has lit his lamp.

"No, I don't mind talking about it," she says finally. "I get all workaholic and try not to think about it. I guess that's the wrong way. . . . I *should* talk about it. I suppose I'm still in mourning. I know I have to break free. . . . Oh, go on and light your pipe. I can tell you've been itching to have a smoke."

"Ah, yes, I have been fidgeting. If I may." When I light up, I feel more relaxed. She sits beside me, only a touch away, staring at the sea, her profile pensive in the golden twilight.

"Chris came up here from Montana during the Vietnam War. Anti-war activist, though of course he got called a draft-dodger. I was seventeen when I married him—can you believe that? We had a quickie ceremony with a marriage commissioner, then our friends came over for the formal reception. Not so formal—we did acid all night. Our friends—I hardly see them now, most of them are stockbrokers, or run fast-food franchises, though one of them's a pretty good musician. Anyway, we were all determined to go back to the land, so we started a commune here on Garibaldi. I know this all sounds silly to you. . . . Are you laughing at me?"

"It is so hard to picture you as a flower child, Margaret."

She laughs in turn; again I think of bells. "Chris and I were the only ones to *stay* on the land. Chris was a natural farmer. He really did love the land. Everything about it, rural and wild. So do I. Real tree-hugger. Do you ever actually *hug* a tree? I do that sometimes. We're petitioning the government to reject that Evergreen Estates by-law, by the way. Do I dare ask you to add your name? Or did I read that you were in sympathy—"

"I distinctly told that woolly-eared reporter I was opposed. Many things on this island get lost in translation."

"Yes, you're the subject of some vicious gossip these days, aren't you?"

Finally, a chance to make earnest defence. "I was literally kidnapped by that woman and nearly raped. I escaped with my virginity bruised but intact."

"But how could you resist her?" She is smiling, teasing me.

"I still have nightmares."

"No, I never believed any of that stuff. I saw you on the boat out there with her. You looked really scared."

"Should I put a light on?" The shell of night has closed upon us.

"I like the dark. Gosh, I can't remember in years when I've sat down for more than ten minutes like this. What did you say about that agreeable condition of doing nothing? You're right. It feels good."

From high above, the steady bleat of a searching nighthawk. Our galaxy glows bright and thick in the moonless night, and the evening star seems blinding. I feel oddly light-headed. *A drowsy numbness pains my sense.* . . .

Distantly comes a sound of civilization, and it takes me a moment to realize it's my telephone. In the dark of my house, I stumble against a chair before finding the phone.

"What time is it there?" It's Deborah on a bad line, my daughter far abroad.

"Deborah, how good to hear from you. It's close to ten o'clock. What time is it wherever you are?"

"We're in Rome and it's six in the morning. I wanted to reach you before you went to bed."

"How wonderful. Rome. My spiritual home."

"You sound awfully happy."

"And why shouldn't I be? It is a marvellous summer night and stars fill the sky. How is the European jaunt, my dear? You are faring well? And Nicholas is busy and young Nick well?"

"We've been having a wonderful . . . Dad, are you okay? Why are you so happy? Look, I hate to be the bearer of . . . But you've heard, haven't you? Well, I *just* heard. About . . . about . . . Is there a divorce happening, or what?"

"Ah, yes, it seems dear Annabelle is in love with some effete Nazi from Düsseldorf—"

"François bloody Roehlig. He's fifteen years *younger* than her."

"She always wanted a son, and he probably needs a mother. I've wished her a future of unadulterated bliss. Give me a number where I can reach you—I am entertaining someone."

"You haven't been drinking?"

"I have been sipping only upon the sweet dew of poetry and fine conversation."

"With whom? Who are you entertaining?"

"The neighbour lady."

A pause from Rome. "Ah, the widow Blake . . . Whoa, just a minute here, what is going on, Dad? Now, don't tell me you are suddenly getting a *life*. Margaret Blake? You said she was some kind of militant busybody, you told me . . . I'll hang up. I love you. I'll call you when you're not, you know, *engaged*."

I find my way through the darkness to the porch and to Margaret.

"That was my daughter."

Margaret nods, but seems so lost in her silence that I fear intruding further upon it. I sit beside her, and the divan creaks. In dim outline against the sky, I make out her work-lined, handsome face. Again I try to picture this solemn woman in her youth, long-haired and barefoot and wild. I have a sense from her of immense strength. The confession I'd made to

Rimbold returns to me: *It's a shameful thought, but I think I'm attracted to dominant women.*

"Your voice carries awfully well. I couldn't help hear . . . you're getting a divorce?"

"The marriage died many years ago. I only recently became aware of that."

My guest has a right to more than this: she has shared *her* former life. But I cannot bring myself to speak of Annabelle; it will only depress me. It would take more courage than I possess to tell Margaret of my physical failings as a husband, my impotence.

"Deborah is your one child?"

"The light of my life."

"And are you happy? Like you told her?"

"Growing happier by the minute in your company." A bold compliment, daringly offered.

"You're awfully charming, you know, when you're not playing the big shot."

"Do I come across that way?"

"A little bit. You probably don't notice."

But of course I do. Overblown. Donnish and pedantic, Annabelle said. But it's too late in life to undo the curse of who I am.

Another silence. I cannot think what to do with my hands, and I relight my pipe. The fields and the forest have fallen asleep and the sea is windless and still. A blazing meteor: it traces a scar of fire across the sky, and dies.

"A shooting star, how beautiful," she says. And she jumps up. "Let's go for a walk on the beach."

But again, from the house, the instrument of the devil is ringing. My first thought is to ignore it, but its call is insistent. I will be pleasant but short.

"It's George, Arthur. I think I need a little help."

The forest blots out the starlit sky, and darkness enshrouds me as I switch off my headlights. No lights are on in George's house, but I detect the flickering glow of a fireplace.

His house—a rental—is a log cottage in the trees: finely grooved cedar timbers enclosed by plank decking and, above, a shake roof and a bedroom loft with its own balcony. Immense cedars and Douglas firs rise magisterially around it—this small acreage had not been logged since the turn of the century.

The front door is partly open, and its oiled hinges are silent as I step inside. The stale odour of alcohol seems to come at me in gusts. George is sitting by the hearth, feeding sticks into the fire, staring blearily at the flames. Beside him is an ashtray filled with butts. An empty bottle of rye whisky stands on the kitchen table, two other empty bottles on the floor.

I kneel beside him. "You've been having a bit of a time, George."

"I wanna chuck it all." He slurs this.

"Chuck what?"

"The whole damn thing."

"What a ridiculous notion. I wouldn't have a friend to come to. I won't hear of it."

That fetches a grim smile. The case is not totally hopeless. I assume it is only when the last of his drink ran out that he began entertaining such dour thoughts. This is fairly common.

"Is there anything else to drink in the house?"

"Drank it all up." He hiccups. "Scotty, the bastard, won't give me more." Scotty Phillips, the island bootlegger.

"How long has this been going on?"

"Two, three days, I don't know."

I rise and go to the refrigerator, where he keeps his fine-grind coffee. "Where are the filters?"

"First cupboard shelf."

As I get the coffee under way, I blather on about

this and that to keep George's mind off whatever woes belabour him. I suspect a former priest's loss of faith must stick daggers into him from time to time, but something else might be afflicting him, too.

Eureka, I have him chuckling—with an elaborate and unembellished account of the savaging I took in Small Claims Court. Everything has worked out for the best, I assure him. Margaret Blake and I—like children newly met in the school playground—had to have a wrestling match before becoming friends. Though I tell him we made amends, I do not mention how I parted from her tonight, in an anxious fluster of apology and regret. It would not do to let George feel blamed.

Coffee slops from the brim of his mug as he raises it shakily to his lips, his eyes on me. Even through those dilated pupils he seems to be able to read something new and interesting about me.

"Arthur, you have this . . . thousand-mile stare. Kind of a Jehovah's Witness look. You jus' join some kind of sect?"

"I'm fine. Feel vitalized, really, by all this mending of fences. Margaret asked us both over to dinner this Friday night, by the way."

"So I can be a chaperone?"

"What do you mean, George?"

He grins crookedly, a malevolent leer. "Are you planning to make some advances then, old son?"

"Oh, come now, George. I'm too over the hill for that sort of thing. Though I must say we've been getting on quite famously."

George continues his recovery as I prattle about how I was reciting "To a Nightingale" and opened my eyes to see her standing before me with her eggs and tarts. A picture forms in my mind: how stunning she was against the sunset. I kissed her hand before we parted. That took great courage.

But why am I carrying on about Margaret Blake when a comrade sits here in need beside me?

"George, what ails you? Why have you been on a bender? Do you want to talk about it?"

"Crisis of faith. Nothing to hold onto any more." Despite his thickness of tongue, these words sound with a depressing clarity. "Do you have any smokes?"

"Oh, yes, I brought a pack for you." I fish it from my jacket pocket and pass it to him, then fill my pipe and tamp it down. George scrapes a wooden match against the hearth. We work at these simple tasks in silence.

"What is it, George?"

"Guess you haven't heard what some of the wits around here call me. Queen of Prince George, the island fairy."

"I don't quite follow."

"As gay as a butterfly."

I'm stunned, but I remember now his words of stoned confession on my boat. *I coveted my neighbour's ass—that was my sin.*

Hours pass unnoticed as he pours it out—the life of a gay priest: guilt, repentance, broken vows, never absolution enough to heal the wounds of mortal sin. Defrocked after the exposure of a long, illicit relationship, he underwent a fundamental loss of faith.

"Found solace in the bottle. God's plan. Hell with Him. You believe, Arthur? You believe in any of it?"

"I tend to hedge my bets."

"Lily-livered agnostic. Doubt is for cowards. You believe or you don't believe, there's no goddamn in-between. There's no afterlife, only darkness, sweet, empty darkness."

I find such thoughts disturbing, and try to offer some soothing soporifics about life and all its mysteries, though I can see that this only depresses him further. But I get him smiling again with my deadpan account of the tree falling on my garage. Finally, George rises.

"I'm going to bed, Arthur. I'll make it through the night."

He leads me to the door, more sure-footed now, but weary. I believe he will weather the rest of this storm.

"I'll come by and make a hearty breakfast."

From the doorway, we see a lightness in the little patch of sky above, and an early twilight haze creeping about the stout trunks of trees.

"You'd better make that lunch," George says. "Late lunch." He takes my hand. "Thanks for this, Arthur. Thanks for being a friend."

I take his thin frame in my arms and bring him close to me, and hold him until he stops shaking.

δ̂ê

Good afternoon, Dr. Dix.

My, aren't we being formal. Well, how do you do, Professor O'Donnell. Won't you have a seat?

Look at this.

What?

In the theatre section. This ad.

"The Theatre Workshop presents *Switch*. A sassy comedy of manners . . ." Oh, I see: Kimberley Martin's in it.

Can you imagine? She's cashing in on her fame. How can she be taken seriously? A comedy! A week before the trial . . . Jesus, I don't understand this woman.

Though you seem fascinated by her.

Sure. Like a kid at the zoo staring at the man-eating python.

Still on the wagon?

Yep.

Did you phone your father as I suggested?

About the hardest thing I've ever done. He was great, though, couldn't see why all this fuss over such piffle. She led you on, did she? Time you started thinking of settling down, old chap. He should talk. The old boy actually seemed a little relieved. Probably thought I was gay. . . . You're all dressed up. Going out for dinner?

I am, as a matter of fact.

You look smart. Didn't know you had such pretty ankles.

Well, why don't you sit over there where you don't have to look at them?

Sorry.

It's all right. I'm flattered.

You're not married, are you? I'm not prying; I heard that somewhere.

I'm a lesbian.

Oh.

Well, don't sit there like a nervous rabbit. I'm not dangerous.

I feel stupid.

For assuming I was straight? Or for wanting to screw me?

I guess I'm incredibly transparent.

But that's good.

Do you have a partner?

Her name is Molly. She's a computer programmer.

It's working out?

She takes my abrasiveness quite well.

You don't have any trouble with relationships.

Well, I don't have a long record of one-night stands.

Jane, you believe I'm innocent, don't you?

I don't think I should be rendering verdicts at this stage in therapy.

It's important to me.

Innocence is much too vague a term. In its sense

of virtuous, you can render your own verdict. It also means naïve—you should be sent away for *that*.

Jane, don't give me a stall. I'm not asking for a treatise on the meaning of innocence.

Okay, Jonathan. Well, oddly enough, I do believe you are innocent. You're not in the pattern. The rapist is into a misogynistic control trip. You like women. Your weapon of choice is charm. Though many women would call seduction a form of rape.

I know those women. They teach in our women's studies department. They also think rape is committed whenever a dirty joke is told.

Jonathan, I know the subject of your sexuality seems to rub at your tender spot, but I'd like to work with you on it a little more.

I can handle it.

Do you ever see yourself as having any . . . shall we say, performance problems?

Boy, you're . . . Premature ejaculation, I suppose. Sometimes I just can't hold on.

And then is there a problem after that?

How do you mean?

Getting a second erection.

Jane, this is incredibly awkward.

I don't think you ought to be embarrassed.

Yes, well, it does happen.

A lot?

Well, yes. Is it a big deal?

I would imagine it's fairly common among men. Premature ejaculation followed by a rather long period of enervation. I had a case once: a guy who always came on so strong with his wife he lost his erection. I advised a little creative role-playing. Psychodrama: each becomes the other. It tends to stretch things out when one becomes aware of his partner's need for pleasure.

I've had enough creative role-playing.

What do you mean?

Nothing, I guess.

Hmm. Jonathan, here you are in your late thirties without having even *attempted* a permanent relationship. Does that say anything to you?

Says I pay the single-rate income tax.

Says you're insecure about marriage. Worried you can't perform. As a means of raising your self-esteem, you develop a bit of a Don Juan complex. One-night stands. Wham, bam, thank you, ma'am, and Mr. Studley doffs his hat and limply leaves the stage. And can't find the courage to even call her the next morning.

The truth isn't quite as bleak, Jane. Sometimes I maintain very well.

And how do you do it?

A couple of scotches and some lingering foreplay.

You're defending like crazy, Jonathan.

§§

By Friday evening George has managed to crawl from his pit of despair and is his former jesting, cynical self: his gaiety at Margaret's dinner table does not seem forced. I suspect he is stoned on his powerful marijuana, an analgesic that blurs his inner pain.

Our hostess—to my utter lack of surprise—is as deft in the kitchen as she is in the yard, and her roasted chicken is beyond compare. All through dinner I am like a fumbling child, unable to utter intelligible words. I can't fathom what is wrong with me—my concern about George's state of mind has me distracted, I suppose.

Margaret's busy house comes complete with her lazy cat and her slightly more energetic spaniel, Slappy, whose role is to guard the house from invading livestock. The furnishings are worn but comfortable, though hinting of a former hippieness: a few twigs-and-branches chairs, doubtless made by some artisan friend; an ornate brass hookah decorating a corner; glass crystals that slowly twist in the air behind sun-dappled windows, their reflections dancing upon the walls.

Poster art adorns these walls: political, hortatory. Greenpeace demands we save the whales; "No Clearcuts" insist the Friends of Clayoquot Sound. Yet another sign simply commands that we L-O-V-E. What? Who? Those four frightening letters on that weathered poster seem from another age; the 1960s, a time of boldness when people were unashamed of passion.

An eclectic library: nature books, whodunits, leftist political tracts, a few classics—they speak of a mind untrained but curious.

Margaret insists we take dessert and coffee on the porch so George and I can smoke. I find myself babbling, filling the evening air with a recounting of the O'Donnell case. Margaret listens transfixed, punctuating my account with gentle profanities: "Good Lord," "Merciful God." Her eyes are wide; her mouth is open, a shocked O.

George rolls a marijuana cigarette during this. He lights it, takes a deep drag, and blows out a thunderhead of sweet-smelling smoke, then offers it to us. Margaret shakes her head. "I think I forgot how, George." I decline as well.

"By the way, Arthur," he says, "I saw Kimberley Martin's name in an ad for a play. Vancouver summer theatre. A sassy comedy, that's what the ad said."

"It sounds appalling," I say.

"Maybe you'd like to take Margaret. Wouldn't a sassy night in the city be a lark for both of you?"

George is playing the matchmaker with distressing boldness, and my awkwardness manifests itself in strained, unnatural laughter. Desperately, I continue the tale of my client's *Walpurgisnacht* of wanton love with Kimberley Martin, but this turns out to be doubly embarrassing: sassier than any play, and in the telling of it I sound like a decrepit roué.

At the end of this, an agony of silence. Then Margaret says, "Good *Lord*."

Have I disgusted her? She is making a face, a grimace, a little moue. But suddenly it widens into a brilliant smile, and she tosses her head back and laughs. Her face is perfectly framed against the glowing evening sky. I feel a faint shiver run through me and I endure a light-headed sensation, a tightness of the heart. For the briefest moment I fear I have suffered another stroke. But it is something else, a most odd, unnatural feeling.

When George makes his departure, he squeezes my arm in a comradely way, a silent gesture telling me I am not to worry about him: he's back on track. Margaret rejects my offer to help with the dishes, and discreetly smothers a yawn. Eleven o'clock, I realize, is a late time for a farmer who daily arises to the calling of roosters, and the gentleman in me has me on my feet, collecting the remains of the bowl of salad I humbly contributed to her feast.

All the while I prattle lamely about how pleasant was the evening, how bountiful her table, how . . . how . . . Oh, mighty Beauchamp, show some grit.

"And how lovely and gracious was the hostess tonight."

"You're very kind."

She stands before me at the doorway, smiling with opened lips.

I hesitate. I falter. I flee.

At home I plunge into my favourite chair and sit in the dark stillness of my house. The only sounds are the complaints of the freezer and the soft scuttling of a mouse in the kitchen.

I am trapped in a moment in time. I retain a photograph of her, laughing, silhouetted against the sky at twilight. I cannot erase this picture.

My heart seems to be beating very hard. What shape is it in? Perhaps I should see Doc Dooley again.

Our heat wave continues unabated into August, but my well is fed by a deep aquifer and so my garden prospers, tended by flower-crowned Ceres, of whom Virgil justly exhorts: "In solemn lays, exalt your rural queen's immortal praise." Ah, yes, she causes peas to grow fat and carrots to swell. Here on the left, a row of juicy heads is forming on the lettuce; near the fence, my corn stands soldier tall.

My beard continues to flourish as well. I must soon have it tended or I will look like Moses. With the exception of the beard, I am still condensing in size, thanks to my daily regimen of outdoor work and a gardener's diet that is varied only by the occasional farm-fresh egg and my hoarded but diminishing collection of Margaret's black currant tarts, ambrosial in their delicacy.

I now realize that the strange sensation that overcame me at Margaret's house was clearly caused by Rimbold's secondary smoke. Garibaldi Gold: a potent physic. It seems to work for George, for his spirits have remained at least artificially high these last several days. I have yet to muster courage enough to sample one of the cigarettes he gave me—they are kept hidden in the fridge in my cookie tin.

Margaret has been using her tractor to scoop post holes for her new fence, and since I have been clearing some brush in the area we frequently meet at our respective work sites. We help each other. I learn how to run a tractor. We take breaks from our toil for tea or lemonade. We make Zoller jokes and plot our next foray against Evergreen Estates. She teaches me about the wild things that grow: the camas bulbs that can be cooked, the salal berries that make excellent jelly, the vanilla leaves that insects spurn.

She is candid, holds nothing in, gossips with a wicked sharpness of tongue. I enjoy her abrasiveness, her strutting contempt of whom she calls her "enemies." She is bracing, refreshing, different. Compare her to the woman of my previous life—who hid many thoughts and feelings and led many secret lives. But Annabelle has been receding from me; her picture is becoming hazy, and she no longer haunts my shameful dreams.

I truly like Margaret Blake. And I think she likes me. We are in a state of like. That's all that's going on.

❦

Dear Mr. Brown,

You will recall that I arranged to see Dr. Curtis Mallard, the philosophy teacher whom Professor O'Donnell dealt with so harshly in a recent book review. I have come away from that meeting finding myself in agreement with many of Professor O'Donnell's adjectives, in particular "bloated" and "pompous." I will add another: "vindictive." Dr. Mallard does not forgive.

He insisted on showing me several more kindly reviews and engaged in a long, confusing defence of his work, while assailing Professor O'Donnell in language that I would have expected no philosopher to use, and also expressing glee at his archenemy's recent fall from fortune.

In short, he was willing to be of what assistance he could, though mainly he offered speculation about Professor O'Donnell's sexual excesses, much of which seemed unlikely. He did, however, lead me to the name of a former mistress of the man I investigate. Her name is Dominique Lander, a past visiting professor in the fine arts department of the university, a painter who—as I have discovered upon a visit to a gallery—is known for her dark, erotic art. It was widely rumoured, Dr. Mallard told me, that she is an avid student of sadomasochistic sexual practices. Examples of her works seem to bear this out.

I have learned she now resides in the mountainous interior of this province—near a village called Slocan—and I will go there immediately. In the meantime, I will also spend more time in the library in an effort to master the intricacies of what is known in the trade as S and M. The concept is truly beyond me.

It might be worth noting that Professor O'Donnell's only break from routine last week was his attendance at a Thursday evening performance of a play called *Switch* at the Granville Island Theatre Workshop in which, as you are obviously aware, Miss Martin plays a role. Perhaps there was nothing so unusual about Mr. O'Donnell's presence there—he was probably curious. While I was unable myself to buy a ticket—the theatre is small and the production popular—I did wait outside until it emptied. You will be pleased to know that the audience—excepting Professor O'Donnell and a few people with picket signs—seemed smiling and happy, and had an enjoyable time.

I remain faithfully,
Francisco (Frank) Sierra

৯৬

To whom it may concern,

I am Dominique Lander. I live at Rural Route 1, Bellflower Road, Slocan. I write this in support of my friend and former lover, Hon. Jonathan Shaun O'Donnell.

I met Jonathan two years ago at a reception for new faculty at U.B.C., where I was commencing a term as visiting lecturer in fine arts. I told him I wanted to fuck him, and we went to my rented studio in Kitsilano, where we did so. We fell in love and continued to meet there for the purpose of sex two or three days a week for seven months, after which I returned here to the Slocan Valley.

As a form of play before we fucked we would often paint each other's bodies. On frequent occasions we engaged in bondage and discipline. (This is often called sadomasochism, but that is a misleading term for what are properly seen as acts of affection. Pain is after all just another aspect of love. Death itself is erotic.)

Although the routines varied, a common element involved Jonathan tying me up to the bed and spanking me with his hand. I therefore do not believe that if he tied Kimberley Martin to the bed it was for any other reason than to engage in a ritual he enjoyed prior to fucking. He has never harmed a person in his life. I hope this information will assist him in his case, for I know that he is innocent.

Signed:
Dominique Lander

Witness: Francisco Sierra

♦♦

On this second Sunday of August, clouds decorate the horizon, but above Garibaldi the sky remains blue, the sun unrelentingly hot. The "spell" is what everyone is talking about at the ferry dock today. "Longest spell I can remember since '85." "Don't think this spell is gonna end till October."

Kurt Zoller is fluttering like a butterfly about the fringes of this crowd—local elections are set for this fall, and our trustee has been seeking the opinion of the grass roots, testing the waters before deciding whether he has any hope of re-election.

He strolls towards me, fidgeting with the straps of his life jacket. "Mr. Bo-champ, good morning. We got another hot one, eh?"

"Ah, our esteemed trustee. This drought must be keeping your little waterworks company hopping."

Zoller recently began a business tanking water up to his neighbours in Evergreen Estates, and he is reputed to gouge. This may have lost him a few votes, especially because he is seen as profiting from the spell.

"It's a service to my fellow islanders." He drops his voice and bends to me. "But I hear rumbles. Some people can't handle the idea of a businessman with initiative. Ford didn't build an auto empire without taking his opportunities. If it hadn't been me, somebody else would of done it, an off-islander."

I wonder if he is not sweltering in that heavy life jacket. Margaret and I have decided it is a kind of mother's blanket.

"You are merely adhering to the time-honoured ethics of capitalism, Mr. Zoller."

"Thank you."

I like the way he insists on misinterpreting my sarcasm. He is still convinced I am his unswerving ally.

"I'm meeting some bureaucrats from the city." Zoller continues to speak in the hushed tone of an international spy. "Government hydrologists. Coming over here to check water-table levels. This is how they spend our taxes."

"Ah, yes. The government is always interfering in matters that don't concern it."

"Can you think of some legal move to head them off, like a sort of injunction?"

"Not offhand, Mr. Zoller."

From behind me comes the nasal mewl of Nelson Forbish. "Hey, Kurt, I heard the government might put a freeze on the new subdivision. You got any word on that?"

Forbish wears his usual headgear, the porkpie hat. He is sucking the contents of a can of grape soda through a straw.

"Arthur here said it better than I could. They're always sticking their nose into other people's private places."

Forbish produces his notepad. "They say there's gonna be an investigation into, um—they call it . . . a possible malfeasance."

"No comment."

"Well, hey, I ain't accusing you of anything, I just asked what you know."

"I know nothing." Zoller's eyes are narrowed to defensive slits. He tightens the straps of his life jacket.

Not Now Nelson slurps up the last of his grape soda with a long, rasping gurgle. "So, are you going to sue Margaret Blake?"

"For what?"

"Saying you were in bed with the developers, that they paid you off. I thought you were going to sue her for slander."

"Well, I'm still thinking hard about it."

"Think he's got any kind of case there, Mr. Beauchamp?"

"If people ran to the courts over every word said in the heat of debate, the system would self-destruct." I am hoping Zoller will take this as a word of advice from his confidant to abandon thoughts of suing: Margaret may have seriously misspoke. She has confided she had no ammunition for her charge.

"Yeah, but do you think he's got a case? On what you know?"

Forbish surprises me, showing hitherto unrevealed

reportorial skills, a doggedness. Perhaps I have mis-read this clumsy stout. Does within hide a skinny streak of cleverness?

"I, too, know nothing."

"So would you be acting for Mrs. Blake if Kurt here sued her?"

"Nelson, the ferry is arriving."

"Like I hear you been, um, talking to her."

"Not now, Nelson."

"A lot. Over the fence and like that." Kin to gro-tesque Silenus, half-man, half-goat, he is the peeping satyr of Garibaldi Island. "Maybe you're doing more than talking, eh?" A bawdy wink.

Zoller's expression is one of confusion: the full im-pact of betrayal hasn't hit home.

"I am afraid I must flee your riveting company, Nelson—I have a friend to meet."

"I hear she's thinking of running for trustee this fall."

This is true, though told to me in secret. But secrets never seem to survive on this island.

As Forbish ambles off, Zoller stares at me with the expression of a soul mate betrayed. I slink away ashamed, the Quisling of Garibaldi.

The ferry groans wearily into its slip and spews the cyclists out. Augustina then disembarks by foot, greet-ing me with a hug.

"You seem pretty pleased with yourself, Arthur."

"Why do you say that, my dear?"

"The funny smile. Look like you swallowed a ca-nary."

"But I'm merely happy to see you."

We bump off in my truck towards Potter's Road. Stoney and Dog are whaling away with hammers as we pull in. They are still showing up on weekends, demonstrating a tenaciousness to the cause of my ga-rage that I'd not believed I'd see—though they take long cannabis breaks, wandering about the yard and into the woods. Most of the framing is up now. The Rolls is back in Stoney's shop, and I don't often think about it.

Augustina and I assemble briefs, notes, and transcripts on the dining-room table.

"I have reams of stuff from the client—I spent a whole day with him. I don't know . . . sometimes I wonder if he isn't a little kinky. It's as if he's hiding something. Anyway, let's see, I talked to a cocaine expert, pharmacologist from the university. Too many variables, so he can't conclude Kimberley was feigning sleep, but says coke's a powerful stimulant and it *does* cause a strange reaction in some people. But we've lost the element of surprise: Paula Yi met with the prosecutor."

"Please ensure the Crown subpoenas Miss Yi. She seems reluctant, and we can't have her wandering off. Those bruises on Kimberley's wrists and ankles worry me. I can't bring myself to believe they were self-inflicted."

"Well . . . injuries. She was drunk, falling down. . . ."

"It doesn't quite wash. Can we get a peek at Kimberley's polygraph test? One often finds unexpected blips on the graphs that the examiner has disregarded."

"It won't be easy."

"Then we'll seek a disclosure order from my old friend Justice Sprogue, who knows all about the perils of polygraphy. He once wrote a brief on it."

"Okay, I'll bring some cases. The pre-trial is this Wednesday. He wants to do it in his chambers, informal, no gowns."

"That's fine by me."

"And I got a call from Dr. Werner Mundt at the forensic clinic—you know him, don't you?"

"Ah, yes, we were friends once." Annabelle had had a rather public affair with him, and I sense Augustina now remembers this, for she seems embarrassed. "What did he want?"

"Well, he's offering to be an expert witness."

"Slavering at the thought, no doubt. He likes the limelight."

"Well, he just published a paper about a so-called rape fantasy, and he expostulated on it for an hour. You see, certain women have these 'male aggression masturbation reveries.' They enjoy the thought of being forced so they can abandon responsibility for their own sexual pleasure. As Kimberley would put it: Gag me."

"I think we'll take a pass on Dr. Mundt."

A few years ago I might have held my nose and plunged ahead, but I suppose I have become soft. Surely one of the reasons I deserted the courthouse for Garibaldi Island was to escape the foul excesses of the law. Again I ask myself: Why did I give in to a moment of weakness and undertake this trial?

The windows are open on this hot day, and we continue to talk strategies to the clatter of hammers and saws. At times I find my mind wandering.

"Arthur, you have this moony stare."

"Oh, sorry, I guess I lost the train. . . ."

"You feeling okay?"

"Splendid. Finding it a little hard to get back in uniform, that's all."

I soon tire of reading the voluminous treatises on law and evidence Augustina has compiled, and lead her outside, where I compel her to admire my garden; then we do a quick inspection of the building site. Stoney waves from a ladder, a cigarette and several nails clenched between his lips. The newly framed garage looks sturdy enough. I have decided once again to forgive Stoney. His eerily occult ability to cause calamities wherever he goes is surely counterbalanced by his good intentions. In token of this, I have agreed on a fair contract price with the boys and give them weekly draws: I cannot see them starve.

A tour of my acreage—up and over the yellow-grass bluffs, down through the shade of my conifer forest—leads Augustina and me to a path I cannot recall having seen before, but it must be the shortcut Stoney takes on the many days when the master mechanic can't get his car started. Farther along is my own well-tromped path—to the pasture where I have been clearing brush and helping with the fencing.

"My, you've been doing a lot of work."

I absently pluck a pale blue blossom from a corn-flower and twirl the stem between my fingers. I feel a vague . . . not unease, a sense of absence. Something missing here, cut out of the frame.

"Arthur? Hello."

My mind is adrift; I realize Augustina has been talking to me. "I'm sorry, you were saying?"

"It's getting near ferry time, I should go. Are you all right?"

"Tip top."

"Why are you staring at that house?"

"Oh, no reason."

"You're acting awfully strange."

She is looking at me anxiously. What in the world is she going on about? Movement behind the kitchen window: is that Margaret? Her dog runs out, evicting a flapping, clucking hen.

"I'm fine, Augustina. I'm just . . . happy." I begin walking her back to my truck. "I'll see you Wednesday for the pre-trial."

"Did you want me to pick you up at the seaplane dock?"

"Oh, we'll just take a taxi."

Augustina continues to stare at me. "*We'll* take a taxi?"

I hear my words coming in short, breathless sentences. "Margaret Blake is joining me. We're taking a little break from the routines. My neighbour. She's usually out here. She has animals to look after, so we'll fly back that evening, of course."

Augustina seems to be fighting a smile now. "Of course. Otherwise you'd have to spend the night together."

"Oh, dear, nothing like that is happening. She's just a good friend. All very platonic."

As we drive to the ferry, Augustina sits silently smiling, as if she holds a secret. Finally she says, "Do you know what, Arthur?"

"What?"

"I think you're in love. I think you're head over heels."

The use of the L-word startles me. I sputter, "Nonsense. What a preposterous notion."

"I'm the world's foremost expert, Arthur. I've been there and back too many times."

I smile at her jest. I shake my head. "Completely out of the question."

"Why are you red in the face?"

"I'm not. I'm just ruddy from the exertion of our little hike."

"I think it's sweet."

After I drop her off at the dock, I enjoy a good laugh over this.

In love. What an idea.

A fondness exists, yes, even a strong fancy. But love? Complete with stardust in the eyes? With the legendary pounding of the heart and the lightly skipping feet?

Absurd.

ॐॐ

That evening, alone in darkening night, I practise tai chi movements on the lawn. I make tea. I walk on the beach. I study a purple starfish clinging to the rocks. I listen to the soft sounds of night. And all the while I debate within the curious verdict Augustina rendered.

No, it is inconceivable, I am not some fuzzy-cheeked adolescent but a mature sixty-two-year-old. I am beyond such banality.

But why do I have this sense of having been rendered into some glutinous form of paste?

Have I been denying a truth evident to others? Surely I have not plunged into that monstrous abyss of which the poets sing. No, it is beyond the pale.

But again my inner senses are assaulted by a picture burned into memory: Margaret on her porch, silhouetted against the sunset, the chiming carillon of her laughter. How . . . different I felt at that moment. I assumed it was Rimbold's secondary smoke that overcame me, but was it the tuneful twang of Cupid's mighty bow?

No, this cannot, dare not be love. Love becomes physically complicated. Love must be consummated, but this could never be. I am a man disarmed, enfeebled, ineffectual, incapable. Gag me. . . .

Ah, yes, if it be any manner of love it is the passion of weakness for strength, the puerile ardour of a masochist seeking a dominatrix who castrates her own pigs and mops the courtroom floor with Arthur Beauchamp; yes, indeed, that is the kind of woman Beauchamp seeks in order to satisfy his aberrant desires.

Am I in love? I fear I am. Woe to Arthur Ramsgate Beauchamp. Weaponless, he can only want but never have.

Abed, I dream the spell is over. I am naked in the softly falling rain, my wrists and ankles bound. A slender woman haunts the shadows. Though tied and helpless, I am overcome with desire for her. Later I awake with—is it possible? is it real?—a tumescent penis? As sleep overcomes me again, I am not sure whether this *phallus erectus* is only a chimera sent to mock me.

Good morning, Kimberley. You look weary on this nice sunny day.

Morning, Dr. Kropinski. Ouch. Tied one on yesterday. After the show we all went to Bridge's. I guess we were celebrating.

Over the success of the show, yes?

Yeah, we're on the front page.

I saw that.

What do they call themselves? Citizens for Decency, something like that.

You do not worry the play will be closed down?

By those morons? Bunch of dweebs with their picket signs. But we drank a lot of toasts to them—we're getting sold-out houses. And guess who I keep seeing in the audience? Twice I spotted him trying to look small in one of the back rows as we were taking our bows. Professor Jonathan O'Donnell. Creepy, huh?

How odd.

Scary, kind of. Everyone else was applauding . . . but he looked . . . I don't know. Depressed. What kind of stuff does he think he's pulling anyway? Probably trying to put a hex on. Well, what did you think of the play?

I thought you were very good.

Thank you.

You received the best laughs.

A little racy, though, hey? What did your wife think?

I am afraid Penny found it too rich for her blood. Well, she is a little conservative, yes? An old-fashioned Jewish upbringing . . .

Oh, dear, I had one of those, too, only Catholic. All that's left is the religious guilt, I'm afraid. Well, *my* significant other hasn't seen it yet, though he read that prissy review where they called it obscene—right next to our pictures. Was he ever torqued. I'm not going back to his place until he apologizes.

You have been staying in your apartment?

I don't need all the distractions. The play runs another week, and then I've only got four or five days to get ready for the trial, which I don't think I'm up for—I wish it would just go away. I'm going to come out looking like . . . I don't know.

Why?

Oh, Pat Blueman dropped on me that apparently I did some cocaine that night I was at O'Donnell's house.

Cocaine . . .

I snorted some in the rec room with Egan Chornicky and that Paula woman. I must have been fairly loaded, I don't *do* coke. Maybe twice in my life. I guess I just kept quiet because I didn't dream it would come out. But Paula spilled the beans to Patricia, who gave me royal shit for not telling her, and the defence knows about it.

Did this drug affect you?

Not really. Well, maybe I got a little wild and crazy, it's after that I changed into O'Donnell's suit.

And now this may come out in court?

Remy—he'll have another wig-out. And it could make it tough to get articles. Maybe I'll become a star of stage and screen instead. There's a chance the play will move to Toronto this fall. . . . Oh, hey, we may have the goods on O'Donnell now. Pat Blueman . . . can I tell you a secret?

Everything you tell me is secret, yes?

I called her, got her to come down and join us last night, at Bridge's. She's so lonely, you know—I try to get her out where she can meet eligibles. Well, she was in such a *good* mood. O'Donnell—

she made me swear not to tell anyone—but the guy is right out of the Marquis de Sade. She has a witness under subpoena with whom Jonathan had this *ritual,* she calls it, where he tied her up *and* painted her before getting it on. In her own acrylics, or whatever—she's an artist. Dominique the dominatrix.

Oh, my. How did they find her?

Patricia wouldn't say. I always knew there was a sicko psyche hiding inside Jonathan. I could tell it just looking into his eyes. They were always so sad. Hiding some deep, dark, horrible secret. I mean, I'm sort of modern sexually, I like to do different things. I like a little theatre with it, maybe, but not *kink*—we're talking pre-Remy here, he's pretty traditional about sex. God, I just thought—maybe his defence is going to be that he was so drunk he thought I was Dominique.

I think that is not likely.

I want to see his expression when she walks into court. What's the deal with this bondage stuff, Dr. Kropinski? Why do people do it?

I have not seen much of the material on this. But involved I think are scripted rituals of whipping, spanking, and so on, interspersed with episodes of tenderness and loving. It is clearly so that some people—mostly men, I think—seek their sexual stimulation that way. An unhealthy compulsion either to dominate or play the slave. I have seen reports about normal persons, intelligent, well born, who have gone into therapy for this. Significant antecedents like childhood trauma will play some role, yes? But it is not always easy to trace the connection. It may have something to do with the buttock fetish: *Gesässerotik,* it is called. Fetishes usually come from a submerged sexual impression from early childhood, and so I think there is a similar root for bondage practices.

It's basically a form of play, though, right? Theatre. I mean, you see all these ads. Women who offer a service—discipline care providers. So there must be this *need*. I guess it's better some bozo gets his rocks off by paddling someone's bum than going home all repressed and knocking his wife's teeth out. Anyway . . .

Why are you laughing?

Oh, I was just remembering last night. Patricia had a few, and did this hilarious imitation of Arthur Beauchamp. Snapping his suspenders and reciting from the *Merchant of Venice,* trying to wring tears from the jury. "Mercy falleth as the gentle rain from heaven." Something like that. I guess we should get to work.

All right.

I've had more dreams. I just wish they'd stop.

I would prefer to see them come out.

I know. Healthier for me if I could just spew it out. I get this gaggy feeling, this nausea, I'm afraid that if I think about it I'll throw up.

All your dreams seem to end with you cowering against a wall, then feeling . . .

I can't talk about it. I can't.

Okay. Tell me, have you thought any more about being hypnotized?

I guess I'm afraid of losing control, getting hysterical.

Do you not think you need to remember? After the play is over, you have a four-day period before the trial?

Yes.

And when do you take the witness stand?

Next Wednesday, I think.

What about this weekend? You could come for dinner on Saturday—I find evenings are better, and you will be more relaxed in a home setting.

And I'm to get hypnotized? Do you put me to sleep?

Actually, I may bring you awake.

꒰꒱

The charter flutters into Beauchamp Bay and chugs towards the little dock where I stand with Margaret, who is smiling but tense. She is smartly dressed, a fawn suit, her skirt hemmed daringly high. I am more casual, the more bohemian of the two in my denim and sandals. All my suits are at the cleaners in Vancouver, so I am accepting Wally Sprogue at his word there will be no dress code. And why not make a statement? Why not say I am no longer a slave to the conventions of the city?

"You're sure he can get that machine up off the water again?" says Margaret, who has admitted to a fear of flying. She has never been in a small airplane.

I am still too unnerved to confess my feelings for her. There exists an abiding fear of rejection. And I simply do not know how to start: I do not remember how to do this. Assuming I once knew.

And I so fear the shame of failure if I try.

Margaret grips my wrist as the aircraft groans from the water. I thrill at the fierceness of her touch. I tell the pilot to circle Garibaldi, and I enjoy Margaret's enjoyment, drink deeply of her experience, her eagle's view of her farm, our rustic island, the evil Evergreen Estates. Then the inlets, other islands, the cold green waters of Georgia Strait, the approaching city spires.

She turns from the window and blesses me with a smile that causes my inner core to melt.

I remember our first encounter, on the ferry: Margaret thrusting a petition at me, expecting a rebuff. *I don't suppose you'd care to sign this.* I recall the scorn on her face as she sized me up for precisely what I was—a rube from the city, still reeking of it, a transgressor upon the fair soil of Garibaldi Island. I found her somewhat attractive—lissome and lean, peppy, intense of eye—but she has been transformed in my mesmerized mind into a person of measureless beauty: handsomely wrinkled by the sun, dirt often under the fingernails, hands toughened by honest work, no phony eyelashes, no painted toes, no false heart—earthy and elegant and real.

A tragic dilemma arises from my state of rapture; one of its prongs is of course my own peculiar fear of flying—performance anxiety is how George Rimbold put it. The other problem is that Margaret is also in love. To her honour and my chagrin, she remains bound to the memory of her husband, a man about whom she incessantly speaks. I am playing second fiddle to a ghost.

So, sadly—but perhaps for the better—it appears obvious that Margaret does not return my feelings. I expect she sees me as an avuncular figure, an older friendly adviser with whom she can freely talk of past love and flush her system of pent-up sorrow.

My mind awash with these thoughts, I suddenly realize we are enshrouded within the city's walls. We dip between two container ships, plough across the turbid waters of Burrard Inlet, and taxi to the dock.

I extend a hand to help Margaret from the plane, and again at her touch feel a wilting sensation. Our eyes meet: can she read the horrible truth in my adoring puppy eyes? Or does she just regard me as that friendly old fellow Arthur Beauchamp, her pal, her neighbour, her sharer of fences and secrets?

How do I win her from her husband?

Our taxi takes us first to the downtown shopping complexes, where Margaret alights—she will spend the morning buying household goods. I remind her that we are to meet for lunch at Chez Forget before attending the matinée performance of *Switch*.

"I'll be there." She takes a deep breath, blows me a kiss, and melts into the crowds.

Switch. How crass of me to invite her to a bawdy farce. But George Rimbold eventually teased me into asking her. "You wouldn't be interested, would you?" I said.. "Well, I might be," she replied.

My taxi drops me off at the Nelson Street entrance of the law courts. Here in this building—more greenhouse than courthouse, a vast atrium with potted trees and a roof of glass—will unfold the final chapter of the Queen versus Jonathan Shaun O'Donnell. Only two weeks to the start of the trial: how well prepared am I? My powers of concentration seem decimated. I must focus on this trial or, befuddled by my emotions, I may end up sacrificing a client. I must will myself to keep my thoughts from the woman who lives next door.

In the lobby, court staff stare at me in puzzlement, as persons might who aren't quite sure they know this old fellow, this rumpled, bearded beatnik. Friends wave from a distance, but avoid coming closer, perhaps fearful I will ask for spare change.

In the barristers' lounge, Augustina Sage is having coffee with Patricia Blueman, who looks me over as I sit beside her.

"You here for the farmers' convention, Arthur?"

"My suits are at the cleaners. Wally won't mind, I'm sure."

"Patricia has some new witnesses," says Augustina, looking a little dour. She passes me a photocopied statement.

Patricia explains, "Dominique Lander is a former U.B.C. art instructor who had an affair with your client. She's a bondage freak. It's evidence of previous consistent behaviour. Proves he has a history of tying up his partners."

I quickly glance through the brief handwritten statement of this Dominique Lander. I try to hide both my surprise and my dismay. A line draws my attention: *Pain is after all just another aspect of love.* I recall the dream of a few nights ago, the bound wrists, the risen phallus.

"And when did Dominique Lander crawl from the woodwork?"

But then I notice the signature of the witness to her statement: Francisco Sierra, a person known to me, a private detective with a reputation for artfulness.

"Who hired Mr. Sierra?"

"We didn't."

"Who, then?"

"Mr. Sierra refuses to say."

The possibilities do not seem limitless. I catch Augustina's eye and can tell she shares my thought: one senses the heavy hand of the wealthy fiancé at work. Would he stoop to buying a witness?

"We will want to interview Miss Lander, of course."

"Yes, I'll set it up."

"And who are the other late additions to the cast?"

"Paula Yi. Whom you've talked to, so you don't need her statement."

"You'll be calling her, I presume, to say Kimberley was severely intoxicated on cocaine?"

"I'll be ready for it." There is a firm edge to her voice. "And we also have Dr. Hawthorne's housekeeper—the police really did a raggedy-ass job, they didn't interview everyone they should have. Mrs. McIntosh called to tell me she heard screams from the adjoining house."

Augustina glances at me, and I can tell she shares my vexation: these important items of disclosure are being sprung at us very late.

"Anything else forthcoming at this eleventh hour?"

"We're adding counts of confinement and kidnapping."

"Oh, come *on*," says Augustina.

"Ah, yes, the scatter-gun approach. Throw enough excrement in the hope that some of it will stick." I am furious and rise abruptly. "Let us see Mr. Justice Sprogue."

En route to his chambers, Augustina gives me a playful nudge. "That nice Mrs. Blake—is she getting you all fired up?"

Walter Sprogue is a young fifty, a gentleman of both robust girth and temperament, with a vanity to match. But he is jolly and expansive. He peeks for a moment at Augustina's ankles as we sink into overstuffed chairs in his chambers.

"Jeans and sandals, Beauchamp? Ah, the retired life. You poor bugger, I hear they pulled you from your life of ease for this."

"Not at all, Wally. I jumped at the chance. Desperately wanted to see your first criminal trial."

"You wanted to see if I would gum it up. Very likely I will. The first thing they teach you is to stay out of the arena and above the fray. Very hard when you're an old hand at the counsel table."

"Ah, yes, they're sending the new judges to school, aren't they?"

"Six weeks of my summer. Sensitivity training is a big part of it. We had some intense sessions. Worked with two counsellors, very bright young ladies . . . ah, women. Not ashamed to admit I had my consciousness raised a bit. You don't know what garbage is sitting around inside you when you start out. Rigid, traditionalist notions."

Wally has an oddly placid look about him, as of one recently brainwashed. But he has probably benefited from his gender-sensitivity training. Though married, he has a reputation as a rascal with women, and I recall him once being roundly slapped at a cocktail party.

"Anyway, to matters at hand, let us have some time estimates."

"Roughly four or five days for the Crown's case," says Patricia Blueman. "Depending on how long Mr. Beauchamp takes with my witnesses. I don't know anything about the defence case. I presume Mr. O'Donnell will be on the stand for some time."

I do not bite. "The case opens on Monday, August thirty-first. The Labour Day weekend follows. Two weeks seem about right."

"Well, I intend to move things along. You'll find I don't waste time. Issues of law, Patricia?"

"A voir dire on an oral statement by the accused to an officer. And an issue of previous consistent behaviour."

"My learned friend will have a fight on her hands over that," I say.

Augustina says, "And we'd like to see the polygraph test results."

"Any objection?"

"Yes," says Patricia. "I don't get to see anything from the defence, of course, but that's our wonderful system of justice."

"Well, let's set aside a couple of days at the beginning so you can slug it out between you," Wally says. "I don't suppose there's any chance we will not be going ahead?"

"Not a whisper of a chance," Patricia says.

"Unless Miss Martin repents," I say.

Wally looks at me reproachfully. "*Ms.* Martin," he says. M-i-z.

As anxious as a teenager on a first date, I arrive at Chez Forget well before the appointed hour. Pierre whisks me to my usual table. "Even without the suit I still recognize you. So with you and Madame Beauchamp it is splitsville, eh? Yes, *d'accord*, I know about this. Madame was in here with her boyfriend, not much of a trade for you, maybe you have the better deal. Who is it, Monsieur Beauchamp, that you dine with today? A beautiful woman, eh?"

I respond with a non-committal smile. Two perfect roses sit in a vase. *Déjà vu*: during my final sad sharing of that table with Annabelle, she fiddled with roses while our marriage burned.

I am on edge as I wait for Margaret, sipping a wineless spritzer. A fear bedevils me that escorting her to the matinée of *Switch* might turn out to be a social error of tragic magnitude. Does one woo a proper lady by exposing her to bawdiness on a stage? But Margaret was keen to see the complainant in person: she is hooked on the trial.

I ask Pierre to bring the phone, and I call Augustina, who was to have tracked down Jon O'Donnell.

"Yes, Arthur, I reached him by phone. He says he has something important on this afternoon, so he can't meet me right away."

"What about the screams the housekeeper heard?"

"He says she must be imagining them."

"What did he say about Dominique Lander?"

"He didn't want to talk on the phone. He sounded pretty stressed out."

"I can well appreciate that." Jonathan's reticence makes me very uneasy about this business with the S and M artist. "Call me after you've talked more fully with Jonathan. Tonight?"

"Can't—I'm off to the Slocan Valley to see this Dominique person."

"When you can."

I will leave this issue with my competent junior; I seem unable to focus upon it. Where is Margaret? What if she is wandering lost in the bowels of one of those underground downtown malls? Confused by the city, has she blundered into the seamier side of town? Or perhaps she has hired a taxi driver newly arrived from Uttar Pradesh and they are lost in the suburbs.

But lo, here she arrives, bearing many shopping bags. Pierre winks at me, then darts to her side, taking her bags, from one of which she retrieves a package.

I rise, and she leans and kisses me on the cheek. Uncle Arthur.

"I am Pierre Forget, your charming host. And you are the beautiful young lady Monsieur Beauchamp cannot stop talking about." He settles her into a chair. "Monsieur Beauchamp will have the lamb, and for the lady I recommend the salmon. It is exquisite. I will bring aperitifs." He bustles off.

Margaret opens her package and presents me with an illustrated T-shirt. "End the Rape," it shouts. A giant chain-cut fir is toppling.

"I had to buy it for you."

How lovely of her. "End the rape. I shall have to wear it in court."

"How did it go?"

"I was extremely put out. They threw some last-minute witnesses at us. We can't demand an adjournment or we'd risk losing a good judge."

"And are these new witnesses a big problem?"

"I'm not quite sure. My assistant will be interviewing one this week." I tell her of Dominique Lander's reputed role as O'Donnell's former partner, her expertise in "bondage and discipline," as she prefers to call it.

Margaret's eyes grow wide. "Tell me everything over the lamb and salmon."

But I am again remembering the dream in which I was tied and gagged and ravenous with desire. What might Dr. Freud make of it? Do I repress secret, sordid inclinations? Or is this trial too much with me? *Pain is but an aspect of love.*

Margaret studies the menu with seeming alarm. "These prices. Well, you're paying. I'm glad I'm old-fashioned about that."

"Would you like wine? You can always rely on the house Chardonnay."

"I'm not much of a drinker." She looks about this small, fussily decorated bistro. "We could never afford restaurants like this. Chris and me."

Even from our sixth-row orchestra seats I have difficulty concentrating upon the action of *Switch,* a plotless, pointless endeavour in which a few young people run about the set stumbling into each other as they answer phones and door chimes while talking in a kind of ribald sexual code I cannot decipher. For no reason I can fathom, people keep coming to the door, a Jehovah's Witness, a political canvasser, a Girl Guide with cookies.

But the brickbats I toss come from a minority of one. Even Margaret is joining in the laughter.

The Theatre Workshop is housed in one of those corrugated metal buildings on Granville Island—a style of architecture inspired perhaps by fish-processing plants—and the air-conditioning isn't working. We are at oven temperature on a broiling August afternoon. My problems of concentration arise not just from the heat but because Margaret has placed the palm of her right hand on the back of my left one, a moist, warm touching that makes me giddy and hints she is not offended by my company. My arm is hotly frozen; I cannot, dare not move that hand.

But can hers be more than a sisterly caring? Her husband was comfortably seated at our table at Chez Forget. She talked about him through the entrée and dessert. *He wasn't perfect, but he was the best man I'd ever known. Hell, he was the only one.*

How do I challenge a phantom to a duel over the heart of Margaret Blake?

The performers on stage have been waiting not for

Godot but for Kimberley Martin, who makes a late, loud entrance, all long legs and high boots, taking charge, impish and imperious. She lacks the polish of experience, but despite being trapped within this crude vehicle is charmingly deft and owns an instinctive sense of timing.

A backdrop rises, revealing a large hot tub on a platform. The actors begin languidly disrobing, and the curtain falls on the first act.

"I can't help laughing—it's really off the wall," Margaret says, and she removes her hand from mine.

As we rise to make our way out, I catch sight, near the back of the theatre, of Jonathan O'Donnell, slouching in his seat, looking glum. If he sees me, he pretends not to notice. This was his important afternoon engagement? Upon being confronted with the spectre of Dominique Lander, he attends the theatre? I am put out. His presence here might be taken to imply a morbid interest in his accuser. I will have a word with him when occasion allows.

Outside, we are encountered by the baleful scowls of picketers with their angrily scrawled reviews.

Margaret shakes her head. "There are so many *important* causes."

I can't get over the fact that Jonathan is here. What if Kimberley Martin notices him and informs Crown and jury? Will they conjure an image of a stalker and his victim? But thoughts of O'Donnell atomize into nothingness: Margaret takes my arm and urges me to stroll with her.

"I can't make head or tail of this play, Margaret. What theatrical purpose is served by all those characters coming to the door?"

"I think we're being asked to compare the moral corruption going on inside with the innocent world outside."

"Ah, yes, I see." Obviously there are levels of subtlety here that are beyond the simple workings of my mind.

Margaret studies one of the protesters, a stout woman in checked slacks whose face is aflame with makeup. "Do I look as silly as that when I'm off on one of *my* campaigns?"

Hardly. In fact, she looks incredibly beautiful at this moment. The sun is in her hair. Her lines have softened; there is something erotic about her stance, her hand on her hip, one leg thrust sideways.

"Your Kimberley is pretty sexy."

"She gets quite well into her role."

"Chris was into amateur theatre, did you know that?"

I light my pipe.

The last act is even more banal than the first, relieved only by the sight of Kimberley Martin in the full flower of her twenty-three years jumping naked from the hot tub, grabbing a towel, and running to answer yet another chiming of the door. This time it's the nosy neighbour.

Near the end, some suggestive moments occur in the hot tub that cause a matronly lady in the seat next to us to wriggle with what I assume is discomfort.

Our charter whisks us quickly back to Garibaldi, and I have Margaret at her doorstep at six p.m., as the shadows of evening are growing long. From behind her house come the squawk and baying of hungry animals. "I have to feed them. Would you like to come in and wait? We could have a coffee . . . or are you exhausted?"

I would like to come in and wait. But she is hinting I ought not to. She has many duties. She is giving Uncle Arthur an out. I must tell her I'm exhausted.

"It's been a full day."

"Oh. Well . . . I enjoyed myself a lot."

"As did I."

"Please come for dinner this weekend."

"I'd be most delighted."

I tell my feet that it is time to go. She smiles. I smile. She hugs me. We kiss clumsily, lips slightly misaligned, hers partly imbedded in my beard, but I taste the softness, the moistness of them, and suddenly I am overcome by unreasoning fear.

I run from her like a frantic cat.

In the morning, George Rimbold comes unannounced. He has observed I am pale, gaunt, distracted. It is time to go fishing. It is time to talk: there is a soul to be saved.

After we anchor out, I tell him the story of my swollen, captive heart. I tell him I am suffering a severe case of *amor proximi*: love of one's neighbour.

He smokes a joint. He keeps a straight face until I finish my soggy confessions.

"Please help me understand. You escorted the divine St. Margaret to a play so raunchy the authorities talk of closing it down. Clearly she was sexually stimulated by this play. Indeed, you poor man, she was dropping hints like they were going out of style. She invited you in to share her hearth and later—I have no doubt—her bed."

"George, it would hardly have gone that far."

"Nonsense, her kiss was a formal invitation to acts of passion. You have rejected the woman who has your heart in her clutches. You are possessed of the devil, my son. Repent at once."

"I was in fear, George. I am obsessed with failure."

"Oh, by all the saints . . . How do you know you'll fail if you don't try it? Arthur, you poor miserable creature, I really think you have simply persuaded yourself you're impotent. All those years of married depression, who can blame you for not getting it up? Maybe you learned to *expect* failure: fear of criticism, fear of desertion—sure and doesn't it all keep getting reinforced?"

"I have felt some urges, I must admit."

"At all events, do you think Margaret would not understand? We all take pleasure in the weakness in others, and women particularly enjoy weakness in men. They see it as a challenge. They cherish their role as healers."

"Three's a crowd, George. Chris Blake stands between us like some kind of . . . duenna."

"Oh, but can't you tell what she's doing? She's letting him go. She speaks of him only to purge pain pent up too long, to get rid of it finally, so she can make room for you."

I am heartened by this. But I tell him about my dreams, the recurring theme of bondage.

"Your dreams are what you fear; they are not what you are."

I think I am also in love with George, in that other, brotherly way. Suddenly I am disgusted with myself. I am snivelling about my self-centred heart to a friend who has deeper troubles, who yearns to fill the emptiness of his soul. I suddenly hunger to make communion with this priest.

"Maybe I should have a smoke of that."

"I'll roll you a fresh one."

But the pot affects me adversely. I become groggy, and we end our fishing trip early.

Later, however, resting on a hammock, I am enveloped in a fuzzy but not unpleasant fog. I read from *Paradise Lost* and find new and lovely meanings. I listen to the Mozart clarinet concerto as if for the first time. I make up speeches to the jury, none of which make sense. I do tai chi: Dance Like a Rainbow. Then I fall asleep in the late afternoon and dream of Margaret Blake climbing naked from a hot tub, running to the door to greet me, and Chris Blake is sitting in the tub, smiling.

Again, later, I have a faded memory of my phallus engorged while I slept, in full, tumescent pride.

৯৬

Dear Arthur,

I've just got back from the Slocan and am scratching this out by hand so I can get it Priority Post to you ASAP. I've given the original tape to my secretary to transcribe, but meanwhile I'm enclosing a copy fresh off my portable stereo. Make of Dominique Lander what you will.

Her studio is actually an old Bluebird bus beside her funky handbuilt-type-house on the Slocan River. She has a male partner who is a bit of an old-fashioned hippie, a lute-maker. It's very 1960s out there in the Slocan. Or something. Spooky, in a way.

Dominique is definitely into her own dark trip: a tendency to slinky black clothing, like she stepped right out of a Charles Addams cartoon, and predictably she paints with great gobs of depressing colours. She's very beautiful, in her witchy way. Pale. Doesn't go out in the sun a lot. She was really almost over-cooperative. At first.

But I have to finish setting the scene, Arthur. Over in the corner there was a stool, and some leather straps and kneepads on it, and a thin cane leaning against it. A little distracting, right? It put me off my form. I forgot to turn the tape on right away, but you won't miss much.

More, later, on Professor O'Donnell's reaction. Okay, play the tape and get back to this letter.

No, I don't mind at all. You can even plug it in if you like.

It has fresh batteries.

I want to help Jonathan. But I will not compromise the truth.

I won't ask you to. Okay, to go back—this detective's name was Mr. Sierra.

A nice little man with an accent. I think he comes from one of those Central American countries that are always at war.

And did he say whom he represented?

Well, as I told you, I assumed he was working for you. For the defence.

Did he *say* that?

He told me he was sworn to silence. But he . . . well, he was being very friendly. I'm sorry. I just thought he was there on Jonathan's behalf. I'm truly sorry about this.

And what did you tell him?

Well, he told me the case against Jonathan looked pretty bad, especially the business about tying up his student. He said it would be useful if the B and D could be explained somehow. He used that expression—"B and D," bondage and discipline—and I assumed he'd got it from Jonathan. And I thought about it. And I realized, yes, I should explain that Jonathan actually had a relationship where we did that regularly as part of our fucking. I thought it would be a good defence for him, proving what he did was a form of ritual play, that he wasn't actually attacking her. But now that you tell me it's only her word against his, I feel terrible. I wouldn't have lied—I could never lie—but I guess I could have said nothing.

Help me with this: you and Professor O'Donnell were into this . . . bondage and discipline?

Yes, I introduced him to it. We played around with different formulas until we found what he liked, which was the basic spanking of the buttocks. Sometimes he wanted to be the bottom and me the top. We often took turns. Have you ever tried it?

Doesn't somehow grab me.

Either you create or you're straight. Ever bite your lover? Everyone does that. Love slaps and bites and scratches. Even tickling—that can be excruciating.

Uh-huh.

No one gets damaged, God gave us ample padding. You only do it out of love, though. You punish what you love not what you hate.

You only hurt the one you love.

Love and pain are twin emotions.

This is getting a little strange, Dominique.

Try it the next time you fuck.

I'll take a rain check. Have you been served with a subpoena for the trial?

I've been told to expect one.

And do you intend to wait around for it?

You mean, what—go to the States for a few weeks? No, I couldn't do that. I will not hide. Anyway, don't you think I should discuss B and D with your jury? To help them understand?

I don't think it can help Jonathan. You said in your written statement you used to paint each other's bodies. What was that about?

He liked to colour my nipples. I covered him once in coral snakes and painted a serpent's head on his cock. We worshipped each other's bodies, why should we not make them more beautiful? Some people wear costumes, some like leather, some like rubber. I like skin. We didn't wear anything.

You introduced him to B and D?

Yes.

And you initiated these sessions?

Usually.

Did he seem to enjoy them?

Of course. And it made for better fucking. He had a problem with shooting off too fast; the playing kept his prick stiff. It spun things out. You know how it is.

I hear you. What else went on?

We played different games, guard and prisoner, master and slave, things like that; sometimes I'd scream a little.

But he began to tire of these games, didn't he?

I wouldn't agree.

You and he had talked of marriage, hadn't you?

Yes, we had a talk.

You actually proposed to him.

I'm a very direct person.

And he declined the offer.

I assume that's what he's told you.

And that's when he began to draw away from you. He began dating other women. . . . Are you able to respond to that? You and he broke up with all sorts of recriminations, isn't that so?

Is that his version?

Is it true?

He was seeing them behind my back. It's one thing I won't stand for. Disloyalty.

Do you feel vengeful?

That's insulting.

I'm sorry. By the way, did Mr. Sierra make you any offers of money?

My expenses.

How much?

This interview is at an end.

Sorry, Arthur, I kind of blew it there. My questions got too loaded.

I think she knew all along Sierra was working for the other side. Even if she's capable of love, I don't think she loves Jon O'Donnell—she wants to get him. I forgot to mention, earlier she was going on about how she was just scraping by, the whole starving-artist thing. Jon O'Donnell told me she was always talking about money and marriage, that she considered him a kind of lifetime arts grant. Obviously she's interested in getting some moolah out of this. I wonder how much her "expenses" are.

Okay, the bad news is she did involve him in what he prefers to call sexual "experimenting," but it was nothing as extensive as Dominique describes. More to please her than anything, he says. The novelty faded—it all got too outlandish for him. He says he's sick to death at having kept Dominique a secret from us—he was hoping she had somehow disappeared from the face of the earth. Of course, he's terrified to tell you.

I wish I knew what to do about her.

Augustina

                         ⚘

It is the last Friday of August, the beginning of a last, lost, hazy weekend before a trial begins for which I feel ill prepared. Oh, I have read the briefs of law prepared by my junior, a woman of inestimable value. And today I am rereading the transcripts, scrawling marginalia upon them, reminders of points to be made. But I lack even an inchoate sense of how I am to defend this case. I cannot put Jonathan on the witness stand—for fear he will hang himself with his own tongue. I must somehow unmake the Crown's case, pick away at it until it crumbles.

But is my heart in it? Why does this chronic prevaricator even deserve a defence? Is he also lying about one final, fundamental matter? My belief in his cause has eroded with the housekeeper's report of screams from next door and with Dominique Lander's sinful revelations, an account of which has just been mailed to me by Augustina. (Also at the general store was a cheery postcard from Annabelle in Bayreuth, where, Mr. Makepeace informed me, her friend Mr. Roehlig "is working as a conductor on *The Flying Dutchman*.")

I may make some hay with this devotee of the learned discipline of pain, but the jury will still be left pondering the Honourable Jonathan's predilection for unnatural forms of Hogarthian lust. They will ask: What in the world was he doing with such a woman if he's not perverted himself? I wonder that myself. We must strive to keep this dangerous abstract artist off the stand.

But in what shape am I to take on this cyclopean monster of a trial? I have occasionally won verdicts when drunk in court—but never on the dreamy lotus leaves of love. Sleepless are my nights, for as soon as I lay down my work, I am buzzing with Margaret. To help me through this time, I have been smoking marijuana from the small supply that George Rimbold gave me. There's something to it after all—it relaxes me, but also helps me focus on my work.

In the evenings, stoned in my club chair, I write corny poems to her. I go for long, lonely walks, mumbling lines from Virgil and Catullus. "What a woman says to her ardent lover should be written in wind and running water. I am love's victim." *Amor proximi.*

Outside, the hammers of Stoney and Dog go tap-tap-TAP. Tap-tap-TAP. Stoney has the radio on in his dilapidated flatbed truck, from which issue commercials, weather reports, jangling rock and roll. I am unable to absorb any more of the testimony of the fumbling Constable Gavin Peake, the blunt Dr. Sanchez. I lay pen and transcript down. Another walk on the beach is in order. Or shall I go tripping through the woods this time on fairy feet?

Good news, said the weatherman. Rain is on the way. The air is musty, prickly, still; cumulus clouds are moving up from the south, scouts for the troops of thunderheads massing at the horizon. I wander into the fir grove and bear not right to the fence of Margaret Blake—my mind seeks peace not turmoil—but left onto the trail Stoney has tramped through my upper meadow, the shortcut to his home and car lot.

Here a smaller trail veers off, a deer path down a recess into an alder bottom, a little hidden dingle I must one day explore—a prospective site for that second orchard I've been planning. As I emerge onto Potter's Road I notice tire tracks leading into the bushes: behind them, a bulky shape, metallic. Closer inspection reveals an RCMP four-wheel van. Potter's Road hardly seems a prime location for a speed trap, and there is no sign of the driver. Nor are homes nearby where he might be visiting. Curious.

I walk a mile or so up the road, then turn back. The police vehicle is still there. I go down the trail again and stop to inspect the deer path more closely: here is not a hoof print but a boot print, and a discarded butt. I work my way down into the little valley. Why is this soil disturbed—and over there, why have those alder saplings been cut down to form a clearing. . . .

Comprehension bathes me in its harsh, incandescent light.

Bob Stonewell, alias Stoney, is practising unlicensed horticulture on my land, doubtless assisted by his henchman, Dog. I recall Stoney's arrogant vaunt after being acquitted last month for a similar crime: *This year my grow ain't on the property. They'll never find it.*

Closer inspection reveals about a dozen three-foot-tall cannabis plants, their branches adorned with illegal clumps of tiny, hairy, sticky leaves. Why am I always taken in by Stoney? Am I so gullible? Well, he is in trouble now, because this small garden of delights has obviously been discovered by the local mountie. No sign of him, however.

I lean down to one of the plants. So this is the magical source of those blurry, pleasant moments I have recently enjoyed. A robust, merry little tree. So sorry to see you go. I fondle one of the hairy clumps and put it to my nose to seek its intoxicating perfume, but I am suddenly aware of a stirring in the salal bushes nearby.

Constable Horace Pound rises from his leafy spying post and walks heavy-footed towards me, clutching a small camera.

"Why, it's Constable Pound. But this isn't the second Tuesday of the month."

"I'm doing this on my own time. You know what's growing here, Mr. Beauchamp? Oh, just a minute, you have the right to remain silent and anything you say may be used as evidence, and you have the right to a lawyer. And the first thing I should ask is do you admit you own this property?"

I smile, enjoying his dry sense of humour: he is having a joke on me. But do I not recall that this fellow is somewhat lacking in wit? He brings out his pad and makes some notes. *I then proceeded to approach the male individual who I found crouching behind a small green plant which I identify as Cannabis sativa.*

"Constable, how long have you been sitting out here?"

"Long enough to see what I saw."

"And what was that?"

"You tending these plants, Mr. Beauchamp. I note for the record there is a bag of WonderGrow fertilizer right over there." He takes a photograph of it, and another of the path to my house.

"And how many weeks have you been doing this?"

"I've been coming here on my days off. Waiting until I can catch the perp in the act."

Stung by Stoney's acquittal, this proud officer has

been assiduously seeking revenge, checking for hidden garden sites near Stoney's land.

"You are a patient man, but not patient enough. You have caught the wrong perp. You know perfectly well that I just stumbled onto these plants."

"You were in personal contact with one of the plants, sir. You held it up to your nose in an act of smelling."

Constable Pound obviously knows he has collared the wrong party. But I fear his long vigils have frustrated him: any perp will do. I hunger to play the common fink, to squeal on the malefactor whose hammer I distantly hear. Tap-tap-TAP. Is that what Pound wants me to do—to cooperate, to roll over for him? This is laughable.

"And do you have a warrant to be on this property?"

I am not particularly elated to find that he does. He shows it to me, and it seems in proper form.

"Do you mind if I check through your house?"

For several seconds I am as silent as guilt. I think of the stash Rimbold left with me. Hidden with the cookies in a twist-top tin container in the fridge. But surely the officer is merely hoping to turn the screws, to encourage me to turn Crown's evidence. I will devise my own unique form of justice for that sorcerer's apprentice Stoney—though I would love to rat on him, to tattle the tale of his many strolls up the path just photographed.

"Of course not," I finally say, finding inner wells of heartiness. He will see Stoney working on the garage. His attention will be diverted and I will have a chance to stash my stash. "Get your vehicle, come by, and we will have tea."

His look is heavy with suspicion. "We'll walk there together if you don't mind, sir." Perhaps he thinks I intend to uproot the evidence and scurry off with it.

When we emerge into my yard, he turns and takes a

picture of the trail we have just exited. I look for Stoney, but he is hidden behind a tree. Dog, however, is sitting on the apex of the roof and peering in our direction. All hammering suddenly stops: just the tinny sound of music from the truck's radio.

Pound turns and takes pictures of the house and garage, but too late to capture Dog, who has already descended from the roof.

As we recommence our journey, I hear an engine ignite and rumble into life. Stoney's creaky flatbed two-ton truck comes into view, Dog at the wheel and beside him, cap slid down almost to his nose, a slouching Stoney. The truck chugs quickly up my driveway and with a roar of acceleration escapes down Potter's Road.

Pound stops in his tracks, uncertain now of his next move. "Who were the individuals in that vehicle?"

"Ah, yes, that would be my work crew."

Constable Pound will get the hint and chase after the perps while the trail is fresh. But he just stands there. The skin on his face seems to tighten, and he takes on the frantic look of a man helpless in the grip of a dilemma. Now he looks at me with a raw hostility, sizing me up, seeking potential for revenge. I can see he wants to blame someone other than himself for the bungling of Operation Stonewell.

And abruptly he turns and races to my back door, entering the house half a minute ahead of me. Aghast, I find him in the kitchen, hurriedly looking through the spice racks, examining a container of oregano, pouring out a sample onto his hand, smelling it. He runs his hands over sills and peeks under teacups, his frenetic search progressing ever closer to the refrigerator.

But of course this coming calamity was foretold; long ago I knew that wherever Stoney goes he lays down a trail of land mines. To have befriended him is to have accepted his curse. I muster in my mind the various defences in law: lack of intent, alibi, automatism, insanity. These will be available, too, upon the charge of murdering Stoney.

Now Margaret Blake's half-ton pickup rolls into the driveway, braking hard near the open kitchen door. She sees me and steps out. "Arthur, I just drove by Stoney's truck; it was parked off the road, and there was a police vehicle in the bushes. I was worried there'd been an accident." Now she enters, and spies the constable crouching at the open fridge door, suddenly immobile, as if frozen into place. "Oh, it's Constable Pound. . . ."

"Ma'am, what did you just say?"

"I said I thought there'd been an accident. Are you hungry? What *are* you doing in the fridge?"

"*Whose* truck was beside my unit?"

"Stoney's."

Constable Pound is faster than a speeding bullet out the door, and runs pell-mell up the path leading to the marijuana plants.

"What *has* been going on, Arthur?"

In partial explanation I pull out the cookie tin and show Margaret the contents: twelve home-baked peanut butter cookies and a plastic bag containing some cannabis cigarettes.

"Not very clever," she says. "Never hide your stash with your homemade cookies. What a character you are. Have you been smoking this?"

"I'm afraid Rimbold turned me on."

The bells of her laughter. "I'll hold onto it in case he comes back." And she finds a better stash, unbuttoning her shirt-top and tucking the pot into the cup between bra and breast. I glimpse a seductive roundness, a flash of untanned flesh. When she catches me staring I blush.

"I always used to get dizzy when I smoked this. Chris liked to get stoned, though."

"Ah, yes. What should I bring for dinner tomorrow?"

"Just yourself."

But will she set the usual three places?

I am alone, doing tai chi warm-ups (Flying Dove Spreads Its Wings), as Constable Pound returns—on foot and in a mood of dejection. He apologizes for his uncivil behaviour earlier. He asks me if he might use my phone to call the local garage: there's a problem with his ignition. The perps, he tells me, have absconded with the evidence. He seeks to know whether I shall be expecting Stoney to return to work today. I tell him I doubt it.

He asks me if I mind keeping this quiet. He doesn't want it reported in the *Echo*.

A hectic Saturday, as I put my little farm to bed for the next two weeks. Early in the morning, the girls from Mop'n'Chop show up to clean my house and receive instructions about the garden, though the drenching rain of last night ought to keep it green, and a grey, lowering sky promises more.

My garage may still not be roofed in by the time I return. Janey Rosekeeper and Ginger Jones think they know where Stoney and Dog are hiding, and will pass on two items of free legal advice: one, say nothing; two, finish the roof before the rains of autumn come.

As the girls work, I prepare a small breakfast: a slice of toast, lightly coated with locally produced marmalade. It is all I can handle. I have a poor appetite these days, and I fear my city suits will hang upon me like beach umbrellas.

As I nibble my toast, Hubbell Meyerson phones from the office to worry me with questions about how well prepared I am. He hints that O'Donnell's "defence team" would feel more comfortable if I spent the weekend in Vancouver working with them.

"Gowan and I are going over the jury list now, weeding out feminists and fundamentalist preachers."

I ask Hubbell to pick up my suits at the dry cleaners and bring them to the office. I remind him I will be homeless in Vancouver, but he has already booked a suite in the Hotel Vancouver. He tells me—by the way—that my divorce is set for early this fall.

After we disconnect, I munch toast and remember Annabelle, happy in the hills of Northern Bavaria, half a world away. This woman who for so long held dominion over me has been nudged from the stage, has slipped through the cracks of my mind.

Was I truly in love with Annabelle or was it only a false sentiment, dutifully felt as a part of the baggage of marriage? Ah, yes, the bonds of matrimony. I grieve at all those wasted years.

I can hear Ginger and Janey gossiping over the noise of the vacuum cleaner. They are talking about who is doing it with whom. I think of doing it with Margaret. I try to picture it, but the scene that plays out in my mind seems graceless, a Chaplinesque farce.

But George Rimbold interrupts these crude ruminations. He is at the door with a salmon.

"The coho are running, my son. This fat fellow was disgorged by the seas only this morning. Five pounds easy."

"I am overcome with envy."

He lays the gleaming, sticky fish atop my kitchen counter. "May I offer you and Margaret this pre-wedding gift."

"We haven't quite planned a date, George."

"Are you not her guest for dinner then? I am providing the main course."

"Then you'll join us."

"Oh, I will not do that. No, I see this as a decisive time in your relationship. You are going off to the wars. She will want to give her soldier something to remember her by."

Savouring his role as mischievous Cupid, George seems almost happier than I have ever seen him. I sense this man of lost religion has managed to come strongly to terms with himself: there is no faith, perhaps, but there are fish.

He stays for coffee, and laughs with knee-slapping glee at my recounting of the close call yesterday over his previous gift to me. Then he retrieves his salmon and trots over to Margaret Blake's house.

The telephone rings again.

"We're back. Thought I'd bug you, find out all the poop."

"Ah, Deborah, safely home from Rome."

"Yeah. Back to work on Monday. And I've got to get one weary world traveller enrolled in Grade Three."

"I can give you the poop next week—I'm coming to Vancouver for the O'Donnell trial."

She insists that tomorrow, Sunday, I stay the night with her and the Nicks before trundling off to my hotel.

"I'd enjoy that."

"How's your life?"

"Rather intense right now."

"How's the widow Blake?"

"We are continuing to mend fences."

"Sounds torrid. Love you, Dad."

I will see the widow Blake tonight, but then not for several days. Could it be possible, I wonder, to finish this trial in a week? And be back for Labour Day. Join her at that most glittering gala of the Garibaldi social scene, the annual fall fair, barbecue, and dance. But if the trial is not wound up by then, I fear I will be too caught up in it to return; I will be drowning in it, unable to come to the surface for a breath of fresh country air.

The girls are finished; the house is gleaming. I pay them extra, and also let them keep the prince's ransom in change Janey found tucked behind the cushions of my club chair.

Another phone call. Gowan Cleaver this time.

"You'll be working against a bummed-out prosecutor, Arthur. I just beat Pat Blueman yesterday on a bank heist. My guy had an alibi as tight as a popcorn fart."

"Congratulations."

"Okay, the jury: we've managed to whittle the list down to about twenty hopefuls. I'm working on the assumption you want a female or two in there for balance, so we've got a couple of housewives, but no self-made women except for one beauty-shop owner—one of the senior partner's wives gets done by her something like ten times a week. There's a guy who's an interior decorator living in the West End, so he's probably gay, and I think we want gay. No Orientals, of course, too law and order. There's one lady you don't want. Hedy Jackson-Blyth, she's the executive director of the Telephone Workers' Fed, active in the women's coalition, vocally pro-choice."

"But she sounds very liberal."

"Not on this issue."

The phone again summons me as I emerge dripping and grumpy from the shower—Cleaver's cynical approach to jury selection has been grating on me—and I take the call in the kitchen as I towel off. I apologize to Augustina for answering with so brusque a voice.

"What are you up to, Arthur?"

"I've been manning a switchboard. Now I'm preparing to go out for dinner."

"Then I'll be brief. Patricia gave me her list of witnesses. She'll be starting right off the bat with Kimberley Martin. Do you want me to make the opening legal arguments? I have all the cases."

"Yes, relieve me of that agony."

"I hope this isn't a problem, but we can't locate Professor O'Donnell. He's supposed to be here helping us prep. I hope he hasn't fallen off the wagon."

Yes, this has been a constant worry: might he succumb to the demons of alcohol as his day of reckoning draws closer? If he breaks under the tension, he also breaks his vow to me, and I have half a mind to leave him in the lurch.

"Send a posse out to find him. I'll be arriving tomorrow in the afternoon."

"Shall I pick you up on this side?"

"Thank you, but I'll be driving in."

"Who are you having dinner with, as if I didn't know? Make sure you bring her flowers."

"But she has a myriad of flowers."

"Bring her flowers."

I dress. I fasten my suspenders, snap them for good luck. I emerge from my house with knocking knees. From my garden, I gather nasturtiums and cornflowers and zinnias, a floral potpourri that clearly lacks an arranger's fussy touch, but makes up for that in sheer size and variety.

I aim myself in the direction of Margaret Blake's house. I march purposely forward.

§§

I'll not disturb you, darling. I'll be reading. Call me if you want coffee or anything.

Thank you, Penny.

The meal was delicious, Mrs. Kropinski.

Thank you, dear.

Please be comfortable, Kimberley. Would you like to lie down on that divan?

So this is your little office-in-home? Comfortable. You've nice taste.

About taste, I do not know. Penny has the taste.

I'm not sure if this hypnotism stuff is going to

work. Trial starting Monday—I'm pretty tense. I'll try.

Fine. And now I want you to unburden yourself. Tell me some of the things that are worrying you.

Oh, Remy has a big catastrophe happening in Guyana, some kind of reagent with cyanide spilled at a gold mine, and it's completely poisoned a river. Remy is going nuts. And, oh, God, Mother is threatening to fly out from Labrador for the trial—I told her no, definitely not. It would be *so* embarrassing. I've always been her good little girl. . . . And what else? I've been getting these *lusts*.

Lusts?

Yeah, I don't know why, maybe Remy isn't . . . Well, he's a little distracted, I guess. I mean, I *like* sex—I think it's healthy. Of course as soon as I say that, here comes the guilt again. Punish me, Father, give me ten Hail Marys. God, *I'm* a masochist. Growing up Catholic you learn to love pain. I was never weaned from Sunday school. . . .

You are frowning. Some thought has struck you?

Yeah, but, I don't know—it just went.

Sunday school . . .

Oh, hey, I found out O'Donnell's seeing a psychiatrist, too.

How did you learn that?

Remy said one of the detectives told him. Do you know a Dr. Jane Dix?

Quite well. For him, a very odd choice.

Why?

She is very active on women's issues.

Hmm. I guess you get the therapist you deserve. Well, maybe she's what he *needs*. She must be having a lot of fun with *his* screwed-up head. His latest addiction is jogging, according to Remy's informed sources. What's the psychological explanation for *that*? Fear, right? He's a scared rabbit. Oh, I'm back with Remy, now, living at his place. He came *crawling.* Oo, that felt good. Apologized for being upset over the play, promised to be more support- ive. He *should,* after all, he's the one who pushed me into this.

How do you mean?

I'm not sure if I would have laid charges. . . . I'm not sure. Remy was all gung-ho.

Are you feeling more relaxed now?

Yeah, I think I'm exhausted from talking.

I am going to move over here. I will just plug this in behind you—

Comfortable?

Yes.

Please let all your muscles go limp, yes? Your whole body. All the tension is gone. Your mind is relaxed. Do not concentrate on anything; just listen to my voice.

Whoo, I feel funny already. Okay, I put myself completely in your hands.

We are doing this together. Cooperation, yes? Not control.

Okay.

I want you to think of sleep now. Think only that one thought. Breathe deeply. Yes, you are be- coming tired, and your eyes are heavy . . . your whole head is heavy, your eyelids are heavy . . . you are perfectly comfortable and you are so drowsy, and you are going to close your eyelids. Your eyes, they are closing, they are closing now, and you are going into a deep sleep, and you will stay fast asleep until I tell you to wake up, yes? I am going to count to ten, and when I reach ten you will take a deep breath and fall completely asleep. But also you will hear my voice. When I speak to you, you will be able to hear. Your eyes feel so-o-o heavy. You are completely relaxed. One, two, three, four, five, six, seven, eight, nine, ten. Take a deep breath. Do you hear me?

Yes.

You may open your eyes if you like.

Okay.

How old are you, Kimberley?

Twenty-three.

Do you remember when you were a little girl?

Yes.

Do you remember what you wanted to be when you grew up?

An actress. I liked to play dress-up.

Now I want you to go back to your childhood, yes? To a time when you are a little girl playing dress-up.

Yes.

How old are you now?

Nine years old. Soon I'll be ten.

Does it make you happy to play dress-up?

Yes, and my mummy lets me play with all her old clothes.

What else do you like to do?

I play with my friends. And I have a little sister, Kelly, and I look after her. And I have a dog named Morgan. And I like school very much. I have puppets, too, Mummy and Daddy gave them to me at Christmas.

Do you remember a time when you were not so happy?

No, I'm a happy girl. Mummy and Daddy say I'm a good girl, too.

Now go back in time, yes? Go back to when you are a little younger and you are not so happy. You are at a time when you are sad.

Yes.

Why are you sad?

Mummy's mad at me.

Why?

Because I don't want to go to Sunday school.

And why don't you want to go?

I don't know. I'm afraid.

Tell me what you are afraid of, Kimberley.

I don't know. I don't know.

How old are you?

I'm eight.

Let us go together to your Sunday school. I will be with you. Let us go back to the week before. What is happening at Sunday school?

I don't want to go there.

Why?

It hurts.

What hurts? . . . Kimberley, what hurts? Do not be afraid.

He hurt me.

I am sorry, I did not hear you so well.

He hurt me so bad.

Who hurt you?

The man that lives near the Sunday school.

Did the man do something?

Dr. Kropinski . . .

It is okay, my dear, I am close by you.

Mummy and Daddy told me not to speak to strangers, and I did, and it's a mortal sin.

Do not be afraid, Kimberley. Tell me what he did.

He said he wanted to show me his bunny rabbits, he has some baby rabbits, and I can see them in a cage, and . . . I'm afraid.

Here. I am holding your hand.

And he pushed me into his shed, and pushed me against the wall, and he has his hand over my mouth and he's dirty and smelly, and . . . and . . . he pulled my pants down and put his thing in me, in my bum, and it hurt so bad. And, and my dress is all dirty, and he called me a little tramp, and he is going to kill me and kill my mummy and daddy if I tell anyone, and I ran, and I fell into a ditch, and got all muddy, and I ran home, and I didn't tell Mummy, I said I fell into a ditch.

Why do you not tell your mother what happened?

'Cause . . . 'cause I don't know.

You do not know?

I stopped 'membering.

You stopped remembering.

Only that I fell.

That is all that you recalled afterwards, yes? But you remember now.

Yes.

You remember that man.

I don't want to, but I 'member.

But it is all over, yes? It is a long time ago and it is all over. You are not afraid any more, are you, Kimberley?

Yes, I am. I'm so scared.

I am going to bring you back now, yes? When I count to three you will wake up. When you wake up, you will remember about the man who hurt you. Do you understand?

Yes.

One, two, three.

Oh, God.

Oh, goodness.

Oh, oh.

Penny, Penny, quick . . . Bring a towel and a basin. . . .

§§

Margaret is sitting on her front veranda, bare-armed and willowy in a light Indian-print dress. One of her pet geese hisses and sticks its tongue out at me as I approach, then stalks off, haughty and disgusted. Margaret smiles, encouraging me to come forward, but my body has stalled five feet from her stoop, my knees locked in sudden dread—she will think I'm a silly oaf when I present my posies from behind my back. Worse, these were living things; I have damaged the environment, clear-cut my flower beds.

"What have you got there?"

I grin lamely, move towards her and lay them in her arms. "For thee the wonder-working earth puts forth sweet flowers."

For a moment she looks critically at my haphazard bouquet, then reaches up and kisses me lightly on the cheek. "How lovely." The soft bells of her voice.

I sit next to her. A few tendrils of delicious smoke drift from the side yard, where Rimbold's coho salmon is resting on a grill in Margaret's brick charcoal stove.

She stares at my flowers, suddenly thoughtful. Please, please, do not tell me that Chris used to give you flowers.

But she says nothing. I am urged to make mindless chatter, to break this logjam of silence. "That opening line came from Lucretius. I must admit to having practised it in front of a mirror before coming over."

She smiles again. "Well, it got the effect it deserves."

This seems ambiguous. Stuffy, donnish Beauchamp has created a classically pompous beginning to the evening. But he cannot control his maundering tongue. "Lucretius was a great philosopher as well as a poet. He is said to have taken a love potion that made him go mad. He took his own advice: 'Embrace, thou fool, a rest that knows no care.' Committed suicide." I am dying like Lucretius, dying standing up; the audience is restless. Old Uncle Arthur, spouting on and on.

"Latin poetry seems awfully appropriate. Have a bloodless Caesar."

She stirs the contents of a pitcher with a celery stalk

and pours a glass for me. I am dry of mouth, and take a big sip. "Tastes like the real thing."

"We'll pretend." She sniffs the flowers, then rises. "I'll find these some water, and check on the fish."

At seven o'clock, the sun, all day confined behind a gloomy shroud, descends to the Pacific Ocean. Ducks waddle among grazing sheep. A rooster crows, confused by the twilight. This Elysian scene should relax me, but I'm too keyed up: as much by an impending major trial as by the fearsome chore of wooing Margaret. Dare I make a formal announcement tonight? *Margaret, my dear, I wonder if I may be allowed to speak of certain matters of the heart.* Oh, pompous Beauchamp, fan your aging embers, find some fire.

I would give my right arm for a very dry martini. . . .

"I guess I've been saving up for this," I say apologetically, spearing the last fresh baby potato. Rimbold's gift is nearly skeletonized. I have been utterly tedious with my vapid encomia of Margaret's exquisite table. My recent loss of appetite, I realize, had as much to do with my own inept cooking as with being lovesick.

Our only light comes from two bulky candles on the dining-room table. This is the way it was, Margaret tells me, in the old days, before the island had power.

"I think of it as a more romantic time," she says, "living without light bulbs."

I feel a twinge of pain. She is thinking about Chris.

Over salad, Margaret tells me she has decided to announce her candidacy for island trustee this fall.

"You'll win in a walk. Kurt Zoller seems vulnerable."

"I don't know. When Chris was trustee, there seemed so much work."

He is at the table, the Banquo of Garibaldi Island.

"You should get all his vote. He's well remembered."

"Mostly by me—I think that's what you mean."

"I wish I had such happy memories."

Out of the blue, aghast to find myself doing so, I begin talking about my own marriage. It is a topic I'd shied away from during our innocent trysts at the fence, uncomfortable with those pathetic twin images of cuckoldom and impotence.

But here I am spouting a self-indulgent history of innocence betrayed, of tearful confession, of breakup, of reconciliation. Of alcoholism. And Annabelle's continuing parade of squalid affairs to which I was so willfully blind—denying the scent of other men's salt and sex upon her.

Margaret's eyes are riveted to mine. Perhaps she has been waiting for me to reveal my inner turmoil, to return in kind what she has so generously given me: her own past, her own marriage.

"For all those years I refused to accept the truth. But her affairs had been going on not so much behind my back as almost in front of my nose—they must have been notorious, the subject of locker-room ribaldry."

"I guess you didn't want to know."

"I think I didn't want to admit to myself that I was the cause of her philandering."

Margaret waits, silently demanding clarification.

"I suppose I was no great shakes as a lover."

Margaret now stands up, quietly gathering the spent plates. I have a feeling she is about to announce the evening is at an end; she is repulsed by my whining confessions.

"Let's take coffee and dessert in the living room," she says. "You can smoke inside if you make a fire." She is blunt, businesslike, and I worry that I am on my way to a ruined evening. Her cat gets up from the rug, sniffs dismissively at my socks, and follows Margaret to the kitchen.

As I walk into the living room I am confronted for an agonizing moment by the poster that reads L-O-V-E. I lower myself onto my knees as if in prayer before the old stone fireplace: no newspaper starter here except a few old *Island Echoes,* and it seems a desecration to burn collectors' items. These cedar shavings and kindling will do.

But the fire is slow to catch, and when Margaret joins me I am still bent to my task. She kneels beside me, placing a tray on the hearth with mugs of coffee and dishes of apple crumble.

"Doesn't want to burn," I say. What kind of man is this? He can't light a fire in either hearth or heart.

"Wood's a little damp." She refrains from taking charge, though I suspect it is her instinct to do so. Has she set me this task as a test of manhood? She is frowning, as if in inner debate. She seems stiff with me, uncomfortable.

"Why do you say you were no great shakes as a lover?"

Bluntness reigns. I pause in my labours. I must tell her I am impotent and be done with it.

I hedge: "Frankly, I couldn't keep up with her in bed."

A flame flickers, a splint of cedar catches, then dies.

"Did you think you were at fault?"

"I must have been."

"Must be godawful to be a man. All that social conditioning. Did you ever think Annabelle might have had an *unhealthy* appetite for sex?"

"I don't know what the standard of comparison is." I add more sticks to my recalcitrant fire: its impotence seems too apt a metaphor for my own. I laugh softly, though at myself.

"I'd say *her* standards were pretty low. I'm sorry if that sounds nasty, but that's how I feel."

She is giving me licence to let go, to unlock, to open the gates of anger. And a few months ago I might have done so, but I realize there is no steam left to blow; all that repressed fury with which I arrived on Garibaldi Island has somehow dissipated and, like this fire, flickers only feebly.

"She gave me my freedom. I hope she is happy with her new lover."

Margaret sips her coffee, but keeps her penetrating grey eyes fixed to mine, digging in, excavating for hidden information. "It sounds as if you were too much in love with her, Arthur."

"Well, actually . . . no."

"No?"

"I thought I was in love. It was something else. My daughter calls it masochism."

"What do you call it?"

"Masochism."

"Oh, come, Arthur. You're so hard on yourself." She frowns. "Don't tell me you've never been in love."

"Not until now."

There is dead silence. She is looking at me with what I perceive to be utter astonishment. Good old Uncle Arthur, the wise adviser from next door, has made a social blunder of astronomic magnitude.

"What do you mean?"

"I am in love now. With you."

She slowly puts down her coffee. I frantically return to my fire, busy myself by constructing a funeral pyre of cedar sticks and twigs. I apply a match. I pray to Vesta, life-giver, goddess of fire and the family hearth. I have just confessed my innermost feelings: do I not have the right to a reaction?

"I think it's catching."

What is? Yes, the fire. Flames leap up.

I find the strength to turn to her. She is sitting, hugging her knees. Why is she smiling? Does she find this so excruciatingly funny?

She takes one of my hands. Her expression is kindly: she will let me down as gently as she can. "You're so damn *shy*. That was such a lovely bouquet. A little scrambled up, though. You'll never be a flower arranger. I wanted to laugh."

And she does laugh now, those tolling bells. I don't know what to make of this laughter. I listen to the fire spit and crackle. I am confused.

"They were lovely, really. I'm an old-fashioned romantic. Give me flowers every time."

She seems to be taking the situation very well, and this has taken the edge off my embarrassment.

She continues to hold my hand. "Arthur, I don't know what to say. I'm just not experienced at this sort of thing. I have to work it through. I mean, I like you a *lot*. Okay?"

A lot. Yes, that will do.

"Remember our stupid little trial? When you burst into laughter at the end of it, I realized there was a great, warm-hearted man hiding behind . . . well, a stuffed shirt, that's what I thought. I've liked you ever since. You've grown on me. Not maybe to the point that, um, you'd like." A long pause, then she utters one simple thrilling word: "Yet."

I am borne away on a magic carpet of hope. More wondrous yet, she kisses me lightly on the lips. "I need some time," she says. "Boy, I'm feeling really flustered."

Still afloat, I am only distantly aware of a sound of a car engine, Margaret's dog barking.

"Oh, perfect," Margaret says, rising, straightening her skirt.

I sit up, blinking. *Amor interruptus*. I am in a fog. Maybe this is not real: I am in a scene from *Switch*, where people keep coming inopportunely to the door. In this case, however, the visitor is at the window. From the flickering light of the fire, I make out a pair of greedy, beady eyes behind the pane. They quickly disappear as the house lights go on, and I hear a high male voice, the cordial nasal whine of Nelson Forbish. The press has arrived to cover this evening's events. Or he's snooping for news not fit to print.

I scramble to my feet too quickly, and suddenly feel quite woozy and out of breath, and I think: Oh, no, not now, not another stroke, and I reach out an arm and clutch the fireplace mantel.

Then it passes. It wasn't my heart, just the sudden lack of oxygen one suffers when standing too quickly.

I'm fine. I'm fine.

Forbish has somehow managed to invite himself in, and as I am settling into a chair by the fire, lighting my pipe, he balloons into view in the dining room, where he pauses to sniff at the leavings of our dinner as might a foraging dog.

"We've just finished eating," says Margaret, who emerges from behind him, making a face at me, miming horror. "But there's some extra dessert. I made a panful of apple crumble."

"Thanks, but I just ate myself," Forbish says. "Maybe one. To be sociable."

"One was what I planned to offer you, Nelson."

Forbish has doffed his porkpie, and fiddles with the rim. "Sorry to interrupt your nice evening and all, Mr. Beauchamp, but I was looking all over for you. Your phone was busy all day, so I checked your place, figured you were over here even though the lights were all off—"

"To the point, Nelson." I am struggling to try to remain solemn.

"I was wondering if you could give me a lift into Vancouver tomorrow. I have to do a run for supplies."

"I don't see why not. I'm taking my truck. I have recently had it made street legal. I have plenty of room."

"You'll need it," says Margaret, who is also working hard to keep a straight face. She hands Forbish his dessert on a paper plate, a hint her gift of apple crumble is intended as take-out food. But he stands his ground.

"So what's up with you folks?" he asks. "I see you're having an intimate evening. Together."

"We've been having a strategy session," I say. "Margaret will be running for trustee this fall. I am managing the campaign."

"Maybe I should do an interview."

"Some time later, Nelson, not now."

"Mm, that's good, even without ice cream. Should be an interesting trial, hey, Mr. Beauchamp?"

"Feel free to attend, if you have the stomach for it."

"And he has," Margaret says. She starts laughing, then claps a hand over her mouth.

Poor Forbish looks hurt. "I can't, I got too many things on my plate." But that plate has long been empty. "That was mighty delicious apple crumble, even though you make fat jokes at my expense. Fair enough, but I'm a big eater and that makes me an expert. I've sat at a lot of tables on this island, and I can honestly say yours is the best."

"Just the best on Garibaldi, Nelson?"

"My newspaper may want to endorse your candidacy."

"God, Nelson, take another piece and get out of here."

Forbish, giggling, plucks another handsome helping from the pan.

Margaret remains helpless with laughter awhile after he leaves. "Yes," she says, "one of those treasured moments."

We return to our fire, to our coffees and our own abandoned desserts. I natter on about my past: life before Garibaldi. I think of it now as a little life, narrow, reclusive, focused on my dreary work as defender of the base, the corrupt, the craven. I bring Margaret up to date on the O'Donnell case, a subject guaranteed to entertain her, hooked as she is on this *opera levant*. She peppers me with questions—she would love to take some of it in, but she has her animals, and the fall fair is next weekend; blue ribbons are to be won.

We talk into the night. Candles gutter out. Night-hawks bleat and owls coo. I remind her I must borrow her alarm clock—I must be up by seven or so. She makes more coffee. She orders up some poetry. I recite a Shakespeare sonnet. She says she loves my voice; it must work wonders in the courtroom. Courtroom? What courtroom? The courts seem as remote as the Kalahari Desert.

In sweet sorrow we finally part—at the unheard-of hour of three o'clock in the morning. She bestows another kiss, more lingering than the first.

I return to my house still savouring the warm softness of those lips.

Yet, she said. She's not ready. Yet.

In bed, I toss for another hour: caffeine and love's adrenalin combine to keep sleep at bay. When it comes, my dreams again lack the customary motif of shame and chains and nakedness. Instead, an absurd panto featuring our hero struggling through a desert of insecurity and doubt towards an ever-receding Margaret Blake. But as she beckons, an obelisk rises from the sands, an artifact from a civilization long thought dead.

Nicholas Braid's upwardly mobile family has recently moved to a high-mortgage zone in West Point Grey: stately houses, sedate, tree-lined streets, tranquil but for the unrelenting growl of mowers, weed trimmers, and hedge clippers. Why do men pause at these tasks to stare as I drive by? Why do mothers call their children into the house? One would think they had never before seen come rattling down their street a purple, rusting 1969 Dodge pickup with the passenger door held on by a rope and bearing a bearded hayseed and his elephantine sidekick, the voyeur Nelson Forbish in a food-stained porkpie hat. Somehow—the mechanics of this remain confusing to me—he has not only persuaded me to lend him the truck for his return to the island but has also cadged an invitation for lunch at my daughter's. Her response when informed by telephone: "Oh, we can handle one of your island characters for an afternoon."

As we pull into the driveway, Nicholas strides out to greet me, but stalls as he takes the measure of Forbish wiggling from the truck. Yes, here to break bread among the Braids is one of those very Garibaldi yokels Nicholas counselled me to beware.

He brings his son forward, but slightly shelters him, "Another Nick. Say hello to Mr. Forbish. Arthur, I have some of that non-alcohol beer you like. The back terrace, gentlemen? Deborah made some appetizers."

One would expect the word "appetizers" to send Forbish rocketing to the back terrace, but he stays behind with Nicky.

"And how are the markets, Nicholas?"

"Bullish. Made the right guesses, I think. Pulled back from the Brown Group just in time. Heard about their little crisis, Arthur? Down in Guyana. Whole mining operation shut down. Cyanide spill. Got into a river. All the piranhas have gone belly up. Looking at a fifty-million-dollar clean-up bill. A certain witness for the prosecution isn't going to be in a good mood."

Deborah, presiding over her canapés, squeals when she sees me. "My God! You look like Robinson Crusoe on a bad hair day."

"Wait'll you see Man Friday," says Nick.

"Jeans, work shirt, those ugly yellow suspenders. You'd *better* get a haircut."

"Ah, well, all my regalia is at the office. I have an

appointment with Roberto tomorrow at nine. One is not to worry."

"Your trial starts at ten."

"Oh, nothing will happen without me. The judge is a patient man and a friend."

But is there not some fear that Wally Sprogue, with his newly trained sensitivity to women, will bend over backwards to the female complainant? (The trial has switched on in my mind. It has been doing this all day, flickering like a badly connected light.)

While Nicholas goes off to tend to his other guest, my daughter draws me onto a sunny patch of lawn to make closer physical inspection. "Actually, you look great, Dad. Trimmed right down."

I beam. "Observe." I demonstrate Snake Creeps Down, the latest tai chi movement I have mastered. "The mind and body are one, and I am at peace. I'm not the man I used to be."

Deborah looks at me uncertainly.

As I pull my pipe and tobacco from a jacket pocket, the little plastic bag with marijuana cigarettes slips out, too, and I barely catch it. I had forgotten it was there—Margaret had returned it last night.

"I'll say you're not the man you used to be. Grass. I gave that up at eighteen. Jesus, Dad, what do you think you're doing, discovering the 1960s or something?"

"How embarrassing."

"Well? Explain yourself." But she finds it hard to be stern; she is laughing.

"Caught in the act."

"I'll say. Second childhood. Are you stoned right now?"

"Of course not."

"Well, there's something about you. You're all so bright-eyed."

"I am happy for the first time in my life." I light my pipe and blow a little smoke ring.

"Since Mother left you. I always knew you'd be happier when you were free. Never thought you'd turn out like *this*. A post-generational, long-haired hippie freak." But she is still grinning, happy for me. "I was shocked when I heard about it, her and that Roehlig, and then I thought, how wonderful, you are finally out from under her."

Abruptly she changes the subject, cross-examining me about Margaret, and though I respond evasively (I fear my daughter is not ready to hear her flower-child father has fallen in love), Deborah cuts to the quick.

"Are you courting her?"

Forbish rounds the bend, scratching his belly, heading for the appetizers.

"Caught your dad there in a dark house with her last night."

"Dad!"

I redden. "It was all quite proper, my dear. Candlelight dinner."

"Must've lasted a long time," Forbish says. "Hear he didn't get home till three in the morning."

"You rogue, Dad." Deborah claps her hands in delight.

Nicholas comes from the house with a portable phone: it's Augustina.

"Jonathan called in. He's at his therapist's office. Last-minute crisis counselling, I guess. He sounded pretty whacked out."

"Sober?"

"I think so."

The tortured wretch has kept his bargain with me and earned his defence. Well, I will try to do him justice. (I am moving into trial mode, I can sense it.)

❦

Thanks for this. I'll pay double overtime.

It's all right. I had nothing to do. I was thinking

about you, actually. The trial tomorrow . . . Did you manage to get your sabbatical moved up?

No. The headmaster gave me three weeks' leave after a cheery speech of support. However, a careful reading between the lines tells me the leave will become permanent if I'm convicted. Jane, I can't sleep. I can't eat. I can't *think*. It's consuming me like some flesh-eating virus.

Would you like me to prescribe more Valium?

No, I'm afraid of it. I'm afraid of going over the edge.

Well, is it just the trial?

Oh, God, it's that, and it's . . . Arthur Beauchamp won't be putting me on the stand. It will be her evidence against my silence. The judge will tell the jury they must not read anything into my failure to testify. They will therefore read something into it. My guilt.

Maybe Kimberley won't be believed.

She'll turn the jury into a screaming lynch mob. She's a brilliant actress, Jane. I've never once seen her flub a line. I saw her ghastly play four times. Two evenings, two matinées. I became an addict, the phantom of the opera, waiting and writhing until the next curtain opening. But as soon as the lights went down I went into a blank-eyed staring trance, missing every punch line, haunted, mesmerized by my tormentor. I couldn't take my eyes off her. It's as if she's cast a spell on me.

The word obsession comes to mind.

I don't know. Maybe I'm trying to piece her together, seeking a clue why she'd do this to me.

Another word is masochistic.

Which brings us to . . . Look, Jane, there's something I want to tell you, it's really bothering me. It's about . . . some of the sick stuff you've been trying to drag kicking and screaming from my psyche. I think I mentioned Dominique Lander to you, the woman I was seeing a few years ago.

Yes, your Bohemian love affair.

Bohemian? Hell, she's from Transylvania. She's a blood-sucking vampire—

Steady.

God, why is this happening to me? I don't mind doing time nearly as much as being a laughing stock for the rest of my life.

Tell me about Dominique Lander.

A pagan princess. A hundred and eighty degrees removed from other women I'd known, beautiful, dark, haunted. Like her art. But intelligent. Devious, I didn't know about until later. We carried on for half a year. Longer. But eventually I became, I don't know, a little nervous about her. She was a clinger, she was like sticky gum, always there, demanding, talking about lifetime commitments.

Which frightened you no end.

I started avoiding her. I began seeing other women.

Is that typically how you run away?

Well, you have to understand, um, the sex was getting a little weird, too. That's really the reason I started backing off. Lovers experiment, I suppose, and it can be fun for a while, it's okay. You said so yourself. You prescribe it: creative role-playing. But this got *really* strange.

Go on.

She was into, ah . . .

Yes?

She's going to be a witness, Jane. She's going to say she and I were into, um, a sort of S and M thing.

I see.

And, uh, we were.

Uh-huh.

I guess it's something I've been having a lot of trouble unloading on you.

You're telling me.

It's embarrassing.

Talk about it.

Okay . . . okay, here it all comes. We had this game, she liked me to tie her up. She was the slave and I was the master. A lot of bare-bottom spanking, and, ah, she liked me to force sex on her, that way, from behind. She would beg, plead, sometimes scream. She liked being whipped with a riding crop. This is hideous. I can't . . .

You didn't enjoy it?

I, ah . . .

Well, can you answer me?

I think I did. It . . . well, it extended things for me. Creative role-playing—that's basically what we were doing, playing out our fantasies. I guess you'd call them sick.

I don't call them sick, Jonathan. Maybe not the role-playing I'd recommend.

Why are you looking at me that way?

Just shifting the paradigm a little bit. And did you ever change roles?

Occasionally.

Did you like being whipped?

No, I . . . I don't know.

Did you prefer that to being the dominant party?

You're the analyst; you tell me.

And these sessions gave you staying power?

Kept me erect.

A riding crop. Isn't that what your father used on you?

Yes . . .

I'm sorry, Jonathan, I can't hear what you're saying.

. . . Hated him.

What?

I hated him.

But you also loved him.

Aw, shit.

Would you like some coffee? We have a lot of work to do today.

❧ PART THREE ❧

Let us live and love, my Lesbia, and value at a penny all the talk of crabbed old men. Suns may set and rise again: for us, when our brief light has set, there's the sleep of perpetual night. Give me a thousand kisses.

—CATULLUS

I awake before dawn after dreams dimly recalled, but pulsing, erotic. I am confused: what is that distant electric buzz that confounds the stark silence I have grown so used to? I am in the city; it breathes raspy outside those windows.

I feel buoyant, rested. I have slept well again. I rise and shower and dress, slip quietly from the house, and walk north to English Bay, to the long, flat beaches of Spanish Banks. I do my tai chi here on the sands of ebb tide, dancing barefoot as the eastern sky begins to colour: face east, raise both hands slowly, turn on the right hand, face north.

North: I am at the centre of the compass of my trial. To the west, above the Point Grey cliffs, the campus and the law school. Facing me, the mountains of the North Shore, dressed in a cloak of cloud. Just beneath those peaks, high in the British Properties, the abode of Clarence de Remy Brown. Lower down, the house of alleged shame where Jon O'Donnell restlessly sleeps. Not far to the east, the former atelier of Dominique Lander.

And beyond, buried amidst those towers gleaming golden in the morning sun: the courts. Where all things will be decided. Where I must play my unwished for role: inquisitor at the *auto-da-fé* of Joan of

Arc, her public burning. This saucy scamp is telling false—I have no choice but to believe that. She, not Jonathan, is the evildoer. I will not abide any other possibility. I must quell any doubts I harbour about his innocence.

Yet I feel uneasy, lacking in confidence. Has the soft life of my island idyll caused me to lose the lust for victory? Formerly, I compensated for a career of impotence in bed with a show of virility in court. Ironically, have recent rigid stirrings in the night rendered me a less virile warrior for justice? I must be bloody, bold, and resolute.

As I walk east—Locarno Beach, Jericho Park, Kitsilano Beach—my thoughts turn to Margaret, to my island, but as I tramp up Burrard Street Bridge, my other, sweeter world begins to melt away. As I find my way into the busy downtown streets, I feel myself begin to mutate into a previous life form. I am becoming a lawyer again.

Roberto whirls dramatically about my unruly thatch with scissors and clippers, hair flying in all directions.

"We don't want to be frightening the jury, do we? Like some mad hermit just down from the hills. Fatherly, that's how we want you. Kindly and wise. But a military cut to the beard—I call this creation the naval commander. We are sending messages of firmness. We are in control."

Augustina Sage stands by, absorbed in one of her briefs of law. Gowan Cleaver is pacing in the hallway outside. Three young articling students are also out there, with valises and book bags. A limousine is parked out front.

"Augustina, you must tell that mob to disperse. I don't want the jury feeling the Crown is outnumbered, or that we've money coming out of our ears. And tell

Gowan to get rid of the limousine. We will take a homely taxi."

She leaves to do this.

"You see, the magic is working," says Roberto. "We *are* in control."

He whirls me around to the mirror. Roberto has re-created me. Commander Beauchamp at the tiller of his leaky man-of-war.

Now I am in my undershorts in the barristers' changing room. I am putting on an iron-fresh white shirt with a wing-tip collar. I am slipping on my black vest. I am tying on my dickey. I am hoisting up my pin-stripe pants, and fastening my suspenders to them—the belt which comes with these pants is meant for a certain former fattie. Finally I don my robe, and I am now in my silks, costumed for the play.

My role, of course, being one of those comic-book heroes in tights and ceremonial capes. And suddenly I *am* feeling surges of a Batmaniacal strength. Perhaps the power of love is adding fuel to the adrenalin that courses through me in a courtroom. *Omnia vincit amor.*

It is ten o'clock as I walk from the dressing room and down a hall empty but for a few lawyers scurrying to their courtrooms. I climb the stately wide staircases of the atrium-lobby to the fifth floor. And I stop as I turn a corner. A vast, milling throng is in the mezzanine seeking entry into this spectacle *ad captandum vulgus*: the prurient, the tantalized, and the merely curious. A flock of young people—probably law students. The Women's Movement seems well represented. Reporters are having their credentials checked by Barney Willit, the brown-uniformed sheriff's officer, so they can be assured of seats.

"Morning, Mr. Beauchamp," he says. "Sold-out

house today. The judge wants everyone sorted out before he opens court. Jury panel's in there now."

I peek inside at the backs of sixty heads, citizens called from home, office, and plant to do their democratic duty. Court staff but no lawyers. Where is Augustina, where the client?

At the end of a hall, by the door to a witness room, I spy Kimberley Martin and Clarence de Remy Brown. Kimberley wears a blue, ankle-length outfit that looks both *chic* and *chère,* but she does not seem as blithe and bouncy as when last observed climbing from a hot tub. In fact, she looks spent, enervated, as she grips the arm of her fiancé. There are dark areas under her eyes. I had not expected she would be under so much stress—or is this a sensitive portrayal of the vandalized maid? Mr. Brown, with his cyanide-spill problems in South America, seems none too happy either. They are in close session with Patricia Blueman and her junior: Gundar Sindelar, a ten-year veteran, squat as a barrel, with the reputation of a pit bull.

Ah, here comes Augustina Sage, up the stairs and weaving through the assemblage.

"Jonathan is one floor down, watching a trial," she says. "I think he was really whacked out after his session with his therapist yesterday. I hope he's ready. Are you?"

"Chomping at the bit."

"Not in some kind of transcendental state of abandon? Did you bring her flowers?" She chucks me under the chin.

"I'm preoccupied only with this trial," I bluster, and quickly change the topic. "How are our chances of getting our hands on that lie detector test?"

"It's iffy. There's that bad case in the Supreme Court."

"And Dominique Lander?"

"Previous similar acts by a rape defendant are admissible to prove a consistent or unique pattern: Ontario Court of Appeal. We're in trouble there."

"Is Miss Lander here?"

"That's her."

A pale, striking woman dressed in black, her features appear pencilled onto her face: a thin line of a mouth, the merest crescent moons for eyebrows. She is at the edge of the crowd, sketching on a large pad, and when she catches Augustina's eye she nods and returns to her art. Augustina's perception is probably accurate: she is a loose cannon and she is here to sink the Commander's ship.

"I'll get Jonathan," says Augustina.

Court 55 has now been opened to the public, and is quickly filling. I make my way in, issuing loud good mornings, and banter a few moments with some of the court staff while I look over the prospective jurors. Canadian lawyers do not enjoy the American luxury of acquainting themselves with jurors through long, friendly cross-examinations; we know only names, addresses, and occupations. A barrister must have his senses tuned to the silent nuances: the smiles and frowns, the bold or timid stances, the presence or lack of eye contact.

Which one is Hedy Jackson-Blyth, the feminist union leader? Gowan Cleaver has scrawled a big "No" against her name.

Patricia Blueman plumps a heavy book bag on her table. "Ready, Arthur?"

"Fiat justitia, ruat caelum."

"Means what?"

"Let justice be done though the heavens fall."

Augustina leads in Jonathan O'Donnell, who seems inert, depressed. He is startled by my smile, my words of cheerful welcome, the vigour of my handshake. (These gestures are heartfelt: his spirits must be buoyed; but there is a cynical side to this—jurors watch lawyers for signs of caring, a belief in innocence.)

I lead Jonathan to the prisoner's dock behind the counsel tables. "Stand tall when you make your plea. Keep your voice firm."

Jonathan vents one deep sigh, then steps into the box.

"I'll fetch the judge," says the court clerk.

The fetching is quick—Wally Sprogue has been waiting in the wings for his grand entrance. He swaggers out, chest swelling under the red-sashed robe that denotes his recently elevated station: a showy display of inflated ego. Feet shuffle and limbs creak as the audience rises then settles back onto benches and chairs.

Sheriff Willit barks the words that for long centuries of the English common law have heralded the beginning of a criminal jury assize, the trial of citizen by citizens: "Oyez, oyez, oyez. All persons having business in this Court of Oyer and Terminer and General Gaol Delivery draw near and give your attention and answer to your names when called."

Ah, history, ah, theatre. We are in the very womb of English law, the time of that hapless ruler Henry III. "Oyez!" calls out the court crier to the citizens attending this grave commission into treasons and felonies committed in this county against His Majesty. *Oyer et terminer,* to hear and determine. In this age of speed and cybernetics, there is comforting tradition in the ancient discipline of law.

Jonathan does stand tall as charges are read and pleas taken to counts of sexual assault, confining, and kidnapping. He is not afraid to look at the jury panel—that is good.

"Not guilty," he says each time, and I am pleased that his voice does not crack.

I rise. "May the defendant be allowed to join me at counsel table?"

Patricia objects: "Accused persons usually remain in the dock."

"I fear she's right, Mr. Beauchamp," Wally says. "Be he pauper or professor, I can't grant special privileges." Should I have expected else from this born-again advocate of equal access? "Are we ready to pick the jury? Let's start with fifteen names, Mr. Sheriff."

Sheriff Willit shakes a wooden box containing cards with names of the panel members, then begins the draw, and ultimately fifteen persons are lined up beside the bench.

The first twelve seem quite an acceptable bunch—an equal mix of the sexes and several youthful faces: youth being preferred in morals cases. All twelve have been vetted by Gowan Cleaver, and have passed scrutiny. But the thirteenth person brought forward is the risky Hedy Jackson-Blyth, who looks bright though stern and distrusting, a woman of about forty, barren of any jewellery, liberated from the curse of female makeup. If any of the first twelve jurors is excused by the judge, she will be the next one sworn. Dare I take a chance that will not happen?

"A moment, m'lord." I attend at the prosecution table. "We can spend a couple of hours at this, Patricia, or we can take the first twelve."

She looks over her copy of the list—a big exclamation mark is beside the name of Jackson-Blyth.

"The first twelve. Okay."

Her assent is too quick, and I have a sense she knows something I don't. And, of course, that is so: when the judge asks if anyone has a legitimate reason to be excused, panellist number three says his mother has just died. "My condolences," says Wally, and he lets him go.

Patricia rises. "With that exception, counsel are agreed to take the first twelve."

Five men, seven women. I have several friendly

faces, and I can only hope Hedy Jackson-Blyth will not be all that adverse to the defence.

When the jurors are comfortable in their seats, Wally recites the boiler plate about their solemn duties: they may return to their homes in the evenings, but must not discuss the evidence outside the jury room. Innocence is presumed. The defence need prove nothing. The Crown must establish guilt beyond a reasonable doubt.

"I expect this trial will go two weeks, but we have legal matters to deal with, so I'm going to let you select your foreperson, and then go back home for—how long? Did we agree on two days?"

I am missing Margaret already. Do we really need two days of opening arguments? Cannot we finish this trial in five days?

I rise. "I hope we can shorten things a bit, m'lord. That's important to the complainant, whose university classes start tomorrow. I also understand her fiancé has a business crisis to attend to—some kind of cyanide spill in a river. If Miss Blueman can agree with me on some minor matters, we might all get out of here by Friday to enjoy a stress-free long weekend." I can see Patricia looking sourly at me while I play the fairy godfather.

"Anything you can do to save time," Wally says, and he orders a brief recess. Patricia and I arrange for a confabulation of counsel in the barristers' lounge. I tell Jonathan to stay put and not to worry.

"I'll be fine," he says. "I think I've been sweating over this more than I've let out. Suffered a morale collapse yesterday, so I had a long session with my therapist. I'm going to have her talk to you, Arthur. She can say some things I can't. I've been a shitty client; I'll try to make it up to you." And he adds, "I've sorted a few things out."

"What might those be?"

"I just have a clearer picture. I know what I have to do."

"What is that?"

"Be honest with myself."

I'm not sure what he means—I would much prefer he be honest with *me*—but I pat him on the shoulder. "I will do my best for you, Jonathan."

"I know that."

Will my best be good enough? If I entertain doubts as to his innocence, how do I convince a jury they should not? His earlier dishonest evasions, the screams heard by the housekeeper, the bizarre rites of sexual arousal with Dominique Lander: these do not inflame a righteous indignation that an innocent soul is entangled in the law's tentacles. Somehow I must resolve my ambiguous feelings about this man.

In the mezzanine, I see Patricia talking with Kimberley Martin, who is still downcast. Is she unwell? Beside her, Clarence de Remy Brown is on his cellular phone. Patricia parts from them and follows me to the lounge.

There, she and her associate, Gundar Sindelar, listen politely to my pitch to jettison Miss Lander. "We'll save a day of argument. An argument you will lose." I feign utter confidence.

"Oh, no, I have previous acts of bondage," Patricia says. "I have all that body-painting she did with O'Donnell."

"Ah, but, Patricia, the judge won't like the chicanery. Clarence de Remy Brown hired a private investigator to track Miss Lander down. Frank Sierra posed as a hireling of the defence to obtain her statement. Walter Sprogue will be furious."

For some reason, this argument seems to be playing to attentive ears. I have a sense that Patricia, who looks contemplative, is—surprisingly—about to bite. She looks at Gundar, but he stubbornly shakes his head.

"I say we go for broke."

I close my files and stuff them in a briefcase. "Let's put it to the judge. He will shortly send Miss Lander packing back to the Slocan."

"Hold it," says Patricia. "What does your client have to say about this bondage stuff with Dominique Lander?"

"You'll have to wait to find out," I say.

"I can always get it out of him in cross." She ponders. "Let me talk to Gundar."

They walk a few paces away, but we can hear low snatches of conversation. "Don't want to give him any grounds of appeal . . . we could keep her in reserve. . . ."

On her return, Patricia says, "Okay, this is the deal. When O'Donnell takes the stand, I'll be asking him if he was into S and M and all this body-painting. I'll call Dominique Lander in rebuttal only if he denies it. Agreed?"

I tell them that now I must speak alone with Augustina. We caucus by a window.

"Exactly what I was about to propose myself," I say, pleased with my craftiness. "If Jonathan doesn't testify, the Crown *can't* call Dominique in rebuttal. That neatly gets rid of her."

For appearances, we spend a few more minutes in quiet discussion, then return to the foe, and ask them to throw the polygraph results into the deal. Patricia protests. I accuse her of having something to hide. Her hasty denials seem suspect. I produce a copy of a recent legal brief on polygraph disclosure—authored by one Walter Sprogue.

After another conference of prosecutors, Patricia finally says, "All right, it's a deal, but you have to undertake not to object to my calling Dominique to contradict your client." She takes no chances, penning our promises to a scrap sheet of paper that we both initial.

Patricia may feel she has the better bargain—she keeps Lander in reserve. But with one swoop I have not only eliminated proof of previous kink but shortened the trial. I am on a fast-track schedule that may yet get me to the fair on time. But I must curb this otiose wanderlust for my island.

I return to the fifth-floor mezzanine and brief Jonathan, who greets this turn of events with an acerbic sense of humour. "Now Dominique is free to sell her story to the tabs. The *National Enquirer* will love it— 'Law Prof Hits Bottom.'"

Court reassembles without the jurors, the next order of business being a voir dire, a trial within a trial to determine whether the jury may hear Jonathan's words to Sergeant Chekoff: "I did no such thing. Of course I touched her. I took her to bed." "Or *put* her to bed"; he wasn't sure at the preliminary inquiry. I do not fancy either version, however exculpatory. I would have preferred silence.

Chekoff is Patricia's sole witness in the voir dire: a man of military bearing with grizzled hair who wasn't particularly keen about making this collar and who failed to caution the suspect.

The officer begins to relate his conversation with Jonathan in his front yard. "Mr. O'Donnell said, 'Is this some kind of practical joke?'"

"How did you respond—"

Wally impatiently cuts Patricia off. "Hold on. Was there a warning given? He was a suspect, wasn't he? A very serious complaint had been made against him, and *recited* to him."

"M'lord, the accused is a law professor. He may be presumed to know his rights."

"Pauper or professor, Ms. Blueman, same rules apply to both. I'll hear from the defence."

"I have case law on the point," says Augustina.

"And I know those cases. The Crown can argue until it's blue in the face on this one."

"Your mind is closed, m'lord?" says Patricia, her tone overpolite.

"Not closed, but only slightly ajar."

He impatiently hears Patricia out before ruling. "The Crown has not proved beyond a reasonable doubt the statements are voluntary. They will not go before the jury. Okay, let's have them in."

"That was too easy," Augustina whispers.

My sense that the trial has got off to a good beginning is eroded by the fact that Hedy Jackson-Blyth is leading the jury in—she has been elected forewoman. As such, she has been elevated from ordinary pawn to influential queen on this human chessboard.

I watch the jurors' faces as Patricia makes her opening address. Eyes grow large and mouths fall open as the salacious allegations are described. I decide I do not like the fourth fellow in the back row: he smirks too much, a smart aleck. Goodman, a young investment broker. A woman in the front row—a nurse, according to the jury list—often smiles, too, but in a different way, with a slight frown, as if she senses absurdity here. Miss Jackson-Blyth is looking distrustfully at Jonathan, who sits with head bowed in the dock, his reading glasses on, occasionally writing notes.

Patricia's opening is a rather flat summation of the evidence she proposes to call, and to her credit she does not use her speech as a platform to flog her case, to win votes for the prosecution.

After she concludes, Wally asks, "Would you like to defer your first witness until after the lunch break?"

"Well, I thought tomorrow—"

I jump up. "Tomorrow? M'lord, we have half an hour left of the *morning* yet. Should we not plough on and allow Miss Martin to get off to her classes?"

"Mr. Beauchamp, you're full of zip today."

"According to my daughter, I'm in my second childhood."

"Maybe that explains it."

The jurors are chuckling—so important to relax them early.

"M'lord," says Patricia, "I hadn't expected Ms. Martin would be needed so early. She hasn't been fully briefed."

I leap at this chance. "If my learned friend needs time to rehearse her witness, can we not proceed with some of the other evidence?"

"Brief her, not rehearse her."

"If she doesn't know her lines by now, she never will."

Patricia is aflame. "M'lord, that's entirely improper! The jury is present!"

"That kind of comment is best reserved for argument, Mr. Beauchamp," warns frowning Wally. "I wonder if counsel will oblige me by taking a few minutes in my chambers."

I suppose I am in for it now. Wally will chide me and prohibit further displays of forensic misbehaviour. But when we enter his chambers, he is chuckling. "Beauchamp, you naughty bugger, I'm going to have to keep an eye on you. Very good opening, Patricia. Brief, to the point; we're sledding right along. Well, this will be a *very* interesting case. Please, sit down."

Wally's eyes rove briefly to Augustina's stockinged knee as she perches, dainty and cross-legged, on the edge of a chair. Melanie, his wife, is of a jealous bent, and with cause.

"This is a manner of date rape that you're alleging," Wally says. "Acquaintance rape, that's the right term, I think. Too much of it going on. I'm not prejudging of course, but a lot of this stuff never even gets reported. Professor and student, boss and secretary—there's still that power imbalance thing between the sexes. We're part of it ourselves, Arthur, it's ingrained in old-timers like us. The patriarchal male hierarchy."

I fear he is warning me that if convicted my client will face the full measure of the law. I hope he does not see Regina versus O'Donnell as a test case—one in which his sentence must send a loud message to the patriarchal dictatorship.

"Now, Patricia, can we call someone other than Ms. Martin? One of the boys in blue? Or, ah, girls. Women." Tangled among the thorn bushes of politically incorrect speech, Wally can find no escape, and silently surrenders.

"I'd like to put in the exhibits first."

"We'll admit all exhibits," I say. "Just show them to the jury, and we'll agree they are what they are."

"You're being awfully accommodating, Arthur. I get suspicious."

The marking of exhibits consumes the remainder of the morning, the jurors examining each item in turn: an outlandish tropical tie and a simple, unadorned gold-cross pendant, larger than I expected, about three inches high. Items seized from O'Donnell's house are tendered: coat, dress, spike heels, pantyhose, panties, bra, pair of small gold earrings, purse, a tube of Shameless lipstick worn to a nubbin, and various bedsheets. Photographs of O'Donnell's home, inside and out, are marked and identified.

Upon adjournment Patricia confers with me. "I'm going to start with the students this afternoon. Your buddy Mr. Stubb first. Unless you need more time to prepare. I wouldn't mind talking with him and Paula Yi a little more."

Obviously it is she who really needs the extra time. I have managed to push her far ahead of schedule. "*Tempus fugit,* my dear. Proceed with your case."

As the room clears, Gundar Sindelar passes me a thin file. "Graphs, transcripts, examiner's report. Mr.

Mackleson is available if you need to talk to him."
The polygraph examiner.

I pass the file to Augustina. "Talk to Mackleson and meet Jonathan and me in my hotel room for lunch."

"Sure. Order me a salad."

Jonathan and I take the stairs down, and walk silently out past the statue of solemn, firm-breasted Themis, goddess of justice and consort of Jupiter, onto the second-storey promenade and its artificial forest and waterfall, then down to busy Robson Square. Only a minute's stroll away is the Hotel Vancouver, grande dame of the city's better inns, a blocky Gothic fortress. My suite on the ninth floor overlooks Georgia Street, the exterior façade guarded by concrete gargoyles, griffins craning their necks, looking malevolently below.

"Gruesome decorations," Jonathan says.

"A conceit of Gothic architecture," I say, and reach into my store of trivia. "Evil spirits, seeing their own images, were thought to be deterred from entering Christendom's grand palaces of worship."

"That one looks a little like Dominique Lander. Bloody woman tried to accost me during the last recess."

"Try to avoid her."

"She's on my side, she said. She wants to help me."

But he seems less than eager to continue this conversation. Nor does he respond to my urgings to expand upon his so-called clearer picture. His mood remains solemn and dark. It is hard not to feel his pain.

When Augustina arrives she spreads several papers and graphs across the desk.

"There's just a little more activity on the charts than I think there should be when the examiner asks the critical questions: Was she raped? Is she telling the truth? I'm no expert. Mackleson is, and he says that's normal, just a natural autonomic response to a stressful memory."

"The actress Kimberley Martin," says Jonathan. "This is her shtick, the violated woman."

"But here, look at this—the lines almost go off the sheet."

All four lines on the graph paper shoot upward at the point she indicates.

"What was the question?"

" 'Were you physically attracted to Professor O'Donnell?' She answered, 'Not really.' Mackleson said she was lying, and so it was a terrific control question."

A sharp intake of breath from behind my shoulder—Jonathan seems unduly startled, but his tone is cynical. "Should I be flattered? Yeah, she's attracted to me, all right. That's why she wants me locked up for about twenty years. Remove the temptation."

I ask Augustina, "Does she know she answered untruthfully?"

"Mackleson didn't tell her. But Patricia is having lunch with her so I imagine it will be discussed. Here's another jump: 'Have you ever been sexually assaulted before?' And she answered, 'Never.' The examiner said Kimberley was emphatic, but he called her big reaction a stress anomaly—there would be no reason for her to lie."

Jonathan says, "Maybe I should take the test."

"To prove your innocence to whom?"

"Well, maybe to you, Arthur," he says with a strained vehemence. Does he question my allegiance to his cause? "I'm sorry, that was a dumb thing to say. I just feel so damn alone sometimes, a non-person, ignored, a neutral object caught up in a clever courtroom game. Why is innocence treated as incidental, a kind of academic irrelevancy? The aim is to work the system, right?—get the bad guy off, who cares if he actually *did* it? Oh, shit, forget it, I'm just shooting off my mouth when I should be down on my knees to you, Arthur. I'm frustrated; I'm scared."

This dithyramb of pent-up grief impresses me as deeply felt. I feel ashamed that he has so obviously tuned into the niggling sense of distrust I have secretly harboured.

Augustina takes his hand. "We're here for you a hundred per cent, Jonathan. You're not alone. You're innocent and we're going to prove it."

She speaks with an earnestness I can't quite summon, but I must make an effort. "Quite so. There can be no question." How sincere does that sound? Yet his emphatic plea, his offer to put his credibility to the test of a machine, argues strongly for his innocence. I must try to put my petty doubts aside.

§§

In the fifth-floor mezzanine, Charles Stubb, our future prime minister, approaches Jonathan and me with a salesman's smile and shakes our hands in turn, speaking in conspiratorial undertones. "Everything going all right? Any last-minute advice?"

Try not to sound bombastic? Avoid long speeches? Beware of coating Jonathan with too much sugar?

"Just don't overdo it, Charles," I say.

"I don't catch your meaning, sir."

Jonathan interprets: "He's telling you not to spread the butter on too thick."

Stubb's protruding ears turn as red as sails at sunset, but the damage to his ego heals promptly—he will make a fine politician. "Sure, I get the point, don't come on too strong."

But as court resumes, Charles Stubb embarks on a pathetic eulogy for Jonathan, sadly ignoring our advice not to fawn over him, describing him as "a man of fierce intellect who is highly respected by students and faculty alike." Patricia works like a sheepdog to keep him in line, cutting him off when he becomes discursive. This is clearly not the fat part of the Crown's case, and she hopes to make his long story short.

Wally, who can't keep his mouth shut, runs interference for the witness, chastising Patricia for amputating the limbs of his answers. I can find no occasion to object: Wally is doing everything for me, my surrogate, my gofer—though I am finding his interruptions time-wasting and annoying.

After Stubb concludes a rambling account of Kimberley tagging doggedly after Jonathan at the dance and after-party, impatient Patricia ushers the witness quickly into Jonathan's Jaguar and up to his house.

"By then I was pretty well the only sober person in the car. I may have had one beer. I'm not a—"

"What about the others?"

"Well, I sure wasn't going to let Professor O'Donnell drive. Paula Yi was okay—she'd had a few, I guess. Egan Chornicky was higher than a kite, and Kimberley was *very* boisterous—I don't know how much she had to drink. I would say a lot."

I watch for reactions from the jury as Stubb tells them about Kimberley's costume change, but only one censorious-looking woman in the front row seems at all offended.

Seated at the back, I am distressed to see, is Dominique Lander, busily sketching. I must advise Patricia that as a possible witness she should not be here; she will cause Jonathan unneeded discomfort.

Patricia asks, "While she was still in her dress, did you notice any bruising on her? Especially her ankles or wrists?"

"I can't say I did."

"Did she ever fall down or bang into anything?"

"Not that I saw."

Those bruises remain the Crown's strongest weapon. How are they to be explained?

Stubb's lame reason for leaving Kimberley behind at Jonathan's house: "She was going to be heading off in another direction anyway."

"Where?"

"Up to her boyfriend's place in the British Properties."

"How do you know that?"

"Well, she told me—"

"Objection," says Wally Sprogue. "That's hearsay." He has risen an inch from his chair, but sheepishly settles back. Wally has forgotten he is no longer a lowly barrister: I cannot help but smile.

"Objection sustained," I say. "Old habits die hard, m'lord."

"Yes. Quite. Carry on, witness." He is flustered; how easily the vain embarrass.

"Anyway, it would make more sense for her to take another cab after she slept it off a little." Stubb adds, "We knew she'd be okay. We knew Professor O'Donnell wouldn't—"

"Thank you. Those are all my questions."

"Let the witness finish," says Wally.

"He wants to answer a question I didn't ask him," Patricia says.

Wally purrs to the young man: "What were you about to say, sir?"

"Professor O'Donnell acted like a gentleman all evening. He would never do a thing like this."

"Thank you. Cross-examination, Mr. Beauchamp?"

I have not liked Stubb's evidence at all. Too glossy, too puffy, too sycophantic. Cross-examination would seem utterly self-serving. "Nothing, thank you."

Stubb walks from the stand looking disappointed; he had more to say. Patricia, in a severe pet, talks heatedly with her assistant, Sindelar, then turns on Wally. "I hope it's clearly on the record that his last little speech was elicited by your lordship."

Wally assumes a hurt expression. "That's what you get for cutting him off. We'll take the mid-afternoon break."

In the mezzanine, Kimberley Martin and Clarence de Remy Brown are chatting with Paula Yi—much too amicably. Miss Yi will be the next witness: a rebel, a feminist, a victim herself of male assault, she must be handled with scrupulous care.

Farther down the hallway I am shocked to observe Jonathan in an altercation with Dominique Lander, who has him backed against a wall. From their expressions, the exchange seems sharp.

Jonathan tries gently to push her away and she slaps his hand. As I advance quickly to intervene, she slaps him again, in the face, then rushes away. I look about for jurors, but thankfully none are present, though others have observed this tatty scene—including Kimberley Martin, seeming quite taken aback.

Jonathan is breathing heavily. "Love taps. It's her way of showing affection. I told her to get out of my life, Arthur, that's all that happened."

The Commander is severe with him. "You will not converse with anyone but your lawyers, do you understand that?"

"*Mea culpa.*"

I am unsure what effect the episode has on Kimberley, but as I pass her on my way back to court she is smiling. A small benefit is derived from the contretemps: Miss Lander does not return to court.

"Call Paula Yi," Patricia says.

Petite Miss Yi enters the courtroom tentatively, obviously nervous. She is dressed casually: jeans and a floppy sweater rolled at the sleeves.

Patricia repeatedly asks Miss Yi to keep her voice up; she is so soft-spoken we must strain to hear. Our untrained puppy of a judge continues to intervene, seeking clarifications, expanding the answers; he will earn a poor reputation if this keeps up. Like a child, a good judge should be seen and not heard.

But my love-addled mind is unable to concentrate—as the scene Miss Yi describes is about to shift from the student dance to the *danse macabre*, my brain shifts, too, blown by a sudden southwesterly down Potter's Road, past Stoney's place to where the chickens freely range upon the road. I pause there to seek Margaret, but she is not to be found.

I feel a need to hear her voice. I require an earnest of faith from her, a reassurance. I must know that her whispered contemplation of the possibility of love has not been scrutinized in the cold, hard light of day, withdrawn, discarded with the morning's compost.

I'm not ready. Yet.

"Mr. Beauchamp?"

Dimly, I hear a voice that doesn't belong in my reveries.

"Do you wish to cross-examine?"

I plummet from the clouds and plop onto my chair at counsel table. One of the trial's most important witnesses is on the stand, and I have missed a vital scene: the snorting of coke in the rumpus room. I look uneasily about. Has anyone noticed I was gone? Augustina, for one. She frowns, a warning look: stop gambolling in those fields of daisies.

I rise in cross-examination with a snap of my suspenders. But I have early trouble finding my bearings. "Miss Yi, I understand you had never met Kimberley Martin or Jonathan O'Donnell before that evening?"

"That is right. That's what I said."

"And they were so friendly at the dance, you thought they were paired off as a couple."

"Yes, I already said that."

"Yes. Now, you told the jury about an interesting episode in the rumpus room."

"Well, no, I didn't."

"We didn't hear anything about a rumpus room,

Mr. Beauchamp," Wally says. "Maybe we should check if that's just water in your pitcher."

This is a disaster. I have taken on the role of the court jester. But worse, has this reluctant witness gone over to the other side? In my confusion, I overreact. "Do you deny it? I'm talking about the cocaine, Miss Yi."

She looks at me with puzzlement. "No, I don't deny it. The prosecutor never asked me."

"Mr. Beauchamp, are we at different trials?" Wally is enjoying this tremendously, spearing me as I writhe on the floor.

"Sixty-two years of losing brain cells may have caught up to me, m'lord. Let's work our way out of this maze, Miss Yi. There *was* an episode in the rumpus room."

"Yes. Sort of between acts."

Meanly, Patricia has left it up to me to call evidence that could injure reputation. "Tell us exactly what happened."

"Well, there was a bathroom break, and Egan Chornicky sort of pointed to his nose."

"His nose?"

"Well, giving me a signal. So I followed him downstairs, into this room with a bar and a pool table. I don't want to get anyone in trouble. . . ." She falters.

"I'll say it for you. Mr. Chornicky produced some cocaine."

"Yes. From a little folded-up envelope, and he laid out some lines on the bar. Chopped them with a penknife."

"Was there conversation?"

"He was pretty drunk. Didn't know whose house he was in, actually."

"That's hearsay," says Wally.

"This is cross-examination."

"I'm afraid it's still hearsay." He smiles at me. He hopes I'll understand.

"Miss Martin joined you, did she not?"

"Yes, and Egan passed her a rolled-up bill and she . . ." Again her voice becomes indistinct.

"She knew what to do with it."

"She did two of the lines."

"There may be some here who are not familiar with the process of doing lines. Would you describe it?"

I finally seem to be on track. As Miss Yi relates to the uninitiated the art of snorting cocaine, I seek reaction from the jury. The smile on the face of Goodman, the broker, hints he needs no schooling. Hedy Jackson-Blyth has the peeved look of one whose bridge partner has trumped her ace. Two stripes of a mood-altering substance about the length and thickness of a match stick have disappeared up the complainant's nose: she will not be seen as the soul of innocence.

"Was this cocaine fairly strong?"

"Yes, Egan said—"

"No," the judge warns. "You can't tell us what someone other than the accused said."

This is wearying. I sigh rather audibly. "You've used cocaine before."

"Yes. Not a lot."

"And in your experience, was it potent?"

"I'd say so."

"Cocaine's a sleep inhibitor, is it not?"

"I think you'll need to call a pharmacologist for that, Mr. Beauchamp," says the judge. "Sorry."

I must keep my temper. "It certainly didn't make you feel sleepy, did it?"

"No, but—"

"It stimulated you—"

"Let her complete her last answer, Mr. Beauchamp."

"I wonder if your lordship would let me do my work here."

Wally looks hurt. "I have to be fair to both sides, you know. What were you about to say, Ms. Yi?"

"Well, Egan passed out in the taxi, so I don't know if it was *that* stimulating."

The whole room laughs. My cross-examination is again in shambles. I am so peeved at Wally that I find myself tottering badly during the balance of my inquiries, and limp to a stale close. "I understand you consider yourself a feminist, Miss Yi." I seek to show that despite sisterly misgivings, she has come here prepared to tell the awful truth about Kimberley Martin.

"Yes, but I don't believe just because a woman gets high means someone has a right to attack her."

Hedy Jackson-Blyth nods in total agreement. My examination ends with that loud clong. I can think of no way to make repairs. The Commander fumbles his way to a chair.

Wally is grinning, too obviously enjoying my discomfiture. "I have a leftover sentencing matter, so I think we'll adjourn for the day."

"That was a disaster," I mumble to Augustina as we flee the courtroom.

She hands me her evidence notes. "In case you missed something," she says sternly. "Make sure you phone Mrs. Blake tonight, okay? Might help keep you alert. If it's okay, I'm having dinner with the client. Keep him sober, guard him from the witch of the Slocan Valley."

"Enjoy yourself." A. R. Beauchamp, Q.C., says this bitterly, still disgusted with this morning's amateur production. Caped hero, indeed. Where was the blood, the boldness?

I retreat ignominiously to my hotel suite. I stare sourly out the window at a gargoyle sticking out its tongue, jeering. I've been out of training too long. My island has made me stupid and soft.

I wait until five-thirty to call Margaret—she will be in the house, preparing her dinner. I let it ring several times—she is probably in the garden or the barn. I picture her rushing to the house, panting as she grabs for the receiver, ah, yes, yearning to hear my voice. But no. No answer.

I try to console myself with a book, but cannot work my way into it and put it down. I order food up. I drink coffee and read the newspaper. I phone Margaret's number again. No answer.

She has a meeting to attend. The Fall Fair Committee. The Save Our Island Committee. She is campaigning for office. She is busy.

I try to get into my book again, but the words slide around on the pages, forming an illegible, muddy paste. I stare out the window: traffic clogs the streets below. The city is turning orange against a sun that sets beyond Garibaldi Island.

She knows where I am staying. She could call me.

I venture out into the fresh evening air. I pause upon the lawns of the Vancouver Art Gallery, kick off my shoes, and swirl slowly about on the grass, fifteen minutes of mind-composing tai chi.

At ten-thirty, back in my room, I phone Margaret again. And still no answer. Why is this early bird out so late?

I pick up Augustina's notes. I put them down. I pee. I shower. I brush my teeth. I go to bed. I fall asleep.

My dreams are visited by old unwanted friends: Messrs. Ridicule and Shame. I stand flaccidly exposed before Wally Sprogue in his golden toga. The executioner stands by, masked and smiling. Guilty, intones the chorus, guilty, guilty. . . .

On this first morning of September a soggy quilt of clouds lays atop the city, obscuring the peaks of the North Shore mountains. As I stand before my hotel window, I feel as gloomy as the sky; yesterday's bout of courtroom impotence has caused me an ill foreboding. And where was Margaret all last night?

"Hurry, Arthur. It's almost ten." Augustina has come to fetch me, armed with umbrellas. I grab a room-service muffin and munch it as we venture out into the drizzle. She sees I am morose, and kindly offers no reviews about the bomb I dropped on opening day.

"I just talked to Patricia—she's going to hold off Kimberley until the afternoon. Egan Chornicky is next; he should be okay, he likes O'Donnell. Then it's Constable Peake, who's on annual leave and wants to rejoin his wife in Arizona, followed by dashing Clarence de Remy Brown, who's antsy to get down to South America."

"How was your evening with the accused?"

"Like a sort of date, actually. Not romantic, I don't mean that, but we went to a movie after, and had a decaf at his house. He didn't try to tie me up and paddle me. He was being all very witty and sarcastic, but then he got moody. He kept saying, 'I have to do the right thing.' Refused to elaborate."

Inside, we sheathe our umbrellas and swim among a school of reporters, arriving in court to find Egan Chornicky already in the box. A spare, weedy-looking man, he wears a jean jacket that seems in the process of decomposition. A wild thicket of moustache. Unruly blond hair that he constantly sweeps from his eyes as he bends forward in whispered conference with Patricia. As court is called to order, she walks away shaking her head.

Chornicky is quickly in trouble. "I don't have a home address right now," he testifies. "Like, permanent. My landlady and I had a little disagreement."

He is equally unsure about his current occupation. "My job? A short-order cook. I was going to repeat my year in law school, but I got a chance to promote this rock band. I dunno."

His memories of the dance are vague and of little

help to either side. "I was too busy looking after the bar to really notice anything," he says.

"What was Professor O'Donnell drinking?" Patricia asks.

"Stiffs. Doubles."

"What about you?"

"I guess I was looking after myself pretty good. I didn't want to have to lug away any full bottles."

"Tell us what happened after the dance."

"Well, we had this party to go to after, downtown here, and we all sardined into a bunch of cars. I was in there with Kimberley in one car, which Ears was driving—"

"Ears?"

"Charles. Charles Stubb. And we went up to this house, and there was this really large evening going on there, about fifty people, and I guess when they ran out of beer that's when we went to the professor's house. A lot of this was so long ago, I've forgotten what I did remember. Some of it I think I read in the papers. I was pretty zoned."

"Tell us just what you remember."

"I remember going over Lions Gate Bridge. I remember a fairly swish house, I assume it was his, the professor's. Big library and a fire, lots of sort of Elizabethan music. There was some excellent scotch or something doing the rounds."

"Who was with you?"

"I don't know, there were five or six of us. Kimberley for sure, and another good-looking lady."

"Woman," Wally says. "She was a woman."

"Very definitely, your honour. Chinese."

"Southeast Asian Canadian."

"Correct. And there was some kind of cross-dressing thing going on, I remember that Kimberley started, but I didn't get into it. She did some kind of Shakespeare gig. Or that may have been at the other house. I don't remember going home, but I must have."

· 301 ·

Though I can't fathom how he passed his LSATs, I admire this man: he has attained heights denied even to Beauchamp in his prime. The jurors are smiling.

"Okay, Mr. Chornicky, there's been some mention of drugs being used that night. Did you have any cocaine on your person?" It is a subject Patricia cannot avoid now.

"Well, here's where I object on the ground that the question will incriminate me."

"Nothing you say can be used against you," says Wally. He frowns at the witness in warning. "Except on a charge of perjury."

Patricia says, "Okay, what is the answer to my question?"

"Well, the night before, an associate of this band I work with laid on me a little powder which I assumed was cocaine, though I never had it lab-tested or anything. Could've been speed, could have been powdered milk. And I remember I had it on me at the dance."

"Did you consume any?"

"Yeah, here and there."

"Did you ever share it with anyone?"

"With Kimberley and the Chinese girl. I have a little spurt of a memory there. I think they each blew a couple of lines."

"But you don't know if it was cocaine."

"Not for a fact, no."

"Oh, come, Mr. Chornicky, we weren't born yesterday," says Wally, who seems incapable of honouring his pledge to stay out of the arena and above the fray. "Did you really think it might be powdered milk?"

"Well, you do get ripped, but, yeah, it was probably cocaine."

"Surely your supplier told you that's what it was." A tone of impatience: Wally will teach this ruffian a lesson.

"Not really, your honour."

"What exactly did he say?"

"All he said was it was pure Ivory Snow, and had never been stepped on."

"Stepped on?"

"Like, it was very powerful. Never diluted."

"M'lord, has your cross-examination concluded?" Patricia asks. "Or is there more inadmissible evidence you'd like the jury to hear before this finds its way to the Court of Appeal?"

I marvel at her boldness. A shock wave seems to pass through Wally, who has the horrified expression of one who has observed a dead rat in his soup. The magic words, Court of Appeal—their lordships love to put the whip to new judges—seem to cause him to reflect, and he says petulantly, "I was just clarifying, counsel."

Wally is doing such a fine job for the defence that I worry the jury may conclude we sleep together. I'd actually feel more comfortable if he was well on the other side of the bed.

"Your witness," says Patricia. "For what it's worth."

I do not want to risk another debacle by cross-examining Chornicky. I have been dealt good cards and will stand pat. "Thank you. No questions."

"Not many questions left, are there?" Patricia glares at the judge, who has begun to look worried: his fly is open and his bias is showing.

"Call Constable Gavin Peake."

He enters, a cordial, husky boy in blue with an Arizona tan who I sense is not unsympathetic to his fellow white male person in the dock. He tells his tale efficiently, describing his reception by Clarence Brown at a few minutes before six o'clock in the morning, his long wait while the couple conferred, then finally his visit to the bedroom, where he awkwardly accepted

Kimberley's offer to view her scrubbed and bruised bare bosom.

I rise and snap my suspenders for luck. Do this right. No more bumbling, Beauchamp.

"A weird business, constable."

"Yes, sir."

"Not your usual sort of West Vancouver mischief."

"No, sir. Although you'd be surprised."

A sprinkling of laughter from the jury: a hopeful sign some of them may not be taking this case too seriously.

"Mr. Brown was in quite a fury when you showed up, wasn't he?"

"Yes, sir."

"Cursing, carrying on, vowing revenge, that sort of thing?"

"That's right."

Never ask a question without knowing the answer—that is the primary rule of cross-examination. But sometimes it must be broken. " 'I'm going to get that son of a bitch'—did he say something like that?"

"Close."

"How close?"

"He said, 'I'll kill that fucking son of a bitch.' "

"Thank you." A pause to let this surprise gift sink in. "Mr. Brown had a red substance on his hands and clothing, did he not?"

"Yes, some lipstick he got from—"

"Be careful," Wally warns. "That sounds like it could be hearsay."

I give him a warning look: Stay out of my yard. "Let's assume it's this Shameless-brand lipstick he got from being in contact with Miss Martin. On what part of his clothes was it?"

"Well, he had on a white shirt, and the front and sleeves were discoloured. He changed into a fresh shirt before we went up to talk with Miss Martin."

"No lipstick on her?"

"No, sir. She'd bathed."

"It was obvious she had been drinking?"

"I smelled it on her breath, yes."

"From a few feet away."

"Yes."

"Any other signs of intoxication?"

"Her words were somewhat slurred. I had a little trouble getting a sense of what happened."

"You're not alone. Thank you, that is all."

I sit with a grunt of satisfaction. I shot accurately enough, managed to miss my foot.

Augustina seems relieved. "Good show."

At the recess, courtesy requires me to dally awhile with Gowan Cleaver, who has dropped in, gowned, from another courtroom.

"Good God, Arthur, I thought I advised you to avoid that Jackson-Blyth woman at all costs. She's your bloody *foreman*."

"I think I must admit to a tactical blunder. How bad can she be?"

"Well, try on for size an article she wrote in . . . I don't recall, some left-wing rag. I think it was titled 'Assaults the Law Ignores.' About so-called unwanted touching. In the workplace *and* in the home. Ultra-militant stuff: you have to get down and beg for it, that's her attitude. Please, darling, pass the nookie. Anything else is rape."

I proceed outside and hide myself in the gloomy shroud of my pipe smoke.

As the jury returns, Hedy Jackson-Blyth looks at me with puzzlement, as if curious why I would even dream of letting her on the jury. A union boss—she will be arguing that her jurors stand on principle, in solidarity with aggrieved women everywhere.

On the other hand, she may not be sympathetic to

that corporate exploiter Clarence de Remy Brown, who has been known to hire strike-breakers at his northern mines. He, not his future wife, may be the key to winning this juror's heart and mind.

Brown walks in aggressively. As he takes the oath of truth, he thrusts out his wide, dimpled chin like a salute. Patricia leads him through the preliminaries: he is thirty-five, holds a degree in business administration from the University of Alberta, and has been engaged to the complainant for almost a year.

Patricia asks, "Do you know the accused, Professor O'Donnell?"

"I can't say I've had the pleasure." A deep baritone edged with malice. He looks at the man who defiled his spouse-to-be as one might study a turd the family dog had deposited on the rug. "I was aware he was one of Kimberley's teachers."

"During the final week of November last year, where were you?"

"I was in Venezuela. We were negotiating purchases of some mining leases. The trip came up suddenly."

"When did you plan to be back in Vancouver?"

"Early on the Friday, on an overnight from Caracas. I'd promised Kimberley I'd be back for her dance. That turned out not to be possible."

"She was expecting you that morning?"

"Oh, yes, we talked on the phone every day."

His voice alters abruptly: con spirito, tenderness and devotion. On early impression he seems not a man in whom reside deep wells of altruism; there is something mean and crabby behind that manly façade. The jurors, however, seem far too non-judgemental. Instead, curious, perhaps overly impressed— he has wealth, he has looks, he has power.

"Excuse me," says Wally, "you and she talked long-distance every day?"

"At least once or twice."

"Did you talk to her on November twenty-seventh? The day of the dance?"

I am liking this as little as Patricia. We may have to bind and gag our frustrated former counsel.

"We . . . yes, I believe I called her that morning."

"Then she knew you wouldn't be back for the dance."

"Yes, I think I told her I wouldn't be getting in until midnight."

"Thank you," Wally says. Having elicited this un-adulterated hearsay, he looks at me and nods smugly. Does he wish to do my work, or merely impress me?

"May I continue, m'lord?" Patricia says acidly.

"By all means."

"So she was expecting you to be late?"

"Yes, I told her to enjoy the dance and I would go straight home and wait up for her."

"Were you living together?"

"Yes, for the most part. She also has her own apart-ment."

"And when did you get into Vancouver that night?"

"Well, there was a long layover in Seattle so I had our executive aircraft come . . . about one o'clock in the morning, another fifty minutes to my house."

"And was Kimberley there?"

"No, and I knew the dance must be over. I called to her apartment and she wasn't there. I decided she was just out having a good time. I was deathly tired. I tried to stay up, but I fell asleep."

"And were you awakened during the night?" Patri-cia asks.

"Kimberley phoned some time around a quarter af-ter five."

Yet another unwelcome intrusion from the bench: "Now, you know you can't repeat what Ms. Martin said to you. That's hearsay."

"What was her emotional condition?" Patricia asks.

"She was distraught. Hysterical. She wanted me to—"

"There, that's exactly it," says Wally. "She told you something. That's hearsay."

I have had enough of this. It is time for the Commander to move Wally smartly into line. "M'lord, when I decide to object, you will hear it loud and clear. 'Out of the arena and above the fray,' as a wise man once said."

The message is cryptic enough, but Wally looks as if he has been stabbed: I have affronted him before this vast audience. "I wanted to make the ground rules clear. Carry on, Ms. Blueman."

Wally's vanity has been pricked. His sour look says: Don't expect me to do you any more favours, Beauchamp.

With no further flack coming from the bench, Patricia sweeps along at jet speed, taking Brown to the house of the Reverend Dr. Hawthorne, Jonathan's neighbour, where he rescued his lipstick-slathered fiancée.

"When did you first observe these red markings on her?"

"She was wrapped in a blanket, but when we got to the house, she showed me. There were red smears all over the lower half of her body and circles painted around her nipples. Sort of like targets."

"Anything else?"

"Some very prominent bruising on her wrists and her chest."

Hedy Jackson-Blyth's eyes narrow: this is beyond unwanted touching.

"Then what did you do?"

"I tried to settle her down—she was still pretty panicky—and we had some more conversation, and then I called the police. It seemed to take till doomsday to get someone I could talk to. I finally connected with Constable Peake, and he said he would come right over."

"And what was Kimberley doing as you were on the phone?"

"Well, she disappeared upstairs into one of the washrooms, and she bathed and put on her nightgown and went to bed."

Patricia is looking at the clock: almost noon. I think she wants to bring Brown's evidence to a swift close, to avoid building his role as promotion manager for the complainant.

"Briefly, tell us what happened after Constable Peake arrived."

"I had a detailed conversation with him, and then he interviewed Kimberley. He took us to the North Shore Hospital, where she was examined by the doctors. By this time, she had settled down quite a bit, but she was still very angry."

Patricia is awarded a dramatic note upon which to adjourn for lunch. "At whom?" she says with a flourish.

"At him." He points a six-gun at Jonathan, the thumb raised as the hammer.

Tactless and callous, the gesture backfires, and Patricia stalls, seeking to salvage the moment, then says, "No more questions."

As we take the noon break, Jonathan says, "Don't think I'd want to meet that man in a dark alley. Where did we get this judge, Arthur? Institute of Political Correctness?"

"He spent the summer getting his consciousness tuned up."

"God spare us all."

He offers to buy lunch, but I decline. Augustina eagerly accepts—I sense she has begun to enjoy his company too much.

I return to my hotel suite. I telephone Margaret. No

answer. Preparing her pens? Grooming her animals? Or is she purposefully avoiding me, unable to deal with my adolescent crush, my stumbling attempts to pursue her? Will my beloved tree-hugger continue to flee like Daphne from rude Apollo only to transform herself into the unbudging laurel tree of legend? *Abate, fair fugitive, abate thy speed, dismiss thy fears, and turn thy beauteous head. . . .*

༺༻

Before court resumes, Wally again calls us into his chambers. "Beauchamp, I don't particularly enjoy being upbraided before the jury." He is still smarting from this morning's spanking, and has obviously been mulling over his bruises through the lunch break. "I intend to be an activist judge. I will interfere when I feel it's necessary."

"Not during my cross-examination, if you don't mind, Wally."

"When it's necessary. *I'm* running the show here. Let's get back to work." Almost a snarl.

I have underestimated his pridefulness. If we tangle in open court, fine: I will work to a keener edge. Friction pumps me up, and I feel I am finally getting into this trial, freeing myself from the seductive pull of Garibaldi Island.

As court convenes, Brown sits down, checks his watch, then leans forward, ready, the promontory of his chin thrust out like a target he dares me to hit.

I begin with some risky target practice.

"Mr. Brown, you personally picked up the phone and called the police that morning."

"Yes."

"But you did not do so at Miss Martin's behest."

"I called them."

"Miss Martin did not want the police brought in?"

I don't know this as a fact, but all indicators point that way.

"She was very confused."

"She specifically told you she didn't want the police involved."

"Not after I explained to her . . . Can I say that, my lord?"

"Mr. Beauchamp has opened it up," Wally says. "I assume he knows what's he's doing."

A juror smiles at me, the nurse, Mrs. Beiran. She can tell the judge is in a snit.

"We had a discussion. She didn't want to be put through this whole rigmarole . . . this show, what we're going through right now." His voice again takes on that false note of tenderness. "It has caused her a lot of pain."

"Not to mention the pain it's caused you."

"She is the one who was raped, counsel."

"But you are the true complainant. You are the one who insisted that charges be laid."

From the bench, Wally makes a show of shaking his head, letting us all know this line of questioning doesn't wash with him. Too many sexual assaults go unreported.

"I advised her, yes."

"You persuaded her. In fact, there was a heated discussion."

"I advised her."

"I put it to you that you made your point quite firm and clear."

"It's not something about which I would give orders."

"However much you're used to giving them."

"That's uncalled for," Patricia says.

"You don't have to answer that," says Wally.

"Were you upset when you arrived home and found Miss Martin wasn't there?"

"Not particularly."

"On the telephone that morning, you told her to enjoy the dance and you would wait up for her."

"Yes."

"You expected her, as instructed, to come home after the dance?"

"I wasn't *instructing* her, counsel."

Counsel. A form of address one might use to a peon in a boardroom. "You'd been away for a week. You'd made plans to see her that Friday night. She didn't show up. And you weren't upset. Do I have all that correct?"

"She likes to enjoy her parties."

"It wouldn't have been the first time?"

"Not really. She is a very independent spirit."

"Which I hazard is the cause of some friction between you?"

"Not at all. We never fight."

It seems a palpable lie from the mouth of this controlling person. Even Hedy Jackson-Blyth must see that—though she remains expressionless.

"Later on, after you fetched Miss Martin home, were you surprised when she went upstairs and . . . did she have a shower or a bath?"

"Both. Yes, I didn't want her to. But as I say, you can't tell Kimberley what to do."

"Did you have an argument with her about that?"

"I told her . . . I suggested she shouldn't destroy evidence."

"And you had quite a tiff with her?"

"I never touched her. I've never laid a hand on Kimberley."

A firm denial of an unmade accusation. Was there a tussle? Would that explain some of her bruises?

"She asked you not to call the police. You insisted. You told her not to bathe. She insisted. This was not a calm discussion, was it, Mr. Brown?"

"You have to understand, counsel, the state she was

in. She had been to hell and back. She was crying, hardly able to—"

"Answer the question!" The Commander's blared order rebounds from wall to wall within this hushed courtroom.

Brown seems taken aback; he is not used to being dictated to. "We had some words."

"Despite the horrible ordeal she claimed to have suffered, you and she had a fight?"

"I was trying to get her to act rationally, counsel. She was all over the place, confused."

"Understandably. She was drunk, was she not?"

"I didn't think so."

"Oh, come. She was intoxicated, and you know that to be a fact."

"She'd been drinking, but I'd say she was in a state of shock. She managed to explain quite coherently what had happened to her."

"While Constable Peake waited to meet with her, you were up in the bedroom helping her with her story."

"It wasn't a story."

"The jury may feel differently."

"You're bullying the witness, Mr. Beauchamp," Wally says.

I ignore him. "Mr. Brown, is it fair to say you felt the police were lax in handling this case?"

"Lazy *and* lax."

"The accused not visited until several hours later. No arrest made until the afternoon. The complainant poorly interviewed. That bothered you, didn't it?"

"I will definitely agree with you there."

"That's why you hired a private detective to try to dig up some dirt about Professor O'Donnell, isn't it?"

The witness seems about to take offence at this, but surely he must know his footprints are all over the scene. Patricia is in motion, a swirl of black gown: "Objection!"

"What's the basis?" Wally asks.

"It's irrelevant, it's prejudicial, it's . . . Excuse me."

She marches quickly up to me and hotly whispers, "This is out of bounds. You gave an undertaking."

"Read the undertaking," I whisper back. "It says nothing about my not raising this issue."

She realizes that is so. "I agreed not to call Dominique Lander as part of my case. You're taking advantage of that."

"Yes, I am."

"It's unfair."

"Tell it to the judge."

Exasperated, she returns to her table. "This is entirely irrelevant, what the witness did afterwards, whom he hired. Mr. Brown is not on trial."

"Perhaps he ought to be," I say. "Counselling a false report of a crime."

Wally is severe. "That's enough, Mr. Beauchamp, you're taking too much liberty. I don't want to be warning you again."

"*Lapsus linguae,* m'lord." Formerly, I was naughty. Now, I am being warned of possible contempt proceedings. I sense Wally would love to uphold Patricia's objection, if only out of revenge, to prove he is the boss. But he knows he risks facing the wrath of the much-dreaded Court of Appeal.

Lamely, he says, "Let's see where this goes."

"Do you remember the question?" I ask the witness.

Brown has had some time to compose his thoughts, and knows better than to lie. "Did I hire a licensed investigator? Yes, I did. For the very reason I told you. The police weren't doing much of a job."

"And you had him follow my client."

"I believe he did so."

"Everywhere. Home, office, strolls in the park."

"I can't say where he went. You'll have to ask the investigator."

"And you instructed him to find a witness you could use against the accused."

"Whatever he could find."

"And he finally came up with somebody called Dominique Lander?"

The trail I follow is leading me directly across a frozen pond. How thin is the ice? Will I take Jonathan to the bottom with me? But instinct tells me the risk is well taken: there could be treasure on the far shore.

"That was the name he gave me."

"And you instructed him to offer her some money to come here and testify, didn't you?"

Brown shifts, frowns, a witness in trouble, unsure whether I know or am guessing. "Just her expenses."

"How much?" This is the question the avaricious Dominique Lander refused to answer when asked by Augustina. It is one with which Brown is now grappling. He fears I may have proof.

"Five thousand dollars."

"Plus hotels and meals?"

A pause. "Yes."

"Did you consider that a bargain? Hard to buy a witness for less than that these days, isn't it?" And I look Hedy Jackson-Blyth hard in the eyes. "I assume that's more than you're used to paying your strike-breakers."

Patricia is demanding retribution; Wally is warning me one more time. I flee the raging storm and take my chair. "No more questions," I say.

"We'll take the mid-afternoon break," says Wally grumpily.

Augustina grins at me like a monkey. "And I was afraid you'd lost it. You *are* a son of a bitch."

"Thank you, my dear."

As the jury files out, they observe Brown tramp disgusted from the room.

"That is a relationship doomed to hell," says Jonathan. "Poor Kimberley."

I find it odd he feels such consideration for his nemesis. "Stay put, out of his sight."

As Augustina and I head off to the great outdoors for a smoke, we observe evidence of Jonathan's dire prediction: Brown is in animated conference with Kimberley—who is beyond incensed, livid, in fact. She storms off.

"What could that have been about?"

"God knows," says Augustina. "It looks like he's deserting the ship."

Attended by an aide, Brown follows us out the courthouse door, shrugging into a coat for this cool and gloomy day. He marches down the steps, busy on his cell phone, marshalling his corporate empire, damage control in Guyana. He pauses at a waiting Cadillac, turns to us, shakes his head with an air of disgust, and departs.

"Sensitive, understanding guy," says Augustina. "And generous with the expenses. *That's* why Patricia wasn't too keen on calling Dominique."

On our return to the mezzanine, Patricia parts from a still-simmering Kimberley Martin and beckons me to join her in a quiet corner.

"Arthur, I'd like to recess for the rest of the day."

"Kimberley's not ready? Ah, but she had a little spat with her gentleman friend."

"The silly, bloated bastard. He hadn't told her about hiring Frank Sierra."

"And she fired him as stage prompter, did she?"

"She's furious at the deception."

"Are none of your other witnesses available? We have over an hour of this day to while away." I feel sympathy for Kimberley—she is having a difficult time—but I cannot bear to see precious moments wasted.

"Okay, I've had to excuse Dr. Hawthorne; he's not

well. A touch of flu. He's on in years, so we'll make do with his housekeeper. We can read in his evidence from the prelim, if you like."

"Please." He spoke no ill of Jonathan. But I would rather have him here.

"And Mrs. McIntosh is subpoenaed for tomorrow along with the pathologist, Dr. Sanchez, and Sergeant Chekoff. And we'll have the serologist, if you need him."

As she explains this, Kimberley edges closer. For a moment she stands uncertainly just out of range of our voices, then barges in.

"Mr. Beauchamp, we haven't been introduced." She offers her hand: a tight, tense grip. "I've heard wonderful things about you. Mostly from Patricia."

"Ah, but you can never trust what Patricia tells you."

Kimberley offers a game but strained smile. "Pat, I want to go on. Now. I don't want to wait. I'm ready. I'm not ready, but I want to get what's left of my life under way." She turns to me. "He did it, Mr. Beauchamp. He's guilty."

Patricia tries to warn her. "Kimberley—"

But Kimberley won't be hushed. "I'm sorry he did it. I'm almost as sorry as he is. If he could undo the past, I'm sure he would, but we all have to live with what we've done and who we are."

"Aptly put, Miss Martin. Past life is a script that cannot be altered."

From the periphery of my vision I see Jonathan watching us, curious.

"Now, Pat. I'm okay. I can do it."

Is she playing the gallant trouper for my benefit? How difficult it is to read this young woman.

๑๑

"I call Kimberley Martin."

Kimberley walks gracefully up the aisle, her head high. On the stand she takes a deep breath, her chest filling out. She smiles at Wally—his eyes fixed on those swelling breasts—as she accepts his invitation to sit. Wally smiles back, showing teeth, flirting.

As she responds to the opening questions, her voice assumes a firmness. She is led through her personal history: where and when born, parents, sibling, schooling, her plans to finish law school and to wed. Her evidence as to her early dealings with Jonathan varies little from that at the preliminary, but is less emphatic, offers less punch. Often her responses are long and rambling, but just as often curt. Many glances Jonathan's way: usually hostile, but sometimes curious. Occasionally she fails to follow a question, and it must be repeated for her. For all her determination, she is not the feisty young woman who testified at the preliminary inquiry.

But this works for the jury; she has already engaged their sympathies. In fact, I suspect they find her far too likeable. Wally, of course, interjects often and gallantly, spreading his cloak to help the witness cross the puddles, coquetting boldly with this maiden in distress.

Yet Kimberley's evidence is so far none too compelling. Patricia would obviously like to portray Jonathan as a lusting beast circling his prey on campus lawn and in cafeteria, but the picture lacks resolution.

"How often did you and he, ah, bump into each other?"

"It seemed like two, three times a week."

"Did you feel he was stalking you?"

I am on my feet. "That is about the most blatant leading question I have ever had the privilege to hear in a court of law."

But Wally is solicitous. "Try to put it another way, Ms. Blueman." Why is he not rapping her knuckles for this? But he is miffed with me, and is taking out his revenge.

"How would you describe the accused's relationship with you?"

"I thought he was giving me a lot of extra attention. In class and out. It didn't bother me."

This line of questioning seems in danger of fizzing out, but Patricia is relentless. "Did you at any time inform Professor O'Donnell that you were engaged to be married?"

"Yes."

"Did that seem to discourage him?"

Again I rise. "I object to this clearly loaded question."

"I think you're being far too fussy, Mr. Beauchamp," Wally says. "The witness may answer."

Kimberley is emboldened. "He kept coming on."

"You were chair of the social committee that organized the dance?"

"That's right."

"And did you invite any of the faculty?"

"Yes. I personally sold Professor O'Donnell a ticket."

"Why?"

"He was on my list."

"And his response?"

"He said he'd be delighted."

"Around this time what were your feelings about him?"

The witness takes some time answering. She bites her lip.

"I liked him. He was a very good teacher, and that's how I thought of him. Mostly."

While that odd little adverb "mostly" hangs in the air, she locks eyes again with Jonathan: briefly, intensely. Patricia studies the wall clock.

"Good time to break, Ms. Blueman?" Wally asks. "Almost four-thirty."

"M'lord," I say, "can we not carry on until five? I'm sure Miss Martin would like to get a full day in."

"Are you comfortable with that, Ms. Martin?" purrs solicitous Wally. "Do you think you can cope? It's up to you."

"Yes," says Kimberley, "I'd like to get this . . . ordeal over with."

"I quite understand," says Wally.

Augustina leans to me. "I think I'm going to ralph up."

Patricia takes the witness to the Odd Fellows Hall in the Fairview area—Kimberley arrived early to help set up for the dance. She had "a beer or two" with her helpmates and, later when the affair got under way, a rye and 7Up.

"And did the accused show up at this dance?"

"Yes, I would say about nine-thirty. And he came over to where I was, and I asked him if he'd like to dance, and we did that."

This is a more muted version from that on her tapes, in which she said Jonathan made a beeline for her.

"And then he bought me a drink. It seemed a little more powerful than the one I'd had before. It may have been a double. We talked for a while. He asked where Remy was. And I remember we talked about his background, about the British aristocracy—his father's a nobleman of some kind, a viscount, I think. But he came to Canada when he was nine, educated mostly here, except for Oxford . . . well, anyway, that's what we talked about."

She staggers to a halt. I suspect she has been coached not to run on like this, to keep her answers short and pertinent. A hint of a sardonic smile plays on the lips of forewoman Jackson-Blyth, who keeps staring at Jonathan—does she see him as some inflated right-wing aristocrat, boasting of his heritage in an effort to corrupt this trusting student?

Kimberley restarts her engine. "I saw him make several visits to the bar, and then he came up to me and asked if he could have the last dance. I could see he was a little impaired. He took a misstep or two—but even in that condition he's a pretty good dancer, and I told him that, and he said the same to me. He became very complimentary; he liked my dress, said I have taste, said I have a great sense of humour—he went on like that. And then he told me that the lecture theatre filled with a beautiful light every time I walked into it." She reflects. "A brilliant light."

"This is as you were dancing?"

"That's right."

"What did you feel about all these compliments?"

"Well, I was . . . complimented."

Unaccountably she denies Patricia the answer obviously sought: that Jonathan was coming on like a train without brakes.

And with that, the clock strikes five, and Kimberley descends somewhat gracelessly from the witness box, nearly missing a step, her attention focused on Jonathan. She has glanced at him often, perhaps seeking applause from this theatregoer for her latest sterling performance.

During my cross-examination, will Wally continue to swaddle her in protective blankets? I fear if he does I may have no recourse but to engage in a little S and M and smartly spank this unctuous judge's bottom.

Jonathan approaches me, complaining, "Christ, the judge is crawling all over Kimberley."

"Wally has fallen hopelessly in lust. And the object of his attentions seems not to be herself."

"Whoever that is. Arthur, I'm inviting you and Augustina for dinner at the scene of the crime."

"A pleasure, but I may be poor company." I will be restless—my addiction is starting to gnaw again. I desperately need a fix of Margaret Blake.

At the bank of elevators I engage two of the jurors.

"Ah, yes, just another average day in life's weary round, Mrs. Nevers."

"I wouldn't know about *that*." The music of Jamaica in her voice. She is shy but smiling, this dimpled secretary.

"How's the season been, Mr. Lang? Bleak, I hear." He is listed as a fisherman.

"Yeah, it's been bad. They only gave us two days on the sockeye."

I ponder telling him of my own skill with line and lure, but think the better of it: fishing persons—fishers?—are not always fond of amateur depleters of resources.

Back in my room, I call Margaret's number. No answer. No messages from her on the hotel voice mail. She is clearly not prostrate with grief at my absence. A black thought: Is there someone else?

I gaze out into the gloom of downtown Vancouver. Rain pelts my gargoyles. How fare the evil spirits that beset George Rimbold? He answers after a few rings, his voice unnaturally strained—this worries me.

I tell him that my trial is whizzing along and I expect to see him on the weekend.

"I don't think I'll make it to the fair."

"Nonsense."

"Too much merriment going on. It will only depress me. I just bought some real estate, Arthur. First piece of land I've ever owned."

"But that's excellent. Where is it?"

"Plot in the cemetery."

"I hope, George, this is your macabre sense of humour at work."

"Don't worry, Arthur, it's a long-term investment."

To cheer him up, I entertain with a few nuggets from the trial—with some success, I think, because he becomes more spirited in conversation. Finally I ask if he has recently chanced upon Margaret. He has not, but he asks how my weekend evening went with her.

"I offered my heart. It wasn't summarily rejected, but is being held for inspection."

"Sure and she will never return it. She shares your feelings, Arthur, but a lady doesn't blurt them out. She demands to be wooed and pursued."

That, in turn, pumps up my own spirits.

My taxi takes me over Lions Gate and passes by a welter of malls and shops before finding the sanctuary of Jonathan's quiet street, a comfortable neighbourhood of sturdy frame houses buried in the urban rain forest. I alight at 141 Palmer: neo-cubist architecture, three split-levels cascading down a gentle decline that ends at a small gully—dry now in September, though a running brook when Annabelle and I were Jonathan's dinner guests a few winters ago.

I proceed up a stone walkway to the door from which naked, painted Kimberley Martin fled on a cold November night last year. *He's going to kill me.* A nasty dramatic touch or a hasty improvisation? It seems too bizarre that Jonathan would have uttered a death threat, yet unlikely she would make that claim unless her mind had gone careening out of balance.

Augustina's sporty Porsche is in the driveway behind Jonathan's sedan, and it is she who greets me at the door, a glass of wine in one hand, a cigarette in the other, a smoky kiss plump on my lips. I have grown increasingly fond of this excellent person, but I fear for her foolish heart—I have noted it seems to flutter when Jonathan is near.

In the kitchen, bending to a built-in oven, is the accused in an embroidered blue apron. How domestic he appears. Steaks sizzle on a Jenn-Air grill; vegetables are steaming in a colander. Jonathan has arrayed various herbs and seasonings on his work space—like many bachelors, he seems an accomplished chef.

"What a sordid scene of wanton lust this afternoon, Arthur," he says. He mimics Wally: " 'Poor thing, do you think you can cope?' I've met him at a couple of bar functions—he has a repertoire of bedroom jokes. Beneath the shiny new p.c. paint job lurks the same old lecher."

Despite the strain Jonathan must feel, he manages to maintain his cynical sense of humour. I have a sense he has recently resolved some kind of inner struggle, though I also pick up a worrying tone of defeatism. Can it be that he has lost hope, found the peace of surrender? I pray not. It is a contagion I dare not allow to infect my unsatisfied need to believe in his innocence.

He pours me a Perrier and ushers us to his study. "Don't offer to help. I'll call you when it's ready. I've already shown Augustina about; she can be your guide."

His library evidences a catholic taste in literature, along with much history and philosophy and, of course, law. A poetry corner: the complete works of Ovid and Virgil in the ancient language. A three-volume set of Shaw's collected plays, plus a single edition of *Saint Joan*, a thin paperback, looking rumpled and misused, some pages bent. As I riffle through it, a large red smudge catches my eye: Scene Nine.

Augustina studies it. "Not blood. It's lipstick. Shameless."

What to make of this? Anything? Clearly, this script was roughly handled during the amateur theatrics of November twenty-eighth. But Kimberley knew her lines—why would her lipstick be in this book?

"Seize the evidence," I tell her softly. "Don't mention it to Jonathan just yet."

"Why?"

"In case it . . . compromises his defence." Although I'm not sure why it would.

Wordlessly, she puts both copies of the play in her briefcase, then continues showing me about.

"This is the chair where she passed out, quote unquote," Augustina says.

An overstuffed armchair, a matching sofa by it. Over here, a large built-in desk, with a Selectric typewriter. Beside it, a review copy of some heavy tome about law in the Middle Ages. Framed on the wall, a photograph of a smiling, confident-looking older man in hunting gear, holding a dead pheasant by the neck, a bottle of champagne in the other hand.

"Viscount Caraway," says Augustina. "Jonathan says the picture tells it all; he thinks it's funny. He says he only recently brought the photo out from hiding. He and his father have had some kind of a rapprochement."

"How has his father reacted to all of this?"

"With pride, I think."

The viscount was in the news again, I recall, shovelling coals of hell and damnation upon Whitehall for selling Ulster out to Irish popery. It strikes me as cynically apropos that Kimberley Martin is Roman Catholic.

My tour takes me to the fireplace: a spent condom and a few linen sheets met their doom here on November twenty-seventh. Jonathan's panicky incineration of evidence may yet serve him poorly at this trial.

Augustina leads me through the living room—original art on the walls: modern, confusing to my eye—then down to the billiard room: the table covered, cues stacked neatly. A shiny varnished bar—the cocaine chopping block.

Our tour then takes us to the upper level, to a spacious master bedroom with a queen-sized brass bed. Here is where Kimberley did it with Jonathan, as the girls of Mop'n'Chop might put it.

French doors lead to a sundeck at the back. A large window looks out upon a mature weeping willow, obscuring Dr. Hawthorne's house, about forty feet away.

"This is the closet where her clothes were all neatly hanging. That's the suit she put on." Hidden in the back. "The en suite. Nice big bath, a Jacuzzi. Over here, the dresser drawers she snooped in, where she found the famous tie."

Augustina gets up onto the bed, lies face down, her legs splayed, her feet touching the second-to-the-end bedposts, raising a comely blue-jeaned rump. "Try it, Arthur. Oh, I forgot, you're in love with someone else. Actually, it would be really hard if she were resisting. On her back, yeah, no problem. So why would he have tied her face down? Obvious. So he could spank her. I didn't say that." But she abruptly becomes solemn. "Arthur, do you believe he's innocent?"

I hedge: "Innocence is irrelevant. We defend; juries judge."

"Yeah, I know all that, but what's your gut reaction—*is* he innocent?"

"I want to believe he is." But I sense that is not enough for her, too vacillating and weak. "Beyond a moral certainty, I cannot say, but I am determined to give him the benefit of doubt."

That seems not to satisfy her at all. Her face clouds. "He's been terribly wronged, Arthur."

I dare not suggest to her that her judgement might be impaired by the tenderness she obviously feels for the haunted soul we defend. Yet, I, too, have grown in my regard for this brother in pain—almost more than I dare to admit.

What did George Rimbold say? *You believe or you don't believe, there's no goddamn in-between.* I cannot be agnostic as to Jonathan's innocence; I *must* believe.

The food is excellent, the conversation intense, and it continues over compote and coffee. We discuss strategies: how to pry Wally Sprogue from Kimberley's bosom; how to cross-examine her—unrelenting politeness or the dentist's drills and needles? Were inhibitions so enfeebled through the cocktail mix of cocaine and alcohol that she succumbed to repressed desires? Augustina has talked to experts, one of whom is under subpoena, but it's an area of risky forensics that we may wish not to touch.

Have we missed anything? Are there clues floating about like gossamer too indistinct to see? Or are we looking in the wrong direction? I say nothing about the Shameless blotch on the text of Shaw's play. I'm still unsure what to make of it.

Jonathan tells me his psychiatrist, Dr. Jane Dix, will be attending tomorrow, and I am advised to spend some quality time with her. But he continues to be reluctant to say how she may be of use. She will not know the court's rules of engagement and may urge some inappropriate mental defence.

Jonathan can't seem to stop ruminating the mystery of Kimberley Martin. "She's a complex puzzle. Amazing woman. Bloody awesome, in fact. Too vibrant. Too damn *real*. Why can't I hate her? I can't find my anger; maybe I've buried it too deep."

I am perplexed by his forbearance. The wrongly accused usually tend to flare in indignation at their tormentors, but Jonathan seems to flounder in a swamp of . . . what? Not self-pity. Self-reproach, maybe, or shame.

"Actually, I feel a sort of sick admiration for the skilful way she's managed to trash my life." A wry smile. "I'm like a rat worried into a corner, trapped in a dead-end maze. A blameless rat, for what that's worth. I can't *prove* my innocence." He seems to be working up one of his heads of steam.

"The law does not require you to do so, Jonathan," I say softly.

"The law is an ass." His fist thuds the table; coffee slops; forks and spoons bounce. Augustina looks alarmed. "The *law*. The *law*! I'm trapped in the bloody *clutches* of the law. Presumption of innocence, reasonable doubt, grand precepts, aren't they? It's a system of beautifully constructed bullshit. The rule of law that I shove down innocent throats, that I teach and preach and supposedly celebrate, has reared back at me like some monstrous, rabid animal. It won't allow me to clear my name! If I continue to play dead like this I'll be chewed alive. Jesus bloody Christ, at least if I fight, I may have a ten-per-cent survival chance."

I down a last draught of decaffeinated coffee, wait until he cools down. "What are you saying, Jonathan?"

"I'm saying that this gag order is choking me. Even in the unlikely event I'm not *proved* guilty, I'll still be subjected for the rest of my life to a kind of universal smirking disbelief. But I can't defend myself, can I? Somebody give me the reasons one more time."

Augustina takes his hand, gently unballs his fisted fingers. "Jonathan, don't be so damn pessimistic. You're not going to hang unless you provide the rope."

I explain again to him. There are a dozen reasons for not putting him on the stand: he must admit to a guilty mind—his frantic efforts to destroy or alter crucial evidence, the sheets, the condoms, the dry-cleaned suit. None of this could they prove without his generous help. He could be trapped within the coils of his many lies. But, most perilous, the dangerous Dominique Lander would be unleashed against us in rebuttal.

"Miss Lander may find pleasure under the whip, but the lash of rejection bites deeper. She abominates you with the kind of venom that only a disorganized mind can concoct. She is determined to destroy you and will enjoy an immense sadistic thrill in doing so. No, Jonathan, you are to be acquitted by your silence."

He calms himself, sadly shakes his head. "There's no other way of keeping her off the stand?"

"That's the ultimate effect of our arrangement with the Crown. If you don't testify, neither does she."

"And nobody hears that you played master-and-slave games with that weirdo," Augustina says. "Wouldn't you rather have people smirking than laughing out loud?"

He smiles ruefully. "I've really done it to myself. What a pathetic jerk I've been." He sighs. "God save me."

"He will," says Augustina. "Won't you, Arthur?"

Our after-dinner conversation has not only enervated me but inculcated an almost morbid fear that I may fail in the godlike trust imposed on me. And now I have returned to my hotel too late to try Margaret once again, and this causes me to descend into a yawning chasm of emptiness and loneliness. *Love and pain are twin emotions.*

I crawl into bed and fall into a fretful sleep.

And then she calls.

"Arthur? Is it too late?"

I look at the bedside clock: a few minutes after midnight. "Not at all." I am suddenly wide awake, my body pulsing.

"Were you sleeping? Don't lie to make me feel good. Fall Fair Committee, two nights in a row. They were still going at it when I left. People were at each other's throats. That ridiculous Leanna Sawyer started it all. You know her. Bossy Jesus freak? Wanted no *beer* on the grounds. No beer at the fall fair? I told her she was nuts."

She needs to vent steam, and I insist she does so on my dime, so I disconnect and call her back. She talks nonstop for twenty minutes, an exuberant rhapsody: I am on her side, cheering her on, clucking with displeasure at the chicanery of her enemies.

"How's the trial coming?"

I talk until I am almost hoarse, reciting the entire encyclopaedia of the last two days, my gaffes, my triumphs, my hopes and fears.

At the end of this, I ask her if she could find the time to visit Rimbold. "He needs cheering up."

"You're an awfully kind man, Arthur. For a lawyer."

"I think of you a great deal, Margaret. I'm afraid I've been drifting off in court a bit."

"I think of you a lot, too. I do."

I nestle the phone onto its hook and crawl under the covers with a silly smile on my face. . . .

I am strolling with Margaret across the fair grounds: she applauds at the sight of a blue-ribboned entry in the organic category. I have won for best zucchini.

৯৬

The Commander is seated at the counsel table doodling two tiny words on a pad of paper: "I do, I do." *I think of you a lot, too. I do.*

But my mind must wander no longer down Potter's Road. The star performer has retaken the witness box and all other main players are present, *sans* Remy, who has apparently rushed off to his Guyana gold fields. As we commence, the activist judge beams down at her, a full moon lighting her way so she doesn't trip over any roots.

Recommencing her evidence, Kimberley is pensive,

brief with her answers. But intermittently a different personality seems to take over, and she brightens, and when she does so rambles incautiously, as is her wont. She is resolute enough considering that her fiancé has abandoned her in a time of need for business others could do.

The jury, too, must be seeing stress fractures in their relationship. They are quiet, attentive, and, I sense, neutral; they are waiting to hear the other side, the unflinching denials by O'Donnell of her atrocious slanders. Hearing no rebuttal, will they conclude Jonathan's silence means assent? Will Wally Sprogue then throw the book in vigorous affirmation of his belief in class and gender equity? *As her professor, you were in a position of unique trust. I sentence you to fourteen years.*

Patricia escorts Kimberley from the dance to the West End party to the scene of the crime. The witness goes there without prodding, running unleashed like a frisky dog as she describes the bantering over cognac and Benedictine, then the parlour-game production of *Saint Joan.* I am reminded of that smudge of lipstick in the rumpled paperback. Perhaps, for some obscure reason, she put the page to her face.

"And that went on for about twenty minutes, and then we took a break. Professor O'Donnell was going through his CDs, looking for some suitable music, baroque or medieval, or whatever, and I think Charles had to go to the bathroom, and . . . well, I followed Egan and Paula downstairs to a kind of billiards room."

"And what happened there?" Patricia asks. She has clearly decided to bite the bullet, to blunt my own fire during cross-examination.

"We had some cocaine."

I interrupt; I want the jury's full attention. "Since this junket to the rumpus room was omitted from her evidence at the preliminary, we will want to take careful notes."

"Take your time, Ms. Martin," Wally says.

"Who produced this cocaine?" Patricia asks.

"Egan Chornicky. He had a little envelope of it."

"How much did you consume?"

"A line. I'm sure that's all. I guess I had just a little too much to drink, because normally, unless . . ." Her voice falters. "I'm not a user. I mean, I've done it a few times. It's around a fair bit, you know, among some people in the theatre crowd."

There is an earnest pathos to this apology, and it rings true. I do not remotely see Kimberley as a drug-dependent personality—and I am all too familiar with the type.

"It's not something you do," Wally repeats for the jury's benefit, anxious to rehabilitate her.

"No. I normally don't like drugs."

Wally nods sagely. He is anxious to shelve this awkward incident; the innocent are prone to error. He asks Kimberley if she might enjoy a little break.

"Yes, thank you."

After judge and jury leave, Jonathan draws me aside and introduces me to Dr. Jane Dix, who has been sitting behind him in the gallery. She is in her mid-thirties: petite and perky, deep-set blue eyes, extremely close-cropped, straw-coloured hair.

"I cancelled my patients today," she says. "I thought this might be more gripping."

"She's here to analyse the judge's masturbation fantasies," Jonathan says.

"Poor Jonathan," she says. "I think you're jealous." She gives him a friendly poke, then turns to me. "We'll have a chance to talk?"

"Certainly."

As court reassembles, Kimberley's handlers huddle with her at the prosecution table; they want the complainant to strut her stuff, to come out swinging. She takes a deep breath as court is called to order, then mounts the stand and sits with chin uplifted. She looks resolute now, much fortified by Wally's kindly ministering.

We now follow her from rumpus room to second-floor bedroom to en suite washroom: "to answer nature's call" is her euphemism. While upstairs, she struck upon the "not-so-brilliant idea" of dressing in male clothing for the next scene of *Saint Joan.* Wally edges closer to the witness, hunching forward as she describes looking through Jonathan's clothes, stripping to her underwear, changing into his suit.

Her reasoning for playing this game of dress-up seems lost on some of the jurors. Kimberley's cheeks glow slightly, an innocent blush, as she recounts her impertinent impersonation of Jonathan.

The play proceeds. The fire awaits in the marketplace outside the castle of Rouen, wherein stands the heretic saint, chained at her inquisition—a trial within this trial. Just before she recants her confession, she falls asleep. Why then? Why does this boisterous actress suddenly spark out at the play's dramatic apogee? The jury must surely suspect, as I believe, there is an element of stagecraft here.

Jeanne d'Arc awakes to find on fire not herself but her law professor, in full bloom of lust, seeking to lance his trussed love slave from behind, successfully locating the generally preferred aperture, then trying in vain a less elegant route. Kimberley's account of her rude awakening is brisk if not eager, and we are subjected to no histrionics about how utterly degraded she feels to speak of such matters. This story of erotic abuse is so blunt in its telling that it jerks no tears, though Wally is frowning and has stopped taking notes. Here is the accused *in flagrante delicto.* Here is a woman cruelly abused by an agent of the patriarchy.

But do I pick up a faint aroma of scepticism wafting from some members of my jury? There is shuffling, a cough or two. Miss Jackson-Blyth is looking down at her hands and seems unhappy—the complainant has let the side down.

O'Donnell visits the washroom, and as he fills the tub Kimberley frees herself and flees. Her testimony becomes more spirited now; the major obstacle on her course has been cleared and she is racing for the finish line. A brief stop at the neighbour's house, then her lover arrives and whisks her away.

She showered, she bathed, and—heard here for the first time—she douched. She is not defensive about any of this. "All I could think of was winning back my body from him; it felt stained—it *was* stained. The lipstick looked like blood. And I just had to clean his smell from me." This last note is harsh, unexpected. She is returning Jonathan's stare now, bellicose. "I mean, I really felt I had something sickening done to me. By a man I'd respected."

I should rise to complain about these *ex gratia* calumnies, but content myself with a loud grunt of displeasure.

"Is that an objection, Mr. Beauchamp?" Wally asks.

"Merely a petty critique, m'lord, of an otherwise bravura performance."

Patricia scrambles to her feet needlessly; her witness proves able to protect herself. "I am speaking what I *know* is the truth, Mr. Beauchamp."

"Truth is known only to God, Miss Martin."

"I think your client needs help."

I am taken aback by her tartness and can summon up no quick rejoinder. Wally's hearty intervention makes matters worse: "She got you right back, Mr. Beauchamp."

Odd how such a reasonably competent lawyer can turn into such a toad of a judge. My nose has been bloodied, but I must keep my temper.

Patricia wraps up with a brief excursus to the production of *Switch*. Did the witness ever see the accused in the audience?

"At least four times. He kept staring at me. Like he's doing right now."

"Your witness," Patricia says.

A nice touch upon which to conclude. Miss Martin's combativeness is restored and fully functional. It is nearly twelve-thirty, lunch break. I rise.

"How are you feeling, Miss Martin?"

"Right now? A little hungry. I missed breakfast."

"Then enjoy your lunch. This afternoon we have work to do."

She smiles. "I'll be ready."

I am impressed as much as troubled by her new-found confidence.

I change from my costume, then brave the day: the clouds are still answering nature's call, gently voiding rain. The spell is over; I need not worry about returning to a withered garden, though the damp weather augurs poorly for the fair.

I proceed down Pender Street to Chinatown, then to Gastown, the city's old section, its red-brick bottleneck. Some old instinct leads me into skid road, to a century-old square brick building on Cordova Street, where I observe a moment of silence. This was my storefront office during my drunken two-year hiatus from Tragger, Inglis, Bullingham. Separated then from Annabelle, I slept in the suite upstairs. The lowest point in my life.

How sorry I feel for my former self. How glad I am not he.

While court assembles, I am witness to yet one more unblinking duel between Jonathan in the dock and Kimberley Martin in the witness stand. What messages are being telegraphed here? There is a stubborn set to the accused's face and Kimberley appears no less determined: haughty and imperious. This seeming struggle for dominance ends as court is called to order. Kimberley turns to gaze upon me, direct, defiant.

I open with a blunt and dangerous question, but I carry insurance on it. "Miss Martin, will you agree you were physically attracted to Professor O'Donnell?"

Obviously she is not expecting such a bold thrust, and she hedges: "When?"

"In the weeks and days prior to the dance."

"Was I physically attracted to him?"

"Yes, that was my question."

There occurs one of those empty silences that are often more telling than answers. The witness is in a bind: she knows she lied to the lie detector. She opts—boldly, though too late—to be candid. "Yes, I was."

"Physically."

"Yes. That doesn't mean I wanted to jump in bed with him."

"But you had reveries about that, didn't you?"

"What I dream about is personal." But the brightness that taints her cheeks is mute proof. The jurors and I follow her eyes as she looks for help to Patricia, who knows better than to jump in, to overprotect, to prolong this. But predictably, Kimberley's self-appointed guardian rides to the rescue from the bench, six-shooters blazing.

"Surely her dreams aren't relevant here, Mr. Beauchamp."

I give in to my irritation with this judge, speak with a sharpness that gives Wally fair warning that my fuse is short. "With respect, m'lord, you are in error. Her dreams are at the very crux of this case."

Wally remains silent for a while, then repents. "Well, I suppose. . . . Okay, let's hear how this develops."

"You had daydreams about Professor O'Donnell, did you not?"

"I hardly think I was the only one. Most of the women in the class thought he was interesting. There was lots of talk about him, some, you know, speculation. Single man with a brain, unusual background."

"Son of a British viscount, Rhodes Scholar, widely published author and critic."

"Yes, all of that."

"Were these dreams of yours erotic?"

Again she reddens. "Yes. But I mean . . ." She sighs. "Yes." A helpless shrug. "Dreams are dreams; life is different."

She says that rather sadly. Life is different; life is Remy.

"Yet you were engaged to be married."

"You make it sound . . . I was in love, Mr. Beauchamp. I *am* in love."

She has lost some poise. She looks down at her hands, at the diamond on her finger, furtively glances at Jonathan, then me. Those shifting eyes speak to me not of love but of some smaller, second-rate passion.

"In the course of the months Professor O'Donnell was teaching you, he made no physical advances?"

"Not really."

"Not really or not at all?"

"I wasn't aware of any."

Why do I sense she might have been disappointed by that? "No improper suggestions?"

"No."

"His conduct was gentlemanly throughout?"

"I don't deny that. Until the end."

This prompts a soft snigger from some coarse soul in the gallery.

"I think you once described him as a fantastic teacher."

"He was very good."

"And you felt he paid you extra attention, beyond the common lot of students—did you mind that?"

"No."

"He helped you after classes with your work?"

"Yes."

"And that's what a fantastic teacher might do."

"Okay. Yes."

"Yes. You were not a straight-A student."

"No, I wasn't exactly at the top of the class."

"And the course he taught in property law was especially difficult."

"I was having trouble with it."

"So you were grateful for this extra attention."

"Well, he wasn't giving it to all the other students."

"But he did to those who needed it, yes?"

"Maybe. Okay."

We now have a gentle rhythm working here. No doubt Patricia Blueman—who has taken on a crabbed, anxious look—has instructed her not to joust with me, to be forthright. A chastened Wally is giving me free rein for the time being. The courtroom is as still as a graveyard.

"And, to be fair, you often approached him on your own after class."

"A couple of times."

"It worked both ways, yes? A student-tutor friendship developed, is that fair to say?"

"A sort of friendship."

"It didn't shock you that he would join you for coffee from time to time."

"Not really."

"In fact you were quite encouraging to him."

"I don't know if that's how he read it."

"But is that how you wrote it?"

Kimberley can still her tongue no longer. "Mr. Beauchamp, I know what's in your mind, but I definitely wasn't pursuing him. I clearly let him know I was engaged. I suppose we flirted, it's something the opposite sexes *do,* but, you know, there's a line you agree not to cross, and . . . well, that's how it was."

"Fair enough, you flirted with him."

She sighs. "It wasn't one-sided. There weren't, you know, any expectations."

But were there base motives? The jury may find it unworthy of me to suggest she sought to charm her way to a passing grade. Jurors are neither dull-witted nor forgiving to counsel who belabour the obvious.

"You told us about visiting his office for some career counselling?"

"That's right."

"How did that come about?"

"I'd told him I was interested in family law. He asked me to come up and see him. He talked of everything but my career: my general interests outside law; what I did in my spare time."

"A professional adviser ought to know your interests outside law?"

"I thought he was being a little personal. Questions like was I going to have a family, and was I worried about conflict between marriage and career. As a Catholic, did I believe in birth control, that was another thing he asked."

I wait until this non-responsive speech peters out. "Miss Martin, do they still teach the rules of cross-examination in law school?"

"Yes."

"Please remember them. Kindly refrain from answering questions I haven't asked."

"I'm sorry."

Wally leans towards her, smiling. "I'm afraid Mr. Beauchamp's being a little persnickety about the rules, Ms. Martin. But just do your best. Would you like a break?

"No, I'm fine, thank you."

This dainty palaver allows me a moment to inspect

my jury, and I earn some eye contact, a smile or two. I think the Commander has their respect.

"You told us Professor O'Donnell was on your list to be invited to the dance."

"Yes. We had tickets to sell."

"Who prepared that list?"

"The social committee."

"And who was chairperson of that committee?"

She responds to my slightly mocking tone with a grin; she is recovering. "I was. But I also asked three other professors."

"And you found a moment to be alone with him?"

"Yes."

"And you asked him to save a dance for you?"

"There was nothing sinister about that. It was just friendly talk."

"Did you ask the other three professors to save you a dance?"

"They were all women, Mr. Beauchamp."

I turn to the jury, chuckling with them, accepting my lumps. Patricia grins broadly, too, but no one is enjoying this more than my self-important former friend, the judge.

"Miss Martin, did you tell my client that you'd be coming to the dance unescorted?"

"I . . . well, not like that. I mentioned Remy was in South America."

"He wasn't due back until the night of the dance?"

"That's right. A late flight."

"How long had he been gone?"

"A week."

"So you must have been pining for him."

She searches my expression for a sardonic tilt of eyebrow, but finds it deadpan.

"Yes, I was missing him. I had lots of things to occupy me, though. The dance. My play."

"Ah, yes. For several weeks you had been rehearsing for a student production of *Saint Joan*."

"Since September."

"And you were immersed in this play, were you not?"

"Totally. I think I bit off too much."

"You were leading lady."

"Leading woman," says Wally.

"Female lead," says Kimberley.

Wally is noticeably taken aback, the corrector corrected. Kimberley flicks a little smile at me—conspiratorial, as if we are sharing a secret. I am finding her dangerously disarming.

"Did your fiancé ever complain that so little time was reserved for him?"

"Oh, no, he keeps himself very busy, too. I mean, we were engaged, but we had our own lives. We *have* our own lives. That's important to us both."

"And do you intend to continue in that independent spirit after marriage?"

"As far as I'm concerned."

From this firmly stated response I once more sniff the sweaty scent of premarital discord—this strong-willed female lead has been arguing for her civil rights within marriage. No doubt her illiberal boyfriend has asserted a more doctrinaire philosophy.

Jonathan is looking contemplative, leaning back, his arms folded. He never lets his eyes stray from the witness.

"At times you live with your gentleman friend. At other times you stay in an apartment. Am I right?"

"It's just . . . convenient."

I find myself suddenly hard of hearing. "Excuse me—it's what?"

"Sometimes it's convenient to have your own place, that's all."

The utter vagueness of that word seems telling.

"Convenient in what way?"

"Sometimes . . . I have to be alone."

I strike a contemplative pose and study my jury.

Goodman's brows are raised, in speculation or distrust. Is he seeking to share with me, man to man, his doubts as to her loyalty to her lover? But I can't imagine she keeps a trysting place.

I spend several minutes probing her relationship with Remy, mainly to draw a reasonably unromantic sketch of a hard-nosed businessman—but also one who entertains his betrothed on his yacht and flies her first class to a rented villa in the Italian Alps.

Finally, Kimberley remonstrates: "I'm not in love with his money, Mr. Beauchamp. I'm in love with a fine, generous man."

Would this response pass a polygraph test?

She repeats, emphatically, "I am *not* marrying him for his money."

"I am sure you would not consciously do so."

Patricia breaks her long silence. "This has nothing to do with anything."

"Mr. Beauchamp, you're wandering far afield," Wally says. "We are interested in West Vancouver, not villas in Lake Como."

"I am merely bringing out the many reasons she isn't bored to tears by Mr. Brown."

Patricia complains again, "That's a very unfair and totally nasty innuendo, m'lord."

"Mr. Beauchamp, you're going over the line. I don't want to have to warn you again. We'll take our break now. Ms. Martin, I'm afraid that while you are under cross-examination, however long it lasts, you must not speak to anyone about this case. Anyone. That includes the prosecutors."

"I understand that."

"I'm sure you do. Ten minutes."

"You're on the right track, Arthur," Augustina says. "She had the hots for him; Remy is a moneyed bore."

"The point has been made?"

"Yeah, I've been watching the jury."

"But the jury likes her?"

"They like her, Arthur, but they don't buy her."

Kimberley is across the courtroom, sipping water, watching us. She looks far too relaxed. Has Remy's absence lessened the pressure on her? Are they enjoying a little time apart together? I catch her eye and she smiles. Despite all my nagging at her, I think she likes me. It is rather unsettling.

Then she looks at Jonathan, and the smile clicks off.

৯ঙ

When court resumes, Kimberley seems a little more guarded, though still composed and alert. I snap my suspenders, take a sip of water, and wait for the room to become silent.

"Let us return to the dance, Miss Martin."

"Sure."

"In the days of my youth, it was common for a young lady to reserve the last dance for someone upon whom she might have set her heart."

She laughs, and I have to smile.

"That did sound over-embroidered, but you have my point? Or have times changed?"

"Times have changed, Mr. Beauchamp."

"Ah, well, I'm a child of an earlier era. But tell me, did no one else ask to have that last dance with you?"

"Set of dances. They don't have just a last dance any more, Mr. Beauchamp."

"I amend the question—what is the answer?"

She hesitates. "Yes, I . . . Yes."

"But you turned these suitors down."

"Well, I didn't want to dance any more. . . ." But that line of response does not quite work for her. She shrugs.

"You were waiting for Professor O'Donnell to ask you, weren't you?"

· 343 ·

"Not exactly."

"Come, Miss Martin."

"Well . . . okay. I wasn't going to turn him away if he asked, let's say that."

"And as the two of you were dancing you mentioned there was a party afterwards, and you invited him to it. Am I correct?"

"I think I only inquired if he was going."

"The chairperson of the social committee didn't stay to help clean the tables after the dance?"

"I thought I'd come back the next morning."

"Yes. You were enjoying yourself immensely."

"I was having a good time."

"And wanted it to continue."

"I guess I did."

"Remy would have to wait."

"Well, Mr. Beauchamp, I guess Remy and I are just not old-fashioned enough for you. Relationships are different today. He's a very modern person; we're a modern couple, and I knew he'd understand. And I'd been working nonstop: classes, rehearsals, organizing this dance, and I just wanted to . . . let my hair down."

"And you'd had a few drinks by now."

"A few."

"And a few more at this house in the West End."

"A couple."

"As Mr. Chornicky might phrase it, you were pretty zoned."

"I think I was holding it."

"And your flirting with Professor O'Donnell—did it continue at this party?"

"You make it sound . . . No, we both circulated."

"But you got back in his car with him."

"I was heading up to West Vancouver, too. I thought of continuing on in the taxi, but I decided, okay, I'd like to see his house, and . . ." Again, she shrugs.

"And Cinderella didn't want the ball to end."

"However you want to put it."

"Thoroughly modern Remy would understand."

"I believed he would."

"Did you try to phone him?"

"Well, at the house party there was a line-up for the telephone."

"No line-up for Professor O'Donnell's phone, however."

"By that time—it's the small hours now. . . . Remy can't sleep on airplanes, so I assumed he'd turned in."

"As the hours passed, you suffered no niggling worries that your fiancé might be concerned about you?"

A long silence. "A little, maybe."

I return her silence. She cannot hold my gaze, and bites her lip and looks up high at the ceiling. Wally is giving me more breathing room now; I feel I am getting along quite nicely. A quick perusal of the jurors; Augustina is right: they like the way she offers her wares, but they aren't ready to buy. Even Miss Jackson-Blyth is looking uncomfortable. Goodman, the investment broker, has the set expression of one who knows the games such wily women play.

"At Professor O'Donnell's house, you enjoyed a heaping glass of cognac and Benedictine."

"I don't think I ever finished it."

"Followed by some of Mr. Chornicky's excellent cocaine. You tooted . . . Is that the right word, 'toot'?"

"I suppose so," she says wearily.

"Two lines of it, according to Miss Yi."

"I thought it was one."

"It helped you let more hair down?"

"A little more energy, that's all I noticed."

"You didn't mention this cocaine in any of your early interviews?"

"Frankly, I didn't want to get Egan in trouble."

"Frankly, I suspect, you hoped no one would come forward with the incident."

"I didn't think it was that big a deal."

"And this cocaine put you right to sleep, did it?"

"I'm sure it had worn off."

"In half an hour?"

"Well, maybe I just passed out, Mr. Beauchamp, I don't know. I remember feeling a little dizzy, and I closed my eyes. I heard voices, and I couldn't make sense of them."

"Ah, yes, but Jeanne d'Arc made sense of hers."

"Well, these definitely weren't from God. Everything just went black."

It is nearing lunch. I will add a touch of pepper to this debate to whet the jury's appetite.

"Now, you claim you woke up naked, ankles tied to a bed."

"Exactly."

"But that never really happened, did it?"

"It did, Mr. Beauchamp. It really did."

"You went willingly to bed with him, didn't you?"

"I certainly did not."

"You desired him."

"Mr. Beauchamp, I was engaged. I believe in sexual loyalty."

"You pretended to sleep; you found yourself alone with him. He was receptive to your advances—"

"*My* advances!"

"Yes, your advances."

"Your memory is better than mine, Mr. Beauchamp."

"There indeed seems to be a major gap in yours, Miss Martin."

She doesn't respond to this, and only bites her lip again, frowning, as if trying to fill in that gap.

"This is what I am putting to you, Miss Martin: As he leaned over you with a blanket, you suddenly opened your eyes. You put your arms around him and you kissed him deeply."

"That is quite wrong."

"You took off your earrings and laid them on the table, and you continued to embrace him."

"I deny that."

I turn up the volume control to full stentorian vigour. "You went upstairs. The two of you undressed. You hung your clothes up. And then you threw yourself upon him, embracing his naked body. You made passionate love—"

"That's an absolute lie!" Kimberley shouts. She waves her arm with an exasperated gesture, knocking over her glass of water, dousing the front of her dress.

"I think we had best adjourn for the day," says Wally. The heat of the moment is too much for him; he flees.

As Kimberley bends over near the witness stand, dabbing at her skirt with tissues, Jonathan appears from behind me. He extends to her a folded light-blue handkerchief. To my astonishment she accepts it, though without word or expression.

"It's not a flag of surrender, Kimberley," Jonathan says, and draws me aside and speaks with an air of weariness. "I want to give evidence, Arthur."

I am not sure I have heard him correctly. I have him repeat it, then I respond: "Over my dead body."

"I can't stay silent in the face of her lies."

"It's a good thing your psychiatrist is here, Jonathan. She can have your head examined immediately."

"Talk to her, Arthur."

I sigh. "I'll go change. Meet me across the street at the El Beau Room."

We are subpoenaed into chambers, where we find Wally in shirt sleeves, changing into his suit. He refuses to look at me, still aggrieved.

"This sort of intimidation doesn't sit well with me,

Beauchamp. I'd handle her differently were I defending. Kid gloves."

"I am reminded of a saying: 'Nothing is given so profusely as advice.' "

Wally looks as if he is about to square off with me, but Patricia intercedes. "Arthur, Mrs. McIntosh is anxious to get back to Reverend Hawthorne. He's at home with a temperature. Can we do her first thing in the morning?"

"No, I do not want my cross of Kimberley Martin blunted by delay."

Wally grumbles, "We'll just carry on in the normal way, then."

I must make amends to his pouting lordship. "What do you say, Patricia, shall we invite our esteemed judge out to dinner tonight?"

"I'll make that a joint submission."

"Okay, Wally? You and the four lawyers. And bring Melanie. We'll let *our* hair down a bit. Like the old days."

Wally stands before his dressing-bureau mirror, adjusting his tie. "Well, we *were* planning to have dinner out. . . ."

"Splendid," I say. "Pierre's. I'll reserve for six at seven-thirty."

❦

The El Beau Room is the bar at which in former times I held dionysiac court, regaling friends with drunken, salty wit. I recognize many cronies here: lawyers, court staff, sheriffs, a former crooked constable I once defended, now in real estate.

Jonathan is alone at a table. I ask him what happened to Dr. Dix.

"She had an emergency, seriously ill patient. She'd like to meet you this evening."

I tell him of my dinner arrangements. Tomorrow, he urges.

"What can she tell me that you can't?"

"Why I need to give evidence."

I shake my head in disbelief. "This is the right thing you are so set on doing? Jonathan, the trial is finally on the proper course. Read the jury. They are in doubt. It is a reasonable doubt. When they learn that no sperm was found within her, that doubt could expand exponentially. Rape with a condom? How unlikely that will seem."

"She claims she took a douche, Arthur. Only I can prove we used a condom. . . . Look, what's the through line for the rest of Kimberley's cross-examination?"

"What do you think it is?"

Jonathan takes a deep breath. "Okay. The drunken couple have boisterous, bruising sex. They fall asleep. She awakes. Hangover and reality set in. She panics when she realizes how late it is. Her fiancé is the spoiled heir to a fortune. She doesn't want him to know she made love to her professor on Remy's first night back. She doesn't quite have both oars in the water yet, and scripts this ridiculous scenario whereby she is tied and raped and defaced with a tube of Shameless lipstick. She runs next door: A, to secure a witness, and B, to call Remy. She never expects charges will be laid, but a battle royal ensues over the issue. Remy grabs her by the wrists to control her, and bruises her up some more."

"And is that how it was?"

"I'd like you to talk to Jane."

"I'll meet with her tomorrow."

Obviously, Dr. Dix will be his surrogate truth-teller and, I fear, the bearer of unwelcome news he cannot himself impart.

Back in my room, I try to quell the disquiet I feel about Jonathan's absurd urge to tell the jury . . .

what? Are we yet to have another amended history? Why can't Jonathan simply keep his mouth shut and stick to one perfectly satisfactory if inoperative version of the truth?

I am quite prepared to resign as counsel if he refuses my advice. Let that be an end to it.

I attend to a more important matter, a little toot of my favourite non-prescription drug. This evening Margaret is by her phone. As always I savour that pleasant numbing sensation when I hear her voice. She is cheerful, through worried about the weather: more rain is forecast on the weekend for gloomy Garibaldi.

She describes a typical island day: one of her geese escaped down Potter's Road and attacked a cyclist; Stoney and Dog are back on the job, but are still hiding from the law, sleeping on air mattresses in my garage; Kurt Zoller has had to shut down his water tanking business and is "wandering around with some rip-off logger trying to bribe people to clear-cut their lots." After she concludes her report she asks for mine.

"It's looking very good. I am starting to smell acquittal from this jury." There commences an hour-long strutting gasconade as I boastfully describe my *pas de deux* with Kimberley Martin. But I am fair: I give my fencing opponent the points she earned, the touchés. I also tell Margaret of my client's eagerness to bare all, his crisis of conscience—if that is what it is.

"But isn't that what the jury should hear—the truth?"

How do I respond without seeming the sleazy lawyer? Truth, disagreeable truth. Does it play a part in the theatre of court? Saint Joan burned in the flames of truth and so, I fear, may Jonathan.

" 'Liars when they speak the truth are not believed.' Aristotle."

"Don't hide behind your dead philosophers. What

is that other thing you always say? Truth does not blush. I mean, honesty is a kind of important concept, isn't it? And if it means so much to your client, shouldn't it be important to you?"

More important than winning? I shy from the topic with some ambiguity about life being a constant search for truth. I ask her if she has yet gone to see George.

"I'll do that tonight."

I want to put her to the test. I want to whisper through trembling lips those daunting three little words. But I would barely survive rejection: the mumbled apology, the vague promise to "think" about it.

After we disconnect, I try to reach George Rimbold. But after several hollow, distant rings, I hang up.

Probably starved, though I am unclear about that (for one in love, hunger seems a mere irritant)—I embark on a tramp through the dense West End, between high-rises that hide the murky sky, at twilight the colour of lead. Tomorrow, Thursday, the remaining witnesses will testify. Friday, final addresses. At day's end the jury will go out to discuss reasonable doubt. By Saturday morning I will be on the *Queen of Prince George*. This will be so.

I make my way to Denman Street, near the beaches of English Bay, and when I arrive at Chez Forget I find Pierre fluttering over Augustina, Patricia, and Gundar, telling them what they will have as entrées. He waves me forward, scolds me. "Mr. Beauchamp, I do not forgive you. Two hours' notice of a reservation for six. This is not some cheap joint where you can just walk in for a bowl of soup. As punishment you will have the tenderloin. It will cost you."

Wally and his wife have not yet arrived. Gundar

Sindelar is wrestling with a monstrous martini; the women share a bottle of pricey Bordeaux. Everyone knows that my generous client, the Faculty Association, will be picking up the tab tonight. Patricia will protest, for form, but the Attorney-General doesn't honour chits for fancy dinners.

I settle in beside Augustina, who looks quite alluring tonight, leggy in a brief skirt. I must find a quiet moment tonight to tell her of O'Donnell's mad urge to testify.

"Excellent performance today, Arthur," Patricia says. "But it ain't over until the horizontally challenged woman sings." She seems too buoyant for one whose vessel seems so close to foundering. "Kimberley's bearing up pretty well, I'd say, and we've still got Mrs. McIntosh. Come on, Arthur, let me get rid of her; she's nagging me."

In a giving mood, I relent. It is uncaring of me to keep the good Mrs. McIntosh from her employer's bedside, so tomorrow Patricia may call her as the first item of business. I am still unsure how I will deal with the screams from next door; I must think of something.

We consume escargots and paté until Walter and Melanie Sprogue finally arrive: both seem out of sorts, their clenched, false smiles giving evidence of a recent zealous exchange of words.

"Sorry," Wally says. "Heavy traffic." He has had a few preparatory drinks: I can smell his breath as he helps Melanie into a chair next to me. In her mid-forties, she is a tense woman who hides emotions behind heavy makeup.

"You sit beside the great one. I'll join the ordinary mortals." Wally squeezes in between his wife and Patricia. "Boy, girl, boy, girl. I think I'll start off with one of those." He points to Gundar's power martini.

"Go easy, Walter," Melanie warns. She turns to me. "He has already knocked back three scotches."

I try to divert her with innocuous chitchat, but she proves an inattentive audience, watching Wally like a nervous cat as he slavers at Augustina from across the table and slugs back a couple of martinis. After our food orders are taken, he holds forth: it's the old Wally, pre-sensitized.

"You're going to have to buttress your case, Patricia, or it's going to be your word against Beauchamp's. No question, that Kimberley is a bright young thing. Candid. Charming. But when O'Donnell takes the stand—well, he's a man of prestige. Hard to picture him doing this terrible thing, tying someone up and reaming her from behind."

"Darling," says Melanie. "Your mouth."

"He may have seduced her, but that's short of a crime. And if that's all he did, I guess in a way you can't blame him. Hard for a guy to keep his belt buckled when a banquet like that is spread for him."

"Please, Walter."

A nervous silence as Wally reaches for the wine, slopping some as he tops up his glass.

"I think you've had enough, Walter."

Now he refills Augustina's glass, and boldly winks at her. His political correctness in full remission, he entertains with a racy joke that only Gundar laughs at. While he engages for a while with the prosecutors, I confer with Augustina, who looks alarmed when I relate my discussion with Jonathan.

"It's that shrink he's seeing. She has him all confused. I'll straighten him out."

Wally is studying the wine list. "How many for white and how many for red?"

As we feast into the night, Wally attains truly Chornickian heights: two massive martinis and much Bordeaux and cognac, and now he is insisting on, as he calls it, a Kimberley Martin: a dollop of Benedictine in his snifter.

"Hey, Arturo, I saw your divorce on the list the other day: coming up in a few weeks. Bet you can hardly wait—free again, eh? Thank God a'mighty."

"Walter, shut up!"

"Hey, I'm jus' having fun, why's everyone so uptight?"

He navigates his way around the table, and bends, wobbling, between me and Augustina, supporting himself with an arm around my shoulders. "This guy's a weenie. I jus' love him. My pal, my ol' pal. We had our little spats, eh, ol' buddy? All forgotten. Hey, how'm I doing? Conshidering it's my rookie trial."

"You're doing fine, Wally."

"I try. I do my best." A repulsive little tear glistens in one eye. I fear he is about to become maudlin.

Melanie rises. "Walter, we're going home."

"I wanna be fair. Justice mush not only be seen but done."

Suddenly Augustina starts, then sits there frozen. It will seem obvious to a careful observer that Wally has reached up and touched someone.

Melanie is such a careful observer. "You can do your pig act when we get home, Walter."

"Evening's *young*. I got my Kimbly Martin coming."

"Walter!"

A hush descends. Nearby patrons pretend to avert their eyes. Wally slowly straightens up, slightly losing his balance, taking his wife's arm for support.

"Yesh. Yes. Time to go."

Melanie marches the sobriety-deprived judge smartly out, and we wait until they are on the street before we all give in to the rudest of laughter. Such moments fire the coals of my resolve to maintain my lifetime pledge.

"Where did he get you?" Patricia asks.

"It was just a thigh shot. His aim was grossly impaired."

More peals of laughter.

"Boy, girl, boy, girl," mimics Patricia. "Les' all have another Bimberly Martin. Hard for a guy to shay no when that cherry pie is spread on a platter." She has his voice down pat. I applaud.

But it is also time for me to go. I must ready myself for tomorrow, for Kimberley, for Mrs. McIntosh and Dr. Sanchez, the screams and the bruises. I brush aside offers of rides. I bribe Pierre and his staff lavishly, hinting at my displeasure were I to read anything untoward in the gossip columns, and I walk out into the cold drizzle, suddenly tired. I wave down a taxi.

ॐ

My message light is blinking, an urgent, rhythmic throb. Midnight. Who calls? Now I hear a recorded message from Margaret.

A deep unease wells up within me as I listen to her halting broken phrases. "Arthur, I don't . . . I don't know how to tell you . . ."

A stab of fear: I am being rejected by voice mail.

Her voice continues. "It's awful. I'm still at George's . . ."

Oh, dear God. But I pray futilely, too late, to the deity he denied: George Rimbold has committed the final sacrilege.

Her voice becomes tearful. "Oh, Arthur, he hanged himself. From a balcony post. We're all over here now, neighbours, his friends in A.A. Doc Dooley is here. Call me."

I had sent Margaret on a tragic mission and she found him swinging from a rope. The call came in three hours ago. She will not yet be asleep. She answers immediately.

"Oh, Arthur, I'm a wreck."

I am, too. I must be strong for her. "Is someone with you?"

"No. But that's okay. I'm just . . . I found him, you know."

"Yes. I don't know if it helps, Margaret, but you know you have my love."

"It helps." She sniffles.

"Had he been drinking?"

"Yes. There was an empty bottle."

I lay my shattered frame upon the bed and close my eyes. "I was deaf to what he said. He told me he'd just bought a graveyard plot, and wasn't going to make it to the fair."

"Arthur, he left a will. Just a note, really. He . . . thanked all his friends for their support, and asked forgiveness." From whom? Not God. "He wanted you to have . . . well, his words were: 'I give to my dear and noble friend Arthur Beauchamp my fishing gear, my blessing and my love.' Everything else to the A.A."

As she describes her busy, grisly night, ridding herself of it all, she becomes more composed. I ask her what arrangements have been made.

"Doc Dooley is going to call it natural causes so we won't have all sorts of police and coroners. He says, 'I think we should just pop good old George in the ground quickly tomorrow.' We're not to talk to anyone. What's tomorrow? Thursday. Well, we'll be doing it in the afternoon. There'll be a sort of A.A. honour guard. They asked about you."

"I'll be there."

⚜

I awaken dense of brain from a black, dreamless night, but the fog clears and I am left with a sickly sense of loss. A man I have learned to love is dead. I must survive this day; I must not bring my sorrows to court: they could be misread. I reserve a one o'clock charter with Harbour Air, then slog through the rain to the law courts, only to learn the judge has ordered a late start.

"He's on his way," says Sheriff Willit. "Traffic problems is what he said."

Augustina and the two prosecutors appear the worse for last night's wear, and doubtless Wally will be a shambles. Near me, Jonathan is conferring with Dr. Dix. In the gallery, watching them with narrowed eyes, is Kimberley Martin, seated next to a slight, balding gentleman of about sixty-five, in a navy-blue suit of a dated style. Shrewd eyes under an imposing beetle brow. This cannot be her father: too old world. Her psychiatrist? On her tapes she had mentioned therapy for her "awful nightmares."

I have seen him before. Yes, it comes back: an expert witness in a trial I did many years ago, a gentle, honourable professional, widely respected. I confirm his identity with Jane Dix: Dr. Benjamin Kropinski. "He was my mentor, actually." The therapists' eyes meet; both smile.

"Have you a few minutes now, Mr. Beauchamp?" Dr. Dix says.

I really do not want to confer with her. I suspect we will argue. George's death has put me in a grim mood. "They tell me the judge is on his way. What about lunch? No, that won't do, I have a funeral. . . . Tomorrow morning?" I invite her for breakfast in my hotel; I will be in a better frame of mind by then, prepared to deal with this interfering psychiatrist and her bad advice to Jonathan.

I explain to Patricia why I must be absent this afternoon. "Wally will be only *too* happy to take the rest of the day off," she says. But I insist that the trial continue without me: Augustina can do the remaining minor witnesses; Kimberley can be deferred until tomorrow.

Wally Sprogue must be taking the scenic route:

forty minutes pass before his bleary-eyed lordship finally struggles up to the bench. He makes no apology for his lateness or explanation for his condition. Indeed, he can barely seem to talk—he will not be much of a nuisance factor today.

Kimberley is excused so that we may hear from Mrs. McIntosh, a tall, severe-looking woman in her mid-sixties, her hair done up like a large ball of knitting wool. She has the thin, grim-lipped look of one who disapproves of hanky-panky.

I order myself to pay attention, not to think of George entering the cold, cold ground, as Patricia leads Mrs. McIntosh through her resumé. She came from Scotland when she was eighteen, married to an older man who has since passed away. A former health-care worker and an active churchgoer, she has served Reverend Hawthorne for the last nineteen of his eighty years. She lives in. She is devoted to the retired bishop.

"When did you go to bed that night?"

"I settled the reverend in at about nine o'clock—a little early for him, but he hadn't had his nap. And then I went up."

"His bed is on the main floor?"

"Yes. Mine is on the second floor, to the rear."

"And is it as shown in these photos?" Patricia directs her attention to two photographs taken a day after the event: the first one showing the witness's immaculately kept bedroom, its window facing the second floor of Jonathan's house; the other offering a better view from that window. We see a small corner of Jonathan's master bedroom window opposite, the remainder of it obscured by a not-quite-leafless weeping willow.

"I read for about an hour, then I turned the light out and went to sleep. I don't sleep soundly—I always have half an ear tuned to sounds from below. The reverend likes to sneak into the fridge when he thinks I'm asleep."

"Did anything disturb you during the night?"

"Yes, in the wee hours Professor O'Donnell came home with a group of friends, and then I heard some laughter from next door, raised voices. And after a while a taxi came and picked three people up. Two men and a woman."

Augustina whispers, "This wasn't in her statement."

"It's minor," I say.

"Did you see that taxi?"

"Yes, from my window. Well, I was quite disgusted—one of the men urinated on the lawn. And I fell asleep again, and then another noise woke me."

"Tell us about that."

"Well, I always keep my window open for the air. And I heard these voices, but I couldn't make out what they were saying."

An urgent voice in my ear: "Arthur, we have to call a stop to this. Her statement only mentioned screams."

Do I object? Do I let the jury know I am nervous about this evidence? How bad can it be?

"Could you tell where these voices were coming from?"

"From Professor O'Donnell's house, right from his bedroom opposite. His window was partly open, and the curtains weren't drawn. It was dark in there, but there was a light on in the bathroom next to it. I could just make out someone moving in the bedroom—but I couldn't say if it was a man or a woman."

None of this is damaging yet. Helpful, if anything. I should be a coiled spring, but my wits aren't sharp today, much blunted by the loss of a friend.

"Then what did you hear?"

"Well, I heard a few slaps. And Professor

O'Donnell said, 'I am Satan and you are a naughty, naughty girl.' "

Satan? Naughty girl? With all the calm I can muster, I rise. "M'lord, a matter has arisen about which my learned friend and I should have a friendly chat. A minor oversight." Minor, indeed—does the jury hear the quaking in my voice? I have allowed Mrs. McIntosh to open Pandora's box, and all its evil moths are winging forth.

Even in his condition, Wally can tell I am unnerved, and offers a look of pity as he adjourns court. Among the jurors: shocked expressions, grins. When the last of them leaves, my own smile snaps shut and I stalk to the prosecution table.

"Where have your ethics gone? Lawyers have been disbarred for less than this."

Patricia looks astonished. "What are you talking about?"

"Non-disclosure. This *booby-trap*." I wave my copy of Mrs. McIntosh's statement in her face. "Where does it say Satan? Where are the naughty, naughty girls?"

"You *did* get her second statement, didn't you?"

"You mean the one your secretary forgot to mail?"

"I put it right into the hands of Gowan Cleaver. We did a trial together last week."

I am speechless, apoplectic.

"Oh, dear, Arthur, I was wondering why you were *so* confident. I had to do her second interview myself, after the pretrial. Well, I told you how the police weren't really busting their asses, Arthur. Gowan screwed up? Well, it was a rough trial, must have slipped his mind." She finds a clean copy, three typewritten pages. "Take all the time you need." She sees the whiteness in my face; she feels sorry for me.

Augustina and I spend a few tense minutes huddled over the housekeeper's bad news. Here on the second page are the words that have torpedoed the Commander's ship: "There were some slapping noises, and then I heard him say something about being Satan, and he shouted at her, 'You are a naughty, naughty girl.' " I turn to the last page, knowing the worst is not over. "I heard the girl's voice pleading, and she went on for several minutes, whimpering and begging. 'Don't,' she said. 'Oh, please, don't.' Then several minutes later I heard her scream loudly, about three or four times." Then silence. And a few minutes later, Kimberley came calling with her frantic hue and cry.

"You have to go after her, Arthur. She's a snoop and a liar."

The entire jury denies me eye contact as they file in: I have betrayed them, sold them a slick bill of goods. Astonishingly, Jonathan seems impassive, either unconcerned or in shock or simply beyond hope as he gazes at Mrs. McIntosh over his half-moon glasses. Wally finally graces us with his presence, gingerly easing into his chair.

Fear wonderfully concentrates the mind, and I behold Mrs. McIntosh in chilled, bright focus as she continues her evidence. "She was arguing with him, pleading with him to let her go. She was saying, 'Stop, Jonathan, stop! Please help me, God. Please don't make me.' Words like that. And, 'You're torturing me.' I remember that very clearly. Well, I couldn't make out *all* her words. Then I heard nothing for a while until she started screaming. I was afraid she was going to wake Dr. Hawthorne."

"Were you concerned in any other way?"

"I was confused. I didn't know what to do."

Shortly after, she heard a commotion at the front door. "I could hear her very clearly. She said, 'Help, he's going to kill me.' " Hurrying downstairs, she found the reverend fully awake and entertaining a naked, hysterical young woman decorated lavishly with lipstick.

Mrs. McIntosh identifies the blanket in which she

wrapped Kimberley, then it is passed among the jurors: smears of the blood-red tone called Shameless. "After she settled down, she kept apologizing. She didn't want the police. She wanted her fiancé. That's what she said."

"Aside from the lipstick, did you notice any injuries, bruises?"

"To be honest, I didn't. The blanket covered her."

"Your witness, Mr. Beauchamp."

Wally turns to me with a hangdog expression. He hasn't had the strength to make any notes today. With a pleading look, he says, "Do you need an adjournment, Mr. Beauchamp?"

I contemplate this offer. "No, m'lord." I blatantly lie: "I am prepared."

As I stand, Augustina makes a discreet fist—release the dogs of war, the gesture says. The Commander takes on a sour, frowning countenance as he confronts this priggish peeping Tomasina. Let the jury think I find her testimony all too unbelievable.

"After you first heard these so-called screams from the neighbouring house, you didn't call the police?"

"I wasn't quite sure what was going on."

"But even when she later came by hysterically and claimed someone was trying to kill her, you didn't immediately call 911?" I am aware of a brittle edge in my voice. I am exceedingly—perhaps perilously—upset, in danger of taking out on the witness all my rage at Gowan Cleaver.

"No. I asked her and she said not to. Mr. Brown came quickly. He seemed like a person used to taking charge."

"She was intoxicated, wasn't she?"

"Yes, I suspect she was. I could smell it on her."

"And incoherent."

"The poor lass was very upset."

"From the photographs it appears that your window is a few feet away from the head of your bed."

"Yes."

"Then how did you observe the arrival of this car full of people?"

"Well, I got out of bed."

"And you would have had to poke your head out the window to obtain a clear view."

"Well . . . yes."

"And later you heard laughter, loud talk, the sound of people having a good time?"

"There was some kind of social gathering."

"I take it you again rose from your bed in order to see the taxi pick up the three people."

"I would have, yes."

"Exactly how many times *did* you get out of bed to look out your window?"

"Well, my sleep was disturbed several times that night."

"Did you ever sleep at all, Mrs. McIntosh?" I could offend the jury carrying on in this sneering manner. But it is win or lose with this witness.

"Not very soundly, as I've admitted."

"And when you heard these two voices later, you again got out of bed to look?"

"Yes."

"And you tried to peer across into Professor O'Donnell's bedroom?"

"Well, yes, I suppose I did."

I take my copies of the photographs to the witness stand. Mrs. McIntosh is stiff and nervous as I point out that the willow tree blocks her view of Jonathan's bedroom window.

"Yes, but if you scrunch down a wee bit, right to the ledge, you can see better."

"Ah. And that would be your normal vantage point when you are trying to peek into Professor O'Donnell's bedroom?"

"No—"

"M'lord," Patricia complains, "that's an unfair—"

Wally, his headache presumably well settled in, cuts her off curtly. "This is cross-examination. Continue, Mr. Beauchamp."

I walk back to counsel table. I must zero in on the weakest link in her evidence. "None of this business was mentioned in your first statement to the police, was it?"

"We had only a brief visit from them. Dr. Hawthorne told me to answer their questions and say nothing more, and that's what I did. They seemed more interested in what he had to say."

"It was only when you later talked to the prosecutor that these unusual details filtered out, this business about slapping and Satan and the naughty girl."

"I called Miss Blueman. I said I had something I wanted to add."

"Do you mean something you thought up in the interim?"

"No, sir. It was not that way at all."

"Something you'd imagined?"

"I did *not* imagine it." She speaks with a prim vehemence.

"The slaps you claim to have heard didn't elicit screams, did they?"

"What do you mean?"

"The screams you think you heard came several minutes later."

"Yes, that's true. . . ." She hesitates, and I make the mistake of not breaking her train of thought. "No, that's not *quite* true. I remember now there was another scream earlier on, very loud and drawn out." She looks at me in triumph, a point scored.

This is going nowhere. She is too emphatic. Where is the solution to this woman? "By the way, you had also been reading a book that night?"

"Yes."

"What book was it?"

"A novel. I forget the name."

"What sort of book?"

"Romance."

"Ah." I react as if this answer has deep significance. "You enjoy such novels?"

"And others."

"Do the female characters in these books ever scream with passion, Mrs. McIntosh?"

She reddens. "Yes, I suppose."

"Have you ever actually *heard* screams of passion?"

"No, I . . . not really."

"Well, you must know they may be mistaken for screams of fear?"

"No, I don't know that."

"But based on your reading experience you do know that lovers will say all manner of things to each other when they are in passionate embrace?"

"I suppose so."

"A woman might do something to prompt her lover to call her a naughty girl."

"It was not said in that way. It was very loud."

"You're sure that was the word, 'naughty'?"

She hesitates. "Naughty, I think." Now she amends, "No, a wicked girl. A wicked, wicked girl, that's what he said."

The ground continues to collapse from under me. I am losing what remains of the jury's sympathy. Their faces are cold, hard, unforgiving.

"And you are aware that when a couple engages in vigorous intercourse, their bodies will slap together?"

"I don't know, really." She is beet red. I am overdoing this. But I am obsessed, irrational.

"And these pleading sounds—could you have mistaken them for something else?"

"Like what?"

"Like the piteous groans of lovers demanding more from each other."

"I don't know."

"Thank you, that is all."

Wally must be looking for a chance for a ten-minute kip on his couch because he orders a break. I descend slowly into my chair beside Augustina. "Well?"

"I don't know, Arthur. It doesn't sound like something she read in a Harlequin."

"My cross was bloody awful, wasn't it?"

"Well, it felt, you know, a little mocking."

It had been mean and small. I have pulled off a disaster. The Commander of the *Titanic* is going down with all hands on board. Maybe I do need to talk to that psychiatrist—from her couch.

In any case I should meet with her before I finish cross-examining Kimberley Martin. I lean across to Patricia's table. "Let's read in Dr. Hawthorne's testimony after the break and adjourn for lunch."

She accedes. In great need of nicotine, I skip out, weaving through the muted throng in the mezzanine. They seem appropriately embarrassed for me.

Outside, I light up, alone, dejected. I shall have a reward posted for Cleaver's body, dead or alive. Had this lonely spinster's statement shown up in timely fashion, I might have been better prepared to discredit her. Did she impress as a prying, lying shrew or a godly, caring nursemaid?

Back in court, I continue to berate myself through the lengthening break—the judge has stolen an extra ten minutes—and remain glum as court resumes and Dr. Hawthorne's previous evidence is read into the record. O'Donnell, the jurors learn, is a gentleman against whom has never been heard an ill-mannered word. Such praise is surely lost on them. They are thinking of slaps and screams. Miss Jackson-Blyth looks upon Jonathan as if he has just risen dripping from the swamp. I have lost Mrs. Beiran, the nurse, and even the broker Goodman looks entirely too uncomfortable.

At twelve o'clock, Wally adjourns court and wearily slogs his way out to his chambers.

I stare down at my open copy of the Criminal Code. Section 272. "Everyone who, in committing a sexual assault, causes bodily harm to the complainant is liable to imprisonment for a term not exceeding fourteen years."

Jonathan pats me on the shoulder. "Tough morning. Thing that really bothers me is Kimberley hasn't returned my handkerchief." He laughs hollowly at this weak jest, then leaves to enjoy what freedom is left for him. Dr. Jane Dix retrieves a small briefcase and begins to follow him out, then turns to me with the oddest little smile.

"See you for breakfast," she says.

Morosely, I accept Augustina's invitation to drive me in her Porsche to Coal Harbour. En route, I am too choked with grief to utter anything but imprecations to the gods to punish Gowan Cleaver.

"I saw him this morning," Augustina says. "Coming out of court after a Charter argument. Looking pretty cocky until I told him about his little lapse."

What retribution might be appropriate? I think of the punishment of Ixion, bound by writhing snakes to a revolving wheel of fire through all eternity.

"You're comfortable about this afternoon?" I ask.

"Sure. I'm doing only three witnesses. And Wally's in such bad straits I don't have to worry about him bugging me. Do we need anything from the serologist?"

"No. He will merely say the sheets and clothing

seized at Jonathan's house bore no stains of semen or lipstick." But the sheets also were freshly washed: will the jurors smell something besides Rinso?

"Any advice on handling Sergeant Chekoff?" she asks.

"He's liable to say anything to help us. But he'll be piqued that Patricia, not he, obtained the house-keeper's damning statement, so be careful. Bring out the fact Jonathan was cooperative and courteous, a man with nothing to hide. You've examined Rosa Sanchez before."

Dr. Sanchez is a frequent visitor to our courts and can be depended upon to be blunt and fair, though doubtless the Crown will dwell tenderly on every minor bruise.

"The left shin, where the skin was broken, that's the only injury of consequence."

"How do we explain it, Arthur? How do we explain the bruises on her wrists and ankles? The ones on her breasts? They weren't noticed by Mrs. McIntosh, so do you think Remy did it?"

"It may be the best we have to offer." They fought—that has been established. But will the jury buy the theory these were not merely verbal fisticuffs? Why would she lie, why remain engaged to such a brute? "Is there any other option?"

"Self-inflicted? Just like her paint job? How's this: When Kimberley realized Remy was determined to call the cops, she bruised herself against the bathtub to make her story look good."

But is she so conniving? Though I pride myself on an intuitive talent for reading people (other than, of course, myself), I still have no firm handle on Kimberley Martin.

"I guess these are more like rope burns, though, aren't they, Arthur? There has to be a better answer." I sense she is disappointed in Jonathan, distrustful

· 368 ·

now, feeling victimized again by her own foolish heart.

She blows me a kiss as I board my plane. "Pass that on to Mrs. Blake for me."

The little aircraft chugs into the harbour and throttles into the wind, lugging this sad sack back to Beauchamp Bay on Potter's Road.

჻

From the air, my island looks sombre under a drizzling, mournful sky; fields and forests of bereavement. We spin above my plot of land: there, that is my home, that is my garden, that is Stoney waving from a garage still unroofed. That is my life, one that I solemnly swore not to forsake. The gods are punishing me for breaking my oath, for my arrogance in having taken on this dismal trial.

And there—that is Margaret Blake standing on my dock. A simple black dress, a sad smile: she looks beautiful beyond imagining.

As I step onto my dock she comes to my arms, holding me tight. But she looks at me without offering her lips. "You okay?"

"I blame myself. I ignored the warnings. I should have been here for him."

"Don't do that to yourself, Arthur. What could have driven him to this?"

"He died from a loss of faith." *There's no afterlife, only darkness, sweet, empty darkness.*

I tell the pilot to wait, and we proceed towards the house.

"The death of a friend certainly puts a bad day in court into perspective."

"I heard something on the radio. The naughty-girl bit."

The merest hint of fall is upon Garibaldi, swatches of yellow on the big-leaf maples, colourful mush-

· 369 ·

rooms poking through the earth, purple and yellow and orange. The garden is weedy and needs a sound harvesting. A lazy pock-pock of hammers, as Stoney and Dog fix shakes to the garage roof.

"Don't be too impressed. They didn't get going until they saw the plane come in."

I frown. "Not much progress."

"Too much dope."

Their belongings are scattered about. They have moved into my garage like squatters. Where's my old pickup? I remember: I'd left it in the care of Nelson Forbish.

Stoney clambers down. "What do you think of it so far? An architectural classic. Hey, man, you're a sight for sore eyes. Listen, do you think me and Dog can get a little draw?"

"How is the Rolls?"

Stoney is evasive. "Oh, well, yeah, it's coming. Had to send out to the factory for a new steering wheel."

That might take a few years. "No sign of Constable Pound, I take it?"

"Naw. He knows I'm under your protection."

After I grease his palm, Margaret takes me by the hand and leads me to her house. "I'll make a sandwich." She turns to appraise me. "You look like a stranger in that suit."

After a handful of days she can barely remember what I look like. Why does she seem so cautious and formal with me? But surely that has to do with the pall that enshrouds us.

The Garibaldi graveyard is behind the community church in a vale bordered by the looping tresses of cedar trees. Several dozen locals have gathered here, many of whom barely knew the deceased. But death is an event of moment on a small island, and even Kurt

Zoller is here, looking overly solemn in a shiny new life jacket. Near a station wagon that doubles as a hearse, a young woman is playing an Irish harp, another blowing softly on a flute.

Nelson Forbish waddles up to me, playing nervously with the rim of his porkpie hat. "About your truck, Mr. Beauchamp—I'm afraid it kinda broke down. I had to have it towed off the ferry."

"It's unimportant, Nelson." A minor death.

He seems relieved. "Hey, I heard all about your trial on the news. What do you think your client's gonna get?"

Without responding, I desert him for the graveside. My comrades from A.A. are all here: they have built a simple casket and reserved a spot for me as pallbearer. We lift George from the back of the station wagon and carry him to his recently deeded land, and we lay his ravaged soul to rest there.

Everyone is looking at me, waiting. To call upon Proverbs or Revelations would be discourteous to George. I choose Lucretius: "O miserable minds of men. O blind hearts. In what darkness of life, in what dangers you spend this little span of years." And I cannot continue. I am weeping.

Afterwards, Emily Lemay invites us all down to the Brig for the wake, where those who are able toast George with rum and those who are not raise their sodas high. As Margaret drives us back to Potter's Road, we are quiet, in our separate, sad worlds.

We stroll about her farm, joined by her dog, her cat, and a strutting goose. She leads me to a sturdy new gate in our fence. "I kind of fancied it up."

And such a lovely gate it is, entwined with willow wands, a simple lockless latch, hinges oiled to swing easily open. It seems an invitation, a shortcut to her house and heart. . . .

She vaults onto the split-cedar fence and takes my hand. "All right, tell me about the trial."

I relate the devastating evidence of Mrs. McIntosh. She nods in sympathy, then says, "Well, you have one thing going for you."

"What's that?"

"Kimberley didn't remember anything about being slapped or any threats or pleading with him."

"Or Satan or the wicked, wicked girl." Of course. So preoccupied with my angst, I have missed the obvious. This apparent black hole in Kimberley's memory had been action-filled, bustling. Either that, or Mrs. McIntosh *was* reliving one of her bodice-ripping novels.

"Getting slapped would sure wake *me* up. Even if I'd passed out."

"How on God's green earth did I let that slip by me? *Why* doesn't Kimberley remember? I could kiss you."

"Well . . ."

I stare at her numbly, feeling myself being slowly drawn into the deep silver cups of her eyes. I raise myself to her perch, and she bends to my lips and caresses my face with her fingertips. Her animals are staring at us, curious, expectant.

"I love you, Margaret."

"I know. It feels a little scary, Arthur. I'm a little . . ."

"You don't have to say anything." No, I don't want her to finish that thought; leave me some hope and dignity.

"I'm just a little afraid of fooling myself, I think. Or maybe of losing control. I have to . . . let it settle in."

Love is not an impetuous matter for the widow of Christopher Blake. It is not given freely, but hoarded, conserved like her precious rain forests. I am content that she keeps an open mind, and I will continue assiduously to follow my mentor's advice: *She demands to be wooed and pursued.* How cocky and confident was

George Rimbold about my prospects. *Too* confident? Did the gay priest understand women so well?

But I must return to my plane before dark. At my wharf, she holds me tight, her breasts and hips pressing warm against me, and I feel prickles, a flutter in my loins, a want.

"Will I see you on Saturday?" she asks.

"I don't know right now."

"Try to come. Even for a little while."

What do I read in those mercury eyes? Affection? Or the self-reproach of one who cannot return the clumsy love I lavish upon her? It feels a little scary . . . I am pushing too hard, an amateur at love.

Before evening falls, I have time-travelled to the brawny, busy city and am back in my lonely hotel suite, communing with my gargoyles. The vicissitudes of the day have sapped my strength and spirit. I do not look forward to the morrow. But the practice of advocacy is a demanding mistress, and I must bow to her whip. I call Augustina to ask how she fared this afternoon.

"Pretty well. Didn't step on any land mines. Wally could barely stay awake—he looked ghastlier as the day wore on—so we adjourned Dr. Sanchez until tomorrow morning. Sergeant Chekoff was fine. We have a nice little picture of Jonathan out there raking his leaves, looking puzzled by his visit."

"And the jury?"

"I don't know, Arthur. They want something from us. Only two people really know what went on in that bedroom. . . ."

"And since Kimberley doesn't seem to remember, they are waiting for Jonathan to fill the void."

"Something like that."

But why doesn't Kimberley remember?

Mrs. McIntosh's apocalyptic revelations have panicked a jury I had been confident would acquit. Shall I be forced to put Jonathan on the stand after all? I would need the entire weekend to prepare him. Patricia will probably pick away at him for two days: she is an effective cross-examiner and he will be exposed to ferocious attack. Then we will doubtless hear Dominique Lander speak of Jonathan's proclivity to paint bound bodies before coitus. Then come the counsel addresses, and finally the judge's charge to the jury— we'll be another week.

But Rimbold is with me again, gazing down at me from wherever his heaven may be, with his sad, cynical smile, his wisdom. *Your dreams are what you fear; they are not what you are.*

Couldn't you at least have stuck around until the end of the trial, George? Until I got back, until I could talk reason to you before you refunded to your absent God His one most bounteous gift? Ah, George, thank you for the fishing gear. Thank you for the pot.

I roll a joint to his memory and smoke it, then in a tossing sleep descend to Hades, in a chariot drawn by Pluto's coal-black steeds, and there I see George being taken by the current of the Lethe, the river of oblivion.

A buffet breakfast is offered daily in a salon down the hall from my room, and that is where I have arranged to meet Dr. Jane Dix. This encounter, which earlier I considered a waste of valuable time, now seems crucial: ground has shifted; we are no longer on terra firma.

I find the young psychiatrist waiting for me in a secluded alcove of the salon, away from the chatter and clicking cups of a table of conventioneers.

She stands, shakes my hand briskly.

"I understand you lost a friend. I'm sorry. Tell me about him."

She seems brusque, yet intelligent and kind. She nods in sympathy as I talk about my sardonic, wise guru, relate his history, recall our friendship. She gently prods me about Garibaldi, and I tell her briefly of my life there, but I am stiff with this lively-eyed therapist, afraid of revealing the warps in my psyche.

"You're tired of playing lawyer?"

"This will be my last case."

"You seem incredibly good at it."

"Life has more to offer, Dr. Dix."

"Jane, please. And what *does* life offer you?"

"Peace and poetry and fresh potatoes."

"Garibaldi isn't just an escape from the courtroom? Some convenient harbour?"

This percipient woman is daring me to be open. "Indeed not. I have found life on Garibaldi amply fulfilling."

I fetch a coffee service on a tray, with croissants and jam and plates of fruit. "What do you have in?" I ask.

She studies me for a while, as I am poised with the cream jug. "White, no sugar. You seem very formal in your ways, Arthur. Gentlemanly."

"Fussy and stuffy, I'm told."

"I don't see that for one second. Though I sense a private school in the background."

"That's too insightful of you." I feel awkward about her blunt forays into my life. Is she planning to peel off my layers of protective skin in search of the repressed weakling inside? She obviously knows I'm an A.A. member. Jonathan has probably told her about my career as a cuckold, the recent fracturing of my marriage.

"Jonathan went to the usual snobby boarding schools, of course," she says. "Did they use corporal punishment at yours?"

"Liberally applied to that fatty area Shakespeare calls the afternoon of the body."

"Societally accepted S and M. Sometimes the scars stay there for life."

In defence, I turn the mirror to her. "And what are the pertinent details of *your* life?"

"I'm a contrary radical feminist lesbian with a chip on my shoulder."

This forces a smile from me. But time is fleeting. "What did you think of Mrs. McIntosh, Jane?"

"Unfulfilled fantasies of love starring the next-door neighbour. An initial refusal to believe her love object could do this. Disappointment and anger blossoming into a desire for revenge. So she decides to tell the whole story."

"A truthful one?"

"I think so."

I grimace.

"Cheer up," she says, and she removes a file from her briefcase. "I've transcribed several of my sessions with Jonathan. He insists that you peruse them. Some interesting papers and articles here, too." Her eyes undress me. "I take it you know something about bondage, Arthur."

Dare I tell her about my recurring dreams? "It's a form of theatre, I suppose."

"Yes, much like your courtrooms. Those can be theatres of pain, too, from what I've observed. I want to talk about pain with you, Arthur."

I nod glumly. She continues.

"Pain is everywhere: in life, in law, in art. The dying swan, the tortured face of the flamenco dancer, El Greco's Christ on the cross. The bad guy getting shot off his horse, murder mysteries, cop shows—we entertain ourselves with pain. Violence and sex sell toothpaste. We love it. We can't get enough of it. Forgive me: I've been doing a lot of thinking and reading in the last few days, and I've got a whole treatise."

"Just carry on," I say. It is obvious now where this is leading. All faith in Jonathan has flown: clearly, Dominique Lander is telling more truth than I cared to believe.

Jane shuffles through some of her articles, finds a page. She talks between sips of coffee and little bites of cantaloupe.

"Havelock Ellis: Pain is an aspect of the love of life. We're all haunted by it, all living things. We live constantly next to it, waiting for it, fearing it, yet thrilled by it. The pain of love hurts as sharply as the pain of a wound to the body; tears of pain are indistinguishable from tears of joy." She looks up from her papers. "This all leads to a theory, okay? There's no solid answer, but there are reasons people get into B and D, bondage and discipline. Pain excites. It arouses just as sex does: increased pulse and blood pressure and muscular tension, hyperventilation. So it can be a kind of turn-on. An aphrodisiac. It may be aberrant, but we're not dealing with psychopathy here or inordinate cruelty."

She has much to say that is fascinating, but where do we go with it?

"Bondage is theatre, Arthur, but with a purpose. Hidden drives and desires are handled as play; demands of fantasy are met. Postponement and delay, begging, stalling, they're all part of the game. The bondee maybe doesn't truly enjoy the pain, but she or he is stimulated by the constraint, the sense of helplessness, the thrill of the unknown."

"Where do these hidden drives and desires come from?"

"At a sort of basic sensory level, there's an interesting biological explanation: pain releases endorphins in the brain—and they're addictive, like opiates. The long-distance runner breaks through the pain, gets a little hit of endorphin." She reflects. "Probably why

Jonathan took up running. Let me give you a sociological perspective."

She finds another paper, glances for a moment at it, looks up. "S and M patterns are imbedded in our culture—socially, we value aggression, the dynamic of dominance and submission. Our gender relationships are set up in that framework—the male is traditionally dominant, the female reluctant and submissive."

"Ah, but the times, I have learned, are changing."

"Not that much. Okay, I also read one interesting theory about masochism serving as a guilt-relieving system: the punishment gives expiation for the sin of sexuality. The masochist knows that if anything sexually forbidden happens, it's not her or his fault. Sometimes it never develops into scripted play: the prototypical case of the masochistic man and the cold, calculating woman—he satisfies his unconscious wish to be mistreated. It's not that uncommon—the desire for domination by an authoritarian partner."

A brilliant aperçu from someone who knows nothing of my relationship with Annabelle. I cannot look at her squarely, and play with my coffee spoon. Clearly, she notices my agitation, and doubtless adds a mental paragraph to her file on me.

"Actually, bondage can be a way of dealing with male impotency."

I take too large a gulp of coffee and feel it sear my throat. Her bright blue eyes are fixed on mine, which are veiled and guilty.

"Our culture is hard on men: all the demands—assertion, aggression, control. Can't blame a guy if he just wants out. Easier on him if his partner takes full responsibility. Tie me up. Have your will with me. Excite me. I've had a hard day at the office. Okay, so, Jonathan grew up in an old, old culture—he was trained from early on in the chauvinistic arts. He tries, but he's trapped within his father. Which brings me to a more clinical perspective. We're getting to the nitty-gritty here: the eroticizing of childhood pain. A traumatic event in childhood can trigger B and D behaviour patterns. Or general day-to-day abuse by a parent can accumulate and bring about an adaptive response. Kids escape from physical pain by romantic daydreaming. Sexual imagery. Masturbation. When you eroticize your suffering it sort of imprints."

We are running out of time: court sits in fifteen minutes. She sees me check my watch, and speaks more rapidly, urgently.

"Jonathan's father regularly beat him until he was nearly ten—that's when his mother brought him to Canada. Jonathan denies this was abuse—just strict British discipline. Anyway, there were other processes going on. A father who couldn't express love. Just tons of ambivalence towards the great Lord Caraway. An older, favoured brother. A great deal of rebellion on the younger sibling's part, which manifested itself in attention-seeking behaviour: mostly truancy. If Daddy continues to ignore me, I'll be bad and he'll whip me—and they'd finally interact and little Jonnie would get the attention he sought, his substitute for love. He received one particularly harsh whaling after he walked into his parents' bedroom and found them making love. So you have a pretty fair picture."

"Of what?"

"Of someone who understands his problem better now, and wants to deal with it and *can* deal with it."

"We must go."

"Here, take this file." I slip it into my briefcase. "He wants to take the witness stand, Arthur. He *needs* to. He wants to unload. Everything."

"Let's talk about it on the way."

I rise. She takes my hand, stilling me.

"He has to, Arthur. He needs to live with himself."

"But does he need to live in a ten-by-ten cell? There are a dozen reasons to keep him off the stand, not the least of which is an annoying flaw in him that your acute mind must have observed: he handles truth poorly."

"He didn't rape her."

"But I assume he told you he tied Kimberley up."

"It was play."

"And do you believe that?"

"I do. We had a powerful session on Sunday. He's gone through a deep personal epiphany, Arthur."

As I usher Jane into court, I realize we have far from finished our conversation, and I am even further from formulating new strategies. I must buy time. The defence must regroup, reorganize, rethink its handling of Kimberley Martin. "You look like doom," Augustina says as I join her at counsel table.

"Jonathan is consumed by a compulsion to bare all in an orgy of truth-telling." I hear Margaret taunting me: *But isn't that what the jury should hear—the truth?*

I have no time to elucidate, for Hedy Jackson-Blyth is leading in the jury—she has the intrepid look of a firm believer, one whose mind will not be altered.

His lordship takes his seat at the bench, well recovered now, but looking remarkably like a recalcitrant child expecting to be sent to his room, still smarting with embarrassment over the fool's role he played two nights ago. Hopefully, he will be eager to return to the great one's good books and not try to cross my path today.

"Ms. Foreperson, members of the jury, good morning." He nods at them in greeting, then turns to counsel and says with what seems forced cheer, "Well, what do we have on the menu? I don't think Mr. Beauchamp is finished with the complainant."

"Yes, but Dr. Sanchez is still here," says Patricia. "I think she's in a hurry to get back to the hospital."

Augustina will cross-examine her; I am anxious to use the time to read Jane's interview transcripts. "No problem," I say. "Let us hear from the good doctor."

Wally smiles sunnily upon me: he has forgiven the past. "That's white of you, Mr. Beauchamp."

A long moment occurs while I await the redness, the sputter, the realization he has spoken with great linguistic imprudence. But he seems blissfully unaware of his clanger and fails to observe Mrs. Nevers, the one black person on the jury, looking at him in shock. Nor can he conceive why Patricia is staring dumbly at him.

"Well? Let's get the show on the road, Ms. Blueman."

I have no time to further relish this malapropos moment, and listen with only half an ear to the evidence of the pathologist, a plump, grey-haired Salvadoran refugee, as I pore through Jane Dix's portfolio of pain.

While I read the underlined selections from Jonathan's interviews, Dr. Sanchez's words and phrases float by, just within my aural range: abrasion, haematoma, reddened areas, chafed epidermal tissue.

The condensed transcripts give a graphic history of the conquest of Jonathan's inner self, his gradual loss of defences, the bludgeoning of his walls, the capture of the helpless survivor within. I break away from this as Augustina begins her cross of Dr. Sanchez: it is a skilful bandaging act, minimizing the bruising, hinting at a possible source in drunken sexual horseplay.

But some jurors are frowning. Too much is being asked of them. Wally remains outside the arena, though making a great show of his attentiveness.

"Dr. Sanchez, you took a swab from deep within her vagina?"

"Yes."

"And you searched microscopically for sperm?"

"For a long time, yes."

"And what did the absence of sperm tell you?"

"That she had not had intercourse with ejaculation for at least the last twenty-four hours—unless an impervious prophylactic device had been employed."

"By that you mean a condom."

"Yes."

"Had the complainant taken a douche a few hours earlier, would that in any way alter your opinion?"

"No, Miss Sage. I would still have expected to find motile sperm."

I return to the transcripts, to the disassembling of O'Donnell, rebel son of the tyrant Viscount Caraway. Jane has excerpted dozens of pages from her final interview with Jonathan—only last Sunday. The final uncut version of the truth. I am struck by a phrase: *A stolen kiss, the slightest touch of lip on lip, that was my crime.*

I read for several minutes until Dr. Sanchez leaves the stand. "That's the final witness, m'lord," says Patricia. "But I expect my learned friend has more questions of Kimberley Martin."

"We'll break now," says Wally. "Ten minutes."

The room clears. "Very nice work with the pathologist, Augustina. Excuse me for a few minutes."

She watches me, puzzled, as I reach into her briefcase and draw out the paperback reprint of *Saint Joan.* I open it to the lipstick smudge. I stare at it, a blood-red blot upon the scene in which Joan revokes her recantation and is sentenced to burn. The author instructs: *The glow and flicker of fire can now be seen reddening the May daylight.*

I turn quickly back to Jane's final interview.

There's just a whole load of stuff she just doesn't remember.

What do you mean?

Or for some reason remembers it differently from me.

Why do you want to give her that out?

· 382 ·

But why *doesn't she remember?*

Yes, Kimberley, why? I watch her bend to Dr. Benjamin Kropinski in whispered consultation. Jonathan is also looking upon her, with an expression of deep melancholy.

I return to my reading, calling upon the counsel of Minerva, goddess of wisdom, for the solution to Jonathan, to Kimberley, for a means to storm the gates of Ilium and bring home victory's booty.

♨

Upon the jury's return, I rise with a false show of enthusiasm, shamming an eagerness to continue my cross of the complainant. Kimberley wins an encouraging nod from Dr. Kropinski, then takes several long-legged strides to the witness box. I am somewhat taken aback at her choice of attire this morning: a vermilion dress too tightly revealing, too daring for this solemn occasion; a belted waist, a callipygian show of rump. Perhaps she intends to continue her seduction of Walter Sprogue. He nods at her; they exchange smiles. The maid of Orleans has him in the sight of her crossbow.

"I'm sorry we've delayed you again, Miss Martin," I say.

"That's fine." She shakes her curls, leans not back but forward: the confident witness.

"We're all trying to figure out what went on during the small hours of November twenty-eighth, so I'm just going to bandy a few ideas about."

"Whatever. Sure."

" 'He's going to kill me.' There's no doubt you spoke those words, Miss Martin, but I'm going to ask you to think about this and be fair. In truth, you don't feel your life was threatened?"

She ponders her answer. "No, I guess not. When he

was filling the bathtub, I had this flash I might be drowned or something. But it was just a panic thing."

"It's a big Jacuzzi bathtub, isn't it? You looked at it?"

"Earlier, yes."

"Big enough for two."

"I noticed that."

"You don't recall Professor O'Donnell inviting you to join him in it?"

"I do not." Said firmly.

"Though he did say something at the time."

The witness pauses. "I didn't really catch it."

"You've told us your wrists were bound together—with a bathrobe cord?"

"I remember it felt silky."

"And your ankles were tied to bedposts?"

"Yes. I don't know with what. I think he used a couple of his ties."

"You have no memory of that."

"No."

"Nor of undressing a second time."

"No."

"Nor of hanging up your undergarments."

"No."

"Nor of making love."

"Not in the usual sense, Mr. Beauchamp."

"You have no memory of a condom."

"None."

"No memory of being tied up."

"No."

"If that happened, it didn't awake you."

"No. But it must have happened."

"No memory of being slapped or spanked?"

"No. I'm sorry."

"Surely that would have awakened you had it occurred?"

"I think so."

Fine. A good answer. We are getting along like a

Sunday drive. Do I dare chance a tricky detour down the dark, twisted valley of kink? Do I have a choice?

"You say you awoke as the accused was behind you, raising your hips, and entering you."

"Then trying to sodomize me."

"You screamed, you say."

"I screamed and twisted away."

"Do you remember seeing an empty bottle of wine near the bed?"

"No."

"You don't recall drinking wine between acts of love?"

"Mr. Beauchamp, I don't think it's possible either to drink wine or make love when you're unconscious."

"The bindings that you can't describe—they don't appear to have been tied very tightly."

"I had to struggle quite a bit. I mean, I was really frantic, twisting and pulling at these things with my teeth. And something was really chafing my ankle. It was like going through a living nightmare."

"A nightmare?"

"A nightmare."

I know something about nightmares. What incubi haunted this fair young woman's sleep? Suddenly I feel light-headed, a brief trance of revelation, an afflatus of truth, my own epiphany. I know I will take that dangerous detour.

She is looking apprehensively at me, waiting.

"You've had nightmares before."

"Bad ones, yes."

"For which you've received therapy."

"That's right."

"From your psychiatrist—who is here in court."

"Dr. Kropinski. He helped me remember . . . an episode."

Have you ever been sexually assaulted before? To that question on the polygraph she had answered,

"Never," though the graph seemed to contradict her. A stress anomaly, said the examiner.

"He helped you remember this only recently?"

"Yes. Last weekend."

My voice softens. "Forgive me, Miss Martin, I don't want to aggravate old wounds, but by any chance did that episode have to do with your being attacked by a man when you were younger?"

She nods. The answer doesn't record, but that is enough. The defence can endure the sympathy this must earn her.

"How did Dr. Kropinski help you bring this back?"

"Hypnosis. He made me relive it."

"You were amnesic?"

"Yes."

Wally's eyes are laden with concern. Do I want to go further with this? Amnesia . . . I pause a long while, thinking. "Bear with me, Miss Martin. I'm sure this is difficult. But how old were you when you faced this ordeal?"

"Eight. And I didn't quite *face* it, Mr. Beauchamp." She is unblinking, head thrust high, brave and tough beyond measure. But I feel all her masked pain.

"He came at you from behind, I take it."

"I was sodomized."

I pause. I reflect. I look at Dr. Kropinski in the gallery. Our eyes meet. Together, we understand. Now I must take that irreversible path. I walk over to the exhibit table. In a plastic envelope, the tube of Shameless lipstick. In another, her heavy gold pendant.

"You wore this that whole night?"

"The cross? Yes."

"Might not its blunt points have bruised your breasts?"

"I'm not sure how."

"In the throes of lovemaking perhaps? With his body pressed against yours?"

"Really, Mr. Beauchamp—" Patricia says.

"You're assuming a scenario the witness doesn't admit to," Wally says. He has deserted his Commander again, his eyes still hot on the witness.

"Quite so," I say amiably. "Quite so. Miss Martin, if indeed you were struggling with bonds of some kind, frantically twisting and pulling as you say, bruising to wrists and ankles would likely then occur?" *Audentes fortuna iuvat,* Virgil wrote. *Fortune favours the daring.*

After a long moment, she says, "Possibly."

"Let's assume your ankles were fastened to bedposts with neckties. Might that chafing you suffered to your ankle be a result of something metallic? A tie clip or stud?"

She pauses, thinking. "Maybe . . ."

"Miss Martin, before you blanked out, what scene of *Saint Joan* were you and your friends performing?"

"The last scene. The inquisition. Up to the point Joan confessed."

"During this scene her ankles were chained?"

"Um, yes. We used shackles in the play."

"And were her hands bound, too?"

"I . . . yes. A loose chain."

"Yes. And after she confesses, she recants. An angry clamour ensues among her accusers. She is accused of being of the devil, a member of Satan."

"Yes."

"She is called a wicked girl."

"I believe so."

"Not a naughty girl—a wicked girl."

"Well, I see you have the play."

It is before me, open to the smudge. I carry it to the witness stand and lay it in front of her.

"This is what you were reading from that night?"

"Probably. If you got it from his library. I didn't read from it, though. I knew the lines."

"Ah, but there's a red smudge here on page eighty-nine—do you see that?"

I lift it high so the jury can see.

"A blot of Shameless lipstick, Miss Martin?"

"I don't know. Possibly."

"Should we have it tested?"

"It looks like the same shade."

Patricia intercedes. "M'lord, there's no proof about where this book came from, who handled it—"

Wally, deeply engrossed now, cuts her off summarily. "Overruled."

"And how do you think it got on the page?"

"I don't know."

"You hadn't quite got to this part in the play when your unconscious mind took over, had you?"

"I don't think so."

"Do you remember this book being on the bed?"

A long pause. "I'm not sure. Was it there? I . . . gosh, I . . ."

"Yes?"

"No, it's gone."

"What's gone?"

"I . . . I just thought I had a brief glimmer." She frowns, struggling with some faint image, buried deep in memory. "No, I don't remember."

"Miss Martin, did not the play continue after the other students had left?"

"I'm sorry. What are you saying?"

I take a deep breath. I am beyond cross-examination: this is Jonathan's truth, the reckless defence I am bound to now. "Miss Martin, I'm saying the play continued. I'm saying it continued in bed, as you drank wine and made love. I'm saying the cross you wore around your neck was the cross you clutched as the flames leaped up: the flames that he and you replicated upon your nether regions with lipstick. I'm saying the bed to which you were bound was your pyre, and the fire that consumed you was the fire of passion."

My speech echoes, fades into an eerie stillness.

Augustina's eyes bug in astonishment at my sudden tactical veer.

"Prove it," Kimberley says, a flat, blunt challenge.

I look over at Dr. Kropinski, who seems intensely engaged in our dialogue. I look for help at Augustina, Jonathan, Jane Dix. But the only advice I hear is from the dulcet coaxing voice of Margaret Blake. *But isn't that what the jury should hear—the truth?*

I return to Kimberley. "The proof resides with you, Miss Martin."

"I'm saying if you have an accusation, prove it."

My voice softens. "I'm not accusing you of lying. I'm saying you were amnesic for these events. An event occurred which triggered that amnesia."

She remains stubborn. "All I ask is that you prove it."

"May I have your help to do so?"

She hesitates. "In what way?"

"You trust Dr. Kropinski, don't you?"

"With all my heart."

I must take the chance. "Will you allow him to hypnotize you again, here in court?"

Boldly, she says, "Yes. I want to know."

"Then why don't we do that right now?"

"Whoa," says Patricia, rushing to her feet. "This isn't . . . I think we should have the jury out."

"Hold everything," says Wally, suddenly enjoying this. "You're proposing to do what, Mr. Beauchamp?"

"To restore the witness's memory."

He looks at me dubiously. "You're sure?"

"My client wants the truth to be told."

"I'd like to see counsel in my chambers."

❧

My body feels tight with the tension of my gamble as the court clerk leads us into chambers.

"Might make some legal history here," Wally says, pleased at the prospect. He waves us into chairs. "Bring in the court reporter," he tells his clerk. "Let's put this on record—it's too important. Anyone like coffee?"

"No, thank you," says Patricia, surly, sensing that Wally's scales might not be balanced on this issue. Gundar Sindelar loyally declines as well, while Augustina and I are almost fulsome in our expressions of gratitude for the coffee Wally pours from his Thermos.

"We're playing around with a young woman's life if we do this," Patricia complains.

"Ah-ah, wait for the reporter."

When the clerk returns with the official reporter and her shorthand machine, Wally plumps onto his chair, sits back, and raises his feet onto his desk. "All right, Patricia, you were saying?"

"It's dangerous. No one knows what trauma this could cause Kimberley."

"She seems willing," Wally says. "She's obviously a strong woman."

"We can't . . . I'd have to talk to Dr. Kropinski, I'm sure he'll warn against it. There's no precedent at all for a thing like this."

"Ah, but there is, my dear. In these very courts. Regina versus Welch, an amnesic woman accused of murdering an abusive husband, as I recall. Famous case in its day. She was placed under hypnosis in court; the jury found for her in self-defence."

But Patricia holds firm. "You can't put her through this in front of all those people."

"She seems used to audiences." Wally has again lapsed into an adversarial role, arguing, not listening. "Thrives on them, in fact, that's my impression. She consented in open court; how can you go against the complainant's instructions?"

"She blurted that out. I'm sure she'll reconsider.

Wally, I know she's under cross, but she *is* entitled to some advice about an undertaking this serious."

"No, she can't talk about the case to anyone: it's one of the sacred rules of cross-examination. We don't want a mistrial, do we? What do you say, Arthur, you're being awfully quiet about this."

"I'm curious as to why anyone would not want the truth to be heard in open court."

"Excellent point. Seems to me, Patricia, Arthur's taking a hell of a risk here, more than you. What if she doesn't go under, just *pretends* to be in a state of hypnosis? Arthur could get screwed in the . . . it could boomerang badly on him."

Patricia must by now understand that hers is an argument she is not about to win. "There should be a trial run. In proper surroundings. Not some circus."

The proposed compromise, I sense, has Wally wavering. I finish my coffee and stand, anxious to terminate this session. "The defence will consent to this: Dr. Kropinski may be allowed to advise Kimberley as to the possible consequences of our experiment. They may not otherwise talk about the evidence. There is to be no trial run that could turn into a dress rehearsal."

"That's white of you, Mr. Beauchamp," says Patricia in a deep voice, mimicking Wally.

Wally frowns. "White . . . that's rather . . ." He hesitates and turns a chalky shade himself. "Did I say something like that in court? Oh, dear. Madam reporter, would you consult your notes about that, and, ah, we'll adjourn now. We'll proceed on that basis, the one Arthur suggested. So ordered." He is most flustered. "Now, when do we want to do this?"

It is almost noon. "Let us all first try to enjoy a bit of lunch," I say.

But lunch isn't greeted with much appetite, though it's not the fault of the plump shrimp that stare at me mournfully from the tray brought up to my room. I am still too disoriented from the morning's many swift turns—capricious gusts have blown this trial off its poorly plotted course.

Augustina is by the window of my suite, picking at her salad, studying Jane Dix's transcripts, reading voraciously by the noonday light. The sky is still busy with moving cloud, but they've shredded here and there, offering sneak peaks of blue, though more rain is forecast.

Jonathan is elsewhere, alone, jogging the seawall— we plan to spend the entire weekend with him, testing the evidence he's to give on Monday. Kimberley is with Dr. Kropinski, talking process—I have come away from a meeting with him much reinforced in my sense that he is utterly fair and sincere.

Truth is a kind of important concept, isn't it? Yes, as Margaret reminded me, truth does not blush. But shall Arthur Beauchamp? He will retire from the courts in either triumph or ignominy; if Kimberley's truth differs from Jonathan's, as recorded in those transcripts, I shall have pulled off the greatest blunder since Prometheus brought fire to earth and was condemned to satisfy the eternal appetite of a liver-gobbling vulture.

Augustina finally looks up from the transcripts. "He's lied to us before."

Too true. Sexual relations with Kimberley? "I did no such thing." The lipstick on her body? "Sleepwalking, nightmares, a tab of acid in her B and B." Did he tie her up? "Christ, no. What for?" The screams the housekeeper heard? "She must be imagining them."

"But this is different, isn't it?" she says, rising, handing a transcript to me, Jonathan's tale of his and Kimberley's passion play. I absorb myself in it once again.

. . . She was still being Joan of Arc, and I was her torturer. I know that's how she understood it. We were *laughing*. It wasn't something planned or talked about. We just slid into it as we were necking on the bed, the final scene. She had this gold crucifix around her neck; it was the cross Joan held as she burned.

Why the lipstick, Jonathan?

To portray the flames in which she burned. Psychodrama. Creative role-playing.

This was after you first made love.

Yes. We both climaxed.

And you couldn't get an erection after that?

Not until . . .

Until you tied her up.

To the stake. She wanted to be face up at first, supine. And we . . . we made love again that way. With some, ah, cunnilingus, and—wow, this isn't easy—she was so hot, Jane, incredibly ready for sex. She came again. I wasn't quite up to it the second go-round, so to speak, so I had no condom, but I guess I had a reasonable facsimile of an erection. Then she said, "Turn me over."

In the meantime, you were still play-acting?

I'm telling you, Jane, she was getting a kick out of it. She prayed to God and then screamed as I painted the flames upon her—Christ, she's a wonderful actor—and then she'd break into these low, sexy peals of laughter . . . why? At the absurdity of it all? At the sheer fun of it? Some reason. Jane, she was having the goddamnest time of her life. I was, too. Then something changed in her.

In what way?

God knows; I don't. I went to the bathroom, put on another condom—because I felt . . . I was ready again. And when I got back to the bed, I remember I said something to her, and she didn't respond. And I saw her eyes were closed, but she was smiling that amazing smile she has, and I made the assumption she was awake. And I kneeled between her legs and lifted her buttocks, and . . . well, uh, performed the sex act. Went into her.

Do you now think she was asleep? Passed out?

I now believe she was. I think I started to realize soon afterwards. Anyway, she started to scream and struggle.

But not in play?

As I told you, she's a wonderful actor. I thought this was an Emmy performance. She was fighting me, trying to pull her legs and arms free, but she'd done that before in play, though not as vigorously, and I slipped out, and I still thought we were just fooling around, and I guess I tried to come into her again, and had trouble finding the right . . . um . . .

Orifice.

Yes. She must have thought I was trying to enter the, ah, wrong place. I wasn't, honestly. My aim was impaired. But I guess I must have probed her there a little and, she, ah, she went absolutely berserk, totally unglued.

What was she saying during this?

She was screaming, pleading. "Please, don't. Stop." And she was crying. And she wasn't laughing any more. And so I backed off, and I was a little worried now, because she suddenly had this wild, haggard expression. And I remember saying something to the effect, would she like to join me in a tub for two, and . . . then I went to the bathroom again, took off the safe, disposed of it, began filling the tub . . . I may have taken a whiz. Probably. Anyway, when I got back, no Kimberley. I ran through the house—no sign of her. I looked outside. She'd vanished. But the lights were on at the Hawthorne house. And that's when I panicked. I bathed, I burned everything. I didn't sleep that night.

Why did you feel such guilt?

I raped her, Jane. An unconscious woman cannot consent.

What are you going to do about it?

What I have to do. I can't keep running from lie to lie. There's no end to that road. . . .

The stage has been set with new furniture: two padded armchairs purloined from the barristers' lounge. They face each other, near the counsel tables. Kimberley Martin waits in the mezzanine to be called. The ground rules for our venture into the subconscious have been agreed upon in camera.

As he mounts the dais, Wally seems to be in grieving, possibly for himself. "Members of the jury, regrettably it has been brought to my attention that I said a very foolish thing this morning. Now, when I remarked that it was white of Mr. Beauchamp to convenience a witness, I want to impress on everyone that I meant that word, 'white,' in the sense of being virtuous, pure, and of course it had nothing to do with skin colour, though I can see how that meaning might be taken. Mr. Beauchamp could be black, brown, or green for that matter, and it frankly wouldn't make any difference to me."

Forewoman Jackson-Blyth looks skintily at the judge, unimpressed with these ill-prepared remarks. Augustina leans to me. "How deep a hole does he need to dig for himself?"

Wally shrugs away the awkward episode and turns to matters at hand. He tells the jury Dr. Kropinski will be called by the defence as a witness. After some preliminary evidence, he and Kimberley will assume the chairs provided and the lights will be dimmed to near darkness. "And anyone who feels they may have an urge to whisper or cough will absent themselves immediately or face my full wrath. Mr. Beauchamp?"

"I call Dr. Benjamin Kropinski."

The psychiatrist nods politely to me, bows with old-country courtesy to the judge, and takes the stand. I draw from him his considerable qualifications: former professor at the University of Bern, member of many learned societies, author of several papers on hypnosis therapy.

I ask him if he has advised Kimberley about the process to be undertaken.

"Yes. She is prepared to do this."

"It helps in that she is a good subject for hypnosis?"

"Exactly so."

He testifies he has been treating Kimberley for six months, assisting her in dealing with a "recurring hysteria associated with dreams triggered by events blocked from memory." He describes his therapeutic approach, summarizes his history of treatment, and tells of a session at his home one recent evening when Kimberley literally threw up and expelled a ghastly demon from her childhood.

I spend a few minutes with the doctor edifying the jury as to the various sources of amnesia—the most common of which is my old friend, substance intoxication: "which may have played a significant role here." But the core factor was "emotional trauma memory loss syndrome"—more simply, traumatic amnesia.

"The mind does not wish to know. The victim blocks the pain, which is buried beneath memory's surface."

"And do you hold an opinion as to whether Miss Martin is amnesic about events related to this trial?"

"I hold that opinion."

"Please take one of these chairs, doctor." I turn to Sheriff Willit. "Be so kind as to lower the lights and escort Miss Martin in."

The lights slowly go down as Kimberley enters and cruises up the aisle, legs swishing beneath her tight vermilion sheathe: Diana the huntress, goddess of the moon, ghostlike in the growing gloom. An oblique peek in Jonathan's direction, a tentative smile for me, and she claims her chair, crossing her legs, hitching down her skirt.

Dr. Kropinski turns to me. "We shall proceed, yes?"

"Please," I say. The room is in near blackness now, but for the soft glow of lamps on Wally's bench and the court reporter's table.

"Kimberley, you are aware fully what we are trying to do," Dr. Kropinski begins.

"Yes, I am," she says in a soft, unwavering voice.

"You are in a courtroom with many people."

"I understand that. I am only going to look at you."

"You will hear only me?"

"Yes."

"You are relaxed, comfortable?"

"Sure. Under the circumstances."

After receiving a few more assurances of her preparedness, this gentle doctor of the mind commences a seductive, lulling mantra, a soft cloud of words that causes Kimberley's body to go visibly slack and seems to make my own eyelids heavy. He tells his patient that at the count of ten she will fall asleep—yet a part of her will be awake, observant solely to his voice.

". . . Nine . . . ten."

Silence.

"Kimberley?"

"Yes." The word floats from her lips.

"You can open your eyes now."

They seem to slide languorously open; a peculiar softness is in them.

"Where are we?"

"I believe we are in a courtroom." The sluggish voice of one just aroused from slumber.

"Please only listen to my voice. Only talk to me."

"I am doing that."

"In this trial, we are talking about something that happened last year, yes?"

"Yes."

"After a dance."

"Yes."

"Let us go back to that time. Will you go there with me?"

"All right."

"It is the night of November twenty-seventh. After the dance there is a party, and later you are at a house with some friends, yes?"

"Professor O'Donnell's house."

"It is late at night, yes?"

"I don't know what time it is."

"Around three o'clock—"

She interrupts. "Oh, my God, Remy will think I'm lying somewhere in an alley." Her voice has abruptly altered in rhythm and tone, sprightly now, a slight slurring of consonants. "Gosh, I think I'm a little drunk. Woo, I don't norm'lly drink this much."

"You and the others have been reading from a play—"

Again she cuts him off, spreading her arms theatrically, lamenting: " 'If only I could hear the larks in the sunshine, the blessed, blessed church bells that send my angels' voices floating on the wind.' Shaw's such an ol' curmudgeon, but he can be poetic when he wants. What happened to my glass? Glass? It's like drinking from a vase. I have to sit down. I'm spinning. Shouldn't've done that toot, Remy would *not* approve, the ol' sourpuss. He'll be fast asleep now. I should call him. Where's the phone? Not in here. There was one by Jonathan's bed. I wonder if this is his favourite brown suit. I'm afraid to ask him where he got the tie—in a joke shop? His father's a scream, no wonder he hid that picture under his socks. Choking a pheasant!"

She is wandering aimlessly over the windswept moors, free-associating, clearly out of anyone's control, including Dr. Kropinski's. He seems a little confounded at having set free this talkative genie.

"How come the inquisitor gets all the long speeches in this scene? Am I feeling ridiculous in this suit, or what? I better go up and change, get on my way. Hi, Remy, I spent all my money and had to walk home. That won't do. I don' wanna know the time."

Dr. Kropinski seems to have decided not to cork this gushing pour of words.

"Charles, you're *so* pathetic. All night sucking up to the inquisitor, grabbing the seat right beside him— you're totally ignoring your date, you ass. I don't think she likes me, thinks I'm some kinda prima donna. Oh, why don't they just all go home? What's going on with me anyway? Feeling so glazed over. Hot flashes. On fire. Too much firewater. Why did I do that coke, I *never* . . . Oh, God, Remy will have a fucking *bird*. . . ."

She seems to have utterly exposed herself to us, naked of mind, candid almost beyond belief. But where is her discursive patter taking us? Now she giggles.

"What are you laughing at?"

"Oh, back when we were dancing, he . . . he had a kind of hard on. I bumped into it, had to pretend I didn't notice."

Is this good, bad, indifferent? Wally, craning down at her, seems to stiffen, too. I can almost feel the heat behind me from Jonathan's embarrassment.

Dr. Kropinski says, "Excuse me for a second, my dear," then approaches me in whispered conference.

"This is, I fear, unusual. She becomes her former self with a vivid personal reliving one rarely sees. But her discourse is scattered. I think it is the setting, too many people—she senses their energy; it confuses her. Do I carry on, yes?"

"Your patient is not in harm?"

"I think she is strong enough for this."

"Please proceed."

But a gremlin of worry is teasing me. What if she is affecting this garrulous hypnotic state? Is this talented female lead, with all her vivid reliving, seeking to salvage honour and marriage, seizing on this chance to make final credible proof of her complaint? Has she mentally armed herself against falling under the hypnotizer's spell in a ruse to seduce Ms. Foreperson and her crew with a siren's song?

And in her gusto to take up my challenge to restore her memory is she also beguiling me? The Commander, unlike Ulysses, is not tied to the mast as he seeks passage between the rocks of doom. Is it gullible Beauchamp who has been mesmerized today? But surely my fears are telling me false. I have never encountered a witness so open and gregarious, so generous with her feelings. . . .

But now a change comes over her, a sadness. Her eyes close; her voice begins to falter.

"You said they wouldn't torture me . . . you lied. . . ." A long silence follows. A strangled cough from a juror, then the court is silent as death.

"Where are you now, dear?"

"At his house . . . I think."

"Who said they wouldn't torture you?"

"The holy church . . ." She opens her eyes wide, and suddenly her contralto becomes a child soprano, stubborn, frightened. "I won't go to Sunday school.

Please don't make me. I'm a good girl, Mother, I'm a good girl."

Dr. Kropinski tries to get her attention. "Kimberley—"

But she is jumping around, lost in a childhood time warp. "I just wanna see the bunnies. Please, don't." The pleading of a terrified girl. "Don't, oh, please, *please*. That hurts! Help me! Oh, help me!"

"Kimberley, you are with me. You are a woman of twenty-three. You are fine now." I sense her immediate relief at hearing her therapist's voice. She relaxes, offers a weak smile.

"You are fine?"

"Yes. Thank you."

I can't bear to look at the jury, to assess their reaction. My eyes are glued to the witness. Is this an act? It cannot be. I dare not believe she could effect such brilliant disguise. If so, I will prostrate myself at her feet in admiration.

"Come back with me to Jonathan's house. Did you fall asleep?"

"I think I did."

"What is happening when you wake up?"

Now her eyes close again, and her deeper woman's voice interrupts. "I'm on his bed. . . ." Suddenly she is wailing, "I'm tied up! He's hurting me! Blood! Blood! I'm bleeding!" She is struggling in her chair, shaking, now working feverishly with invisible bonds. "He's going to drown me!" She begins to heave herself from the chair and then abruptly stops, suspends herself, seems to float, then slowly subsides back, breathing heavily, staring into space. Dr. Kropinski looks quickly at me, with concern, as a deep silence falls heavy upon the room, time slowly flowing, Kimberley breathing more gently now.

"Where are you?" asks the doctor.

"I am in the courtroom," she says dully. "I want to end this now. Please."

Dr. Kropinski looks at Wally, who nods, giving assent. I am fearful of objecting, of making some hazardous intrusion into her trance, but I want to cry out: No, no, we must not end this. What have we accomplished? An entire room of memories remains unfurnished.

"I will count to three, yes—"

I hear my voice, low, urgent: "Not yet. Take her back. Back to Jonathan's parlour."

Though her eyes are open now, they are looking only at Dr. Kropinski. "I don't want to go back . . . I don't want to know."

Wally appears about to intervene, and I am half on my feet, palms flat on the table. "She *needs* to know," I say.

The doctor raises a hand to still me. "Do you not want to remember, Kimberley?" he asks her.

She shakes her head in sadness.

Dr. Kropinski sighs. Clearly, he now intends to bring her out of her fugue state.

I speak to her directly now. "Be brave, Kimberley. Remember, you are Saint Joan."

Unexpectedly, she responds with a chipper voice. "I am, you know. I feel like Joan sometimes. Leader of men." She laughs. "Poor things, bewildered by a woman. Jonathan, too, he keeps looking funny at me, like he doesn't understand. . . . God, when are those characters going to *leave*?"

Dr. Kropinski seems encouraged to proceed. "Why do you want them to leave?"

"I just want to be alone with him, just for a minute. . . . We wouldn't actually, I wouldn't stay long. . . ." Her voice grows weary.

"Kimberley?"

"Yes."

"Don't sleep. You are on a sofa. Tell me what is happening before you fall asleep."

Kimberley closes her eyes and frowns in concentration. "Do I sleep?" she says softly. "I don't think so . . . I hear voices. They are whispering to me: Stay, fly away, stay, fly away. Two minutes alone with him . . . we'll just talk. That's time enough, that's an eternity. A never-to-be-repeated kiss at the door, telling him that I . . . so he will know what might have been. They *are* going, goodbye, goodbye, the taxi is here. Go with them. Fly away, fly away. I . . . Jonathan . . ." And abruptly her memories short-circuit again, and she wails, "He's gonna kill Mummy and Daddy, Dr. Kropinski!"

In despair, I fully expect he will now free her from her transfixed state—she is in much difficulty again, crying. But I am startled by a curt change in this sage healer's bedside manner. He seems determined now to break through the barriers that block her memory, speaks as to a fussing child. "Stop crying. Be strong. You are a healthy, vigorous woman. What happens now as the others leave Jonathan's house?"

A silence. Then in a husky voice, Kimberley says, "I know you are there, Jonathan. You think I am asleep, but I can smell you, I can hear you breathing." Now she whimpers, "Don't . . . oh, don't . . . Please."

Are her sparks about to jump the gap again? Dr. Kropinski has clearly decided he cannot leave her in trauma's limbo and orders, "Stay with Jonathan! What is he doing?"

"Please, I can't . . ."

Dr. Kropinski's tone is flat and insistent. "What does Jonathan do to you, Kimberley?"

"Fly away, fly away," she whispers.

"Kimberley, please—"

Plaintively, "I can't remember!"

A shocked stillness. Then a voice from behind me, Jonathan's, rasping and choked. "I kiss you, Kimberley. I kiss your lips."

The courtroom, silent until this moment, shuffles with whisper and movement.

Kimberley's eyes grow wide in astonishment. "Yes. Yes. Jonathan . . ." Her eyes close again, tight. "You kiss me . . . yes, a kiss, and a kiss again, and now our night can never end, we have it forever. Jonathan, kiss me, kiss me." She hugs her arms to her chest. "God, I want you, I want you. Oh, *damn*, I want you."

Augustina whispers, "Timber." Finally I dare a glance at the jury. They are riveted, their mouths gaping. Wally, too, is welded to his chair.

"Touch me, touch me . . . Stop. No, don't stop. Oh, God. Stop. Don't. Not yet." Now a playful tone: "Bad timing, Jonathan. The end of November is the middle of the month." She giggles—then a sudden hot peal of laughter as she mimes undressing. "This stupid suit. Where did you get this tie anyway? I'm not going to make it up those stairs, I can hardly *walk*. Oh, kiss me first." Huskier: "Oh, that feels . . . oh . . ." Her arms are folded over her heaving chest.

If Dr. Kropinski can't stem the flow of this erotic haemorrhaging, he will vault beyond it. "Kimberley, you are upstairs in the bedroom now. You have had sex, yes? Next, what is happening?"

She jumps ahead and pours forth a gallimaufry of naked revelry and Shavian theatre: "You said you wouldn't torture me! You said . . . Oh, God, Jonathan, I think this is almost too weird. No, do it. Tie me to the stake. 'Light your fire: do you think I dread it as much as the life of a rat in a hole?' Light *my* fire. Your line, and pass the wine. 'Perpetual imprisonment! Am I not to be set free?' Ouch, Jonathan, there's something scraping . . . Softer, softer, that's better. Oh, God, Jonathan, what are you . . . Oh, God, don't. Not with the mouth. That's not fair, I can't move, I can't . . . I can't . . ."

The psychiatrist attempts to interrupt, but Kimberley's torrid stream of consciousness will not be dammed. "Jonathan, I can't hold *on*. Come inside me.

Yes, you can. Oh, please, don't. Oh, my God! Stop! Oh, Jonathan!"

"You *must* return to the courtroom, Kimberley."

Perhaps she doesn't hear him, so lost in bliss is she, writhing, her hips moving with sensuous rhythm, her legs splayed apart. Dr. Kropinski rises hurriedly from his chair and moves to her.

"Kimberley . . ."

"Oh, please help me, God! Yes, yes, there, there! Oh, yes. Right *there*! Oh, God, *yes*!" An exuberant scream of fulfillment.

"Kimberley, please." He is gently shaking her by the shoulder.

She sighs deeply. "Wow."

"You're back in the courtroom with me. Do you understand?"

"Sure." She giggles. "He looked so *funny*, Dr. Kropinski. He had lipstick all over his face. I laughed and laughed. And you know what? He turned me around on my tummy and *spanked* me." She emits another gay peal; then, as if disappointed that her merriment has been met with silence, frowns and shrugs. "I guess you had to be there."

"You will awake. At the count of three you will awake."

She sighs. "Will I remember?"

"You will remember."

"Oh, dear."

"One, two, three."

When she comes to, she is clearly puzzled for a moment. Then her face expands in surprise, eyes enlarging, mouth opened in a silent gasp, and she brings both hands to her mouth, covering it, then her entire face. Fingers part, and she peeks between them, at Patricia.

"Gag me," she says.

She flashes a quick look at Jonathan as a muted

shade of Shameless red continues to rise up her throat and cheeks.

The lights go on. Wally Sprogue, flushed, too, a sheen of sweat upon his forehead, adjourns court breathlessly. Most of the jurors seem shell-shocked as they retreat from their bunker, but the doughty Hedy Jackson-Blyth casts an accusing look at me, as if I have pulled off some unworthy stunt, destroying a young woman for the sake of a mere acquittal.

Kimberley is now being led out by Dr. Kropinski, a protective arm around her shoulders. One of her hands is still clasped over her eyes, but with the other she pulls from an open handbag a large blue handkerchief—her gift from Jonathan—and veils her face with it. Jonathan is looking at her with immense solemnity and awe.

The audience files out, stupefied, silent. Beside me, Augustina is trying to hide a secret smile as she studies Jonathan, who is still dazedly staring at the emptying court.

Patricia shakes my hand. "Win some, lose some. You were brilliant, of course, you son of a bitch."

"Nonsense. You were much the sharper of us. Managed to fumble my way through it, that's all."

"I'll enter a stay."

"If you'd be so kind, may we have a formal verdict from the jury?"

"You're entitled to that. Help me drown my sorrows in the El Beau Room?"

"I'm sorry, I may have to run for the ferry."

All but a few of the audience have left—a young man remains, eyes closed, head lolling, an accidental victim of Dr. Kropinski. We watch as Sheriff Willit shakes him awake.

Jonathan hugs Jane Dix, then offers his hand to me. "Arthur, I can't tell you. . . ." He is lost for words. "I'll talk to you later, I'm numb." What is this curious, distant glitter in his eyes? Not relief, not joy . . . something more potent. He blinks damply, parts hurriedly from me, and races from court, deserting Jane, who looks bewildered at this sudden retreat. Too much manly pride to permit a show of tears?

"Judge would like to see counsel," says the clerk.

The courtroom door opens again, and here comes a beaming Gowan Cleaver, hand outstretched.

"I'll meet you in chambers," says Augustina, and she beats a hasty retreat, leaving me to deal with the miscreant. Gowan heartily grasps my hand.

"So I hear O'Donnell gives great head. Everyone in the building is talking about it. Fantastic coup, Arthur."

"Finished your argument, Gowan?"

"Just."

"Then do me a favour."

"Yours is but to ask."

"I'd like you to run down to the nearest florist and buy five dozen roses for Augustina Sage."

"Arthur, that's asking a bit much. Christ, we can get one of the students . . ."

I scribble a note on the back of a business card, and hand it to him. "We'll be in Wally's chambers. You may leave them with his clerk."

"Look, I'm sorry about that screw-up. . . ."

I walk off. This minor chore seems an insufficient purgatory, but Gowan has found me in a generous mood.

A boisterous Wally brings a bottle of single malt from his bar, offers rounds to the non-teetotallers, a more-than-generous dollop for himself.

"Your chap likes to spice it up with a little kink, I gather. A spanking good time, eh? Yes, I figured it out almost from the beginning. Obvious as a billboard that she never really blacked out on that couch. No, she fell asleep later, on the bed, during a pause in their games. Freaked out when she was jumped from behind, brought the whole childhood trauma back. Of course Beauchamp had to make a big production of it. Overdid things a bit, I thought; I might have handled it another way, but what the hell."

Comfortable, slouched in a chair, I refuse to be baited by Wally in his effort to sand the gloss from my victory. "I've underestimated you, Wally. You saw through our little scheme."

Augustina shrugs helplessly in agreement.

"I know you only too well, Beauchamp. So what's the right way to end this?"

"May I suggest you direct the jury to acquit."

"Fair enough."

A directed acquittal—the remedy *de rigueur* when the case blows up in Her Majesty's face—will be bloodless and quick. No speeches, no laborious lectures on the law, no deliberation, no choice, no delay. I have a five o'clock ferry.

After we work out the mechanics of this, Patricia gulps down her whisky. "I'm going to tend to Kimberley."

Gundar joins in the escape, but Wally seems in no hurry to dismiss Augustina and me and tops her glass. "Must be distracting, Beauchamp, having such an attractive young woman at your side all week. I'd find it damn hard to keep my mind on business. Not that appearance makes a difference, of course. Inappropriate to judge people by their looks. Kimberley Martin, for instance, a bit of a fluffhead, don't you think? Her boyfriend's a handsome chap, but essentially a prick. I'd tell your client to take a long holiday, Beauchamp. Remy doesn't seem the forgiving type."

I rise. "Time presses, Wally. I must get ready to go." The *Queen of Prince George* leaves in an hour and a half. I doubt that I will find a charter on a long weekend.

"Returning to your alternative lifestyle, eh, Beauchamp? My guess is we'll see you back here when the novelty wanes."

When Augustina also seeks to take her leave, Wally waves her over to her seat. "Stay, stay. Don't fly away. I was going to take you out for a drink, Beauchamp, but I guess I'll just have to make do with your junior."

Augustina tries to wiggle out of this. "Gee, Wally, I'd like to, but . . ." A furtive glance at me; she's trying to devise a credible excuse.

But just then the clerk walks in, almost buried in roses of a myriad hues. "For you, Miss Sage. They were just delivered."

Augustina gapes at them, enfolds them in her arms. "Who the hell?" She finds my business card, reads the flipside aloud: " 'Friendship is the breathing rose, with sweets in every fold.' Oh, Arthur, you dear lovely man."

"Oliver Wendell Holmes. It seemed appropriate: his son was one of the great judges of our century." I leave unspoken the inference we are not in the presence of similar greatness. We bid sweet adieu to his forlornly smiling lordship and walk out arm in arm.

In the corridor, reporters throng me like squawking chickens, hungry for their sound bites. I bid them have patience until proceedings formally close.

The two psychiatrists are in the mezzanine, in earnest colloquy. Jonathan is pacing, head down, absorbed in other worlds until I arrest his attention.

"We're moving for a directed verdict," I tell him.

"Great," he says absently. "Is she still here?"

"Who?"

"Kimberley."

"Why?"

"I think I need to talk to her."

"That would be most unwise. Clarence de Remy Brown may not approve of your having further intercourse—social though it may be—with his fiancée. Let sleeping dogs lie."

"I just want to tell her I have no ill feelings. And to apologize for putting her in such an awkward position . . . rephrase that, embarrassing situation." He himself seems much embarrassed.

"I advise against it."

But there she appears, with Patricia, emerging downcast from the witness room: she no longer has eyes for Jonathan. Patricia leads her to court, and as Jonathan steps forward I grasp his elbow, restraining my restive steed from galloping off to her. I wait for Augustina, who has rushed off somewhere to put her flowers in water; then we lead in our client.

The jurors fumble into their seats, still shaken—all but the forewoman, Jackson-Blyth, and the broker, Goodman. The former is frowning, the latter, smiling.

Wally Sprogue, so recently outduelled by me on the fields of chivalry, looks as if he's been pouting. "Ms. Blueman?"

"Ms. Martin can be excused from the stand?"

"No one has any more questions? Very well, the witness is excused from court." Kimberley, sitting behind Patricia, makes no motion to leave. Tight of lip and stiff of neck, she seems determined to brazen it out for the trial's denouement.

Patricia formally closes her case. "That is all the evidence for the Crown, m'lord."

Wally turns to the jury. "Ms. Foreperson, jury members: the charges before you require proof the complainant did not consent. When the evidence points entirely in the opposite direction—and I think you will agree there was consent here *beyond* a reasonable doubt—it becomes the judge's duty to direct the jury to find the defendant not guilty on all counts. I so direct you. I take it you do not need to retire and consider that verdict." He smiles unctuously. But Hedy Jackson-Blyth has raised a hand. "Ms. Foreperson, you have a question?"

She rises with a look that intimates she feels male mischief is occurring here. "The defendant kissed her while he thought she was unconscious. He admitted that. Are you saying that is not a sexual assault?" She has a firm, emphatic way of making a point, doubtless perfected in union halls. The other jurors shuffle awkwardly—they do not seem in support of their leader. Goodman is grimacing, expressing disgust.

"Madam, we are not debating societal mores here," Wally retorts—perhaps too quickly, but he is cranky: his word has been challenged.

"No, I just want it clear. Can a woman consent to being kissed unawares, when she has her eyes closed? Or are there different kinds of consent?"

Wally is about to say something, then pauses, reflects. This feminist spear-thrower may have aimed her political dart too correctly: right down Wally's affirmatively acting throat. "Well . . ." he says. "Strictly speaking, no, it's not *true* consent, but . . ." He struggles, a hint of panic in his eyes.

"I'm not saying it's a serious type of assault, but wouldn't it be a very bad precedent? I don't know if I could play a part in it, your honour. Unless you're sure that's what the law says." She can barely keep the scorn from her voice.

He turns to me for rescue. "There's a principle that applies to this, isn't there, Mr. Beauchamp?"

"*De minimis non curat lex*. The law does not concern itself with trifles."

Jackson-Blyth will not let up. "Well, if unwanted touching is a trifle—"

But Kimberley sharply breaks into this disputation, her voice fierce. "Oh, for God's sake, I *wanted* him to kiss me. And it wasn't any trifle."

Someone gasps. Jackson-Blyth reddens. "I'm

sorry," she says. She looks around at her frowning comrades. "Well, I guess the verdict is not guilty." They nod. She sits awkwardly, ruffled.

"Very good," says Wally. "Now, before we adjourn—can I have the jury's attention?"

They are distracted by Kimberley, who is slowly gaining her feet. She takes a deep breath, regards Jonathan for a moment, then begins to glide out, head high, curls dancing.

"A final word of thanks to you, members of the jury. You have made sacrifices to serve your country, giving up home, family, and work place. . . ."

No one is listening to this saccharine dirge. They are watching Kimberley make an about-face at the doorway. She smiles gamely, blows a campy kiss to the audience, raises her arms in theatrical surrender, and departs.

". . . I could tell by your faces you had an obvious grip on the issues. . . ."

Wally stalls as Jonathan rises and walks quickly up the aisle.

"And, ah, I observed you paid attention throughout. . . ."

Heads are turned as Jonathan accelerates towards the door and disappears, sending it shut with a thud.

His audience lost, Wally sighs. "That's all. We'll adjourn."

"What the hell's with Jon?" Augustina asks.

"He has madly rushed off on an ill-advised mission to seek Kimberley's understanding and mercy. Go in pursuit, quickly. Put the collar on him and don't let him talk to reporters."

They are all in the mezzanine, demanding, threatening, circling us like jackals. I toss them a few bones, homilies about our noble system of justice and its pursuit of truth; I express pleasure in the exoneration of innocence and I pray that both parties involved in this minor fuss will heal their wounds and enjoy tranquil lives and splendid careers.

But as we work our way to the edge of the crowd, I see Kimberley, unattended, slip from a witness room, glance in our direction, then step quickly down a deserted corridor. Between bobbing heads I glimpse Jonathan hurrying after her. I lean to Augustina's ear: "There he goes."

She takes off in pursuit while I make my way down the stairs, bloviating to the press about all manner of nonsense, finally escaping into the sanctum of the gentlemen's robing room. There, the Commander hurriedly stuffs his costume into a locker and throws on some casual clothes. Four-thirty. I shall never make it to the ferry for its milk run to the islands. Woe: I shall have to delay may return to both island and woman of my heart until the morning.

But relax, Beauchamp. Haste takes a heavy toll of the heart. The morning boat will haul me home well before noon, even running late. I shall call Margaret and explain. And why not spend a few good moments in the El Beau Room with friends, basking in victory's glow?

Waiting outside my room, in amiable conversation, are Augustina Sage and Dr. Jane Dix.

"Jonathan gave me the slip, Arthur." Augustina shrugs helplessly. "A very deliberate one. I yelled to him from across the street. He ignored me."

I lead them into my suite. Augustina bends to my mini-bar, finds a fruit punch for me, then pulls out a half-bottle of champagne. The cork pops, and she ducks from a spray of fizz.

"They went off in a taxi. Jonathan and Kimberley."

"In a taxi!"

My stunned expression prompts Jane to smile. "I

only see good coming from it. They have a great deal to say to each other. Lots of bandaging to do."

This clever doctor of the mind has prescribed too well and often for me to take issue with her. My sexually challenged client has high degrees from Oxford; I must assume he knows what he's doing.

"I must apologize to you, Jane. I was too cynical. I preferred silence to truth. But has the truth made Jonathan free?"

"He no longer has to hide. Can't be free in a closet."

"Extraordinary, this seeming urgency to run off and make amends with a woman who put him through nine months of hell. I suppose a permanent cease-fire will not hurt his chances before the U.B.C. ethics panel."

"You *are* cynical," Jane says. "I don't believe he's thinking about his career right now. There's something else about Jonathan you should know. I only came to fully realize it while I was watching him in court."

Our glasses clink. I hesitate before sipping.

"What should I know?"

"He went to her play four times. I thought at first it was a persecution obsession. But it's a rather healthier emotion than that. Though he managed for the longest while to blind himself to it."

My face must seem to her a blur of incomprehension.

Augustina explains, "He's totally gone on her, Arthur, that's what Jane's telling you."

Jane nods. "Took him a while to figure it out. Heavy denial. At some point today—as she was testifying, I think—the light just came flooding in."

Augustina says, "You saw the way he kept staring at her all week . . . totally bewitched. Mad about her." She tweaks my beard and winks. "You should know what it's like, lover." She tosses back her champagne. "Guess he was just flirting with me. We'll see you in a few minutes, Arthur. Everyone's waiting in the El Beau Room."

❦

After they depart, I undress, assailed by my own odours, the dense acid smell of a hard day's toil for justice. Outside: a grey mattress of cloud. But from a thin break in the west, a peep of sun; a yellow slash illumines the high mountain forests across the inlet.

The latest aperçu from Jane Dix has me confounded—yet the clues were all present: Jonathan's confusion, depression, obsession. But never hatred, that evil antonym of love. To his credit he had never cried out for vengeance, for injury, for hurt. *Why can't I hate her? I can't find my anger; maybe I've buried it too deep.* He'd buried not his anger but his heart.

Ah, love. Who can comprehend the madness inflicted by Venus's poisoned arrows? Who can survive and not be blinded? "It is vain to look for a defence against lightning," Publilius Syrus said. Poor Jonathan, who must now suffer the curse of unrequited love.

But I must pursue my own heart. . . .

Margaret's phone rings too often, but I am finally rewarded by her liquid, gay hello.

"How *exciting.* It was on the five o'clock news. I want to hear it all, every second of it. When do you get here?"

"The morning ferry, should I survive that long."

"I'll wait." She says this with entirely too much cheer. "We're short on manpower, can you supervise some of the children's games? The three-legged race and stuff?"

"Of course."

"Oh, and we have a guest artist coming, a wonderful classical guitarist. Excuse me. Have to lay the phone down. I'm running a tub. I just can't undo a bra with one hand."

A tiny, tickling electrical surge passes through me. Suddenly I am overwhelmed by an erotic image: I picture her unclasping that brassière, arms twisted behind her back, the straps gliding from her shoulders. . . .

I look down in awe. I have an erection as stiff as a salute.

My cronies and I celebrate around a long table at the El Beau Room: Patricia and Gundar bravely nursing their wounds, Augustina—suffering a slightly bruised heart—on her way to tying one on. Sheriff, court clerk, and stenographer are here, as well as two of the jurors: Mr. Lang, the fishing person, and the broker Goodman. We are missing Wally, who for some reason has elected for home and family.

"It looked for a while like we had a fight on our hands," Goodman is telling me. "Isn't there some defence where a guy's so drunk he can't help himself?"

I am barely listening to him. Tomorrow, the eight o'clock ferry. By noon, *Dei gratia*, I will be paired off with Margaret at the egg-toss contest. Later, after the barbecue, after the dance, another chance to woo her by her blazing hearth?

My chat with Margaret—she in her tub, I wandering about consumed with erotic fantasy—is still setting off tingles, erogenous pops in my loins. How exuberant I feel; I cannot remember such libidinous yearnings since my youth. But I am saving it, hoarding it in the audacious hope that Margaret may ultimately fall prey to my dogged pursuit.

Finally, all but the lawyers leave. We tarry, order

food, relive our trial. Patricia comically apes a fogbound appeal court judge.

As I am about to rise, an agitated man in a business suit approaches. I remember him: the footman who'd been attending Clarence de Remy Brown the day he left for Guyana. He clears his throat and interrupts Patricia's parody.

"Excuse me, but, ah, can anyone tell me where Miss Martin is?"

Silence. None dares look at him. But Patricia sighs, rises, follows him to the front door, where Remy himself appears, looking cranky and confused after a long flight, a gift-wrapped package in his arms. I decide to go out by another door.

Outside, the air has turned keen and sweet. The sky has cleared. Suspended above is a fattening harvest moon.

⸎ PART FOUR ⸎

No one regards what is before his feet;
we all gaze at the stars.

—QUINTUS ENNIUS

The sun's first rays brush the mountain peaks across the inlet, their wreathes of clouds made rosy by the slanting September light. Arcing over the North Shore mists, a faint rainbow: *Iris gliding through the purple air, When loosely girt her dazzling mantle flows.*

There will be time enough to sing the songs of Flaccus. I am already packed, my suitcase heavier by several pounds. A gift arrived in my room last night: a compact disc player, CDs of Shakespeare's entire *oeuvre* for the stage, a note in Jonathan's scrawl: "For this relief, much thanks."

My phone rings. The office limousine awaits below to fetch me to the ferry. (My rolling stock is now sorely depleted, so I shall be truckless and footloose on Garibaldi.)

And now I am aboard the *Queen of Prince George* as she furrows through tossing waves towards those green hills rising from the inner sea. Ah, the beautiful Isles of the Blest, the heaven of the ancients, where the gods transport the virtuous to live in blissful eternity: thither go I, the finally and forever retired lawyer, reborn as a tiller of soil. On some distant future day, let my obituary read: Though skilled in court, A. R. Beauchamp was ultimately better known for his stirring feats as a farmer.

Obituary . . . George comes back to me. How I would have loved to regale that darling man with my tales of near calamity and triumph. My return home will not be without some grief.

A few of my fellow islanders are out here on the upper starboard side (permanents, like me), and I am of course besieged with all manner of questions and comments about my trial, the outcome of which is the subject of blaring headlines in the morning dailies.

But Kurt Zoller has more important matters on his mind. As he sidles up to me, he asks, "Know why we always run out of water? The trees drink most of it up." He leans to my ear. "They compete with us for the necessaries of life."

His water delivery service having been rained out, he has traded his tank truck for a heavy-duty van, newly stencilled with the logo of a toppling fir tree and the words: "Zoller's Tree Service. Ecologically Sensitive Landscaping."

"I'm tired of helping people, Mr. Bo-champ, so I'm going to let Margaret Blake be trustee for a while. We'll see how people like it when she puts the clock back. You still friendly with her? Beware. She'll turn on you. That's all I can say." It is as if he holds some dire secret, though his words sound more of a curse than a warning.

The wind has whipped up, and the *Queen of Prince George* is rocking slightly, the tides of Active Pass churning beneath us. Clouds scud along the eastern sky, massing against the mountains above Vancouver, fleeing the hot September sun under which our islands bask.

A lanky fellow of middle years—a long blond-grey ponytail, a sad, sensitive look to him—squats on the deck, expertly fingering the strings and struts of a guitar. A sprightly Vivaldi sonata.

When he concludes, I clap my hands.

"You're most kind." His smile is natural, unlaboured.

We introduce ourselves. Malcolm Lorenz, a name I recall from somewhere, perhaps on the radio, a CBC music program. This must be the classical guitarist Margaret mentioned, our fall fair guest artist.

He joins me at the railing. "I saw your picture all over the front pages this morning. Oddest damn trial, must have been fun. Congratulations. You have a place on Garibaldi, Arthur?"

"I do, indeed."

"Spent five years off and on there. Fifteen-year-old runaway who thought he could change the world on acid and mushrooms. Do you know Margaret Blake?"

"She's my neighbour."

"Heard of the Earthseed Commune? That was us. We hadn't the faintest idea what we were doing, except for Chris and Margaret—they had the green thumbs. They lasted it out."

He's an engaging man, with an interesting history—but why does he make me nervous? "Did Margaret invite you?"

"Sort of. I just came back from a tour of East Africa. Canada Council funding, raise money for Rwandan refugees, that sort of thing. The idea is to keep me from starvation, too. I called Margaret, thought I'd pay her a visit, and she asked me over to do a free gig. Sounds like fun."

"It does, indeed."

"Haven't seen her since Chris's funeral. I admired Chris. Still very fond of Margaret."

"Malcolm, I know Margaret would be absolutely delighted if you would join us at the lamb barbecue."

He flicks the quickest little look at me, then his eyes settle on the horizon, the small green islands dappling it. I fixate on a quartet of gulls hanging rigidly in the vessel's slipstream. The gulls lose formation and wheel away as the ferry heaves to port, rounding the beacon off East Point, heading into the ferry slip, where gathers the usual crowd of weekend greeters. On the car deck, cyclists strap on helmets, mount their bikes, and the boat's metal gates begin to yawn open.

Observing my suitcase, Malcolm rightly infers I am without a vehicle. I accept his offer of a lift. He seems a gentle person, and in normal circumstances I would like him. He has qualities I both admire and lack: charm and panache. Therefore, he worries me.

On the car deck, Zoller is tying on his life jacket for the risky drive onto the ferry dock. "Guess the island hasn't changed much," Malcolm says. "Different characters, that's all."

I sling my suitcase into the back of his old Volkswagen van. He also has a bag. Clearly he is proposing to stay the night. Where? Has Margaret offered him her couch (or worse)? Should I let him know Garibaldi boasts a few charming bed and breakfast inns— or might he prefer one of the funky cabins at the Brig? No wedding band decorates a finger. But I am being absurd. He and Margaret are friends of long standing; only an unhealthy jealousy would read anything base in a friendly reunion.

Stranded near the dock is my old rattletrap truck, which I foolishly lent to Nelson Forbish. I suppose it was too much to expect that Stoney might have had it serviced and running for my arrival. Perhaps he can offer another loaner.

As we pass the entrance to her bar, Emily Lemay waves. She is dressed grandly for the fair, sun glinting off her shiny satin dress.

"My God, is that Emily? She stole my sixteen-year-old virginity, that woman." Malcolm laughs, begins talking in a relaxed drawl about the old days. There was no bar then; he and his fellow hippies used to smuggle their beer and whisky from the American islands. "No electricity, no car ferry, no cops, no paved roads, *nada*. We lied to ourselves: this is paradise, we said, and we're not insanely bored."

I listen to his reminiscences with a tight smile as we bump up Centre Road. He obliges me by stopping at the general store, where Mr. Makepeace hands me a week's worth of junk mail and a postcard from Bayreuth. "Your ex is coming back for the winter season. Going to be doing *Hansel and Gretel* at Christmas."

How blurred in memory has Annabelle become; how lightly throbs the pain of yesterday. I hope she has found happiness with her *Musikmeister*. (I expect flouncy François Roehlig shares my curious passion for strong-willed women. He has the advantage of youth and may last her out.)

A quick run up Potter's Road, and while I dash into the house, Malcolm wanders across the yard. Someone has delivered George Rimbold's fishing gear. Its presence beside my unlocked door causes another brief pang of loss. I quickly change into country garb and return outside to find Malcolm gazing wistfully over the fence at his former homestead.

Now we head towards Breadloaf Hill to the fair grounds. Cars line the road as we come around the final switchback atop the hill, where a couple of hundred smiling islanders have gathered, all bedecked in their country finery. To whom do I report to take on the duty of overseer of children's games? Where is Margaret?

A stage has been slapped up by the wall of the community hall and trophy winners are being summoned to it. Best handicrafts, best goats, best float in this morning's parade. The master of ceremonies, Scotty Phillips (island bootlegger, respected businessman, president of the local Lions Club), has an unnaturally loud voice, which he delights in amplifying through the microphone.

"Best overall veggies. Who wants to guess?"

Ah, there she is at the front, walking sprightly up the steps to the stage, accepting a trophy in the shape of a phallic corncob.

"Bloody obscene," Malcolm says. He laughs: a throaty, sensual sound.

"Now, you just stay right here, Margaret," Scotty booms. "You got three more coming in a row."

I am exuberant in my applause each time, easily outdoing Malcolm, who probably must protect his sensitive hands.

"Egg toss coming up in ten minutes," Scotty announces, "so choose your partners." Margaret flits from the stage with her booty, then turns and starts when we descend upon her.

"Arthur, goodness, you made me jump. Malcolm, it's so good to see you. How are you?" She seems flustered and, laden with her trophies, hugs me awkwardly. After I relieve her of them, she takes Malcolm in a disturbingly close embrace.

"You look great," he says as they part.

"A few years older, not much wiser."

"I'd been meaning to come over. Too busy picking up all the pieces." Pieces of what? He is not talking about broken china. . . .

"So. You've met. You two." Margaret seems unable to find words. "Okay, well, um, I'm off duty at last, let's go sit down. It's been a crazy day. Already it's been a crazy day."

Trilling like a nervous songbird, she takes us each by an arm and marches us to a roped-off area near the crown of Breadloaf Hill, where we sit on makeshift benches. Ginger Jones, our waitress, serves us beer and pop. "Watch out," she whispers to me. "Emily's on the prowl." She looks the three of us over, sees possibilities for scandal here; who will make it with whom?

Malcolm hefts the corncob trophy. "Where's the battery compartment?"

From Margaret's throat issues a raunchy chortle. I laugh nervously.

The emcee's booming voice: "Arthur Beauchamp. Arthur Beauchamp. Wanted at the kiddies' three-legged race."

"Hurry back," Margaret says. She waves me away and leans towards Malcolm. I hear her say, "What was Africa like?"

I have passed out one red ribbon, one blue ribbon—and, to the ten third-place winning teams of the three-legged race, ten white ribbons (the judicious practice on Garibaldi: no child may be allowed to return home without a share of glory). I have presided as marshal over the tug of war (a titanic struggle during which seven-year-old Peggy Kane bit ten-year-old Ronnie Cruller on the hand, causing his team to lose). I have wisely refereed the scarecrow contest, awarding the cherished Rosekeeper Trophy to twelve-year-old Winston Bigelow for his clever rendering of a black-robed vampire (carrot-fanged, the mouth drooling catsup).

Between events, I wander about, seeking vantage points to observe Margaret and Malcolm: they haven't moved from their table except to fetch more beer, and they are far too gay and chatty. But they have former times to share, a pot of memories to stir up.

The fair organizers, duly impressed by my Solomon-like adjudications for the children's games, reward me with a substitute's role as judge of the pie-baking contest (replacing Nelson Forbish, who is in the first-aid tent, sickened on caramel apples and candy floss). I am led to a table laden with a dozen succulent entries, apple, rhubarb, blueberry, lightly crusted, oozing their syrups. I nibble at each, muttering words of praise, wondering why my appetite has suddenly vanished. When will I be allowed a little uninterrupted taste of Margaret? When does Malcolm go off to play his guitar?

I pin a ribbon on the proud chest of Mrs. Nancy Stiles, creator of a zesty concoction of apple and blackberry, and I wander off again. They are still in the beer gardens, absorbed in each other. I feel a stranger, outside their space. I am exhausted from the tension of this much-anticipated day, dispirited, my energy sapped by jealous worry. *Beware. She'll turn on you.*

The day's brightness has begun to fade, and a brisk evening breeze has whipped up, tossing scraps of paper across the lawns, sending smoke spiralling from the barbecue pit behind the community hall, where a queue has formed for the sacrificial lambs. I stroll past the volunteer fire fighters and their polished old red truck, past the RCMP exhibit, a canopied anti-drug display. It is deserted but for Stoney, who is standing in the lee of the wind, brazenly lighting a hand-rolled cigarette. He joins me, his breath reeking of marijuana.

"You gotta catch this sunset, man."

Lethargically, I follow him past the beer gardens, our passage unnoticed by Margaret and Malcolm, who are laughing over some ancient escapade at the Earthseed Commune.

The sunsets from Breadloaf Hill are fairly held to be among the finest on the island; barren of all but a few Garry oaks, our knoll offers a vast canvas south and west, beyond islands and channels to the green spine of Vancouver Island and the towering snowy tops of Olympic Park.

But the sunset is disappointing; the wind has chased the clouds, and we see only the darkening sky and the red orb of the sun. It disappears behind the sea like fading hope, and blinks out like a light bulb. Three ravens flap darkly past our view like winged omens, uttering imprecations, gliding, swooping, then disappearing among the steeples of Douglas firs below us.

Now comes a distant guitar melody, and I turn and see Malcolm Lorenz at the microphone, entertaining folks who have filled their plates and are nestling down on blankets before the stage.

"You been home yet?" says Stoney.

"I stopped in quickly."

"Did you, ah, check the garage?"

I have come to recognize a certain inflection to Stoney's voice when he is about to announce one of his catastrophes. There have been ill auguries: the sudden cold breeze, the ravens with their raucous warnings, Zoller with his curse.

"Why?"

"Well, 'cause we finished the roof. Dog and me worked day and night. Lots of overtime. Won't cost you extra."

In that case, he is hustling for a big tip. But I am relieved that his news is good. "I'll do an inspection in the morning."

Stoney clears his throat. "Only one other thing . . ."

I wait for him to complete. Deer have breached the garden fence. The house has collapsed. Stoney's garage burned down, with the Phantom V inside it.

But Stoney just shrugs and walks away. "Well, you'll find out."

I utter a soft oath. I am about to pursue him, but hesitate when I hear Margaret's voice from behind me.

"Here you are."

She peeks mischievously from behind a scraggly oak tree, a child playing hide and seek. Laughing, she hugs the tree. I fear she has had a little too much to drink. Now she is at the top of the knoll, looking out at the sunset's afterglow. She spreads her arms, empress of all she surveys. She is flushed—with the beer she drank? Or has Malcolm kindled more than memories?

"I'm feeling so spaced out today."

A poor drinker, she seems flighty, gawky in her movements.

"Let's go down and listen to Malcolm, then we can eat and dance and you can tell me all about the trial." She takes my arm. "How are you feeling, you look a little blue."

"Hangover from the trial, I suspect." I wonder if I remember how to dance. Doubtless Malcolm is lithe of foot, with antelope-like grace.

We park ourselves at a picnic table near the stage. Malcolm's eyes are closed as he plays a melodic largo, to which Margaret listens raptly. Suddenly, I am shivering. I wonder if I should tramp back to the house and get a sweater. I wonder if I need even bother coming back. Why spoil Margaret's good time? Thanks to the ministering of Uncle Arthur, she is freed of her fixation upon her husband, and now her heart can pursue other goals.

But I am being made irrational by that baneful by-product of love we call jealousy. I am confused by my emotions, made ill by them: a paranoid neurosis. She missed me—she told me that on the telephone. *I think of you a lot, too*—that's what she said.

They're just good friends.

Now I must fill our plates before the food disappears. As Malcolm begins a final encore, I slip away to join a line-up that is still crawling sluglike towards the food table. And I am suddenly feeling an old need. I am suffering the same kind of niggling urge for strong drink that visited me during Annabelle's frequent bouts of perfidy.

But now Emily Lemay joins me, planting an impertinent wet kiss on my lips that tastes of peach brandy.

I ask if her current swain is present, the tugboat operator.

"Ancient history. Found out he had one in every port. By the time he got back here he was too beat to do anything. Not that he ever did much anyway. Some day, I'd like to meet a man. Someone who can keep up."

Though Emily continues to flirt with blatant gusto, my own recent rumblings of potency have stilled; the loins do not stir, I do not rise to her challenge. Pressing against me with thigh and bosom, she leans to my ear with a secret: "That Malcolm Lorenz—he sure knew how to keep it up."

As the server slaps chunks of meat on my three plates, I feel a queasy loss of appetite.

I make my escape from Emily. I see the Garibaldi Blues Band tuning up on stage. Malcolm has disappeared from it . . . and Margaret has vanished from her place at our picnic table.

I lay food and cutlery down, and search for them in the community hall, where Margaret must be showing Malcolm her prize veggies. Inside, I wander among tables arrayed with produce and handicrafts. No sign of them here. The door that exits to the parking lot is open, and after taking no more than two steps outside it I am brought to a sudden stall. In a sheltered alcove near the parking lot Margaret and Malcolm are in close embrace, passionately kissing.

I slowly retreat into the hall. I feel my heart racing, breaking, shattering. I fly away, I fly away.

☙❧

I am sitting in the darkness, all lights off but that of the moon, which sneaks through my window like a cold-hearted thief. I am rigid in my club chair, paralysed with grief, too emotionally withered for tears to come.

I hear a distant pounding of bass, a whine of amplified guitar, rising and falling, carried on the harsh wind from Breadloaf Hill. Outside my open window, trees sway in the breeze under the ghostly light of the moon. (What further evil has been visited upon me? Stoney knows. *You'll find out.*)

How could I have ever conceived I was a masochist? I dread the kind of hurt for which I have found but one effective antidote. Isn't that so, Annabelle? Was that not your experience? I tend to drown pain. I cannot handle it. Not this particular kind, a bastinado I feel up into my very guts.

And now I am suffering a thirst I have not felt for years. But it *has* been years. I wonder if I am now able to handle alcohol. Finally, after nine years of abstinence, can I control my old addiction?

The moon sends a long, shivering slice of light across the choppy waters of the bay, Diana's arrow. They were entwined like vines. Had their mouths been open as they kissed? Ah, love and pain are twin sisters indeed and delight in torturing their bound and helpless victims.

At the sound of a vehicle entering the yard next door I snap to attention like a man on the rack. A barking dog. A male voice. Her tinkling laughter. I close my eyes and clasp my hands over my ears, yet I see and hear them gaily entering her house, Slappy the spaniel dancing around their ankles, showing them the way to the bedroom.

I rise and stroll in a not-quite aimless fashion around the house, through the living room to the kitchen, where, behind a cupboard door, stands a bottle of Seagram's, recently purchased and set aside for entertaining.

I pluck this precious, dangerous cargo from its hiding place. A dram or two, that's all. I seek not oblivion in these amber waters; a minor deadening of the nerves will suffice, a slight surcease of care. Clearly, I have beaten my addiction. If I can just get through this night . . . why, tomorrow I will be back on top of things. In my garden, harvesting my brussels sprouts.

I open the bottle. I sniff, sucking in its pungent ethers. Spirits, light my fire. Burn me, burn the pain away.

You are possessed of the devil, my son. Repent at once.

George, leave me alone.

You are an alcoholic.

No longer.

Bullshit!

The bottle tilts. But my hand is restrained by a power that seems almost physical: the grip of the ministering angel Rimbold, descended from the A.A. chapter above.

Say it!

I am an alcoholic.

The sweet, addicting syrup flows into the sink and down the drain.

Ah, you impious bastard, George, I am a stronger man than this. I will survive. *I will.*

And then I feel the weakness subside. A strength, a peace, comes over me. I have survived loss before. I have plunged into the fire of love and I have lived. I am truly not the whimpering invertebrate I used to be. Perhaps all those years of sweaty labour to conserve a bad marriage have given me muscle. Or perhaps like my rutabagas I have grown healthy and hardy in the gardens of Garibaldi. Have I not just won a notorious trial? Have I not attracted the lurid attentions of Emily Lemay? Yes, I am feeling quite possessed. Unruffled. Calm.

I slip on a wool sweater and walk outside among the rays and shadows of the moon. I shall not think of Margaret.

(But now I see her in its solemn face, hear her in the

whispering wind in the trees, in the scolding slap of waves upon the beach.)

I stroll down the path to the water, and to prove my courage I glance at Margaret's house. It is in utter blackness. I am strong. I will survive. But unbidden comes a vision of heated naked bodies, and I am nauseated by it and speed to the ocean's edge. I stand there for a few moments panting, but nothing comes up.

I stare at the sea for a long and wretched time: the moonlit dancing waves, the foam-whipped channel, flickering lights on distant islands, the star-fat sky. I become aware of a distinct feeling of dampness around my toes and realize the tide has been flowing, saturating my shoes.

Now something is tugging at my pant cuffs. Am I about to be eaten alive by crabs? It seems a sufficiently ignominious way to end it all. I turn, and Slappy licks my hand.

"What the *hell* are you doing?" Margaret is at the top of the path, under the arbutus tree, looking down at me.

Slowly, I turn to face her. She starts to come down the trail, wobbling, lightly impaired by her several beers. "Talking to yourself, wandering into the ocean. Why did you run off anyway?"

My feet are wet and I am paralysed.

"I looked all around for you." She stops about a yard in front of me, studies me for signs of injury or mental illness.

"I, uh, I'm sorry, I just thought you and Malcolm wanted to be alone for a while."

Slappy keeps tugging at me, and I follow him to dry land.

Margaret takes my hand and looks searchingly at me. "Oh, Arthur, I think I hurt you tonight. I know what happened."

"What happened?"

"You saw me kissing him goodbye in the parking lot."

"Kissing him . . . goodbye?" I croak.

"He had to get the nine o'clock, but insisted on coming by to look at the house. I really couldn't say no. Anyway, he took off right after that for the ferry. I looked for your car—why didn't you bring it to the fair?"

"My car?" I am in utter confusion.

"You haven't looked in your garage?"

Zombie-like, I let her lead me there: the Phantom V proudly squats within, festooned with ribbons.

"Stoney drove it in the parade this morning, didn't he tell you? That's a steering wheel from an old Massey-Harris tractor."

I have managed to loosen up enough to laugh a little, though with the slight edge of hysteria.

She turns to face me and takes both my hands. "I'm sorry about . . . you know, the thing you saw with Malcolm. He, ah, really leaned into me."

"I will admit to a raging jealousy. It was unworthy of me and insulting to you."

"Yes, well, I felt very awkward all day. Not used to all that male energy. I suppose he was coming on a little. I told him I couldn't put him up."

"I read your feelings differently."

"You boob. It wasn't that much of a kiss."

As she presses her lips to mine I smell a pleasant beery aftertaste. Her mouth works mine apart and her tongue searches deeply into it and I am intoxicated by the delicious womanly scent of her body, by her narcotic exhalations. Her hips close with mine, gently shimmying, and I am transported, rabid with desire, and I melt in her heat, feel myself diving, diving, into the flames of passion. . . .

"*That's* a kiss," she whispers huskily in my ear.

Her eyes shine into mine, hot as liquid silver, glistening in the moonlight. "You didn't really have to try so hard, Arthur."

And she grabs a fistful of woollen sweater and marches her willing captive to the house.

༄ ༄

Dear Patricia,

I suppose you're absolutely agog with speculation. What happened to that empty-headed sex slave anyway? Kidnapped? Joined a cult? Wandering amnesic through the lanes of Katmandu? None of the above. No, I've changed my name and I'm starring in a smash Broadway production that just opened to rave reviews.

In my dreams.

Yes, the postmark says Domfront, Normandy, France. That's in the apple country, not the wine country. (I've become a nut for calvados.) The town is on a hill, and it's incredibly ancient, all cobbly with narrow, leaning buildings and wiggly streets leading to the ruins of a castle, circa sixteen something. It's just crawling with old fortresses and stuff around here. Some major heart-attack restaurants, too—everything is served in some kind of obscene cream sauce or other. I'm going to become a total butterball.

The villa is on an escarpment. From the window where I write, orchards are spread out below me for miles, absolutely dripping with apples. Lots of calorie-burning little roads to explore by foot.

Got an off-season deal on this place. Four floors, lots of secret little parlours, all sort of rococo. La Maison de la Resistance is what the owner calls it—in honour of a French resister who hid out Allied airmen here during the war. Which is sort of what we're doing, hiding out, waiting for the liberation.

Let's not let Remy know where I am, okay? I

assume he has my telegram, which I sent almost immediately when we got to Paris (ah, Paris, ah, romance, the cafés, the galleries, the strolls under the moon by the Seine). I'll deal with him, with it, with everything when I get my strength back. I'm getting there. Another week here and I'll be able to take on King Kong. I'll bring you a bottle of ten-year-old calvados when I return to face the music.

I've promised Jonathan not to mix it with Benedictine.

Anyway, let's face it, it wouldn't have worked. Remy needs some kind of fluttery society matron. But he's beautiful to look at, and he'll find some nice little money-hungry starlet to worship helpless at his feet.

Jonathan has impeccable French, which aids in our forays into the countryside. We went up to St-Malo on a scooter; that was fun. Enchanted castle rising from the sea. What else? Pilgrimage to Rouen, where Joan was martyred. "Sometimes I actually think I'm Joan of Arc." Did I say something like that in the courtroom? Jonathan says I did. How fucking arrogant. Joan of Arc is still burning with embarrassment over her porno gig in Court 55. You may not recognize me when I get back to Vancouver, but I'll be the one with the bag over her head.

That'll be next week—Jonathan's leave extends to the middle of the month, and I'm going to finish off my last year. We're not ashamed; we'll brazen it out. Anyone who makes a smart crack gets flunked.

Do you know where we spent the first night? Up at Grouse, in my cabin. We snuck down the next morning and caught a flight to Paris.

(Okay, I can tell you're impatient. I'll fill in the gap.)

The scene is an obscure little bar in Chinatown.

HE: There is something else I have to get off my chest.

SHE: (nervously biting her lip) What?

HE: I don't know how to say this.

(She fiddles with her swizzle stick.)

HE: I love you.

SHE: (in shock) Oh, God.

HE: For what it's worth.

SHE: (increased agitation) Oh, God.

HE: (frowning) What's the matter?

SHE: (facing up to the truth) Dr. Kropinski had a final piece of advice. . . .

HE: Well, what did he tell you?

SHE: To ask myself why I see you so often in my dreams.

Next scene is a little cabin on the mountain. Clothes are lying helter-skelter on the floor. By the flickering light of a fireplace we make out two bodies joyfully writhing on a rug.

We've talked about the M-word, but we're going to try living together before we make any legal binding commitments. (And speaking of binding, no we don't! But what the hey, I'm always into a little safe-sex fantasy. He knows not to jump me from behind, though.) He also understands my need for independence, my space. So I get his library—that parlour of debauchery—to study in; he gets the broom closet and kitchen. (Bonus: Hon. Jon loves to cook!) We'll have his-and-her closets, bathrooms, and psychiatrists. Share the bed.

How's your love life? Check out that starving actor I tried to line you up with. Light a fire.

Fondly,
Kimberley

ACKNOWLEDGMENTS

A few writers and other friends are owed
no small debt of gratitude. Ann Ireland's sage
comments were invaluable in keeping the
manuscript on track. Brian Brett and Doug Small
offered critical perspectives. Ellen Seligman
edited with characteristic craft and insight.

ABOUT THE AUTHOR

WILLIAM DEVERELL started a law practice in British Columbia in 1964, following a career as a journalist. He is a founding member and a past president of the B.C. Civil Liberties Association. His first novel, *Needles,* won the Seal First Novel Award and, since then, he has published eight novels including, most recently, *Street Legal: The Betrayal* and *Kill All the Lawyers,* as well as a non-fiction book, *Fatal Cruise,* based on a bizarre and high-profile murder case in which he served as defence counsel. William Deverell wrote the pilot for and created the popular CBC-TV series *Street Legal,* and he has written several screenplays. He is a former chair of the Writers' Union of Canada and served as Visiting Professor of Creative Writing, University of Victoria.

He lives on Pender Island in British Columbia, and winters in Costa Rica.